THE ISKRA INCIDENT

THE ISKRA INCIDENT

**Colonel Jimmie H. Butler,
USAF (Ret.)**

DUTTON NEW YORK

DUTTON
Published by the Penguin Group
Penguin Books USA Inc., 375 Hudson Street, New York, New York 10014, U.S.A.
Penguin Books Ltd, 27 Wrights Lane, London W8 5TZ, England
Penguin Books Australia Ltd, Ringwood, Victoria, Australia
Penguin Books Canada Ltd, 2801 John Street, Markham, Ontario, Canada L3R 1B4
Penguin Books (N.Z.) Ltd, 182-190 Wairau Road, Auckland 10, New Zealand

Penguin Books Ltd, Registered Offices: Harmondsworth, Middlesex, England

First published by Dutton, an imprint of New American Library,
a division of Penguin Books USA Inc.
Distributed in Canada by McClelland & Stewart Inc.

First Printing, September, 1990
10 9 8 7 6 5 4 3 2 1

 REGISTERED TRADEMARK—MARCA REGISTRADA

Library of Congress Cataloging-in-Publication Data

Butler, Jimmie H.
    The Iskra incident / Jimmie H. Butler.
      p.   cm.
    ISBN 0-525-24898-6
    I. Title.
PS3552.U82618I85   1990
813'.54—dc20   90-5743
                                    CIP

Printed in the United States of America
Set in Times Roman
Designed by Nissa Knuth-Cassidy

PUBLISHER'S NOTE
This is a work of fiction. Names, characters, places, and incidents either are the product
of the author's imagination or are used fictitiously, and any resemblance to actual persons,
living or dead, events, or locales is entirely coincidental.

In Memory of Dale

* * * * * * * * * * *

Special thanks to Mr. Paul Gillette (*Carmela* and *Play Misty for Me*) for his continued guidance and encouragement. Paul's friendship and his expertise as a teacher were extremely helpful throughout the development of *The Iskra Incident*.

Chapter 1

Monday Morning, 6:25 a.m.
Vladivostok Local Time

A BLIZZARD OF GROWING INTENSITY WHIPPED GUSTY WINDS ACROSS THE
military airfield at Vladivostok. In the pre-dawn darkness of a December morning, the only activity centered on an Il-62 jetliner that sat
quietly on an icy parking ramp. At first glance, the plane appeared to
be a typical Aeroflot airliner servicing the port city in eastern Siberia.
However, inside the airplane some of the most powerful men in the
Soviet Union waited impatiently to continue their journey from Moscow to San Francisco.

Lance-Corporal Mikhail Dolenko of the Russian Army was the
guard stationed at the stairway to the plane. For more than an hour
he had stood next to the ice-coated railing. Now small icicles glistened beneath his eyebrows. When he exhaled, the moisture froze
immediately in the coarse cloth covering his mouth and nose. He
fought the cold for as long as possible. Then he moved next to the
roaring generator that supplied the electrical power to the aircraft.

The thick pàdding of his headgear and the frozen scarf that covered
most of his face did little to protect him from the noise and fumes of
the generator. After a few moments he had trouble keeping his
thoughts clear. But he needed the heat and would risk the fumes.
Shifting from one foot to the other no longer affected the numbness
below his ankles. He realized he was nearing frostbite.

Passengers had boarded almost an hour before, just after the ground
crew had finished refueling. Although Dolenko had expected an immediate departure, the KGB official assigned to the flight had kept
the entry stairs in place. The maintenance personnel had long since
retreated to the warmth of the hangar and a nearby maintenance van,
so Dolenko surmised that the aircraft did not need additional servicing. Obviously, someone else—someone of importance—still needed
to board the Il-62.

Finally Dolenko noticed that the falling snow near the corner of the
hangar was shimmering in the light from approaching vehicles. He

1

forced his stiff fingers to grasp the automatic weapon that hung from the strap over his shoulder, then he trudged to the base of the stairway. Moments later, two black Volga sedans reached the aircraft.

Colonel Tolkachev, the head of security, emerged quickly from the second car and crunched through the fresh snow. "Be ready!"

Dolenko saluted, but the colonel ignored the salute, concentrating instead on the lead Volga and its occupants. The driver jumped from the car, pulled two heavy leather suitcases from the trunk, and struggled up the icy stairs with the luggage.

Moments later, a short man wearing a dark overcoat stepped from the car. "I'll take care of it when I get there," he said to someone who remained inside.

Dolenko strained to see who was in the car, but his view was obscured by the fogged windows and by the man in the dark coat. As the man turned awkwardly toward the stairway, Dolenko stepped to one side as if moving out of the way. He hoped to get a look at the man in the car before the door closed.

The man in the dark coat stepped toward the aircraft. As he walked, he methodically dragged his right foot. A metal brace scraped across the ice, occasionally cutting through to the concrete—*crunch-scrape, crunch-scrape.*

Dolenko felt a chill more threatening than that of the Siberian winter. The man with the brace was Victor Solomenkov, the number-two man in the KGB. Dolenko's concerns about freezing were forgotten. He was terrified at the thought of doing anything that might gain the disapproval of the crippled man.

As Solomenkov reached the stairs, Colonel Tolkachev saluted smartly. Solomenkov nodded in response, then gave Dolenko no more than a passing glance with eyes blurred by the intense cold. As Solomenkov climbed the stairway, Dolenko felt great relief, quite satisfied to stand unnoticed in the cold for a few more minutes.

An old man, obviously one of the high-ranking dignitaries who had boarded the aircraft earlier, met Solomenkov at the door. "Where are they? What are you doing here?" The old man shouted both questions in rapid succession, and his voice crackled with age and anger.

Dolenko held his breath and listened. However, he could not hear Solomenkov's answer above the combined roar of the wind and the generator.

As the KGB leader limped aboard, the old man said, "We will wait no longer!"

Dolenko could not see the old man's face, but was grateful for the decision.

Within minutes the jetliner taxied from its parking place and disappeared into the snowy darkness. Colonel Tolkachev, promising hot coffee to the guards and ground crewmen, directed everyone toward the hangar.

Dolenko went happily, even though his morning's work was not yet complete. When he stepped through the doorway, he was blinded by the glaring lights inside. Someone offered to take his weapon, and Dolenko handed over the rifle without hesitation. He was too stiff and cold to care as he slowly removed his gloves and unwrapped the frozen scarf.

When he turned to retrieve his weapon, Dolenko discovered it had been stacked with others. The stack was under the watchful eyes of a huge sergeant who wore a distinctive uniform. Dolenko looked around. The only men still carrying weapons were dressed similarly in the uniform of an elite Moscow-based unit.

Dolenko tried to show no more concern than the other guards and ground crewmen, but he wondered why these men had come to Vladivostok. The unexpected turn of events worried him. As he took a tin cup full of steaming coffee, Dolenko heard the roar of the departing jetliner. The rumble echoed through the cavernous hangar, drawing his thoughts to the aircraft and its passengers.

In addition to being a soldier in the Soviet Army, Dolenko was an agent for American intelligence. He wondered how long he and the others would be detained. He was eager to tell his superiors about the man with the crippled leg joining the flight to San Francisco.

A few hours later and forty-five hundred miles away, air traffic controller Karl Wilson leaned back from his radarscope at the FAA's Oakland Center. Wilson had passed his only active aircraft to the approach controller at San Francisco International Airport.

Enjoying an unusually quiet night, he took the opportunity to light a cigarette. Normally he handled a rush of coast-to-coast flights, which reached San Francisco during his shift. This evening the rush had not materialized. A fierce storm had slowed or grounded air traffic at every major airport northeast of Kansas City. A second storm system was moving inland from the Pacific.

Wilson expected the remaining two hours of his shift to be routine: a handful of international flights into San Francisco and a few military cargo jets flying in and out of Travis Air Force Base, northeast of the Bay. He took a taste of coffee he had set aside earlier. The coffee was cold, so he dropped the cup into the trash and got fresh coffee from a machine near the far wall.

When Wilson returned to his console, he checked a new set of data describing his next inbound flight. The information on the console jumped out at him. Call sign: Soviet National One. Routing: Inbound at flight level four-one-zero (forty-one thousand feet) nonstop from Vladivostok, U.S.S.R., to San Francisco International Airport. Remarks: Diplomatic Flight Clearance with a Delta Victor code one. A distinguished visitor with the rank of head of state was aboard.

Crushing out his cigarette, Wilson pulled his chair closer to the console. He selected a radarscope display that would show more of the ocean off the coast, and the image changed quickly. The outline of California reappeared, but smaller and farther right than before. With the skill of a veteran controller, Wilson checked the last reported position and time for Soviet National One, then mentally projected the aircraft forward to what should be its current location.

He looked among the faint grid lines of latitude and longitude displayed on the scope—but there was no radar blip at the estimated position.

He read the estimated time of arrival and coordinates for the next checkpoint on the flight plan. Computing back from that point to the current position produced the same answer. Still no radar blip—the screen was blank within thirty miles of his estimated position for Soviet National One.

The time of the last reported position was less than thirty minutes old, so he was not sure what had happened. However, he was certain that if Soviet National One was still flying, the aircraft would not remain lost for long. The aircraft's next checkpoint was on the boundary of the Coastal Air Defense Identification Zone (ADIZ), a buffer zone of airspace nearly three hundred miles wide covering the western approaches to the United States. U.S. Air Force radars tracked all aircraft entering the ADIZ, correlating their positions with flight plans filed before takeoff. Though he was unsure where Soviet National One was at the moment, he was confident that the Air Force controllers knew.

He wanted to locate the aircraft before getting a call from the Air Force, so he typed additional inputs into his keyboard. He requested information on the entire flight plan and the navigational equipment on the Soviet aircraft.

Accurately navigating an aircraft over the North Pacific routes could be a challenge, even though recent advances in inertial and satellite-based navigational systems had solved most of the problems. After leaving Japan—or Siberia in this case—navigators had few good checkpoints and had to contend with a jet stream made up of winds sometimes stronger than two hundred knots in the winter. When high clouds combined with equipment failures, errors of more than one hundred nautical miles were possible. When such problems were encountered, the flight crew added the phrase "position unreliable" to each questionable position report. He checked. That caveat was absent from the reports from Soviet National One, so he assumed the navigational equipment was working properly.

He also assumed that the Soviet navigator had gotten a good navigational fix when Soviet National One had flown near the American base at Shemya, in the Aleutian Islands. After passing Shemya, however, the aircraft had not been near land for more than two thousand miles.

Just as the computer screen displayed the information he had requested, a special tone in his headset told him the missing aircraft had been found. Before looking at his telephone control-panel, he knew that the button for the hot line to the USAF Air Defense Center was blinking.

"Oakland," he said, answering the hot line.

"This is Guardian," the controller at the Air Force radar site said. "We have an unidentified aircraft approaching the coastal ADIZ at flight level four-one-zero. Do you have a positive ID?"

Wilson searched nearer the ADIZ. "I've been trying to locate— Holy shit!" He discovered the missing radar blip almost on the ADIZ boundary.

"You got it, Oakland. If that's Soviet National One, she's seventy-two miles left of course." An error to the left put the airliner closer to northern California than it should have been.

"National One's inbound at flight level four-one-zero," Wilson said, "but they haven't checked in with Oakland Center."

"Guess we'd better send someone out to take a look, just to make sure the Russians didn't substitute a bomber or cruise-missile carrier."

"Fat chance," Wilson said, hoping but not expecting to talk the Air Force controller out of scrambling the fighter interceptors. "They're on a diplomatic clearance with some high-level DVs on board, so you'll just be wasting gas."

"A DIP clearance doesn't cut it when you're seventy miles off course at the ADIZ. The Russian president should get himself a better navigator."

"Understand," Wilson said.

The Air Force controller added, "Please advise the appropriate Oakland Center controllers that we're activating the Howell Air Force Base climb-corridor, surface to fifty thousand feet—Air Defense Priority—at time, twenty-two twelve hours, Pacific Standard."

"Roger," Wilson said as he made an entry in his special events log, then tried to contact Soviet National One.

Navigational errors were not rare on the North Pacific routes, so he felt no sense of foreboding. The Air Force response was necessary, but Wilson was confident that the errant aircraft would be visually identified as Soviet National One and not a military craft about to start World War III. Instead he worried about the resulting paperwork that might keep him busy well beyond midnight.

Within minutes of Guardian's decision to scramble interceptors, USAF Captain Eduard Benes steered his F-15 Eagle along a high-speed taxiway. Nearing the main runway at Howell Air Force Base, he pushed the throttles from military thrust into afterburner. Trailing twin cones of blue-white flames, his aircraft knifed through the drizzle and fog, accelerating to nearly one hundred knots by the time he reached the runway. First Lieutenant Larry Walker followed closely behind in a second Eagle.

Once he was airborne, Benes turned his aircraft west and raised the nose to avoid going supersonic over California's central valley. Rocketing skyward at more than twenty thousand feet per minute through dense clouds, he relaxed comfortably in the ejection seat. At thirty thousand feet, the fighters broke out of the darkness of the storm into the brightness of a full moon reflected off a solid floor of cloud tops. Except for mild turbulence around twenty thousand feet, the climb to forty-seven thousand feet was uneventful. Walker pulled in tight, a few feet behind and below the wing tip on the lead F-15 as both fighters raced toward the unidentified aircraft.

By the time the two Eagles had streaked across the cloud-covered coastline, Wilson was in radio contact with Soviet National One.

Standard communications were in use. The American pilots were in contact with Guardian on an Air Force frequency. The Soviet aircraft and the FAA controller at Oakland Center were using an FAA air traffic control frequency. The hot line between Guardian and Karl Wilson at Oakland was a third link, which could advise the fighter pilots on contacts between the Russian aircraft and Oakland Center.

Benes was relieved to learn that the Soviet aircraft was responding to directions from the air traffic controller. If the Soviet pilot were avoiding normal FAA contacts and trying to evade detection, Benes' mission would take on an entirely different cast. In that case, he would race in with missiles armed, prepared for a fight.

In this case, he expected a routine intercept. Aided by the light of the full moon, he would pull in close enough to see the big "CCCP" markings of the official Soviet airline. He anticipated no problem in visually identifying the aircraft as an Ilyushin Il-62. With four jet engines mounted on the aft part of the fuselage instead of under the wings, the Il-62 was easy to distinguish from most other aircraft. He relaxed as the mission became more like a training sortie than an air-defense emergency. His only regret now was that he had needlessly missed the ending of the Sunday Night Movie he had been watching when the Klaxon had sounded.

He adjusted the controls on his radar, locking the electronics of his Eagle onto the return of the approaching Soviet craft. With the advanced radar on the F-15, he could fly the rest of the mission without help from Guardian.

When Soviet National One was sixty miles ahead, Guardian told Benes that Oakland Center had cleared the airliner to descend to flight level two-seven-zero.

"Damn," Benes said, the word not going beyond his oxygen mask. He needed to make the visual identification before the aircraft disappeared into the clouds so he decided to expedite the intercept. Pushing the throttles into afterburner, he called out to his wingman, "Eagle flight, burner, now!"

Benes felt the familiar, jolting acceleration as raw fuel sprayed into the tailpipes. He eased the control stick forward, lowering the nose of his Eagle. Airspeed quickly accelerated to one and a half times the speed of sound so he reduced thrust to maintain Mach 1.5 as the altimeter reading decreased from forty-seven thousand feet. He switched his radar to a short-range setting. Only the Soviet aircraft and a large storm cell showed on his radar.

When the Soviet aircraft was twenty-five miles ahead and more than a mile beneath the fighters, Benes said, "Spread it out and stand by for a rapid one-eighty to the left." Approaching head-on at a closure rate of more than twice the speed of sound, the aircraft were just over a minute apart. Watching Walker's Eagle edge back and slide to the right, well out of the way for the reversal of course, he eased out his Eagle's speed brake.

As soon as he was satisfied that Walker would not overrun him, Benes rolled his F-15 upside-down to get a better look at the area below. Careful timing and a high-G turn would be necessary to maneuver the F-15s in trail behind the incoming Soviet aircraft.

He spotted navigational lights just above the cloud tops. "Nav lights, eleven-thirty low at about five miles."

He chopped the throttles to idle and popped the speed brake fully open to slow his fighter. The Eagle shuddered, decelerating quickly into the subsonic range. Shoulder straps held him just above the cockpit canopy as he strained to keep the lights in sight. The Soviet aircraft was nearly in the clouds, so he delayed his turn. He would overshoot some, but might be able to make the identification as he crossed over almost perpendicular to the other aircraft. At the latest possible instant, he rolled the Eagle into a screaming turn.

Straining against the G-forces that threatened to blind him, Benes fought to make out the outline of the aircraft streaking by below him. He was almost overhead when the lights flickered a final time, then disappeared as the dark, swept-wing form dropped into the glistening white clouds. He tried to retain the image. Was the aircraft an Il-62? Or a Backfire bomber with wings swept back for a supersonic attack? Or was the fleeting form a cruise-missile carrier, substituted for the airliner somewhere off the Kamchatka Peninsula?

He had not seen enough to be sure. "Damn! Did you get an ID, Larry?"

"Negative, Lead. She dropped into the clouds before I was close enough."

Benes rolled out of the diving turn and continued the pursuit. His fighter swooped into the clouds with Walker skidding through a sweeping turn a safe distance behind. Using the Eagle's radar, Benes closed to within two miles of Soviet National One. He wanted to stay near enough to move in for a quick ID if the aircraft broke into the clear between cloud layers. When he leveled just below twenty-seven thousand feet, however, he discovered that the clouds remained as solid as those he had climbed through over central California.

All he could see in the clouds beyond his canopy were the ghostly reflections of the lights of his aircraft.

Minutes later, he noticed that the Soviet aircraft had started descending again. He eased back on the throttles and let the nose of his Eagle drop.

Before he had a chance to ask Guardian about the change, the Air Force controller called, "Eagle flight, be advised, Oakland Center has cleared Soviet National One down to twelve thousand."

"We're sticking with her," Benes answered, "but still no visual contact."

He crosschecked his instruments with the navigational charts. Point Reyes, ahead and to the left, was a picturesque coastal peninsula nearly separated from California by the San Andreas fault. Benes considered the irony. He was pursuing a Soviet airplane toward an area boasting the Russian River, Sebastopol, and other remnants of Russian settlements that had been established for sea otter hunting in the early 1800s. His thoughts of Russians—past and present—were interrupted by a radio call from his wingman.

"What's happening, Lead?" Walker's tone was excited.

Benes did not answer. Instead he scanned his displays to see if he could figure out what had caused Walker's concern. Immediately he saw the answer—the Soviet aircraft's speed and rate of descent had increased. The unseen aircraft was falling away rapidly from the pursuing Eagles.

This could be the real thing! he thought for the first time since takeoff. If the aircraft were a hostile intruder, it could be racing to reach the pre-calculated points from which the pilot would launch his nuclear missiles. He felt a surge of adrenaline like none he had experienced since nearly colliding with an F-16 six months earlier.

He shoved the navigational chart onto the glare shield beside the heads-up display. Pushing the stick and throttles forward, he unleashed his fighter. With twin cones of fire reflecting off the surrounding clouds, the F-15 plummeted in pursuit of the Soviet aircraft.

His mind raced, seeking clues to what was happening. He tried to recall details of the intelligence briefing received the previous day when he had come on air defense alert. The briefer had mentioned a Soviet fleet less than a thousand miles from San Francisco. Benes wondered if sneak attacks were underway against other cities, small pieces of a larger plan to catch America by surprise.

The speed of the unidentified aircraft was approaching Mach one, the speed of sound. Speed was a key indicator: An Il-62 was not built for supersonic flight. If the aircraft ahead went supersonic without coming apart, Benes thought, it had to be a Backfire or some other high-performance bomber. He shuddered. A Backfire bomber targeted against San Francisco would be within range at any moment to launch its two AS-6 Kingfish nuclear missiles.

He called out to Walker, "Be awake, Two! Looks like the bogey's evading. Green 'em up for missiles, medium-range!"

Benes swallowed hard as the words seemed to dry his throat. "Green 'em up," pilots' jargon for arming an aircraft to attack, was a command he had given many times on the practice ranges during Red Flag training in Nevada. However, he had never given the command while carrying a set of real missiles in pursuit of a real aircraft. The excitement he felt was exhilarating and terrifying at the same time.

The Eagle accelerated so quickly that the distance to the unidentified aircraft began melting away. He eased back on the throttles and simultaneously moved the weapon selection switch on the side of the throttle to the position for his medium-range missiles. Then he reached forward to the armament panel, selecting weapon station number three. A radar-guided AIM-17X, the first missile he would use, was hanging beneath the corner of the engine inlet.

As he selected the missile, he also pressed the auto-acquisition switch for the radar. The radar immediately searched for a target within ten miles ahead, then locked on to the aircraft he was chasing. He raised the master arming switch from SAFE to ARM. The glowing green of the status lights confirmed that the circuits now were armed for his first missile. Pressing the weapon release button on the control stick was all that was needed to send that missile screaming in for the kill.

He pulled the throttles back even farther. Since he was unsure what kind of aircraft he was following, he wanted to stay at least four miles behind. Each Backfire bomber had a pair of twenty-three-millimeter cannons mounted in its tail. If he was following a Backfire, he wanted to stay out of the range of those cannons. If the Soviets fired something else at him, he wanted a little extra distance to react. Those four miles were not too great for the missiles on the F-15s. Traveling at nearly Mach four, Walker's AIM-17Xs could outrun the AS-6s before the Soviet missiles got out of range.

"If she starts launching cruise missiles," he said to his wingman, "I'll take the mother bird. Get into position to attack any missiles she turns loose."

"Roger, Lead," Walker said. "I'm coming up wide on your left." Walker guided his Eagle toward a position that would let him fire without hitting the lead fighter.

"Eagle One, this is Guardian." Having heard the exchange between the two pilots, the intercept controller showed a new sense of urgency in his voice. "What's going on up there?"

"The Soviet bird's making a run for it!" Benes' voice did not disguise his excitement. "She's in a steep dive through seventeen thousand feet. If she starts launching, we're ready."

In Oakland Center, Karl Wilson noticed the rapid change in the altitude readout for the Soviet airliner. He pushed his boom microphone closer to his lips and slowly pronounced his words: "Soviet National One, this is Oakland Center. Are you having any kind of difficulty?" Wilson wondered if the Russian pilot understood the word "difficulty," so he continued, "Are you having any problems, Soviet National One? Are you in trouble?"

The altitude readout decreased through fourteen thousand feet. Unless the aircraft leveled off immediately, Soviet National One would violate the clearance limit of twelve thousand.

He looked for lower aircraft that might be in the way as he said, "You are not cleared below twelve thousand. Repeat, not below one-two thousand, Soviet National One. Do you copy Oakland Center?"

There was no response. He twisted the selector for his radios to the position marked "Guard." Now broadcasting on emergency frequencies, he spoke more urgently than before, "Soviet National One! Soviet National One! This is Oakland Center on UHF and VHF guard. You are not cleared below one-two thousand! Maintain one-two thousand, Soviet National One. Acknowledge!"

Crushing out his cigarette, he flipped a switch that would alert the shift supervisor to the possible problem.

Benes' Eagle entered the fringes of a winter thunderstorm. Inside the cockpit, he strained against the increased buffeting. He had already evaluated the radar returns from the storm and was confident he could handle the weather.

His fighter shuddered through unseen waves of turbulent air. The jolts might have been jet wash from the preceding aircraft or perhaps just the mixing of conflicting air currents from the storm. Whatever the source, the shaking bounced the navigational chart from its resting place on the right side of the glare shield. His hair-trigger reflexes responded immediately. His gloved hand flashed up from the control stick, catching the chart before it fell below the level of the airspeed indicator.

A simultaneous *flash-boom* lighted his cloud-enclosed surroundings and jolted Benes. For a moment, he was sure he had been attacked.

"Son of a—" His entire world seemed to shift into slow motion as he realized that in reaching for the falling chart he had pressed the weapon release button. The flash was from his AIM-17X missile rocketing away from weapon station three.

His displays confirmed the launch, but he had difficulty seeing those indications. When the bright exhaust of the missile had disappeared into the cloud-filled darkness, most of his night vision had gone with it. For a few seconds he would be nearly blind. Yet in those few seconds he had to interrupt the radar signal that was guiding the missile toward the unidentified aircraft. In panic, he assumed he had a couple of seconds—three at the most—before it would be too late to destroy his missile. He pressed buttons and cycled switches, trying frantically to ensure that the guidance beam was cut off.

The seeker within the missile lost the guidance signal from the F-15, then triggered a destruct command. An instant later one hundred pounds of high explosives transformed the AIM-17X into some five thousand lethal fragments hurtling through the darkness. On his radar scope, the small image of the missile bloomed momentarily, then disappeared just short of the radar return from the diving airliner. He could not see well enough to know whether he had acted in time.

Walker responded before the leader could ask what the wingman had seen. "Lead, did you launch?"

Benes had trouble getting enough moisture in his mouth to answer. He had never been so frightened. "No! I mean, yes. It fired accidentally. Did it look to you like it was destroyed in time?"

The excited voice of Guardian interrupted. "Eagle One, this is

Guardian. Say again about the launch! Has the Soviet aircraft launched cruise missiles?"

"Negative, Guardian. I had an accidental launch of an air-to-air missile. I destroyed my missile. I say again, my missile was destroyed. Any word yet from Oakland as to what this guy's doing?"

"Negative, Eagle. Say again. You did not attack the Soviet aircraft?"

"That's affirmative," Benes said. "I have not attacked, but she's through eight thousand feet, still going down like a bat outta hell. Have they declared an emergency with Oakland?"

"Oakland's heard nothing so far. Keep us posted."

"Roger," Benes said. "Tell Oakland to clear out everything below us. I'm not sure how far down we're going. Break. Larry, what do you think?" The "break" indicated that the latter part of the transmission was for someone else.

"Damn, I don't know," Walker's tone was subdued. "It was awfully close, Ed."

"I still can't see worth shit," Benes said. "Did you see any change in the bird's flight path after the missile detonated?"

"Negative, Lead. She's still steady as a rock."

Benes discovered that by looking near things instead of directly at them, he could work around the blank blob marring the center of his vision. Passing through five thousand feet, he saw that the Soviet aircraft had decreased its rate of descent. Moments later his Eagle dropped through the base of the clouds, barely three thousand feet above the ocean. He jammed the throttles forward and leveled his fighter as he crosschecked the radar return against the area in front of him. Straining to see the other aircraft, he spotted navigational lights ahead and to his right.

He announced, "The Soviet aircraft's in a slow descent out of two thousand and in a shallow right turn."

"You're below our coverage, Eagle," Guardian said. "Are they going to ditch?"

"Looks like it. What does Oakland say?"

Benes moved the master arming switch from ARM to SAFE as he became more convinced that the rapid descent had been caused by mechanical problems.

"Oakland hasn't heard from them since they left twenty-seven thousand."

"I'm trying to catch up for a better look. Break. Safe 'em up, Two."

"What's the sea state, Eagle? Can you tell how bad the waves are?"

Benes banked his aircraft to get a better look. "Negative, Guardian. It's darker than the inside of a cow down here. I'm descending out of two thousand with a northwesterly wind of twenty-seven knots. The ocean's bound to be choppy."

As he closed in, the Soviet airliner continued a slow circle, then rolled out on a northeasterly heading, flying toward the area beneath the original dive. The airliner held the heading and stayed level a few seconds before entering a slow descent.

"Guardian," Benes said, "she's starting down again, about five hundred yards ahead. Break. Have you got her in sight, yet, Two?"

"Negative, Lead," Walker answered. "I'm still in the soup at forty-five hundred."

Guardian asked, "What's happening, Eagle?"

"Tell Oakland I think she's going in."

Even though trailing by only a few hundred yards, Benes could not see enough of the aircraft to identify it. The distance between the lights on the tips of the wings convinced him that the craft was the right size for an Il-62, but he could not tell anything else in the darkness. He focused on the navigational lights that shimmered against the pitch black background of the water. As the lights slipped lower and lower, he was almost mesmerized, allowing his Eagle to match the shallow rate of descent. "She's out of fifteen-hundred feet."

His grip on the control stick tightened involuntarily as he reached with his other hand to wipe sweat from his eyebrows. The sight of the falling lights sent a tingling feeling through his body: The Soviet aircraft, whatever it was, had to be going into the ocean. He switched his oxygen regulator to the emergency setting, hoping to fend off the feeling of nausea that stirred within him.

Moments later, the lights dropped quickly, plunging at last toward the blackness below. Benes watched the lights until a sudden eruption of white engulfed them, extinguishing them forever.

"Holy—What a—" His voice cracked with emotion. "Guardian, she's down. A hell of a splash! I'm going overhead to get a fix on the position."

"Roger, Eagle One. Understand Soviet National One is in the water at twenty-two forty-eight hours, local. Pass me the crash coordinates when you have them. I'm alerting air rescue."

"Roger. You can call 'em out if you want, but it won't make any difference now."

Chapter 2

IN THE HOURS BEFORE SOVIET NATIONAL ONE SLAMMED INTO THE churning ocean, crowds of people had gathered at San Francisco International Airport. As the estimated time of arrival drew near, the clamor in the International Terminal increased with each passing minute until the Christmas music on the public address system was barely audible above the noise of the crowd. The reds, greens, silvers, and golds of holiday decorations contributed a festive atmosphere. However, the presence of hundreds of armed police officers proclaimed the imminent coming of someone other than the Christ child.

On the lower floor, a dual-cordon of officers lined a passageway between a set of doors marked "No Entry—Customs Area" and exits leading to a fleet of limousines. Most of the crowd was restricted to the main floor, where a large glass enclosure divided the long terminal arm leading to the departure gates. The enclosure, which overlooked the baggage carousels in the customs area, allowed people on the main floor to observe arriving passengers who had not yet cleared customs.

Thousands of people had come to the airport to protest or to support the arrival of the Soviet delegation. In an uneasy compromise, local and federal officials had allowed three hundred pro-Soviet and three hundred anti-Soviet demonstrators inside the terminal. Additional lines of police officers on the main floor kept the two groups separated on the opposite sides of the glass enclosure.

Contrasting with the noisy demonstrators, a group of thirty somberly dressed men and women waited quietly near the escalator that led from the main floor down to the exit from customs. These were lesser-ranking officials of the Soviet consulate. The remainder of the gathering consisted of American government officials, conference hosts, city dignitaries, members of the press, and anyone else who could get a pass. Included in that group was U.S. Air Force Colonel Jack Phillips.

14

Quietly observing the activities on the main floor, Jack was still dressed in the three-piece blue suit he had worn on his flight from Washington, D.C. As a member of the Special Operations Division of Air Force Headquarters, he was one of the Pentagon's top experts on Soviet leaders. He had studied the Russian language more than twenty years earlier at the U.S. Air Force Academy, and he had increased his fluency in Russian during the intervening years.

In three years at the Tactical Fighter Weapons Center, he had become the commander of one of the aggressor squadrons assigned to the air-combat training known as Red Flag. In highly realistic aerial war games over the Nevada deserts, he had led his aggressors—pilots flying Soviet-style aircraft—against visiting units from throughout the U.S. Air Force. On each mission, he had flown, thought, and fought like a Soviet pilot, honing skills that remained with him long after he left the aggressor squadron.

Now Jack was on a special assignment to observe a Pan-Pacific Conference scheduled to begin the following day. The highlight of that conference was to be the signing ceremony for a non-aggression treaty involving all nations on the Pacific Rim. He was less interested in the treaty than in the Soviet leaders named to attend the conference. With the exception of Soviet Premier and General Secretary Konstantin Medvalev, the delegation included all the most influential members of the Soviet government and of the Communist Party.

For the next four days, he planned to take full advantage of this extraordinary opportunity to observe the Soviet leaders—particularly Andrei O. Valinen, the Soviet Minister of Defense. The Kremlin's announcement the previous week that Valinen was to be a member of the unprecedented Soviet delegation had taken Jack totally by surprise. Valinen was the last person the colonel had thought would come to America.

Jack checked the time: 10:50 p.m. Shortly, he thought, the flight from Vladivostok should be handed off by Oakland Center to approach control. He wondered if the weather would be a problem. A steady drizzle had been falling an hour ago when he had stored his luggage in his rental car. At least the Soviet pilots would not have to contend with heavy snow like that he had left behind a few hours earlier at Dulles Airport.

Carrying his raincoat, he pushed through the crowd to an elevator that led to the upper floors of the terminal. From a window that had a good view of the airport, he saw a steady rain splashing into puddles on the concrete. With the eyes of an experienced pilot, he looked beyond, checking the visibility and cloud ceiling—two factors that could divert an incoming flight. The landing lights of another aircraft, visible a couple of miles out on its final approach, eliminated his concerns. Additionally, lights on the Oakland side of the bay reflected off clouds in the distance, confirming that neither fog nor heavy rain was a threat to flights arriving within the next half hour.

Back on the main floor, he wandered past the group of Soviets. Before leaving Washington, he had studied dossiers on the officials assigned to the Soviet Consulate in San Francisco. Indicating no special curiosity as he walked by, he identified three minor officials and two KGB agents who were known to work out of the consulate. Although he knew that Soviet Ambassador Sherinin, Secretary of State Winston Shafer, and other dignitaries were waiting in a VIP lounge somewhere in the customs area, Jack had thought he might see some members of Sherinin's staff who had flown from Washington earlier in the day.

Leaving the Russians, he noticed a television news team preparing to broadcast near the glass enclosures that overlooked the customs area. He wondered if the aircraft had arrived already, but a check of his watch showed 10:58—thirteen minutes before the scheduled arrival of Soviet National One.

"Two minutes to air time," a technician with a headset shouted to people in front of the television camera.

Broadcasting in this crowd would be a neat trick, Jack thought, as he pushed through for a closer look.

Floodlights flashed on as another technician checked lighting levels. The sudden increase in illumination drew the attention of the demonstrators. Rival chants, uncoordinated at first, rumbled like an earthquake across the two groups on both sides of the police-lined passageway. When the cameraman from another news team aimed his lights toward the demonstrators, they raised placards and banners toward the ceiling. On one side of the passageway, signs proclaimed: "Welcome Comrades," "Blessings to the Peacemakers," and "Down with Fascist America!" On the other side, placards included, "Free Estonia!" "Murderers Go Home," and "Death to the Murderer Valinen!"

Jack took a second look at the Valinen placard. Its careful lettering was smeared with red, and he wondered if the blood on the sign was real or fake. Turning to the nearby broadcast, he joined a crowd already five or six deep. Everyone's attention was directed toward a sharply dressed man and woman in front of the camera.

Jack recognized the newsman as Alexander Braxton, an acknowledged expert on the Soviet Union and on Soviet-American relations. Even Braxton's many colleagues who did not share his America-first philosophy respected his uncanny ability to interpret Soviet actions.

In his fifties, he had the look of a man well established in the prime of life. His silver blond hair was more carefully styled than that of the attractive woman beside him. Tanned even in mid-December, he had the look of an outdoorsman. A thin scar nearly connecting his eyebrows was the only flaw in his finely chiseled features. His appearances were known for drawing female viewers who cared little about his expertise in Soviet affairs.

More than three decades earlier, he had made his debut before the cameras of a San Francisco television station owned by his stepfather. In the intervening years, Braxton had gained stature as a news commentator and a businessman. Now the television station where he had started was only one piece of his financial empire, which had provided increasing political clout as it had drawn him away from regular broadcasting. A visit to San Francisco by Russian leaders, however, was the type of event that would bring him eagerly in front of the cameras again.

During the Vietnam War, Jack had grown cynical about most newsmen, and his current assignment in Washington had reinforced that cynicism. All the same, he considered Braxton to be a cut above most of the network newsmen. Perhaps, Jack thought, his affinity for this one newsman was because Braxton and he shared common conservative biases about the Soviet leadership. He hoped to have a chance to discuss Soviet affairs with Braxton during the next few days. For the moment, however, Jack found Braxton's associate even more interesting.

"One minute, Mr. Braxton, Ms. Merrill."

Braxton nodded his response to the announcement as he continued studying the papers in his hand. Christine Merrill smiled.

Jack liked her smile, which reminded him vaguely of his former wife. He guessed Christine was in her early thirties. Even in the bedlam of the on-scene location, her suit and makeup were flawless. Her appearance exuded quiet confidence as she awaited her cue. He was impressed by her professional demeanor—as well as her looks. He also was curious about how she would look wearing something more feminine than her "dress for success" outfit. He tried to picture her auburn hair released to fall onto her shoulders instead of being styled atop her head.

He mused for a moment about how pleasant spending a week in San Francisco with someone like her would be instead of with the likes of Andrei Valinen. While Jack enjoyed the excitement of working at the highest levels of the Air Force, the demands of handling crisis after crisis left little time for a personal life or vacations. Seeing this attractive newswoman stirred feelings that he had pushed aside throughout his tour in the Pentagon.

"Ten seconds, Ms. Merrill."

Braxton acknowledged the audience with a pleasant smile as Christine awaited her final cue.

"Good evening. This is Christine Merrill with Alexander C. Braxton at San Francisco International Airport. As you can hear in the background, Alexander and I are only two among thousands. We are here to witness the arrival of the largest group of Soviet officials ever to visit the United States. They are coming to the historical setting where, at the end of this planet's most devastating war, men of good will joined to form the United Nations. This week, representatives of all nations of the Pacific Rim will take another stand against war by signing a non-aggression treaty.

"The idea for such a treaty was initially championed by Japan and slowly took hold among other nations, peace activists, and various disarmament groups on both sides of the Pacific. The real breakthrough came only last month. To everyone's surprise the Soviet Union agreed to periodic on-site inspections of military bases on the Kamchatka Peninsula, on the Kurile Islands, and at Vladivostok.

"Soviet Premier Konstantin Medvalev has demonstrated his firm hold on the reins of power by putting together an impressive delegation of Soviet luminaries for the signing of the treaty. Soviet President Gorshko—the man Medvalev picked last year for the presidency—heads the team. In addition to five Politburo doves, Minister of Defense Valinen and the head of Soviet state security, KGB Chairman Krasnovich, are included in the delegation. Their presence demonstrates the broad support and commitment the treaty has in the Soviet government."

Christine turned toward Braxton and said, "Alex, will this Pan-Pacific Conference and treaty bring us a giant step closer to 'Peace on earth, Good will toward men'?"

Braxton responded with a confident smile and a voice that had just a hint of a European accent, "We'd like to believe that, Christine, but few of us who pray for peace ever count upon the Soviets to answer that prayer."

"Later in this broadcast," Christine said, "we'll show pictures of the Soviet fleet now taking part in worldwide war games only seven hundred miles off the California coast. Alex, on one hand we have a powerful naval force near our shores, and on the other we have what you have called 'the most unlikely delegation ever to set foot outside the Soviet Union.' What does all this really mean?"

"What we're seeing, Christine, is a shift in power of truly historic proportions within the Soviet government."

You're overselling that a little, Jack thought. Signing treaties and complying with them were two separate matters for the Soviets. Also, he was sure Minister of Defense Valinen, who had been forced to join the delegation in spite of his opposition to the treaty, considered his current humiliation to be only a temporary setback.

Braxton continued, "Agreeing to extensive on-site inspections of military facilities is a sharp break with the past and with the paranoia of the Soviet psyche. This treaty is a major defeat for Minister of Defense Valinen and other Soviet hard liners. That's why Premier Medvalev is rushing to sign the treaty while the Soviet military is still conducting impressive exercises. The show of military power is a masterful coverup of the biggest retreat in Soviet policy since the withdrawal from Afghanistan."

Connecting the treaty to the naval exercises was an interesting view, Jack thought. As late as Thanksgiving, no one in America had imagined that the ceremony could be scheduled before Christmas. Braxton's insight offered a plausible reason for why the Soviets had agreed to sign the treaty so quickly.

Braxton continued in a style like that of a favorite instructor: "As far as the delegation is concerned, Christine, we're going to be treated to a veritable Who's Who of the Soviet's powerful elite. Only Premier Medvalev is missing, having chosen to remain in Moscow while his mightiest ministers are abroad."

"Earlier in the week," Christine said, "you singled out Minister of Defense Valinen as the crucial member of this delegation, even though he's not the senior member. What will his presence in San Francisco mean to the American people?"

"Minister Valinen has emerged the loser in the recent Kremlin maneuvering between the Communist Party, the KGB, and the Soviet military. Widely recognized as a hawk among hawks, Minister Valinen had spoken out strongly against the treaty, just as he has condemned every other peace initiative in his seven years as the top military man in the Soviet Union.

"Valinen's presence signals the defeat of the hawks who have dominated Soviet foreign policy since the Cold War began. Valinen has special meaning to all of us who were born in the Eastern European nations that came under Soviet domination after World War II. We simply will never forget Valinen's brutal subjugation of Czechoslovakia that earned him the nickname, Beast of Bratislava, a rallying cry for millions of European refugees.

"So, Christine, every peace-loving American is praying that something good shall come from this historic gathering. But even with the joyous spirit of the Christmas season, many Americans with roots in the countries of Eastern Europe will find it hard not to grab a placard saying 'Valinen Go Home!' and join the demonstrations expected this week while Minister Valinen is in San Francisco."

As Braxton was speaking, Jack's attention was captured by a young man pulling something from a camera case. Jack could not see the object, but he recognized the intense concentration and a narrowing of focus in the eyes—the man was about to attack. Jack pushed past other people as the attacker's hand came up and slashed forward.

The young man shouted, "Fascist, capitalist puppet! Stop your lies!"

Two eggs flew at Braxton. One struck his glasses, knocking them askew. The second hit his shoulder, splattering the yolk across his neck and the lapel of his immaculate blue jacket. With his glasses dangling from one earpiece, the news mogul appeared stunned.

As Jack lunged, he had expected to see a pistol or perhaps an explosive device in the man's hand. Before the assailant could pull anything else from the case, however, Jack struck. Combining a shoulder block with a bear hug, he clamped the arms of the wild-eyed man to his sides, and both men went crashing into a passageway that was roped-off to allow passengers to move through the crowds to the departure gates. As the two landed hard on the floor, the portable posts supporting the ropes clattered around them.

The man beneath the colonel was thirty pounds heavier, but the fall had taken much of the fight out of him. Television cameras from other news teams focused on the struggle, and Jack was nearly blinded by the glare of lights. Seeing policemen rushing forward, he just tried to control the struggling attacker.

The young man continued shouting epithets at Braxton as the police took over. Pushed aside by the growing cluster of uniformed and plain clothes officers, Jack scrambled to his feet. He pulled the hem of his trousers down over one of his black dress boots and brushed off his suit.

Braxton quickly regained his composure as Christine used an expensive-looking scarf to wipe away the worst of the egg mess. Adjusting his glasses, he turned toward his camera with the poise of a battlefield journalist and said, "It'll take more than eggs to keep me from speaking the truth about Andrei O. Valinen and the tyranny he has represented for forty years."

As Jack was retrieving his raincoat, he was startled by an announcement on the public address system. Initially the words had registered only subliminally, but his mind replayed them. "Dr. Baldachi. Dr. Nino Baldachi, call your service immediately."

He was certain of the words even though they nearly were drowned out by the noise. Braxton and his attacker still had the attention of the police, the news crews, and the crowd, so Jack slipped away easily. He checked his watch, then looked for a telephone. If the airliner arrived on schedule, he had little time to lose.

Could there be a misunderstanding? he wondered, pushing through the crowd. Perhaps the name had been similar, but Jack was almost certain the announcer had said Nino Baldachi. Baldachi was a mythical cadet whose presence had been pervasive in the early years of the United States Air Force Academy. The name had been used many times in pranks that became part of the lore of the military school. Jack and Colonel Wes Andrews, a close friend at the Pentagon, had adopted the name as an unofficial signal to be used between them when necessary.

As Jack reached a telephone, he felt a twinge of uneasiness: the open cubicle provided little privacy. He looked around, but no one in the pro-Soviet group seemed to show the least bit of interest in him. Still, he leaned forward, shielding the push buttons from view. He entered the Pentagon's area code, then pressed seven more buttons for a telephone number known to very few.

The second ring was interrupted by someone picking up the phone, and for a few moments the line seemed dead. His organization in the Pentagon was equipped with telephones that prevented transmissions except when someone depressed a button on the handset. So Jack heard nothing through the line until the button was pressed.

"Seven-three-five." A female voice was crisp and professional, saying only the last three numbers Jack had pressed.

"Uh, I'm not sure if there's some kind of mistake, but did someone in the office page Nino Baldachi on the West Coast?"

"Please stand by," she said.

Looking at the demonstrators again, he felt a little foolish. If the call were a mistake, his friend would razz him unmercifully as one more victim of Nino. And if he missed anything significant about the Soviets' arrival because he was wasting time on the telephone, he would be in for far more serious criticism.

In less than a minute, the original voice returned. "Proceed immediately to Alameda Naval Air Station. Call again on their special security line."

"Do you know that the people I'm waiting for haven't arrived yet?" He could not afford to have a misunderstanding send him off just before the arrival of Soviet National One.

"No mistake!" Her voice was firm, with a tinge of impatience.

"But—" he protested. His words were interrupted by a male voice at the Pentagon end.

"Proceed immediately to Alameda! Your plane is in the ocean."

Jack was stunned. He recognized the voice of his boss, General John McClintock, the vice chief of staff of the U.S. Air Force.

"Sir," he responded, thinking of a closer base on the San Francisco side of the bay, "I could get to a secure line at Sunnyvale a little quicker."

"I want you at Alameda," McClintock said firmly, then added, "things are going to get very, very confused where you are within a few minutes. I suggest you get moving now!"

"Roger that. I'm on my way, sir."

Putting on his raincoat as he passed the demonstrators, Jack hurried toward the escalators that led to the parking structure. His mind raced even faster as he tried to imagine why the plane had crashed. As he stepped off the escalator, he overheard a grim-faced man speak into a small radio.

"Get Harvard's car here *right now!* Trojan wants to see him ASAP!"

Exchanging a quick glance with the agent, Jack hurried on. He knew the code words: President Cunningham (Trojan) wanted Secretary of State Shafer (Harvard) to come to the President's estate, which served as the Western White House whenever Cunningham was in San Francisco.

Jack sped north on the Bayshore Freeway and across the Bay Bridge to Oakland. Hoping to learn details of the crash, he tuned a news station on the radio. A reporter at the airport said that there had been a delay in the arrival of Soviet National One. Weather was thought to be the cause.

A half hour later, Jack sped toward the main gate at Alameda Naval Air Station. Exiting the guard house, a large Marine stepped off the curb, partially blocking the car's path. Tires slid on the wet pavement as Jack slammed on the brakes. The only movement the Marine made was dropping his hand onto the pistol on his right hip just before the car stopped inches from his sharply creased trousers.

When he reached the window, he asked, "Your identification, please, sir?"

Jack handed over his military identification card and said, "I'm Air Force Colonel Jack Phillips. I was ordered here to use your communications facilities."

The guard studied the ID card, stared hard at Jack, then checked the information on the back of the card. After a few moments' pause, which seemed to Jack more for effect than for deliberation, the guard snapped to attention and rendered a crisp salute.

"You must have friends in high places, Colonel. We were told to be on the lookout for you."

"I'll need some directions. I'm—"

The guard blew two short blasts on his whistle, and in response, the headlights of a car flashed on in a nearby parking lot.

"Just follow that car, sir. Sergeant Molinelli knows where to take you."

Jack followed the car to the Fleet Intelligence Center, a windowless building near the runways. Razor-style concertina wire topped a twelve-foot fence surrounding the building. High-intensity lights illuminated the fence and the areas between it and the building. As Jack parked his car, he read a warning sign on the fence. The sign declared that the building was a Controlled Access Area. Smaller print gave appropriate references to the United States Code and Department of Defense directives that permitted the use of firearms against intruders.

His ID card, Pentagon entry badge, and official travel orders got him past the two guards at the outside gate. He followed Molinelli inside, past several closed-circuit television cameras and up to the intelligence and communications center on the second floor. For a moment, Jack was puzzled for he had expected to go down into an underground bunker. Then he remembered that the Naval Air Station was built on landfill, virtually surrounded by the waters of San Francisco Bay. The thresholds of the runways were barely nine feet above sea level, and thus most facilities were above ground.

Two armed Marines in separate bulletproof cubicles guarded the entrance to the intelligence and communications center. They were less easily satisfied than the gate guards. After reviewing Jack's credentials, the senior Marine told him he would have to be fingerprinted. Jack wished he had gone to the Air Force base where his Air Force rank would have helped establish his credentials more quickly.

"The vice chief of staff of the Air Force is waiting for a call from me," he said impatiently.

"If he weren't, sir, you wouldn't be inside the perimeter fence without your prints on file."

Molinelli rushed through the procedure as quickly as possible, but Jack regarded the delay with growing irritation. Afterwards, the guard announced his next surprise as Jack was cleaning the black ink from his fingers.

"Without matching prints available, sir, I need to ask questions from your personal security card."

The PSC was a government form on which the individual listed answers and questions made up from obscure background information not readily available to a foreign intelligence service. My card? Jack thought worriedly. It had been five years since he had filled out his PSC. He had no recollection of the questions he had written on the form, and he could not afford a mix-up that would cause additional delays.

"Okay, Colonel. What color was your dog when you were a boy?" The guard referred to a sheet of paper torn from a teletype machine.

"White! I had a white husky." Jack felt better.

The guard continued, "And the dog's name, sir?"

"Shaniko," Jack said, emphasizing the first syllable just as he had when he had spoken to the animal.

The guard seemed unsure whether the response matched the word on the paper.

"Shaniko," Jack said more distinctly. "I named him after a prairie town near my grandfather's ranch in northern Oregon."

"Close enough, sir. How about your best friend during childhood?"

"Dale. My cousin. We were like brothers."

The guard nodded. "One more, sir. The name of your favorite cat?"

"Cat?" Jack was caught by surprise. Noticing the guard studying his reaction, Jack exclaimed, "I don't know why I'd put that on there. I never had a— Is that there?"

The guard smiled. "Just checking, sir."

Jack felt relief and amusement.

"I didn't think you looked like a cat person, Colonel," the guard said, pressing a button on the electronic panel beside him. The button released the lock and sounded a buzzer to alert people in the vault that the door was about to open.

A large room was beyond the door. Dozens of military personnel manned desks and electronic consoles. A map of the Pacific basin covered the front wall, and along the top of the map were clocks labeled Washington, D.C., Alameda, Honolulu, Guam, Tokyo, Manila, and Greenwich, the standard worldwide time reference. Three large cubicles, similar to the soundproofed booths used for hearing tests, lined the wall across the room.

Another guard greeted Jack and advised him to wait inside the middle booth for a call on the classified telephone. When he stepped inside and closed the door, the clicking of computer keyboards and the whining clatter of high-speed printers seemed to cease. The cubicle provided complete privacy for discussing classified information. In less than a minute, the telephone rang.

"Colonel Phillips, sir," he said crisply, just in case General McClintock was on the other end.

"Hello, Jack. Wes Andrews here. Has Randy Jensen joined you yet?"

"I haven't seen him. What in the hell's happening, Wes?"

"We don't have much so far," Andrews said. "The Soviet bird went into the water somewhere near the coast, northwest of San Francisco."

"Anybody survive?"

"Doubtful. Weather's rotten at the crash site."

"Causes?"

"Nobody's speculating. I just hope we didn't knock them down."

"Don't even say that in jest," Jack said. During the drive from San Francisco he had tried to imagine every potential cause for the crash. Though he had considered the possibility of sabotage, an American attack had not occurred to him. He responded with a line that he and Andrews often exchanged whenever they speculated about anything significant. "You sure as hell wouldn't want to see yourself quoted on that in the *Post*."

Andrews ignored the joke and continued very seriously, "We had two F-15s on her when she started down. With Valinen and Krasnovich aboard, that bird made a better target than anything you and I ever went after in North Vietnam."

Jack agreed but did not say so. Valinen's recklessness had caused the hot line between Washington and Moscow to be used on at least three occasions that he knew of. Krasnovich was also a saber-rattler, but his position as head of the KGB was not as powerfal as Valinen's at the head of the military.

"But taking a shot at them isn't worth starting World War III," he said.

"Eliminating that pair might save us all—Stand by. Here's the boss."

Jack waited in silence until the familiar voice of General McClintock boomed through the earpiece. "Got a new job for you, Jack."

"Whatever you need, General."

"We've got one hell of a sensitive problem just off the Golden Gate, and I'got to have answers. I'm sending you to Howell to get the investigation started."

"Howell?" Almost as soon as he said it, Jack realized that the fighters assigned to protect San Francisco would have come from that air base in central California.

"The pair of Eagles that intercepted the Soviet airliner are due on the ground at Howell momentarily. If we can't prove those birds didn't cause the crash, Jack, we may be looking down the barrel of World War III."

Jack was shocked at McClintock's concern and the way he expressed it. The general normally was not a pessimist.

"Surely nobody would jump—"

McClintock interrupted, "Looks like the lead F-15 launched a missile."

A quick whistling sound escaped Jack's lips. He had been away from fighters for nearly three years, but he knew that F-15s seldom missed what they shot at.

McClintock continued, "Our pilot claims he destroyed the missile before it got to the Soviets. I can't overemphasize the importance of coming up with evidence to prove that, Jack."

Jack considered the words carefully. They could be interpreted two ways—as a plea or as a directive. He wondered if, for the first time in their long acquaintance, the general was asking for more than the truth. Jack did not believe that, but he was unsure how to respond. "You do understand, I suppose, that we may end up with nothing more solid than our pilots' testimony."

"That's not the answer we're hoping for, Jack." McClintock paused. "But if that's what you find, that's what I expect you to report."

Jack felt better. "No one's ever accused me of being a yes man."

"That's why I told General Raleigh you were the man for the job," McClintock said, referring to the Air Force chief of staff. "We hope you'll find something to clear the Air Force, Jack, but above all else, we have to get the truth to the President so he can act accordingly. We can't afford any more surprises."

Jack wondered what would happen if the evidence indicated that the missile had struck the Soviet airliner. Certainly if the situation were reversed, there would be demands for President Cunningham to retaliate militarily. "How much time do I have before this all goes public?"

"The FAA's trying to hold off announcing the crash until the President has a chance to go over everything. But that's probably minutes, not hours."

"Before I left the airport," Jack said, "they were trying to hustle Secretary Shafer to the President's estate."

"Getting people together's another problem," McClintock said. "Everyone's so damned scattered. General Raleigh's on his way to a National Security Council meeting."

"Is anyone left in Washington?"

"Almost everyone's in San Francisco. The Vice-President's already at his wife's family home in Beverly Hills, and the secretary of defense is still in Saudi Arabia. Damned poor timing for a crisis!"

"The Soviets haven't broken the story?"

"Ambassador Sherinin's already queried Moscow, but he won't release anything until he gets the okay from the Kremlin."

Jack looked at his watch. "It's late morning in Moscow, so the Soviets have probably gotten their people together."

"Medvalev's likely to have trouble gathering a quorum, too, since his key people were on the plane. Of course he doesn't have Christmas vacations to contend with," he noted, alluding to the fact that the Christmas holiday did not have the same city-emptying effect on Moscow as on the American capital.

"With Valinen and his main 'horse holders' on the airplane," Jack said, "the Soviet military should be confused for a while."

"At least we won't have to worry about him stirring the pot," McClintock said. "There's a chance cooler heads will prevail. I'm sending Captain Jensen with you to Howell to shake down the aircraft and the maintenance records. Is he there yet?"

"Haven't seen him, sir," Jack said, "but I didn't know I was looking for him."

Captain Randy Jensen was a maintenance officer assigned as part of the team supporting Air Force One on the President's trip to San Francisco.

"Any other support you'll need to get started?"

"The tapes," Jack said. "I'd like to get hold of the intercept controller's and the FAA's voice tapes as soon as they're available."

"I've got Wes Andrews working that already. Now, you'd better get on your way."

"Yes, sir. I should be there by—"

"There's a helicopter, with blades turning, waiting outside for you. And, Jack, there's one more thing. In the last few minutes, we sent a set of special orders to the telefax at the comm center in Alameda. In addition to assigning you and Jensen as investigators on behalf of the chief of staff, the orders assign a special code phrase to you to use in the next few hours anyway. In your message-traffic and phone calls, and on any roadblocks the bureaucracy puts in your way, use the words 'Redline Alpha Three' with your name."

Facetiously, Jack said, "Those three words will overcome the bureaucracy, sir?" The suffocating weight of the bureaucracy was a topic the two had discussed many times.

"That may sound like an overstatement, but only two people have a higher priority—President Cunningham is Redline Alpha One and the secretary of defense is two. Anyway, call me when you get to Howell."

Jack left the booth and picked up copies of the special orders. Stepping outside, he heard the familiar *whup-whup-whup* of an idling helicopter. He grabbed his bags from the trunk of his rental car and rushed through a steady rain. The pilot told Jack that Captain Jensen had just entered the main gate of the Naval Air Station.

Settling into a canvas seat and feeling the metallic vibrations of the helicopter, Jack had a moment to consider the enormity of what was happening. Air combat over North Vietnam had provided difficult challenges, but nothing that compared with his current mission. Watching the swirling rain, he felt exhilaration. He also felt the exhaustion that came from flying coast-to-coast after working a twelve-hour day in the Pentagon.

In a few minutes a car carrying Captain Jensen pulled to a stop a few feet beyond the reach of the whirling blades of the helicopter. As Jensen tossed his bags inside and climbed aboard, Jack asked, "Ready for a little excitement, Randy?"

"I don't know what you've got going, Colonel," Jensen said as he shook rain from his hair, "but I'll bet it's not as exciting as what I had going this evening."

"Don't put any big money on that, Randy," Jack said as the helicopter lifted off and banked east through the low clouds toward the Central Valley, "because unfortunately you lose."

Chapter 3

THE HELICOPTER'S SLASHING BLADES SWIRLED FOG IN SPIRAL PATTERNS as the pilot lowered the craft toward a taxiway at Howell Air Force Base. The downwash from the rotors blasted water from puddles on the concrete, mixing that spray with the drizzle that continued to fall.

During the flight from Alameda, the two investigators had changed from civilian clothes. After his experience with the Marines, Jack was glad to be back in uniform. He never needed to establish his competence to anyone who could read the ribbons above his left pocket. Intermingled in six rows beneath his pilot wings were metallic insignias and multicolored ribbons that represented gallantry in combat and exceptionally meritorious service in peacetime.

Despite his lack of sleep, he was ready to get started. As he waited for the pilot to park, he felt the controlled eagerness of a man who thrives under stress.

Trailing behind the "Follow Me" truck, the helicopter taxied through the ghostly yellowish glimmer of high-intensity arc lamps filtered by fog. Finally the pilot parked in front of Base Operations, next to the well-manicured shrubs and grass that separated the concrete parking area from the building. A welcome sign near the sidewalk was decorated with the colorful insignia of Howell's wing and squadrons.

Jack slid open the helicopter door as the roar of the engine died away. The absence of local officials surprised him. The only Howell personnel nearby were maintenance men attaching grounding wires to the helicopter and doing other post-arrival checks.

"I figured someone would greet us," Jack said as he jumped to the concrete.

Jensen handed down a hangup bag and a briefcase. "I imagine they're pretty busy about now, sir."

"If I were the wing commander," Jack said, "I'd sure as hell have someone on hand when the investigating team arrived."

He had decided to debrief the fighter pilots while Jensen went to

29

the aircraft and searched for evidence. Flagging down a nearby Security Police pickup, he showed the driver a copy of the orders from General McClintock. The policeman made a call on his two-way radio, then agreed to take Jensen to the two F-15s, which had been impounded for the investigation. Military protocol dictated that Jack officially inform the wing commander before starting an investigation, and he asked if the commander was at the aircraft.

The security policeman pointed at a staff car parked nearby and said, "That's his car, sir, so I think Colonel Radisson's still in the Command Post."

Jack stiffened when he heard Radisson's name. Angry memories flashed through his mind. For an instant, even thoughts of the Soviet airliner were pushed aside. He doubted that this Radisson could be anyone but the man he knew. A quick look at the welcome sign confirmed his suspicion. Suspended beneath the main sign was a smaller panel that said: "Colonel Robert F. Radisson, Commander."

Normally, Jack did not hold grudges—but he had made an exception in Bob Radisson's case. The two had been young pilots in the final, fire-filled days of the American air offensive over Hanoi. Even that early in Radisson's career, his well-polished combination of ambition, charm, and cunning had increased his influence.

Jack had tolerated Radisson but never respected him. Before those fateful December days in 1972, he had categorized Radisson as someone who was better ignored than bothered with. One deadly afternoon, however, Radisson made a grab for personal glory, violated air discipline, and led his flight of four fighters into a flak trap. Jack had barely survived. His best friend and one other pilot had not. Only Radisson came through unscathed. In the months that followed, Jack tried to nail him with a court-martial. However, the national euphoria accompanying the end of American involvement in the Vietnam War— along with Radisson's charm and connections—caused the charges to be delayed and finally dropped. Thus the issue had been resolved officially, but not personally.

"If I need to reach you, sir," Jensen said as he got into the cab of the security police pickup, "I'll contact the Command Post."

"Command Post?" Remembering the words of the security policeman, Jack added, "Sure. I'll check in later at the aircraft."

He carried his bags into Base Operations and placed them in the aircrew baggage area. He followed a sequence of signs along a dimly lit corridor until he located the Command Post entrance with its steel door, cipher lock, and Restricted Area warning signs. Near the door, a counter extended through the wall below an opening that was barred and shuttered. This was where pilots filed their flight plans and received directions from the duty controller in the Command Post. Jack spotted an electronic buzzer attached to the wall near the counter and pushed the button to summon the controller.

In a few moments he heard the sounds of someone unlatching the panels behind the bars. A captain dressed in olive-drab fatigues shoved the panels aside. Jack could hear voices and machines, but a black curtain kept the busy Command Post hidden from view.

"I'm here from the Pentagon," he said, pushing a copy of his orders across the counter and under the bars. "I need to see your wing commander."

The captain scanned the orders. He did a double-take when he got to the signature of the vice chief of staff of the Air Force. "Sir, I'll check to see if he's available." The captain closed the panels.

Standing alone in the hallway, Jack checked his watch: one-fifty in the morning, more than twenty-two hours since he woke in his Georgetown apartment. He was tired, but the possibility of a face-to-face confrontation with Radisson had him psyched up. He could not have fallen asleep even if there had been a place to lie down.

He leaned against the wall and reached unconsciously for a cigarette. He checked a second pocket, then a third before the frustration of the unsuccessful search interrupted his conscious thoughts. His sudden desire for a cigarette made him even angrier. For years he had been a chain smoker, but he had not had a cigarette in nearly a year. He was frustrated to discover that his suppressed hatred of Radisson had rekindled the habit so rapidly.

Instead of a cigarette, he pulled an irregular piece of metal from his pocket and began rubbing his thumb back and forth across the uneven surface. Less than an inch wide and two inches long, the metal fragment had been part of a Soviet-made antiaircraft shell. For more than a decade, he had carried the fragment wherever he went. Edges once sharp enough to rip flesh now were rounded and blunt—capable only of cutting back through time in his thoughts. Squeezing the fragment in his palm, he realized how much he still hated Bob Radisson and everything Radisson had gotten away with in his career.

Once again he pushed aside angry thoughts. Since talking to General McClintock, he had been mentally preparing a list of questions. Why was the missile fired? Why were the fighters there in the first place? If the airliner had not been shot down, what caused the crash? How much time remained to find answers before the Soviets reacted militarily? How soon would the onslaught of reporters arrive, each in a fierce competition to create the most sinister account of what had happened in the dark skies west of California?

Time was crucial. Though he tried to keep focused on his upcoming interview with the two pilots, he grew ever more impatient. If Radisson had not learned earlier that Jack was en route to investigate, he knew now. Jack's only consolation was the certainty that Radisson was even more disturbed by their unexpected reunion than he had been. Radisson had never forgiven him for filing charges.

He checked his watch. Four minutes had passed. He would wait one more.

Still, nothing happened. He pressed the button and heard the muffled sound of a buzzer somewhere behind the wall. He listened for someone to unlatch the panels but heard nothing. He pushed the button again, holding it ten seconds. His anger increased as he remembered his best friend, Tex Madison, dying on an operating table at an American air base in Thailand.

He waited a few more seconds before depressing the button again. This time he would hold the button until the noise brought results. His other hand squeezed the shell fragment so hard that his forefinger turned blood red, as if threatening to burst under the pressure. He closed his eyes, vividly recalling a fist fight with Radisson in the bar of an officers club in the Philippines. Since the Air Force took a dim view of brawling among its officers, both men had had to help hush the rumors afterwards.

The clatter of the latches told him that someone had returned to the controller's area. As soon as the panels opened, he realized how much louder and more irritating the buzzer was inside the Command Post.

Before the captain could push the panels completely open, Radisson's voice shouted from beyond the curtain. "Tell that idiot out there to get his damned finger off the button!"

The captain looked embarrassed, unsure how to relay that message.

Jack released the button, not because of Radisson, but to relieve the captain from his dilemma. He said in a controlled voice, "Captain, tell your commander that he's delaying an official Air Force investigation."

The captain turned and started to step through a separation in the curtains.

"Tell whoever's out there to stand by. I'm busy."

"Not as busy as you're going to be," Jack said, putting just enough emotion into his voice for Radisson to understand there was no bluff. "I've got a phone call to make on the scrambler. If I have to use the public phone in the lobby, I guarantee you, Colonel, you'll wish that you'd played this a hell of a lot smarter!"

There was no immediate response.

"You've got ten seconds to let me in," he said as he held his watch where he could count off the seconds. When the counter had increased by ten, he roared, "Time's up!"

He flipped the shell fragment upward like a coin, then snatched it from midair with a move almost too quick for the eye to follow. Shoving the piece of metal into his pocket, he stomped from the counter, clicking the heels of his boots into the floor with enough force to be heard beyond the black curtain. As he passed the entry door to the Command Post, a buzzer sounded, indicating that the lock had been released from the inside.

He pivoted and stiff-armed the door, which swung open against the stops with a resounding clang. Everyone's attention was on him as he charged into the Command Post. With his eyes reflecting the fiery anger that filled him, he scanned the room until spotting his adversary. Radisson, immaculately dressed in a tailored flight suit, stood near the black curtain that covered one wall. Their gazes locked, and no one else dared intrude.

Neither man blinked before Jack spoke. "I'm Colonel Phillips from Headquarters, United States Air Force. I'm on an investigation for the vice chief of staff in accordance with Air Force Reg. 120-4. My priority is Redline Alpha Three, and if you don't know what that means, you'd better find out before you think about getting in my way!" He stared at Radisson, visually challenging him to defy.

"You can't just come storming in here and—"

"Do you have an office where we can discuss my requirements?" Jack normally avoided colonel-to-colonel confrontations in front of subordinates.

"This is my office," Radisson said, gesturing with his arms toward the status boards, computers, and people that made up the nerve center of his fighter wing.

"Your choice, Colonel."

"Just because I'm not jumping the instant you—"

"Cut the bullshit. I don't have the time."

"I hope you're not trying to make this another of your famous witch hunts, Phillips. My boys are good, and I don't want you trying to smear them with something left over from the last war."

"I'm not talking years ago," Jack said. "I'm here to investigate what happened tonight!"

"My boys had nothing to do with that bird going down. They were just out working the mission, which is something that may be hard for a staff weenie to understand."

"Your word still isn't good enough. That's why General McClintock sent me here to investigate, Colonel."

A look of rage flashed across Radisson's face, but he maintained control as he walked toward his elevated desk near the center of the room. He stepped onto the platform, which allowed him to look down on Jack instead of being two inches shorter.

"I'm not sure what you think you're going to do here," Radisson said, gesturing toward the phone. "General Harper just called. He'll be here with a full IG team this afternoon."

Damn, Jack thought. Outwardly he concealed his concern about the mention of General Harper, the Air Force inspector general. Harper was one of the sponsors Radisson had cultivated in an effort to promote himself and his career. Jack was confident of his backing, but General McClintock was twenty-five hundred miles away. Radisson would be much harder to keep pinned down once Harper arrived.

"General McClintock wanted me here this morning," Jack said, moving with self-assured strides toward Radisson.

Radisson crossed his arms, playing more to his subordinates than to Jack. "I don't give a damn about any pull you think you have. My orders come through Tactical Air Command, so unless TAC concurs, you get nothing!"

Jack controlled his emotions, but he wanted to grab the front of Radisson's flight suit and yank him from his stage. Radisson was correct about being responsible only to orders coming through his chain of command. However, most officers would have ignored that technicality—especially under the circumstances, and with the signature of the vice chief of staff of the Air Force on the orders that Jack carried. Radisson was stalling, trying to bluff his way into control, and Jack knew it. He also knew he could not keep wasting time.

"Redline Alpha Three! You got that?" Jack shot a hand out, stopping with a pointed finger a couple of inches from Radisson's nose.

Radisson flinched back, almost falling across the desk.

Before he recovered, Jack started toward the booth with the classified telephone and said loud enough for everyone in the Command Post to hear, "You need orders from the TAC commander? I can arrange that. Now, unless the President or the secretary of defense is using your scrambler, it's mine until I'm finished!"

People cleared out of his way as he marched to the booth. He entered, yanked the door shut, and punched the number into the keypad. Then he slumped into the chair, embarrassed to have to bother General McClintock with such pettiness.

The general was not immediately available. As Jack waited, he watched the activity in the Command Post. In spite of the distortion caused by the thickness of the soundproof window, he could read the numbers on the Defense Condition (DEFCON) status board near the ceiling on the front wall. The number four glowed brightly.

DEFCON Four was the level of defense readiness just above the peacetime level of DEFCON Five. American forces had been at DEFCON Four for the last two weeks in response to the worldwide exercise of the Soviet Navy and some war games in Europe. Jack was surprised that the DEFCON had not changed, just in case the Soviets chose a military response to the crash.

After a couple of minutes, McClintock came on the other end of the line.

"Sorry to have to bother you, sir," Jack said, "but I've run into a bit of an internal problem here at Howell."

"I half expected that, Jack. I almost mentioned Colonel Radisson earlier, but I'd hoped that was all behind us."

"I'm afraid not, sir. At this point, unless he receives orders through his chain of command, I'm not going to get much cooperation."

"I guess I'll have to turn up the gain on General Smathers' sensitivity meter." McClintock placed his hand over the mouthpiece of his telephone, directing his next statement to someone else. "Get General Smathers on the TAC hot line."

"Sir, the Command Post here at Howell is still carrying DEFCON Four. Is that a mistake?"

"Not so far," McClintock said. "The Joint Chiefs recommended that we switch to Three and be prepared to go to Two, depending on the Soviet response. But the President said no. He's worried about doing anything that could appear to be an additional provocation beyond the missile that was fired."

Jack was concerned that the President's attempt to avoid a confrontation could increase the danger. The unprecedented scope of the Soviet naval exercise, coupled with the accompanying war games in Eastern Europe, put the Soviet military in an excellent posture for launching a first strike. The only thing missing was a Kremlin decision to attack. "Sounds like we're taking a chance."

"Secretary Shafer and a couple of other advisers convinced the President that a change in DEFCON might be misinterpreted as an indication that we shot down the airliner."

"If I were about to initiate the big one, I'd rather be starting with the Soviet's deployments than where we sit in DEFCON Four."

"Their posture isn't our only problem," McClintock said. "The blizzard moving through the Great Plains has everything north of Omaha in a deep freeze."

The stormy weather in San Francisco, Jack thought, meant more snow throughout the Plains over the next few days. This was a significant concern because of the large percentage of American bomber and missile bases in the Northern Tier, the heartland states near the Canadian border. These bases had the advantage of being at a greater distance from the patrol areas of the Soviet submarines that carried nuclear missiles. The few extra minutes of warning time could allow American bombers and missiles to be launched before the arrival of the sea-launched ballistic missiles of a Soviet first strike.

However, major winter storms temporarily negated the advantage of these northern bases. Snow and ice could paralyze individual bases for hours at a time. Jack knew that the Soviets faced similar problems at an even larger percentage of their bases, but he believed there was one significant difference in the dilemmas facing Soviet and American commanders. If there ever were a first-strike, the Soviets would be launching the attack at a time of their choosing, and the Americans would have to react—in whatever weather and with whatever forces were positioned to fight.

He asked, "Any Soviet response so far, General?"

"About midnight, the ambassador released a short statement announcing that the aircraft had apparently crashed. He made no mention of our fighters or the missile. Our intel experts expect the Soviets to have two Navy ships at the crash site by early afternoon."

Jack found that hard to believe. He knew the Soviets had more than thirty ships exercising between Hawaii and the mainland, but those ships were several hundred miles away. None could reach the California coast in twelve more hours. Even averaging twenty-five knots, a ship would have to have been within 350 nautical miles of San Francisco when the plane crashed.

"Today? You mean at the crash site today?"

"Sure," McClintock said. "I'm talking about the destroyer and sub tender that were nursing their crippled nuclear sub."

Jack had not considered those two ships. Three days earlier, a Victor II-class submarine had surfaced about two hundred miles southwest of San Francisco. Radio messages between the submarine and the Soviet fleet had reported mechanical difficulties as the submarine appeared in danger of sinking in rough seas. Characteristically, the Soviets had declined offers of American assistance. He remembered that pilots of maritime reconnaissance aircraft of the U.S. Navy had reported that crews on the Soviet ships were frantically trying to keep the submarine afloat and get the boat underway again.

McClintock continued. "The *Gnevnyy* and the *Karpaty* are the two closest ships. Having the *Karpaty* nearby is the only good luck we've had so far in this mess. She's the Soviet's most capable submarine rescue ship. Her diving bells and cranes should be exactly what's needed to locate and to raise large sections of the aircraft."

"If our intel people get good pictures of whatever the Soviets bring up," Jack said, "we might get a better idea of what caused the crash."

"We can't wait that long for answers, Jack. Anyway, General Smathers is waiting and you need to get to work."

By the time Jack emerged from the booth, Radisson had regained some of his bravado.

"Well, Colonel," Radisson asked, "just what do you require that we haven't been providing?"

"First of all, I—"

"We're pretty committed right now," Radisson interrupted sarcastically, "but I suppose we can cancel some missions to nursemaid you around."

"Cut the bullshit, Colonel. You've already cost me twenty minutes that I didn't need to waste. I want to see the pilots, and I need a quiet place for oral debriefings."

"They're still at the clinic finishing their flight physicals," Radisson said.

Despite his anger, Jack nodded at that. Regulations required medical checkups after any significant flying incident. "I want to see both pilots as soon as they're finished. In the meantime, I want their postflight debriefing forms and tapes of every word your pilots said from the time they started engines until they shut 'em down."

"Things like that take time," Radisson said. "You'll need to make your request for recordings to the Comm Squadron."

"Get the tapes!" Jack's steely glare did not waver. "Redline Alpha Three! I want a place to sleep that has close access to a secure phone. And I want a car and a map—a base map marked with the location of the two impounded F-15s and where I can interview the pilots."

"Well, I—"

"I want the pilots' records—personnel, flying, physical, and anything else you may have from the time they were born until the moment they strapped on those F-15s last night! Do you read me, Colonel?"

"Anything else you desire, Colonel?" Radisson picked up a clipboard as if he were going to make a large list.

"Affirmative! I need an aeronautical chart of the crash site in relation to San Francisco as well as a copy of all your upchannel reporting messages, particularly safety and public affairs releases."

"Some of those things are privileged information."

"And I have the privilege," Jack said as he waved a copy of his orders in front of Radisson. "I want to get a chop on any additional publicity info you plan to release, and that's an area you'd better not screw up!"

"Looks like you're setting yourself up to be safety officer, censor, flight surgeon, and personnel officer all rolled up into one," Radisson said, making a sweeping gesture toward his desk and chair. "Maybe you'd like to try being the wing commander."

Jack fought the temptation to comment. Instead he repeated slowly and deliberately, "Redline Alpha Three."

Radisson finally broke the exchange of glaring looks. As his eyes darted around the Command Post, everyone returned to normal duties. A master sergeant brought Jack an annotated map and earned a silent reprimand from Radisson.

The longer the telephone remained silent, the more Radisson's confidence seemed to increase. However, the hot line from the TAC Command Post finally rang. A young captain answered, and the color disappeared from his face.

"Sir," the captain said in a voice that suggested he had never before received a telephone call from a four-star general, "it's General Smathers at TAC."

With an exaggerated flourish Radisson grabbed the phone at his desk. He showed the outward confidence of a man about to redeem himself, but he made one serious oversight. He failed to notice the speaker on his telephone was on.

"Good morning, Gen—"

"What in the *hell* are you trying to do?" The deep Southern drawl of the general's voice echoed through the Command Post. Radisson frantically poked his finger at the maze of push buttons. His face reddened as the general continued, "I just had a wire brushing by the vice chief that I won't forget for a long time, so if you have the slightest desire to still be a wing commander at sunrise, you'd—"

Radisson finally succeeded in disengaging the speaker. His contribution to the rest of the conversation was a series of "Yes, sirs," and an unsuccessful "But, sir." When he replaced the receiver, most of the color had drained from his face.

"Sergeant Nolan, get the colonel a vehicle," he said gruffly to the man who earlier had provided the map. Grabbing a stack of teletype messages, he feigned extreme interest in the papers. Without looking at Jack, he continued, "The pilots are due out of their physicals in twenty minutes. They'll be going to the Wing Headquarters building to sign the statements that Flight Safety's working up. The records and other stuff you asked for will be delivered to the Wing Conference Room, which is in the same building. The flying safety officer will show you where." He continued studying the handful of messages as if Jack had never been there.

Sergeant Nolan gave Jack a set of car keys and directions to the car.

"If I were you, Colonel," Jack said before turning away, "I'd learn how to operate that phone—just in case General Smathers needed to give me another call."

Radisson glowered at Jack, but said nothing.

As Jack moved toward the door, he sensed that Sergeant Nolan and most of the others in the room were silently cheering.

Chapter 4

JACK PHILLIPS HATED ACCIDENT INVESTIGATIONS. HE HAD SIFTED through enough crash sites to last a lifetime. During his first investigation he had decided that it was cruel and unusual punishment to make fliers serve on accident investigation boards. A flier's viewpoint, experience, and expertise certainly were needed. However, nothing reminded him more of his mortality than sorting through broken bodies and jagged metal. The distinctive stench of burned jet fuel, scrub brush, and flesh always left him less convinced that the same thing could never happen to him. At least this time, he thought, he didn't have to pick through the remains at a crash site.

Ten minutes after arriving in the wing headquarters, he sat at the end of a large conference table. He held copies of reports the flying safety officer had put together after the initial debriefings of the two fighter pilots. The flying and personnel records of Captain Eduard Benes and First Lieutenant Lawrence G. Walker were stacked next to a coffee cup, an open pack of cigarettes, and an ashtray. A large part of the table beyond was covered by a Tactical Pilotage Chart, with its greens, browns, blues, and purples representing parts of Nevada, California, and the North Pacific Ocean.

Jack lit his third cigarette as he began with Benes' description of the mission. As he read, he wrote notes in a small notebook.

He had not finished studying the report when the two pilots arrived. He told them to make themselves comfortable while he completed his review of the written information. He wanted to keep both pilots with him, thereby forcing each flier to deal quietly with his own thoughts for the last few minutes before the questioning began.

As Jack returned to reading, Captain Benes pushed his hands deeply into the pockets of his flight jacket and paced slowly in front of the windows along one side of the conference room. At six feet, three inches, he was taller than most fighter pilots. His black hair was in disarray, having been crushed once too often by the blue flight cap

40

that now protruded from a lower pocket on his flight suit. He seemed oblivious to the others in the room. Occasionally he stopped to stare into the darkness beyond the window.

Lieutenant Walker sat quietly. He leaned over the table and rested his head on the makeshift pillow he had made out of his flight jacket. Eight inches shorter than Benes, Walker had the compact, muscular build that was ideal for high-G maneuvering in advanced tactical fighters. He appeared to be dozing, but he periodically opened an eye and peeked in Jack's direction.

Walker was not under the same pressure as Benes. Being a wingman was a little like being Vice-President—not a lot of credit, not a lot of blame. In air combat the leader normally got the kills and the glory that went with aerial victories. The leader also carried most of the burden when the flight messed up on its mission. And of course, Walker had not fired the missile.

After reading the reports, Jack checked the flying and personnel records. He found no problems. According to the records, Benes and Walker were good pilots and good officers.

Jack was tempted to interview the two pilots separately, but he did not have time. A joint interview would be quicker with the pilots able to fill in details together that otherwise might be overlooked. By interviewing them at the same time, Jack faced the risk that a coverup would be easier—if there was something to cover up. However, he felt confident that he had the flying experience and the judgment to catch the two young pilots if they chose to lie.

Normally he was supportive of junior officers. In this case, however, he was determined to be just the opposite. Although he did not look forward to the role he had to play, he was prepared to be the meanest son of a bitch Benes and Walker had ever run into—at least until he knew what they knew. He was confident that the pilots would face even tougher grilling once the media learned of their mission—and of the missile. If either Benes or Walker had trouble in the way he told his story, now was the time to bring such troubles into the open.

He took a long last puff on a cigarette and crushed it out in the ashtray. Clearing all hints of friendliness from his expression, he glanced toward Walker, then focused on Benes.

"Okay, gentlemen. I want to hear everything."

Walker raised his head with an expression suggesting he had dozed off. Benes stopped pacing, stood almost at attention, and said, "Everything I know is already in front of you, sir."

"I've been over every word," Jack said, "but now I want to hear you tell it."

Benes looked at his watch as if in protest.

"I know it's late, Captain," Jack said sternly. "I've been up nearly twenty-four hours myself, but we'll stay here however long it takes to get the whole truth."

Benes leaned forward with his hands on the table. He seemed to be struggling to avoid words more blunt than the differences in rank permitted. "The truth's on the paper, sir. We don't have anything to add."

Jack noted the word "we." If Benes were lying, he would want Walker to say as little as possible.

"If there are holes in your story, or in the way you two tell it, I want to find out now."

Benes stood tall and crossed his arms in front of him, taking the stance of a man not often challenged. "Just what kind of holes do you expect to find, Colonel?"

Although Jack fixed Benes with an angry stare, he was pleased. He knew the attitudes of fighter pilots, and Benes' attitude fit. The younger ones were usually cocky and brash, eager to prove themselves, and unwilling to be put down without a fight. Jack was willing to provoke—and even accept—some insubordination from Benes. Anger was what he was after—anger that could release secrets that otherwise might remain hidden.

"Don't play cute with me, Captain. Your finger was on the trigger, not mine."

Benes' hands banged on the table as he again leaned toward his questioner. Raising his voice, Benes said, "You sound like you think I'm lying. Sir, I'm a commissioned officer, and if you—"

"Right now your oath of commission is secondary. Whether you were incompetent, careless, just plain unlucky—or something far worse—you're in today's headlines. You'd damn well better have some solid answers when reporters start jamming their microphones down your throat."

Jack was winging his responses, trying for the right degree of provocation.

"Just how basic do we need to get for you, Colonel?" The tone of Benes' voice reflected more sarcasm than respect.

Jack leaned toward Benes, staring into the eyes of the young pilot. "Let me put things this way, Captain. You two were still learning your ABCs when I was flying F-105s over Hanoi. I was doing my first rat-racing in F-15s about the time you discovered that playing with girls could be even more fun than playing with boys. And I haven't been a staff weenie so long that I've forgotten the kick in the ass you get lighting both burners on an F-15. So if you say something I don't understand, you can trust me to ask." He motioned toward the chair beside Walker and added, "Now get your butt onto that chair, and let's get on with what we came here for."

"Yes, sir!" Benes yanked the chair away from the table. He settled into the chair and started deliberately. "We came off alert on a routine Interception and Identification scramble. We launched at twenty-two twenty hours and made a burner climb to forty-seven thousand. During our climb the controller said he was vectoring us to a bird that had busted the ADIZ by seventy miles."

"Seventy?"

"That's what the controller said."

Walker nodded, indicating that Benes had not exaggerated.

Jack had trouble accepting a navigational error of seventy miles. Soviet National One would have had the best available crew and the best equipment. A seventy-mile error was like the hand-picked crew of Air Force One getting lost with the President on board. Possible, but highly unlikely.

He assumed that the crew on Soviet National One would have used signals from navigational satellites. He would be surprised if the aircraft were not equipped to receive signals from the Soviet's *GLONASS* satellites and from the American *NAVSTAR GPS*. With that data available and properly used, a navigational error of even one mile was unjustified.

Aviation regulations permitted a deviation of only twenty nautical miles from the ADIZ entry point listed in the flight plan a pilot filed before takeoff. Jack easily accepted that a seventy-mile deviation at the ADIZ, such as that by Soviet National One, would result in the warble of Klaxons followed by the roar of F-15 afterburners at the end of a runway.

Jack asked, "Did the controller tell you the aircraft's call sign?"

"He said they assumed the unidentified aircraft was a Soviet airliner."

"Soviet National One?"

"I don't remember if he said that or not."

Watching Benes for any reaction, Jack said, "I'm sure that's already a matter of record—on the controller's voice tapes, I mean." He looked for a flash of panic that might indicate that Benes had not realized all his contacts with the controller had been recorded.

"Then, Colonel," Benes said coldly, "I guess it doesn't matter that I don't remember, does it?" He did not appear to be worried that the tapes would not match what he was saying or had written in his report.

Jack settled into three roles as he listened for every detail. Mentally, he took Benes' place inside the cockpit of the streaking fighter, observing the eerie glow of instrument lights within the darkness of thick clouds. Jack also sought to see beyond that windscreen into the minds of the Soviet pilots. At the same time, he kept his own role, listening for inconsistencies, hints of falseness, or anything else that could trip up Benes in the interviews that would follow.

Benes used his hands as he described the rendezvous with the airliner. When he told of the Soviet aircraft slipping into the cloud tops just as the F-15s got overhead, Jack recognized an opportunity to test the young aviator.

"That's when you armed your weapons?"

"No, that came later when—" A look of anger flashed across Benes' face as he fixed his gaze on Jack. "Of course I didn't arm then. There was no reason to."

"You know who was on the airplane, don't you, Captain?"

"I've heard stories. I—"

"Valinen!" Jack leaned across the table once again. "And a whole planeload of Russian brass. You knew that when you first saw the airplane, didn't you?"

"No! Maybe. Well—"

"Either you did or you didn't, Captain. Which is it?"

"Sure, I'd heard about the big conference," Benes said. "Stories were on TV this evening, but that didn't tell me who was on that airplane."

"Soviet National One! You fly F-15s, and you weren't sharp enough to make the connection, Captain?"

"Not at the time, sir! As far as I was concerned, the mission was just a standard intercept and identify—go take a look and come home."

"And you didn't arm then?"

"If you don't believe me, sir, you can listen to those tapes."

"I will, Captain. I most certainly will."

As Benes continued describing the mission, Jack lit another cigarette and listened until the mention of the unexpected dive by the Soviet aircraft.

"What was your first thought when you realized something was happening?"

"I assumed he was trying to escape."

Jack tried to picture what he would have thought if he had been the F-15 flight leader when an unidentified aircraft radically altered its flight path. Pilots flying VIPs seldom maneuvered unpredictably—combat pilots often did. "Escape? Escape from what? Had you threatened him?"

"Negative, sir!"

Watching for the upcoming reaction, Jack asked, "You hadn't launched yet?"

"That's a negative! Can't we get away from this 'guilty until proven innocent' bit, sir?"

"Look, Captain, lots of folks are going to figure you smoked one up his tailpipe and everything you say is just a coverup."

Benes stood and zipped his flight jacket with an upward jerk. "People can think whatever they choose, Colonel. I know what's the truth, and if the reporters don't buy my story, they can go straight to hell!"

"Right now," Jack said, slamming his fist on the table, "I couldn't care less about reporters. What matters is what the Russians are going to think, and they won't give a damn about your version of the truth."

Frowning, Benes shook his head. Jack waited until the young pilot slumped into the chair and leaned back with his hands shoved deep into the pockets of his jacket.

Jack continued, "Why didn't you assume the Soviet bird was having some kind of mechanical failure instead of escaping?"

"I don't know. You asked for my first reaction, and that's what I gave you."

"We'd had the briefing," Lieutenant Walker said, finally choosing to venture into the fray between the colonel and the captain.

"Briefing?" Jack was uncertain what Walker meant. Once the Klaxon sounded, there was no time for briefings.

"Yes, sir," Walker answered, pulling a notebook from a pocket on his flight suit.

"When we came on alert the day before yesterday, we received a current intelligence briefing. The briefer discussed the Soviet naval exercise and mentioned the Soviet fleet between Hawaii and California."

Jack made a note in his book to review the materials used in the intelligence briefing.

"You need to understand, sir," Benes said, gesturing toward the rows of ribbons above the left pocket of Jack's uniform. "You've been in combat before. I haven't."

Jack nodded. He had seen things get very confusing in air combat. Sometimes the confusion was never straightened out, even after reliving the mission for hours in debriefings and in the bar at the club.

"When his bird started accelerating," Benes said, "I pictured the Soviet pilot putting a cruise missile right on Fisherman's Wharf."

Walker added, "It wouldn't be the first time the call sign of a civilian airliner was used to cover a sneak attack."

Jack agreed. He knew of one instance more than thirty years earlier in the Mideast, but then the world had been in a crisis. "But there weren't any other indicators."

"Besides the fleet," Walker said. "If the Soviets ever do try to take us on, I think they'll attack while they're deployed in an exercise."

Jack agreed again. He was pleased by the young lieutenant's grasp of strategy and military history.

"For all we knew," Benes said, "the same thing was happening near Seattle and Los Angeles. I saw no other choice but to light the burners and prepare to respond to any hostile act."

"Protecting San Francisco is our job," Walker said. He paused. "That's what they sent us up there for."

Jack liked Walker's naïveté and youthful enthusiasm for his job. A few years from now, he thought, Walker's viewpoint would have changed. By then he would have flown a hundred intercepts against a hundred aircraft whose pilots or navigators had been careless.

He would look on his hundred-and-first intercept as another routine flight to put a little fear into a sloppy aircrew. But tonight Walker was right on. His real mission was to be there to protect San Francisco—if necessary.

Benes said, "If you'd been in command, you'd have done the same thing, Colonel."

If their description of the incident was accurate, Jack thought, he would have done exactly the same thing.

"Just how evasive was the aircraft?"

Benes started to answer, then cocked his head to the side as if concentrating on his memories of the frantic dive toward the ocean.

After a few seconds Walker broke the silence. "Just the dive, sir. The heading didn't vary a degree."

"Are you sure?" Jack was surprised. He wondered how much the lieutenant was exaggerating. A constant heading suggested an aircraft under control. Perhaps his answer was part of a broader structure of lies. But if they were lying, Jack thought, they were very convincing.

"No doubt, sir," Walker said, positioning his hands like two aircraft in formation.

He slid his left hand away as he spoke. "When Ed told me to spread the formation so I'd be in position to take on cruise missiles, I checked the heading."

Jack focused on Walker and waited him out.

"You check headings when you fly formation in the clouds, Colonel," Walker said.

He immediately dropped his hands and blushed at having offered such a basic lesson in instrument flying to the veteran pilot across the table. "I mean, the heading was 106 degrees. I banked left for a few seconds to get horizontal separation on Ed. Then I came right back to 106 degrees. That heading kept me with them until they started maneuvering near the water."

Jack could not spot a flaw in Walker's description of his maneuvering in the clouds. Radar and instrument readings were the only tools available for the pilots to keep track of the relative positions of the three aircraft. By turning for a few seconds, Walker positioned his aircraft farther left of Benes. Walker needed some lateral separation before he could fire at the cruise missiles without hitting Benes' Eagle. To maintain that lateral separation, Walker had to stay on a parallel heading. So the lieutenant certainly had reason to know the heading throughout the descent.

"The Soviet's airspeed was pretty stable, too," Benes added.

"How fast?"

"Point nine one, sir," Benes said, indicating that the speed was .91 Mach, or just over nine-tenths of the speed of sound.

"You're sure?"

"I'd been locked onto him from a hundred miles out. During the dive, point nine one is what my instrument readouts told me until we got lower, and he picked up about 350 knots. I wondered if he was going to break the Mach."

Walker nodded in agreement. "We knew that if he went supersonic and didn't come apart, we sure as hell weren't chasing an Il-62."

Jack considered the answers. He would have reached the same conclusions if he had been strapped into one of the F-15s. He made a note to ask the Air Force analysts at the Foreign Technology Division how high the "critical Mach" was for the Il-62.

An aircraft's critical Mach number was the speed at which the passing airflow became supersonic as it accelerated over some part of the aircraft. An aircraft had to be designed for supersonic flight before it could exceed its critical Mach without paying a price. Minor infractions of the speed limit imposed by the laws of aerodynamics could tear off antennas or put premature wrinkles in the aircraft's skin. Major infractions produced a more predictable result—breakup of the aircraft. Point nine one Mach had to be close to the maximum allowable airspeed for the Il-62. Jack was unsure why the Soviet airliner had not gone even faster and broken apart during the descent.

"All indications now are that you *were* chasing an Il-62," Jack said. "I lost a good friend on an aircraft that entered an uncontrollable dive from thirty thousand feet. In that case, the bird broke apart before it ever got to the ground. This one apparently stayed together all the way to the water."

"That's affirmative, sir," Benes said.

The reports of a steady speed and a steady heading troubled the colonel, suggesting two possibilities: an aircraft under control and behaving in a very strange way—or a lie to conceal that the aircraft had been hit by the missile. The first possibility made no sense to him; the second disturbed him, but he decided to postpone any challenges.

"What radio calls did the Soviet pilot make during the descent?"

"I don't know," Benes said. "We weren't operating on his freq."

"You'll have to check the FAA tapes, sir," Walker said. "The Soviets were with Oakland Center. We were working Guardian on a tactical Air Force freq."

"I heard Oakland on Guard," Benes said, reminding Jack that Karl Wilson's calls on the emergency frequency would have been heard by all nearby aircraft. "He told National One not to go below twelve thousand."

"Any acknowledgment?"

"None on Guard, and the bird didn't stop at twelve."

"Maybe they also had radio failure," Walker said.

"Maybe," Jack said.

He was not ready to disregard any reasonable failure or combination of failures on the Soviet aircraft. However, few failures, short of an explosion, would disable all the radios and cause an uncontrollable dive. His breathing deepened as he pictured frantic Russian crew members—some struggling to keep the aircraft from steepening its dive, others immobilized in fear. Instead of radio failure, he could more easily accept that the crew was too busy fighting the problem to take time to talk on the radio.

He picked up the incident report and scanned a paragraph on the second page. Then he focused on Benes. "Tell me about the launch."

Benes made eye contact for an instant, then looked away, shaking his head. His earlier tone of combativeness disappeared. "I wish I had a good answer, sir. I don't know why the missile fired. Maybe a short circuit, but I think I hit the weapon release when I grabbed for a chart that bounced off the glare shield in the turbulence." He took a deep breath, and his voice faded toward a whisper. "All of a sudden there was a bang and a shower of sparks that scared the living hell out of me."

When the young captain's hand emerged from the pocket of his jacket, Jack glimpsed a rosary before the hand disappeared below the table.

"In the first millionth of a second," Benes continued, "I thought they'd gotten me with some rear firing missile my countermeasures gear didn't detect. Then I realized the missile flash was outbound."

Jack studied Benes, listening more for the way the words were expressed rather than for the story itself.

"I was flash-blinded in the center of whatever I tried to look at," Benes explained nervously. "Did you ever try to punch buttons and flip switches you couldn't see, knowing you had half a second?"

"That's why we do blindfold cockpit checks," Jack said, mentioning the training procedure that required pilots to locate all switches without seeing them.

He had not thought of the flash blindness when he read the reports. He realized Benes had faced a real problem immediately after the missile ignited. Night fliers improve their ability to see in the darkness by keeping cockpit lights as dim as possible. The technique sharpens night vision, but makes a pilot vulnerable to unexpected flashes such as lightning. In the few seconds following a bright flash, the results are similar to walking from afternoon sunshine into a darkened movie theater.

"I knew I had to break radar lock on the target," Benes said. "That was fairly routine, but it would've been nice to see what I was doing."

"You believe the missile destroyed itself before reaching the airliner?"

"I hope so, sir. It was close. Lieutenant Walker probably had a better look than I."

Turning to Walker, Jack was disappointed that there was any doubt.

Before Walker could comment, Benes added, "However, I was about four miles in trail. Even if you don't count the time the AIM-17X takes to accelerate to Mach four, the missile needs six seconds to cover four miles. I beat six seconds—by quite a bit."

"The missile disappeared off the scope before reaching the airliner's blip," Walker said. "And there was no change in the airliner's flight path like there would've been if Ed had smoked him."

That sounded better, Jack thought as he asked Benes, "How much time elapsed between launch and destruct?"

Benes paused, then answered, "Two-and-a-half, maybe three seconds at the most."

"Pretty fast reactions," Jack said.

"Seemed pretty slow at the time, sir." The look on Benes' face suggested he was reliving those event-filled seconds.

Jack wondered if Benes had reacted in time. The six-hundred-pound missile did not just disappear when it exploded. Instead it was transformed into thousands of fragments like the one in his pocket. Those pieces continued hurtling forward as they fell to the ocean. Perhaps the missile had hit the Soviet aircraft like a shotgun blast instead of like a bomb in one of the engines. However, if Soviet

National One continued as before, there was a reasonable chance that the fragments passed beneath the plane if they even caught up with it.

He asked, "You still hadn't heard from him or seen him?"

"Negative. Clouds were solid all the way to three thousand. I spotted him visually after I broke out. He'd leveled off and was in a gentle right turn. His lights were all I could see."

"What lights?"

"Nav lights and beacons," Benes answered, referring to the normal external lighting for flights at night.

"How about landing lights? Hadn't he turned those on yet?"

Benes closed his eyes as if picturing the scene. Walker looked confused.

Jack continued, "To illuminate the water. I mean, why in the hell would he be turning if he wasn't picking out a ditching heading?"

"I don't know," Benes answered, "but the landing lights weren't on. They were still off when he hit the water."

"Could you see the ocean's swells and wave patterns without lights?"

"Negative. The only things visible were his lights and the glow of lights from the coast."

"Because you were flash blinded?"

"I don't think so," Benes said. "I could see pretty clearly again by then."

Walker said, "I had good night vision when I broke out of the clouds, and I couldn't see anything in the water."

Benes continued his description of the last few seconds of the flight of Soviet National One, but Jack did not follow the comments. What he had just heard did not make sense. He pictured the Soviet pilots struggling to maintain altitude and to turn the aircraft toward the best heading for ditching. Those pilots should have been trying to illuminate the water ahead of the crippled airliner.

The lights might be a key to the truth, Jack thought. The Soviet pilots—or Benes—had not given enough thought to the landing lights. A pilot preparing to ditch should have aimed the lights toward the water just ahead. Benes' failure to mention the landing lights made his story less credible. No lights sounded more like an aircraft out of control—maybe one that had already been hit by an air-to-air missile. Yet what if Benes and Walker were telling the truth?

"And he started the final plunge on that heading," Benes said.

"What heading?"

"Northeasterly. He'd turned to zero-four-zero and crashed almost under the original flight path toward San Francisco."

That maneuver had not made sense to Jack when he read the incident report, and the maneuver still did not. If Benes' story was not true, Jack thought, the young captain was including more details than he needed.

"How good are the crash coordinates I copied from your report?"

"The location's as good as my inertial nav system," Benes said.

"Could you see well enough in the dark to get a good fix?"

"When I knew she was going in, I pulled in pretty close, but off to the left, so I wouldn't hit any jet wash. By then she'd nosed over into nearly a forty-degree dive, so I had to slow down to keep from overrunning her. I flew a knife-edge pass overhead at three hundred feet just seconds after the crash."

With one wing pointing directly at the water, Jack thought, Benes should have gotten a good look.

Benes continued, "I got a good fix with my nav equipment while the white water was still swirling over the point of impact."

"I got a good cut on Ed's position with my equipment," Walker said. "I worked out the geometry and came up with a crash position within one hundred yards of his direct readout."

After closing his notebook, Jack pulled the irregular fragment from his pocket and rotated the piece of metal between his fingertips. He seemed to be studying the deformed metallic object, but his concentration was on the story he had just heard. He was ready to find out if either pilot would crack under pressure.

"Let me summarize for a moment," Jack said, "and you tell me where I've got things mixed up, okay?"

Benes and Walker nodded.

"You're trailing this unidentified Soviet aircraft in the clouds when the bird starts a mysterious dive. You arm your missiles and somehow manage to fire one but destroy the missile in time. Coming out of the clouds, the other pilot gains enough control to level off and bring his aircraft through a 270-degree turn. Then he loses control, finally diving into the drink under the original flight path. Have I got that all straight?"

"Yes, sir," Benes said as Walker nodded in agreement.

"Where do you think they're going to tear you apart on that story?"

Both pilots looked surprised and neither volunteered an answer.

"I'll have as much luck selling that to the Soviets as I'd have selling Jane Fonda videos to fighter pilots who flew over North Vietnam." Jack continued rotating the piece of scrap metal between his fingers. He fixed his gaze on Walker. "What's a wingman's main responsibility, Lieutenant?"

"Sir?" Walker obviously was surprised by the change in direction of the questioning.

"You heard me."

"Well, sir," Walker said, referring to keeping enemy aircraft from behind the flight leader, "I guess the number one thing is to keep Lead covered. Not let anyone get on his six o'clock." Before Jack could respond, he added, "A wingman's supposed to stick with his leader no matter what happens."

Jack had expected the first part of Walker's answer. The phrasing of the last part caught him off guard. He grasped the metal and squeezed hard until the smoothed-over edges threatened to cut his fingers. He remembered another mission and another wingman and another flight leader. His anger at Radisson and the deadly debacle over Hanoi welled up inside.

"But a good leader shouldn't lead his wingmen into something they can't handle," Jack said. He recalled red tracers and the black puffs of exploding antiaircraft shells in the clear blue sky over Hanoi.

The puzzled looks on the faces of the young pilots told Jack he had just said something out of context.

"I may be junior, sir," Walker said, "but I'm a pretty good stick. Besides—"

"I'm not talking about flying, Lieutenant. I'm talking about blindly backing your leader even when you're on the ground."

Benes dramatically pushed away from the table, dropping his rosary in the process. Anger distorted his face as reached to retrieve the beads.

"Sir, I—" Walker started.

"I'm a strong believer in loyalty to a fellow flier," Jack interrupted, "but your loyalties have to go much higher, Lieutenant. If there's a big coverup here, you're the man who has to stop it."

"But, sir," Walker said, "we've been telling you what happened."

"If I'm lying, Colonel," Benes said in a voice low and heavy with emotion, "you can have my wings!"

"If you're lying, Captain," Jack said quietly, "I'll have more than just your wings." He paused to let his words have their full effect. "You suppose your story would be any different if you'd blown him away?"

"Of course, Colonel! I'd tell the truth to you in that case just as I am telling the truth to you now. What can I say to convince you?"

"I'm not the one you have to convince. You need hard evidence that says you didn't blow the tail off that Il-62."

"Guilty until proven innocent?"

"In the next few hours, there's going to be a rush to judgment."

"Raising the wreckage'll prove our story," Benes said.

"How soon? A week? With that storm, probably at least a couple of weeks." Jack paused, then continued in a voice devoid of emotion and barely audible. "Do you know what time it is in Moscow right now?"

Before Benes could slide the elasticized cuff of his jacket above his watch, Jack answered his own question.

"Early afternoon. And guess what today's hot topic in the Kremlin is—you and your dumb-assed shot in the dark!" He stared intently at Benes. Referring to the classified codes that would direct nuclear strikes against the United States, Jack added, "At this very moment, Medvalev may be passing out the 'GO codes!' "

The sudden onslaught overwhelmed both young pilots. Benes moved to the window. Walker fidgeted with the zipper on the front of his flight suit.

"We're damned lucky Valinen wasn't left in Moscow, because he'd probably have a full 'red force' laydown on us by daybreak. Now blow in my ear one more time, Captain, and tell me about raising wreckage from the North Pacific."

Jack studied both young officers for a sign that either might be about to change his story. He wondered if he should have separated Benes and Walker from the beginning.

"Lieutenant, it's up to you. If there's anything you want to change in your report, now's the—"

The sound of footsteps in the hallway distracted him. A master sergeant in a security police uniform opened the door and said, "Beg your pardon, sir, but I'm Sergeant Rowe and—"

He was interrupted by two civilians who pushed in behind him. Both wore business suits and overcoats belted loosely. Jack had spent enough time in Washington to sense that their civilian clothes were their uniforms. The leader was short and a little overweight. The second man's appearance suggested someone from Army intelligence or perhaps a Marine who had allowed his hair to grow out. Jack jumped to his feet, moving in front of the intruders.

Flashing an identification wallet and badge, the shorter civilian said, "I'm Special Agent O'Donnell of National Security. Are you Phillips?"

Jack did not answer. He slowly buttoned the four buttons on his uniform jacket and continued studying O'Donnell and his companion.

"I'm sorry, Colonel," Sergeant Rowe said.

"No problem," Jack said quietly.

O'Donnell jammed his credentials into his pocket as he read the name tag on Jack's jacket. "Radisson said you were running the show, and I want some answers right now!"

"Let me see your ID," Jack said to O'Donnell. Nodding toward the other civilian, Jack added, "Yours, too."

"Look, Colonel, I'm not—"

"Your ID, now!"

O'Donnell hesitated.

Jack turned to Sergeant Rowe. "How many men do you have with you, Sarge?"

"Two, sir."

Gesturing toward the radio attached to the sergeant's belt, Jack said matter-of-factly, "Make a call and get some more."

As Rowe raised the radio to his lips, O'Donnell angrily retrieved his ID.

With one hand Jack gave a "hold it" signal to Rowe. With the other, he snatched the ID, stared into O'Donnell's eyes, and said, "You're right. I am in charge." He held eye contact until O'Donnell turned away toward his companion.

"Give him your papers!" O'Donnell spat out each word as if the second man had caused the delay.

Jack did not attempt to take the second ID, but concentrated instead on O'Donnell's. The badge was legitimate. The carefully scrolled card had its lettering overlaid across the National Seal: Thomas Edward O'Donnell, Special Investigator. The card was countersigned by the President's national security advisor.

Jack took the ID from the second agent. O'Donnell reached for his, but Jack held both for a side-by-side comparison. He read the name Russell Lee Brown on the second ID card. Returning both wallets, Jack turned to Sergeant Rowe. "You and your people can stand by out in the hallway."

"We don't have much time, Colonel," O'Donnell said crisply.

"Neither do I."

Gesturing toward Benes and Walker, O'Donnell said, "The President needs answers, and your people have them."

"You've talked to the President?" Jack tried to decide whether O'Donnell was name dropping, bluffing, or speaking the truth. He sensed that Brown was uneasy with O'Donnell's claim.

"I have my orders," O'Donnell said. "We have to know what happened out there tonight."

"That's what I was trying to determine before you interrupted. If you can establish the right need to know, I'm sure you can get a copy when my report's completed."

"Don't throw that bureaucracy shit at me, Colonel! I'm not leaving without answers!"

"Maybe. Maybe not," Jack said, still concerned about how legitimate O'Donnell's claim of power was. "Depends on what your questions are."

O'Donnell move toward Benes and Walker. "Why were these two out there in the first place?"

Jack stepped in front, blocking O'Donnell's path to the other pilots. "Standard operating procedures. You can check that with FAA."

"I'm not talking FAA! I'm talking Air Force and Air Force pilots blowing away half the Russian government!"

"It's not our fault if the Soviets can't keep their aircraft in good shape." Jack wondered if O'Donnell was guessing and trying to bluff. "There's no evidence that—"

"We know you shot at least one missile, and maybe two, at the Russians."

Jack could not conceal his surprise that O'Donnell had already learned that a missile was fired. He was stunned by the words "maybe two."

"Until you barged in here," Jack said, "I was investigating—"

"Who gave the orders? That's the number-one question, and I want an answer right now, Colonel Phillips!"

"Their orders come from Colonel Robert Radisson, the local wing commander."

Maybe that answer was dirty pool, Jack thought, but Radisson had probably taken special delight in dumping O'Donnell into the middle of Jack's investigation. Besides, bouncing O'Donnell back to Radisson might buy more time to get his own questions answered as well as the new ones raised by O'Donnell's charges. Was his charge of two missiles some wild speculation or did some national intelligence source know more than Benes had acknowledged? If a second missile had been fired, Jack realized that nothing Benes and Walker said could be accepted without question. Jack also wondered how much he could trust the belligerent intruder.

O'Donnell said angrily, "The Air Force had no damn business operating unilaterally!"

Jack decided that O'Donnell was acting on behalf of interests other than the President's. President Cunningham had more direct ways of determining if there had been a military conspiracy. "I don't know what you're talking about."

"I'm sure not talking about two lieutenants taking pot shots on their own!"

"You're way off base, O'Donnell," Jack said, "and I don't have time for your fantasies."

"You're not going to get away with covering over treason that easily!"

"Treason?"

"The President didn't order an attack, so what you're involved in is treason!"

"That does it," Jack said. "Out!"

"You're making a big mistake, Colonel!"

"Won't be my first one."

"It may be your last!"

"Probably not," Jack said, then turned toward the door. "Sergeant Rowe!"

Jack saw the look of rage in the agent's eyes and sensed that O'Donnell was about to lose control. Brown obviously was worried. Jack shifted his weight, ready to react.

"You can't pull an operation like that independently!" O'Donnell shouted with clenched fists raised. "We had people on that airplane!"

Jack began to understand the rage. "Look—"

"No, Colonel! You look! Do you have any idea how long it takes to get an agent onto the fuckin' Politburo?"

"For chrissakes, Tom," Brown said, grabbing O'Donnell by the arm. "Shut up!"

The reprimand jolted O'Donnell. He brushed away Brown's hand, turned, and stomped out of the room. Sergeant Rowe had to jump out of the doorway to avoid a collision.

"I'm really sorry, Colonel," Brown said. "He's not usually that way."

"You'd better get that guy under control."

Brown nodded, started after O'Donnell, then stopped just short of the doorway. "He had some close personal friends out there. About as close as you dare get in this business."

Chapter 5

Monday Morning, 4:00 a.m.
Pacific Standard Time

JACK WAITED UNTIL THE SOUNDS OF FOOTSTEPS IN THE HALLWAY HAD disappeared, then said, "O'Donnell's not the toughest questioner you'll face in the next couple of days—and he's on our side."

Captain Benes and Lieutenant Walker remained silent, seemingly overwhelmed by the confrontation between O'Donnell and the colonel. Jack felt energized again, but now had even more questions than before. O'Donnell's comments had given the investigation new dimensions that Jack had not anticipated. Intrigued by O'Donnell's slip, Jack was eager to review the passenger list. Even with his knowledge of the Soviet leadership, he did not have a clue to reveal which member of the Politburo could have been an American spy.

Speculation on that subject would have to wait. His immediate concern was O'Donnell's charges of an Air Force plot and the suggestion that Benes had fired a second missile. Firing one missile could be accidental. Firing a second missile indicated a purposeful attack that would justify retaliation by the Soviets.

He needed to disprove the possibility of a second missile before too many people found that a rumor worth exploring. He sat on the edge of the conference table and asked Benes, "Did you fire a second missile?"

"Negative, sir. I came home with all but one."

Jack asked Walker, "How about you?"

The question seemed to surprise him. He slowly shook his head as he answered, "I was ready, and I swear to God I'd have punched them off if the Soviet had started firing." The young lieutenant seemed more involved in reassuring himself that he would have done his duty than in trying to evade the question.

"So you didn't fire?"

"Sir, I was panting so loud in my oxygen mask," Walker said, smiling as he recalled the excitement of the moment, "I probably wouldn't have heard a missile if I'd fired one. But I brought all my missiles home. You can check with maintenance."

"I've already got someone checking," Jack said, hoping that Jensen had gathered enough evidence to prove that only one missile had been fired.

"You seem to have thought of everything, Colonel," Benes said.

"Far from it," Jack answered, recalling O'Donnell's shocking revelation. "I'm sure I'll be thinking up questions over the next couple of days that I should have asked you now."

"If the Russians don't get us before sunrise, sir," Benes said, sarcastically referring to Jack's earlier comment about the possibility of rapid retaliation by the Soviets.

"I had to get your attention," Jack said. Even though he recognized that Benes' overall tone was inappropriate for a captain-to-colonel comment, he knew he had been rough, especially if Benes had been truthful. "There is one more question."

Benes returned to his chair. Walker fidgeted with his gloves.

"Either of you want to change your story?"

Neither pilot answered immediately. Walker looked toward Benes, waiting to take turns. Benes stared at Jack as if they were alone in the room.

"I do *not* lie to fellow officers, sir," Benes said. "Honor is very important in my family." He paused, then looked Jack in the eye. "I do not choose to dishonor the name of my family. I have told the truth."

Jack sensed from the delivery as well as the words that Benes was sincere. Walker waited long enough to be sure that Benes was finished, then said, "I haven't been in the Air Force as long as you have, Colonel, but I swore the same oath you did. We've described the incident just as it happened."

The comments struck a responsive chord. Jack was a modern-day patriot who had continued to serve when patriotism had been out of fashion in America. He liked being part of a brotherhood of honest men and women who were guided by the principle that their word was their bond. Whenever another officer gave his or her word as an officer, the issue became a matter of honor. He placed great credibility in such statements. He also recognized, however, that people outside the brotherhood would be less willing to accept Benes' story on faith alone. Jack hoped he could build up a framework of facts that would make Benes' story more believable than it sounded.

"Okay, gentlemen," Jack said as he closed the notebook. "I accept your word and your reports."

Benes seemed unconvinced. The ambivalence in his expression suggested that he was waiting to see if this were the colonel's next tactic.

Jack continued, "I did just what you would've done if you were sitting on this side of the table. I pressured you for two reasons. I wanted to give you plenty of opportunities to screw up if you were lying. You passed that test. I also had to know how you'll handle hostile questions under pressure."

Benes smiled and said, "Your questions were easy compared to the pressure O'Donnell was laying on you, sir."

"Maybe I should've let you get some real experience with him, but I didn't have the time."

Walker shook his head and said, "We weren't ready to handle someone that irrational."

"Some of the news people you'll face in the next couple of days may seem less rational than O'Donnell. I'm worried about the ones who'll consider your story as their 'once in a career' ticket to break into the big time. They could take the crack O'Donnell made about two missiles and build that into an exposé that'll make you seem more sinister than Valinen."

Benes and Walker looked worried. Benes asked, "How do you think this is going to turn out?"

"You'll have to meet a Flight Evaluation Board that'll consider—"

"Sir, I don't mean for me. I mean, what's going to happen between us and the Russians?"

"Damned if I know," Jack said. "Things would have been a hell of a lot smoother if you'd brought all your missiles home. If the Russians never discover you fired, that'd be okay with me."

Benes' expression brightened as he seemed to consider that possibility for the first time. "Any chance of that?"

"Little or none," Jack said. "Our best chance is to prove the Soviet bird was under control when it came out of the clouds. Control would indicate you destroyed the missile in time."

"The FAA tapes might help," Walker said.

Benes added, "The tapes will show that the Soviets were in trouble before I punched off the missile."

"The tapes may establish the sequence of events," Jack said. "But what we need are the black boxes. They're the best proof of what happened in those last few minutes on Soviet National One."

Walker asked, "How long will the recovery take, sir?"

"Depends. If the water isn't too deep, and if the ocean floor isn't too rugged, and if the wreckage isn't too scattered, and if the storm subsides, and if, and if, and if, and if we're luckier than we deserve to be, we might have the recorders in three or four days."

"Do we have that much time?"

"Probably not," Jack said, then looked at his watch. It was nearly four-ten, and he wanted to look over the aircraft before reporting to General McClintock. "In the meantime, you two'd better get some sleep. I don't know how long we'll be able to keep the media away from you."

"I could use some rest," Benes said, "but I'm not sure I can sleep. Do you have any advice on how to handle the reporters?"

"I'll be there," Jack said, "and I'm sure the Air Staff public affairs people will try to keep the interviews from becoming a media circus. Just stick to the truth, and don't let some reporter goad you into volunteering anything and saying something dumb."

Both pilots got up to leave. Benes hesitated as he reached Jack.

"Thank you, sir," Benes said, extending his hand.

Jack shook hands and patted Benes on the shoulder. "We've still got a long ways to go, Captain." He started gathering the reports and maps, then added, "One more thing, gentlemen. O'Donnell said some things about the Politburo that must not be repeated."

Both pilots nodded their understanding. Benes stepped through the doorway, but Walker stopped.

"If that turkey wants to know what happened," Walker said, "he should be checking with the Russians."

"Why do you say that?"

"That bird was in trouble before Ed did anything," Walker said. "O'Donnell doesn't know that, and you don't really know that, but Ed and I know. No matter how hard everyone leans on us, the real answer is somewhere else."

"They flew out of Vladivostok," Jack said. "Maintenance in eastern Siberia this time of year has to be tough."

"The cause might be as simple as bad maintenance," Walker said, "but something disabled that airplane, and I don't imagine that you've ruled out sabotage yet."

Jack paused. "Frankly, I haven't given much serious thought to sabotage since General McClintock told me you'd fired a missile. I've been worried more about proving what we didn't do than about what someone in Vladivostok might have done."

Benes added from the doorway, "Just remember sir, there are even more people on the other side who'd like to get Valinen than there are on this side."

Jack had thought about sabotage while he was driving between the airport and Alameda. Now without even trying, he could think of three leaders in the Kremlin who would like to see Valinen out of the way. But, he thought, each was also a member of the delegation to the conference. Yet he was convinced that he should give more thought to a Soviet cause—perhaps a time bomb in the tail of the

Il-62. This was one accident investigation where he really wanted to see the pieces of the aircraft.

Before going to the flight line, Jack made a telephone call to check on the tapes of the radio communications. The recording made at the air defense center was being duplicated and should be at the Command Post within an hour. The FAA recording of conversations between Oakland Center and Soviet National One would be delivered to Howell sometime before dawn, if the weather at Oakland and Howell permitted.

Minutes later, he drove through the fog to the flight line. O'Donnell's comment about a second missile made Jack want to see the F-15s before any of the missiles were removed. He hoped he was not too late.

He parked near the open door of a large hangar. Inside the barnlike structure, two F-15s sat wing tip to wing tip, glistening in the artificial light. Red ropes, looping down from short, white stanchions, encircled the aircraft.

Walking toward the planes, he was pleased to see the red streamers beneath the fuselage and the wing pylons. The streamers were attached to safety devices inserted at critical locations on the air-to-air missiles and their armament stations. The missiles were still in place.

An armed guard stood in front of the aircraft beside a small sign that proclaimed, "Controlled Area—Single Point Access Procedures in Effect." Four other guards stood at irregular intervals around the perimeter. At least Radisson had gotten that right, Jack thought. The whole investigation would receive the closest scrutiny, and the sooner everything was under tight control, the better.

Before reaching the entry point, he was hailed by Jensen, who emerged from a maintenance office at the side of the hangar. A smear of grease on his forehead and the ragged-edged collection of papers on his clipboard suggested that Jensen was well into his investigation. His wink and half-smile in response to Jack's greetings indicated things were under control, but not by much.

"I may've gotten us in trouble with one of the local commanders," Jensen said. "He was really hot when he found I was checking out the aircraft. His name's—"

"Radisson," Jack said. "Where do we stand?"

"He wanted to run me out of the area," Jensen said, "but the shift commander for the security police had already seen my orders. The colonel was pissed, but General McClintock's name won the argument."

"Good," Jack said, continuing toward the entry point.

They cleared through the fatigue-clad guard and approached the first F-15. Months had passed since Jack had been close to one of the big fighters. However, the ever-present smell of jet fuel and rubber tires brought back sensations from a thousand other missions on a hundred different parking ramps. Any time he got near an Eagle, Jack experienced the same unmistakable aura of power waiting to be unleashed.

When he saw the bare weapon station at the lower corner of the engine inlet, he did not have to ask which aircraft Benes had flown.

Jensen scanned notes on his clipboard and said, "Everything on the birds checks out as advertised. The photographer finished about an hour ago. As soon as we're sure he's got good prints of everything, we'll down-load the ordnance."

Preserving the evidence was one of the first tasks of accident investigation. The pictures could be critical. Jack said, "I also want a good check of the nav systems as soon as you get power on the birds."

The inertial navigation systems (INSs) automatically kept track of an aircraft's position from before takeoff until after landing. The accuracy of the INSs would help determine the accuracy of the crash coordinates that Benes had reported. Accuracy was important. Even a few miles off the coast, the wreckage of the Russian aircraft could be difficult to locate.

"During postflight checks," Jensen said, "the INSs checked out within a tenth of a mile on both aircraft."

"Good."

Jack walked under the F-15's wing to get a close look at the weapon stations. The missile Benes fired had been attached to the lower, outboard corner of the engine intake. Just aft of the empty station, an AIM-17X missile still hung on weapon station number four. Even in the shadows beneath the massive wing, telltale scorch marks were evident where the missile had been. Jack rubbed his fingers lightly over the cold metal. The dark gray residue of a recent missile launch smeared onto his fingertips.

"We've taken closeup photos of station three," Jensen said.

"Is this weapon station the only one that shows a recent firing?"

"Roger that," Jensen said.

"You checked the rest?"

"The standard alert load's four Sidewinders and four AIM-17s on each bird. The other fifteen missiles are 'all present and accounted for, sir,'" Jensen said as if reporting a squadron present for duty.

Jack moved over to the two Sidewinder missiles attached to weapon station two. He studied the pylon and the attachment hardware for each missile. There was no residue, no indication of anything other than normal erosion of paint due to numerous flights at high speed.

"There's no possibility of a second firing?"

Jensen looked at Jack as if the colonel must not have been listening to the last comment. "The rest of the missiles are still aboard. I wouldn't let them down-load."

"No doubts?"

"None, sir!"

"What do you have that shows these are the right aircraft?"

"I've got copies of the control tower's arrival and departure logs, the maintenance debriefing forms, and the Form 781s on both birds," Jensen said referring to documents that normally verified a flight by aircraft tail number. "The documents all match the mission to these birds."

"Get the originals."

"Sir?"

"I want the original documents," Jack said, "I don't want anyone claiming we have anything that could've been altered."

"No one had much time to alter anything," Jensen said. "The birds stayed at the crash site for a while so the Eagles landed only an hour ahead of us."

"You don't have to convince me. Premier Medvalev's the one who'll want details on what happened to his number-one saber rattler."

Jensen paused, then said, "A coverup would be tough, just from the maintenance point of view. You'd have to involve maintenance supervisors, crew chiefs, and armament technicians. By the time you add in the pilots and the air traffic controllers, you've ended up with a crowd of people who'd have to go along with a coverup."

Jack agreed, doubting that everyone in that group could be kept from telling the truth. And, he thought, Radisson's people would not try such a conspiracy without Radisson being involved. Radisson was brash and capable of deceit, but predictable in one respect—he never took a stand unless he knew which way his boss leaned on an issue. So a plot and a coverup would reach much higher than Radisson.

Jack's thoughts jumped two levels higher in the chain of command to General McClintock, one of the true leaders in the Air Force. Jack knew McClintock well. Unlike Radisson, McClintock was a man of action who took chances when necessary to accomplish the mission. But the general was from the "duty, honor, country" mold and would not tolerate such a conspiracy.

Besides, Jack thought, there had to be smarter ways of getting Valinen. Letting him fly across thousands of miles of ocean, then openly sending up two USAF interceptors to blow him away within sight of California simply did not make sense. Sending fighters out of Alaska to attack the Soviet aircraft while flying through an area not covered by anyone's radar was a much better tactic. That was an explanation even O'Donnell should understand, though Jack could not see the Air Force making that argument on the network news.

Jack scanned the walls of the hangar until he spotted a red cross signifying the location of a first aid kit. "Get some fresh gauze and wipe down the nose of each missile and anywhere else an exhaust plume could have left any residue." While Jensen made notes on his clipboard, Jack continued, "I want more pictures, too—closeups of every missile and every attachment point, before and after the missiles are down-loaded."

Jensen nodded and continued writing.

"By dawn," Jack said, "I want you to be able to prove to General McClintock that there couldn't have been a second missile fired out there tonight."

Jack was inspecting the second Eagle when the guards passed a message. The general wanted another telephone call.

At the Command Post a few minutes later, Jack entered the booth with the secure telephone. Waiting for the call to be put through to the Pentagon, he stretched and yawned. He needed sleep. When the ringing of the telephone broke the stark silence of the enclosed booth, though, it triggered a fresh surge of adrenaline.

"What's the verdict, Jack?"

"The information's not as clean-cut as I'd like, General."

"General Raleigh's still meeting with the National Security Council. He hopes you're finding something plausible, something that doesn't leave the focus on that damned missile."

As Jack summarized what he had learned since arriving at Howell, he withheld the details of the airliner's descent until last. "General, I'm not sure if this final news will make you feel better or worse. Both F-15 pilots make it sound as if the Soviet aircraft wasn't out of control during most of the descent."

"What are you trying to tell me, Jack?"

"If the flight recorders back up what Benes and Walker say, there's no way Benes hit the bird."

The engines on an Il-62 were mounted on the side of the fuselage near the tail. Jack was confident that detonating an AIM-17X in an engine would disable the flight controls for the tail—if it did not actually break the tail from the rest of the aircraft.

"That certainly makes me feel better. Why wouldn't I want to hear that?"

"Until you've got data from the flight recorders or we can get a look at the tailcones on all four engines, claiming the Soviet pilot was in control sounds like a boldfaced lie."

McClintock hesitated, then responded, "If Benes blew most of the tail off the Il-62 and we were trying to cover up the attack, we might try that same line."

"Exactly, sir. We need to see the wreckage."

"The seas are too rough to do much. I'm not counting on any surface debris being recovered before morning. The Navy's scrambling to get a salvage ship under way out of San Diego, but we're probably two days from getting heavy-duty submersibles into the water. The Soviets may actually beat us to getting a good look at the wreckage."

Jack wondered about the depth of the ocean at the crash site. However deep the water was, he knew heavy equipment would be necessary to raise the Il-62's tail section and cockpit to the surface of the choppy North Pacific.

"I've still got my original question, Jack. What happened out there last night?"

"I'm betting horizontal stabilizer," Jack said, making reference to the winglike section of the tail, which controlled climbs and dives. "Probably electrical, hydraulic, or mechanical failure—that is, if we're limiting our guesses to legitimate aircraft failures."

"Legitimate? What else have you got in mind, Jack?"

Jack recognized the general's tone as that used when he was pretty certain of the answer to his question.

"With all the sparring we've seen lately in the Politburo, I'd say it's too early to rule out sabotage." In his assignment in the Pentagon, Jack had followed the Kremlin's internal struggles closely. In spite of the routine secrecy that shrouded all Kremlin actions and the efforts of key Politburo members to disguise their motivations, he felt confident he knew the major alignments. Making reference to the minister of internal affairs (MVD), he continued, "If Yakovin wasn't on the passenger list, I'd wonder if he'd finally screwed up enough courage to go for Valinen."

Aligned with four other opponents of Valinen, Yakovin used his position in internal affairs as a strong power base for occasional challenges of Valinen. Jack had assumed that only the strong hand of Soviet Premier Medvalev had kept the balance and had prevented a final showdown.

"We've gotten a list of everyone on the flight from Moscow to Vladivostok," McClintock said. "So far we don't have any agent reports out of Vladivostok, but I assume Yakovin didn't have any business that would've kept him in eastern Siberia."

Unless Yakovin had advance knowledge of the fate of the airliner, Jack thought. He made a mental note to check the possibility that Yakovin might have stayed in Vladivostok. "General, when do we expect to have any agent reports on Soviet National One's final departure?"

"Right now, the KGB, the MVD, and the military have a tight lid on the whole Vladivostok area, so we may have to wait a day or two."

Jack assumed that Krasnovich's people in state security, Yakovin's people in internal affairs, and Valinen's people in military security were in a frenzy since hearing of the crash. Some would be scrambling for answers, others scrambling for position. "Their tightened security could mean that they suspect sabotage. Reporting that could help get us off the hook."

"Even if they suspect one of their own people blew the tail off that bird, I can't see Premier Medvalev interceding on our behalf."

"Yes, sir. But we can honestly report that the Soviets have tightened what was already very tight security while they investigate. That provides a different focus than the missile. Let members of the media draw their own conclusions."

"That leaves me to sell the story that the missile firing was purely coincidental." McClintock paused. "The more I think about that, the more I don't want to think about that. How about getting back to your legitimate causes?"

"The way I see it," Jack said, "the rapid change in the aircraft's pitch attitude looked like she was making a run on San Francisco."

"But all we've got's our pilot's word on that?"

"Yes, sir. He's got a good record. His effectiveness reports are all top block, and his flying folder shows he's a pretty hot stick on check rides."

"That all may be true," McClintock said, "but it won't impress the Kremlin."

He paused, and Jack heard someone else's voice in the background. "I've got another meeting. But there's one more question. You having problems with anyone besides Bob Radisson?"

McClintock's tone suggested that he already knew the answer, so Jack deliberately understated his response. "A couple of national security folks showed up in the middle of the debriefing. I don't guess I gave them all the answers they were looking for."

McClintock laughed. "We got a call."

Jack considered mentioning O'Donnell's slip about a spy on the Politburo. However, he reasoned that if General McClintock had the right clearance and "need to know," he would already know. If he did not, Jack had no authority to pass on the information.

"Some guy named O'Donnell came in shooting at everything that moved," Jack said. "He believed we'd taken the bird down on purpose. He had a rumor that we might've fired more than one missile."

"Where in the hell did he come up with—We didn't fire more than one, did we, Jack?"

"Negative, sir," Jack said quickly. "I've checked all weapon stations on both Eagles, and there's nothing indicating more than one missile was fired. The pilots say only one was fired."

"What did the guy base his claims on?"

"O'Donnell never said, but he had his information in a hurry. He was on us almost as soon as I settled into the postflight interviews."

"Try to keep him at a distance, Jack, and I'll work the problem from this end. I'd have handled him the same way. I—Stand by again."

Jack appreciated McClintock's support.

"Gotta go, Jack," McClintock said. "General Raleigh's on the other line. You keep on keeping on, but you'd better try to work in some sleep. This thing isn't going to be over in a hurry."

"Yes, sir. The way I feel now, I may not get out of this booth without a nap."

Jack pushed open the door as he tried to decide what to do next. A sergeant was waiting with a portable tape recorder, a tape of the conversations between the two pilots and the military controller, and a copy of the controller's written log. Jack asked the sergeant to locate a second recorder for use when the FAA tape arrived.

At the moment he was unsure how important the tapes or the recorders were. He had been awake for twenty-seven hours. Getting sleep was becoming a higher priority.

Chapter 6

JACK MOVED INTO ONE OF THE BEDROOMS KEPT AVAILABLE AT THE command post for emergencies. The room was small with a bed, nightstand, recliner, and television set taking most of the available floor space. He could have stayed in the VIP section of the Visiting Officer Quarters, but he wanted to be near the secure telephone.

Though tired, he decided to begin reviewing the tape recording he had available. He placed his notebook on the recliner and began the Guardian tape. He removed his boots and was hanging up his coat when the first transmission from the F-15s crackled through the speakers.

"Guardian, this is Eagle, flight of two, out of six thousand for flight level two-three-zero."

Jack recognized the message as the initial check-in with the controller as the two F-15s were rocketing skyward to their clearance limit of twenty-three thousand feet. Even with the distortion caused by an oxygen mask pressed tightly across Benes' nose and cheeks, Jack recognized the voice of the young captain.

"Roger, Eagle Flight, Guardian has you in radar contact. Continue climb to flight level four-seven-zero and maintain a heading of two-seven-five degrees."

A routine beginning, Jack thought as he continued settling in. Benes came across as calm and professional, maybe even a little bored. He did not sound like an assassin on the most daring assignment of his life.

For the next few minutes, little besides static came from the recorder. Guardian was working only the two Eagles, and they required little guidance or conversation as they streaked through the quiet of the night. Benes and Walker were also using the frequency for their interplane conversations, but electronics and radar were doing most of the communicating between the aircraft.

Jack stretched out on the recliner with his notebook in his lap. He mentally placed himself into the cockpit of the lead fighter, but he resisted the temptation to close his eyes.

"Guardian, Oakland."

From his extensive flying background, he recognized the new voice as that of someone at Oakland Center initiating contact with the Air Force controller on a hot line. The new voice was that of Karl Wilson, the FAA controller who was working the Soviet airliner. After Guardian acknowledged, Wilson continued. "Soviet National One has made radio contact and is following my radar vectors into San Francisco."

After Guardian passed that information to Benes, minutes passed without additional words. Jack had trouble fighting off the fatigue. He closed his eyes for a moment. When he opened them again, he was unsure whether he had been asleep or not. He was about to rewind the tape to make sure he had not missed anything when Wilson's voice broke the silence.

"Guardian, be advised that Soviet National One has departed flight level four-one-zero for two-seven-zero."

That message told Jack that if he had fallen asleep, he had slept only seconds. Soviet National One was just leaving its cruising altitude. The significant parts of the tape and the flight were still ahead.

When the Air Force controller reported that Soviet National One was descending, he also added that the Soviet aircraft was straight ahead at sixty miles.

"Eagle flight, burner, now!" Benes advised Walker that they were accelerating the intercept.

That command, Jack thought, corroborated Benes' statement about trying to complete the intercept before the airliner disappeared into the clouds.

Benes told Walker to back off and prepare for a rapid course reversal.

Putting aside his notebook, Jack mentally took the F-15's throttles in his left hand and control stick in his right. He closed his eyes and tried to see the world through the eyes of the young captain. With Benes flying supersonic and the Soviet airliner coming head-on at nearly nine-tenths the speed of sound, those sixty miles would disappear in three minutes or less. Head-on join-ups were the most difficult, especially where time was critical. An error in judgment could take the Eagle from ten miles in front of the airliner to ten miles in trail. The intercepting pilot had to anticipate and stay ahead of his aircraft, no matter how fast he was flying. Jack's breathing deepened just as in the past when he encountered an adversary in the skies.

About two minutes after Benes' call for the F-15s to accelerate using afterburners, Jack rolled his imaginary Eagle inverted. He could almost feel himself hanging upside down with the shoulder straps and lap belt preventing him from falling out of the ejection seat. He strained to see the fleeting image of the Soviet airliner skimming above moonlit clouds.

"Nav lights, eleven-thirty low at about five miles."

The voice startled him and his eyes flashed open. He pictured the other aircraft fifteen seconds ahead, a few thousand feet below. He knew the next few seconds would require extraordinary maneuvering. He tightened his stomach muscles and tensed his legs just as he would to fight off unconsciousness in the upcoming high-G turn.

Benes' excited voice broke the silence. "Damn! Did you get an ID, Larry?"

"Negative, Lead. She dropped into the clouds before I was close enough."

Once again, Jack found those to be the words of pilots intent on identification, not destruction.

He continued listening, but the periods of silence lulled him toward the sleep he desperately needed. He heard Oakland Center announce that the airliner had been cleared down to twelve thousand feet. That exchange did not jolt him like the words of Lieutenant Walker a few moments later.

"What's happening, Lead?"

The words were not as electrifying as the way they were said. A staccato delivery in a higher-pitched voice usually indicated that an aviator had just discovered something. Many times over North Vietnam, Jack had heard the same betrayal of emotion at the sighting of MiGs or surface-to-air missiles.

He recognized a similar increase in emotional intensity in Benes' response. The words seemed to be a genuine reaction to an aircraft suddenly trying to evade.

Benes' order to "Green 'em up for missiles, medium-range!" brought Jack onto the edge of his chair, staring at the speaker on the tape recorder. His excitement increased as the two F-15 pilots exchanged comments and maneuvered into attack formation.

Ominous words of the controller at Oakland Center were barely audible in the background. Broadcasting a warning on the emergency frequency, Wilson said that Soviet National One was not cleared below twelve thousand feet. Jack was straining to hear Oakland Center's words when a knock on the door startled him. He switched off the recorder.

A sergeant delivered the FAA tape recording and the controller's log. They had just arrived from Oakland Center. However, he had not located another recorder for Jack to use in playing the tapes simultaneously.

Jack had heard enough already to be convinced that Benes was not on a preplanned mission to shoot down Valinen's plane. So he decided to continue listening to the tapes individually, sleep a couple of hours, then listen to the tapes together when the second recorder was available. He asked that a noon meeting be scheduled with Colonel Radisson. He was not sure what he would cover, but felt the need to stay up with whatever Radisson was doing.

He closed the door and went to the clock radio on the nightstand. He set the alarm to come on at ten-thirty just in case he fell asleep while listening to the tapes. He switched on the recorder and settled onto the recliner.

"Son of a—" Benes' exclamation pierced the silence of the room.

Jack held his breath, picturing the missile streaking away in the darkness. He listened carefully to the excited words that followed. Besides wanting a feel for the sincerity of Benes' response, he was listening for something else—did Guardian tell Oakland Center a missile had been fired?

He was reluctant to admit even to himself that he wanted an answer to that question. He was not ready to participate in a coverup, if indeed there were anything to cover up. However, he believed that the fewer people who knew of the missile firing, the better.

A few moments later Guardian passed to Oakland Center an urgent request from Benes. The airspace below the plummeting aircraft needed to be cleared of other air traffic. Guardian did not mention the missile.

Jack felt relieved. He went to the recorder to replay the sequence of comments involving the missile.

That sequence also included the discussion between Benes and Walker about whether the missile had been destroyed in time. They sounded uncertain. However, less than five seconds elapsed between Benes' shout in response to the missile firing and his questioning of Walker after destroying the missile. Jack believed Benes had reacted quickly enough, especially considering that Walker had reported no immediate change to the flight path of the airliner.

Each time Jack heard the acknowledgment of the missile launch and the claim that the missile had been destroyed, he became more convinced about the truth and spontaneity of the words. The recordings of the actual radio calls made the incident seem more plausible than the oral and written debriefings had. When he returned to his chair, he let the tape continue and listened for every detail.

"Guardian, Oakland. Do you still have radar contact with Soviet National One?"

"That's affirmative, Oakland—for another thousand feet anyway."

"Be advised, we're still without radio contact, and we lost contact with their radar transponder when National One descended below seven thousand feet."

"Damn!" Jack had hoped that the radar controllers could corroborate Benes' account of the low altitude maneuvering by the Soviet airliner.

Benes reported seeing the Soviet craft for the first time, and Jack found himself swept up in the excitement. He personally had experienced the thrill—and the fear—of chasing another aircraft through the low altitude darkness of moonless nights. Under other circumstances, he had fought to keep a dying aircraft airborne a few more minutes, so he easily pictured the final struggles from both viewpoints.

The action continued with few pauses, and he felt more awake than at any time since he had left San Francisco International Airport. Listening to Benes' description of the low altitude turn, he still was puzzled—there seemed to be no plausible explanation for the turn. That troubled him. Anytime he tried to sort out disparate facts, he had found that "Why?" was often a more important indicator than "What?" Why had the Soviet pilot leveled off at low altitude and made a sweeping turn, taking his airplane away from the coast? Before he could guess at an answer, the chilling impact of the next message jolted him from his unanswered questions.

"Tell Oakland I think she's going in."

Guardian acknowledged, then switched to the hot line. "Oakland, Guardian. Better scramble the Coast Guard. Looks like you've got a crash on your hands!"

"Understand," Wilson said in a tone of calm defeat. He paused, then asked, "You have an estimate of the location?"

"I'll get a confirmation from our pilots," Guardian said. "Best guess at the moment is the 255 degree radial of the Point Reyes VORTAC at about twenty miles." Guardian's reference was in relationship to an air navigational radio on the Point Reyes peninsula. He had estimated the crash at about fifteen miles off the coast, just over forty miles northwest of San Francisco.

"Chaney, this is Guardian."

Jack detected a slight difference in the voice quality and static level on that transmission. He recognized that the Air Force controller had activated another voice circuit. After a short pause, a female voice representing Chaney Air Force Base acknowledged Guardian's call.

Guardian continued, "We have an airliner Mayday at 255 degrees and twenty miles from Point Reyes. Direct an immediate scramble of your air rescue alert force, time twenty-two forty-six local."

Chaney Air Force Base, just north of San Francisco, had a detachment of the Aerospace Rescue and Recovery Service. Scrambling helicopters from Chaney was the logical Air Force response to an aircraft in distress off the coast of central California.

"She's out of fifteen hundred feet." Benes voice sounded frightened.

Even though Jack knew the inevitability of the ending, he was surprised by how quickly the crash happened after Benes' report of the descent from fifteen hundred feet.

"Holy—What a—Guardian, she's down. A hell of a splash! I'm going overhead to get a fix on the position."

Jack found the spontaneity and emotion in Benes' voice convincing. The first part of the transmission had just the right combination of a pilot's concern for fellow fliers; the last portion reflected the more detached professionalism of a man who still had an important job to do. The words, Jack thought, could not have sounded more authentic if Benes had rehearsed them.

The comfort of that thought lasted only an instant, then was chillingly overridden by the frightening possibility that perhaps Benes had rehearsed those statements and all the others.

Enough! He was too tired to deal with the possibility that the tape was a hoax. For the moment, he would accept it. He closed his eyes and listened to the recording, which had evolved primarily into the Air Force controller at Guardian making various notifications and relaying requests to Benes. Jack knew the answer he had to focus on—a plausible explanation that would clear the Air Force and the nation of any direct responsibility for the crash. He stretched to a more comfortable position on the recliner.

The click of the automatic shutoff mechanism on the tape recorder startled him. His eyes flashed open as he woke from the deep sleep that comes from exhaustion. For an instant he did not recognize the small bedroom, but quickly remembered. He had no idea how long he had been asleep. A glance at his watch told him he had been out for less than thirty minutes.

After placing the FAA tape on the recorder, he turned off the overhead light, leaving only the twenty-five-watt illumination from a small lamp by the clock radio. Placing his notebook on the nightstand and stretching out on the bed, he loosened his belt and unfastened a couple of buttons on his blue shirt. He hoped the tape would be exciting enough to keep him awake. The FAA tape was similar to the one made at the Air Force control center, except the FAA recording monitored all communications coming into and out of Karl Wilson's headset at Oakland Center.

The recording began just before Guardian had called Oakland Center to report that the Soviet airliner was seventy-two miles off course. The initial interchange between the controller at Guardian and the voice of Karl Wilson at Oakland Center held Jack's attention for a few moments.

Wilson attempted to contact Soviet National One. Jack listened for a response but heard none. He imagined the interior of the airliner, and fleeting images of the Soviet crew moved through his mind as he visualized the cockpit. He tried to see why they were not answering, but he could not force the images together. After a few minutes and the sixth or seventh call, a heavily accented voice answered in halting English.

"Oakland Center, this is Soviet National One at flight level four-one-zero."

Wilson responded with a radar vector to guide the Soviet airliner toward the air traffic entry points near San Francisco.

Jack sensed having heard those words, but he was not sure if they had been part of a dream or not. Wilson, however, ceased his attempts at contact, so Jack realized that the interchange must have been real.

The recording was quiet for the next few minutes, and Jack drifted in and out of a deeper sleep. His restless dreaming called forth distorted images of the events of the long day. Little in his dreams fit with the occasional interchanges on the tape until Wilson urgently called, "Soviet National One! Soviet National One! This is Oakland Center on UHF and VHF guard. You are not cleared below one-two thousand! Maintain one-two thousand, Soviet National One. Acknowledge!"

The words did not waken Jack. Instead, his breathing quickened as he searched the cockpit for the altimeter. There were scores of gauges and dials, but none seemed to indicate the rapidly decreasing altitude. He looked at his copilot, who was wearing a bemedaled dress uniform of the Soviet Air Force. Jack sensed a grimace on the man's face as the copilot struggled for control, but no recognizable facial details were visible.

Wilson's voice said something about losing radar contact when the airliner had descended through seven thousand feet, and Jack felt the growing panic. He still could not find the altimeter. He looked for the pilot's control yoke, which would permit him to help the copilot pull the plane out of the death dive. There was no yoke, but he located the control stick of an F-15 between himself and the myriad of gauges labeled in Russian. Strange place for a stick instead of a yoke, he thought, but his increasing panic forced him to grab hold.

He grunted and pulled. His efforts combined with those of the faceless copilot and seemed to reduce the descent rate. Jack could find no inside or outside references, however, that would tell him whether or not the aircraft was safe. Nothing seemed to happen until Wilson was told to call the Coast Guard. Ending that transmission were the frightening words Jack tried to deny. "Looks like you've got a crash on your hands!"

Guardian's words terrified him, and he pulled even harder on the control stick. A warbling tone in the background told him that the high rate of descent at such a low altitude had activated a ground proximity warning system. In the blackness beyond the windshield, he saw the turbulent seas reaching up with hands of foamy white. His breath came in gasps. He struggled for control, but sensed this was the airplane he would not survive. He tried to yell at the copilot to pull harder on the yoke, but no words came. He turned to get the copilot's attention and found the bemedaled figure now had the menacing face of Andrei Valinen.

This time the heavily accented voice spoke Russian instead of the halting English heard earlier. The first part of the sentence was almost blocked by the noises of another radio call and the howling sounds of air screaming by the cockpit. For an instant Jack did not understand. Just before the plane hit the water, he recognized Valinen's words as a standard phrase of honor declared by Russian military men—"I serve the Soviet Union!"

Jack threw his arms up and jumped back, trying to avoid the onrushing ocean. His hand knocked his notebook from the nightstand, and he bumped the headboard with his shoulder as he twisted and half rolled. He was still panting and pushing covers away with his feet when he realized he was on the bed. As he sat up, his body tingled with the sensation of all his flesh trying to escape the confines of his skin. His eyes darted around the dimly lit room as he tried to control his breathing and suppress the waves of panic.

He stared at the tape recorder, then bounded from the bed to turn off the machine. He had gone through enough for one day. After hanging up his shirt and trousers, he settled onto the bed and clicked off the light. The room darkened, but already the light of another foggy morning was creeping in around the edge of the shade that covered the window. He was asleep again even before the shuddering feeling of fright had left his chest.

Chapter 7

Monday Morning, 8:35 a.m.
Pacific Standard Time

NOT LONG AFTER JACK SHUT OFF THE RECORDER AT HOWELL AIR FORCE
Base, an overflowing crowd of reporters and cameramen had gathered
for a press conference at San Francisco International Airport. A
spokesman for the Federal Aviation Administration entered the conference room and approached the podium.

"Before I read the prepared statement," he said, squinting to see
through the brightness of the floodlights, "I must remind you that the
FAA and the National Transportation Safety Board are currently
conducting an investigation of the crash. Therefore, I will not be able
to go beyond the prepared statement at this time."

He adjusted the folder he carried, getting the statement out of the
glare of the lights.

Last night at approximately 10:40 p.m., Pacific Standard Time, a
Russian-made Ilyushin Il-62MK airliner with ninety-three people
on board disappeared from Oakland Center's radar screens. The
aircraft, Soviet National One, was approximately sixty-five miles
northwest of San Francisco International Airport. Accompanying
U.S. Air Force pilots reported seeing the airliner impact the Pacific
Ocean at 10:45 approximately twenty miles west of Point Reyes.
FAA air traffic controllers alerted the Coast Guard at that time.

Search and rescue efforts have been in progress since before
midnight. However, the major Pacific storm that battered San
Francisco throughout the night has hampered the search. As of
eight o'clock this morning, there were no reports of survivors.

The flight of Soviet National One originated at Vladivostok,
Russia. The aircraft was flying on a standard International Civil
Aviation Organization flight plan with a destination of San Francisco. Contacts with the aircraft throughout the flight had been
normal until a few minutes before the crash. At that time, the
aircraft entered an excessive rate of descent and did not respond to

76

additional attempts by Oakland Center to contact the aircraft. A listing of passengers and crew members has not yet been released by Soviet authorities. A complete investigation of the crash is underway.

Even before he closed the folder, hands went up throughout the room. A man in the second row boomed, "What caused the crash?"

"A copy of my statement is available at the exits," the spokesman said. "I'm sorry, but that's the limit of the details we have at this time."

Another reporter shouted, "When will you be releasing a passenger list?"

The spokesman had moved from the podium. He hesitated, then stepped back. "The FAA will not make that release. I believe the State Department or the Russian Embassy in Washington will provide a passenger list when next of kin have been notified."

Christine Merrill, the television reporter who had been with Alexander Braxton the evening before, was in the front row. She said, "You mentioned our Air Force was there. Isn't it unusual for Air Force aircraft to escort Soviet planes?"

Again the FAA man hesitated, obviously concerned about getting drawn into more questions.

"You'll have to ask the Air Force about its procedures. I'm really not prepared to speak for the Air Force."

Someone yelled from the back row, "The Air Force only goes after airplanes if there's some kind of problem. Isn't that true?"

Nearer to the front a woman asked, "If our Air Force was involved, why wasn't that admitted last night?" The spokesman did not respond. She called out as he neared the exit, "Can you tell us where we can talk to the Air Force pilots?"

He seemed to ignore that question, too, but as he opened the door, he said, "I'm not sure when the Air Force will make the pilots available, but I believe the intercepting aircraft were flown from Howell Air Force Base."

The reporters were disappointed because they had hoped to get a casualty list confirming which key Russian leaders had died. Generally the FAA statement was a consolidation of information released throughout the night in bulletins from the Western White House. The only new item was the acknowledgment that U.S. Air Force pilots had watched the crash.

As a result, most stories speculated on possible reasons for Air Force involvement. Television reporters took turns posing for their taped reports in front of the FAA shield on a wall near the entryway.

The closing lines for those reports were similar to Christine Merrill's wrap-up. "So ten hours after the crash of Soviet National One, we learn there were eyewitnesses—American pilots who watched the jetliner strike the cold, stormy waters of the Pacific Ocean. Now we have two key questions. Why did the Soviet aircraft crash? And why were American aircraft there when the crash occurred? The Air Force may or may not have an answer to the first question. It certainly has the answer to the second. As of now, the American public does not have either answer. This is Christine Merrill reporting from San Francisco International Airport."

Immediately after the FAA announcement, Howell Air Force Base began receiving telephone requests for information. When Colonel Radisson saw Merrill's summary on a special news report, he knew the reporters and cameramen would not be far behind. He instinctively wanted to take the spotlight, but knew better than to open up to the media on his own. So he picked what seemed to be his best choice. He directed his public affairs officer to announce that nothing could be released without approval of Colonel Phillips, the Pentagon officer in charge of the review of the incident. Radisson was pleased by his ability to deflect the pressure toward Phillips.

A few minutes before ten, however, a telephone call from the Western White House put a new twist on the situation. The duty officer at the Command Post was told that the President wanted the interceptor pilots made available to the press as soon as possible to tell about the crash and to settle the rumors. Also, the Air Force was not to volunteer information about the firing of the missile.

Radisson was delighted. He had always believed that the Air Force was not quite big enough for his talents, so he welcomed the opportunity for national exposure. He had suspected that some in the higher ranks would oppose his promotion to general. So he was convinced that a masterful presentation before the network cameras could silence his critics and might even be a stepping stone to bigger opportunities.

He knew he should inform his superiors before carrying out a directive from the Western White House, but once the people at the Pentagon knew that the Air Force had to make a statement, the generals would choose Phillips to handle the press conference. The thought of his old enemy getting the attention angered Radisson.

Yet there were risks in taking the story before the newsmen, and he never made a major move without considering the risks. The missile firing was the Achilles heel that could turn his potential triumph into an embarrassment. The actions of his pilots were completely clean, otherwise. The real risk was whether any of the reporters knew about the missile. Merrill's statements a few minutes earlier told him that risk was minimal. If she had known about the missile, he thought, she certainly would have offered a third question for the American public to ponder.

The timing was critical for at least two reasons. Once reporters arrived and started asking questions, they were likely to encounter someone who had heard of the empty weapon station on the returning F-15. Second, Phillips asked for a meeting at noon, but could be up and around at any time. Each minute of delay was one minute closer, Radisson thought, to the possibility that the Pentagon or Phillips would find out and either screw up the plans or steal all the credit. Radisson decided that if the news conference happened quickly enough, he could get the glory—Phillips would get the tough questions later when information leaked about the missile.

Radisson swung into action. He called in Captain Wade Lafferty, the base public affairs officer, and told him to draft an official statement about the Soviet crash. After checking to make sure Captain Benes and Lieutenant Walker were available, Radisson chose eleven-hundred hours as the time for the conference. The time might slip some if the reporters were still straggling in from San Francisco, but he wanted to be started well before noon.

Lafferty was to gather the reporters in the crew briefing room of the Base Operations building and get a tentative list of questions. Radisson knew he could not control the questioning, but under the guise of wanting to be sure he would have the answers, he hoped to learn if anyone was aware of the missile. If Lafferty got questions about the missile, Radisson could inform the Pentagon and let them pull Phillips in at the last minute.

Radisson also ordered the Command Post duty officer to prepare a message to Tactical Air Command Headquarters and the Pentagon. The message, which was to be held for Radisson's signature, would report the presidential directive to make the pilots available to the press.

With those actions started, he rushed to his quarters to get a fresh uniform. As he drove away from Base Operations, he noticed that reporters from a local television station were already arriving.

He selected one of his dress uniforms that had been tailored in Washington, D.C. The uniform, and a lightly starched blue shirt, were perfectly pressed. From his closet shelf he picked a pair of black shoes with a mirror-like finish. He always kept those shoes ready to wear when VIPs visited. By the time he returned to Base Operations, he looked like a Hollywood version of the professional officer.

*   *   *

Jack was in a deep sleep at 10:30 when country music from the clock radio echoed loudly off the walls of the small bedroom. He clawed at the offending radio, trying to figure out where he was and why he had such a terrible taste in his mouth. The controls on the radio were hard to locate in the dimly lit room, and he finally grabbed for the cord and yanked the plug from the wall.

Sitting on the edge of the bed, he remembered smoking, then remembered why he had smoked. As he turned on the television, he swore off smoking—again. Rotating the channel selector, Jack found game shows, movies, and pre-Christmas programs. He was relieved that there were no grim-faced commentators talking about a deepening crisis between the United States and the Soviet Union. He called the Command Post to check on the other tape recorder and to verify that he was on Radisson's schedule for noon. A few minutes later, a sergeant delivered the recorder.

He felt terrible, almost worse than if he had not slept at all. After shaving and taking a long shower, he felt more alert as he set up the two recorders. Wanting to review as much of the tapes as possible before his meeting, he turned on the FAA tape from Oakland Center. The tape included the voice transmissions of Karl Wilson, the air traffic controller, and the radio calls that came into his headset. Jack played the tape until he heard the first words from Guardian at the Air Defense Center.

Jack stopped the FAA tape and started the Air Force tape. He played that tape until he got to the same call from Guardian to Oakland Center. Once he synchronized the tapes, he could listen to what both controllers were hearing and saying. He settled into the recliner and listened carefully, hoping to catch anything he missed because of being so tired earlier when he had listened to the tapes.

At 10:45 Colonel Radisson, Captain Benes, and Lieutenant Walker were in the small projection room behind the stage. Captain Lafferty entered from the briefing room and handed Radisson two lists: the names of the reporters and the questions the reporters had submitted. Gesturing toward the briefing room, Lafferty said, "Sir, two more network teams just arrived, so we need about twenty minutes before we can start."

Worried about Phillips, Radisson cried, "Push them hard! I want to start on time." He scanned the names. Before Lafferty could leave, Radisson added, "Is this everyone that's coming?"

"It's a good crowd, sir," Lafferty said, seemingly surprised that Radisson was not pleased. "All the networks are here with remote hookups through the local affiliates, and we've got the wire services and Bay Area newspapers."

"I just figured for the amount of interest this thing's generated, some of the biggies from back East would get off their duffs and be here in person. The only real names I see on this list are Alexander Braxton and Richard Kane's kid, and those two are really just local media."

"Bruce Kane may be young, sir," Lafferty said, "but he's his network's top man on the West Coast."

"Big deal. His old man's the Kane I'd much rather see sitting in the front row."

Richard Kane was the anchorman on his network's nightly news. His son was the West Coast correspondent for the network, having already moved several rungs up the career ladder toward his father's job.

Lafferty was experienced at being unsuccessful in satisfying Radisson under almost any circumstances. "Sir, since the President's still in San Francisco and everyone's still looking for the Russian casualty list, the national anchormen probably felt compelled to stay in the city."

"Right now we're the story," Radisson said in his characteristic tone of self-importance.

"If we were releasing information about the missile firing, sir," Lafferty said, "I'm sure we could have drawn a bigger crowd."

Radisson frowned at Lafferty, but did not argue. "Let me know when you have everything ready."

Lafferty left, and Radisson scanned the list of questions gathered from the waiting reporters. Nothing indicated any knowledge of the missile. He concluded that most of the reporters did not understand enough about air defense operations to ask the right questions. No sweat, he thought, turning his attention to the two young fliers.

"I'll do most of the talking," he said. "You guys should treat this like an inspection. Just answer whatever you're asked, but don't volunteer anything! We're not here to talk about your screw-up out there last night." He looked Benes in the eye to be sure the captain understood that the accidental missile firing was a subject not to be volunteered.

Radisson checked over both pilots, who looked sharp in their neatly pressed flight suits, gold scarves, and spit-shined boots. Their appearance was professional and almost perfect: a long, olive-drab thread hung from the edge of one pocket on Walker's flight suit. When Radisson spotted the thread, he frowned like a mother whose child had just tracked in mud on a freshly cleaned carpet.

"Come on, Lieutenant," he said as he pulled a cigarette lighter from his pocket.

"You don't want to go on national television with cables hanging all over your uniform."

"No, sir!" Walker blushed in response to the reprimand.

"You probably won't have a speaking part in this performance," Radisson said, putting the flame of the lighter to the end of the thread. As the thread burned away and disappeared, he added, "But you don't want to go out there and embarrass the Air Force by looking sloppy."

The colonel's mind jumped to other things almost as soon as the flicker of flame died away. "When we walk out on that stage, we'll be outnumbered better than ten to one. Not great odds even in an F-15, but approach this interview like any other dogfight when you're outnumbered—just get in, do your thing, and get your tail out. These things can be like the middle of that furball with fifty aircraft swirling and turning. Stay in there long enough, and someone'll ram a missile up your ass."

His enthusiasm made it obvious that he was getting psyched up like a star player before the big game. He stepped before a picture and used the glass as a makeshift mirror while he combed his hair. Then holding the door open slightly, he looked out at the reporters, technicians, and cameramen. The flurry of activity continued as technicians struggled to solve last-minute cable and lighting problems.

As he watched, Captain Lafferty stepped onto the stage and got the attention of the reporters. "I'm told everyone will be set in a couple of minutes. Then Colonel Robert Radisson, our wing commander, will present the two fighter pilots who flew last night's mission. Colonel Radisson will make a statement about the mission, and there will be some time afterward for a limited number of questions. I will serve as moderator during the question and answer session."

A few minutes later, a sergeant entered the projection room and said, "Sir, Captain Lafferty says everyone's ready whenever you are."

Radisson nodded and opened the black leather portfolio he had carried from the Command Post. "Stand by a moment, Sergeant. I need this taken to the message center."

Radisson pulled out the message form that had been prepared earlier. He reread the words announcing to headquarters that he had been directed from the Western White House to conduct the press conference. With a dramatic flourish he signed the "Releaser" block on the form. "Okay, Sarge, I've got an Immediate message here that needs to get right out on the teletype."

The sergeant took the message and hurried from the room.

"Pay some attention today, boys," Radisson said, "and you'll learn some valuable lessons about how to get ahead. You've got to recognize which situations require a CYA message. If you don't 'cover your ass' at the right time, you'll be in the hospital the next day getting a buttocks transplant."

Radisson laughed loudly, and Benes chuckled politely. Even as nervous as Walker was, he joined with a broad smile.

"And," Radisson added with great conviction, "timing's critical! If you want the headquarters to intercede, tell them in a hurry. If you don't want the head shed in your way, don't backbrief until it's too late for them to interfere. Getting an Immediate message on the wire as you step on the stage is a personal technique you'll develop when you've been around as long as I have."

Captain Lafferty announced the wing commander's entrance as Radisson, Benes, and Walker came through the door and took seats at a microphone-infested table on the stage. The bright lights brought even greater contrasts between Radisson's immaculately tailored blue uniform and the olive drab flight suits worn by the two pilots. Sparkling noticeably, his silver pilot's wings topped the multicolored collection of ribbons centered above his left breast pocket. Even without rank being considered, his appearance left no doubts about who was the star of the press conference.

Captain Lafferty began his introductory remarks and a summary of the ground rules, but Radisson lifted his hand in a gesture for silence. "Thank you, Captain, but I can handle things from here."

He turned toward the audience and slowly opened the portfolio. Every action was a deliberate step to maintain control. Finally, after as much of a dramatic pause as he felt he could get away with, he glanced at his notes, then looked thoughtfully toward the reporters seated in front of the bank of cameras.

"This is a sad day for Americans as well as for the people of the Soviet Union. We were on the brink of a major step on the path to world peace and away from the threat of nuclear confrontation." He hesitated, thoughtfully, then continued. "Before our formal statement, I want to apologize for the austere accommodations we've offered our many media friends who came all the way from San Francisco. From the moment we became aware of your interest in the Air Force's witnessing of the crash, we've done everything we could to get the story available as quickly as possible. That has, unfortunately, caused us to squeeze you together to accommodate everyone."

He sensed the impatience and restlessness of some reporters and decided that he had better get into the review.

"Last night," he continued, referring to the notes in his portfolio, "at about twenty-two-ten hours, Oakland Center confirmed that Soviet National One was more than seventy miles off course approaching the California coast. Routine procedures call for interceptors to be sent to identify approaching international flights that violate their clearances. . . ."

Radisson's performance also caused restlessness at the Pentagon. General McClintock was shocked to see the news conference. Minutes later, a sergeant in the Command Post at Howell knocked on Jack's door and told him he had a call from the general.

Jack had not finished dressing, so he grabbed a shirt and was still tucking it into his trousers as he hurried down the hall.

He entered the booth for the secure telephone and picked up the receiver. "Good morning, sir. I—"

"What in the hell are you doing out there, Jack?" The professional friendliness that had characterized their earlier discussions was absent from the general's voice.

Jack hesitated, having no idea of what to say.

"The conference, Jack," McClintock continued. "I don't know what you can be thinking of to put Radisson and his two pilots in front of the cameras."

"You've got me a little confused, sir. I have no plans to put them—"

"There's sure as hell confusion somewhere, Jack, because every network in D.C. is carrying a live news conference with those three right now! You know damned well that General Raleigh wants to personally clear any major releases to the media."

Jack was surprised and angry at the same time. "Where are they broadcasting from, sir? Radisson's supposed to check with me before he tries anything like that."

"Somewhere on base," McClintock answered. "I don't care where, but you'd better get there ASAP and minimize our losses!"

Before leaving the Command Post, Jack learned that the news conference was being conducted in another wing of the same building. As he hurried to his room, he kept asking himself, Had there been a leak of information about the missile? He was worried about local reporters, who would see the next few days as a once-in-a-decade opportunity. The crash had put the world's focus on San Francisco like nothing else in recent years. For some reporter, a dramatic accounting of the story could be a ticket out of the journalistic Sleepy Hollow of the West to a news desk in Los Angeles, Washington, or New York.

Once in his room, he turned on the television set as he hurriedly pulled together the rest of his uniform. On the screen he saw Radisson's well-practiced look of self-importance. He paused a moment to watch, still unable to believe Radisson was not savvy enough to stay away from the cameras until cleared by the Air Staff.

Radisson displayed the polished eloquence of a university speech major. Adding the right pauses, he sounded sincere and forthcoming. He was putting on an impressive show. Jack felt resentment and a little envy as he went to the closet and pulled out a clean shirt still wrinkled from being in the hangup bag.

"Now," Radisson said, "we have time for a few questions if there is anything I missed."

Several hands went up immediately. Before Radisson had a chance to select one, Captain Lafferty interceded from his position behind the podium. "As we agreed earlier, I'll designate the questioner. When called on, please identify yourself and—"

"No need to be quite that formal, Captain," Radisson said. Though the expression on his face remained pleasant, the narrowing of his eyes told Lafferty he was expected to be seen but not heard. "I'll field the questions from here."

The first questioner asked, "Can you tell us, Colonel, what caused the Soviet aircraft to be so far off course?"

Radisson was pleased that the question focused on the Soviets. Just like running out the clock at the end of a football game, he thought. The more time used on such questions, the cleaner the whole press conference would be. He put on an expression of thoughtful consideration and paused for as long as he deemed advisable.

"Naturally," he said, "I'm much better able to speak for the outstanding capabilities of our own aircraft. I can only speculate on the source of the Soviet's navigational error. If I were a Soviet accident investigator, I'd focus on three areas: weather, equipment, and personnel." He paused as if trying to be sure he had thought of everything. "I understand Soviet National One was able to fly above most of the weather. The weather wasn't great all the way from Siberia, but nothing that good equipment and good men couldn't handle."

He paused to take a sip of water and give the audience a moment to make notes on his comments. After wiping his lips with his handkerchief, he continued. "The Il-62 is a fairly modern aircraft. Since it carried the Soviet president and members of the Politburo, I'm sure Soviet National One was fitted out with the best navigational equipment the Russians have. They can't match our state-of-the-art electronics, of course, so flying across the open ocean for ten or twelve hours is more of a challenge for them than for our Air Force. Again, if I were a Soviet investigator, I'd certainly pick equipment problems over personnel error as the most likely cause. When their generals choose the crew to fly President Gorshko and Minister Valinen around, I'm certain no 'Ivan the Terribles' are picked for the navigators."

He smiled, pleased with the way he had handled the first question as he called for the next.

"Is there any possibility that Soviet National One could have been drawn off course?"

Radisson asked, "Do you mean on purpose?"

"Yes."

"I can't imagine that happening. There are documented cases where the Soviets have used high-powered navigational beacons to draw our aircraft across the borders in Central Europe and other places. That's their technique, not ours. Besides, Soviet National One already was authorized by an ICAO flight plan and by the FAA to enter our airspace for a landing at San Francisco. There was no reason to try to draw the aircraft off course."

The next questioner asked, "Why is the Air Force investigating the crash of a Soviet aircraft?"

"Why not?" Radisson popped back the answer, then focused more on the question and its potential implications. Before he could modify his answer, a questioner in the second row followed up.

"Isn't that an FAA responsibility?"

"Well, of course!" Radisson tried to disguise being distracted by the previous question. "I'm sure most of you are aware of the FAA statement this morning confirming that they have an investigation in progress."

"So, you're saying that the FAA is investigating and the Air Force is not?"

"Yes," Radisson said firmly.

Questioning looks and the immediate increase in the number of hands in the air made him quickly rethink his answer. He was becoming angry and frustrated as he caught himself thinking about things that had already happened instead of what was actually happening. Such lapses could be fatal in a dogfight and certainly would not do his image any good in this encounter if he did not get on top of the questioning.

"Yes on the FAA," Radisson said slowly and deliberately, "and, yes, the Air Force is investigating. It's routine procedure."

"It's routine to bring a colonel all the way out from the Pentagon to investigate the crash of a plane that doesn't belong to the Air Force?"

Radisson was sorry he had implied earlier that Phillips' presence was so important. "When the plane is full of high-ranking Soviet officials, we're interested. And actually the colonel was not brought out here for the investigation. He was already in the area." He turned to someone on the far side of the audience. "You have a question?"

"Maybe we can summarize. You've said that the Air Force had no role in causing the navigational error, doesn't know anything at all about why Soviet National One mysteriously crashed, and really had no involvement other than going out to intercept the aircraft and witnessing the crash?"

Radisson nodded in agreement throughout. He smiled, pleased to have the questioning back in a more favorable direction. "I'd say that's a pretty good summary."

Bruce Kane, a neatly dressed young reporter said, "No collusion of any kind?"

A strange way to phrase the question, Radisson thought. "Collusion? With whom? Of course not!" He tried to sound as convincing as possible.

Kane continued, "You're telling us, then, that there's no reason that the world should suspect that the Soviet aircraft was shot down by U.S. Air Force fighters?"

"That's definitely not true!" Radisson used his typical bravado to disguise the sudden surge of panic. "That's a pretty dumb question to ask with world tension at a potential flashpoint." He hoped he might embarrass Kane into silence, then turned away. "Mr. Braxton, I believe your hand was the next I saw."

Braxton looked surprised, but obliged. "Colonel, accepting your statement about no Air Force involvement, then in your expert opinion, what caused the Russian airplane to crash?"

"That's a question I wish we had the answer to. Unfortunately, we may never know. The only people who know for sure are still in the cockpit. Once the recorders are recovered—if they are recovered—we may learn things the pilots can no longer tell us. Again, if I were a Soviet accident investigator, Mr. Braxton, I'd focus on three areas: weather, equipment, and personnel."

"So," another questioner asked, "you're saying the Air Force has no idea at all why the plane crashed?"

"We have ideas," Radisson said. "Until the investigations are complete, however, we're just speculating."

Kane had continued to try for Radisson's recognition, but the colonel avoided the young newsman. In the moment of silence after the last answer, Kane shouted, "Can you tell us, Colonel, if Minister Valinen's aircraft was struck by an AIM-17X missile fired from Captain Benes' F-15?"

A murmur rumbled across the crowded room as the cameras zoomed in on Radisson. The color faded from his face just as when he was chewed out during the telephone call from General Smathers. His eyes darted around, focusing momentarily on Benes, who continued looking beyond the cameras and refused to make eye contact.

"Where'd you hear a wild rumor like that?" Radisson's scratchy voice betrayed the dryness in his throat.

"I didn't say there was a rumor, Colonel," Kane said. "I just asked a question, but your response sounds like you're aware of rumors."

"Don't try to put words in my mouth, young man," Radisson said. "We're here this morning to ensure senseless rumors don't get started—rumors that could be extremely dangerous to the national security of the United States."

He looked for other questioners to call on, but everyone else seemed to be waiting for Kane's follow up.

"Then to get away from rumors, Colonel," Kane said dramatically, "can you assure me that *the* AIM-17X missile fired from Captain Benes' F-15 did not strike Minister Valinen's aircraft?"

As Jack ran through the hallways, he removed his name tag and put it into his pocket. Rounding a corner, he saw camera equipment cases scattered in the hall and a group of Air Force personnel crowded around a set of open doors.

He pushed through the crush of people blocking the doorway, and most stepped aside as soon as they spotted the silver eagles of his colonel's rank. On the stage, Captain Benes was carefully discussing the fallen map and the accidental firing of the missile. Other than the trio in the floodlights, the only person Jack recognized was Captain Jensen.

Jack forced his way through to where Jensen stood near the left wall, then whispered, "I can't believe anyone in his right mind would go public before we got everything figured out!"

With the briefing room quiet except for Benes' voice and the whir of cameras, Jack's words carried at least to the smartly dressed woman taking notes in front of Jensen.

Christine Merrill spun around and flashed a look of righteous indignation. "The President directed this news conference!"

Her message stunned the colonel. He could not believe that a man with the political savvy of the President would have risked full public disclosure before all the information was available. However, she had spoken with such conviction that Jack believed her. He maintained eye contact momentarily, recognizing her from the previous evening at the airport. He was tempted to respond to her condescending tone, but decided against it as she seemed to be trying to place where she might have seen him before.

Jensen confirmed her statement with a nod, then added, "Since mid-morning, the press corps has been converging like locusts. The media knew the F-15s had been with the airliner, and some TV people were pushing for a statement to settle the rumors. Colonel Radisson held fast until there was a call from the Western White House."

"I sure don't understand that decision," Jack answered.

"Military mentality," Christine said. "The President's smart enough to support the American public's right to know the truth."

"If you folks aren't careful with your questions," Jack said, "you won't need those notes you're writing."

She looked confused but even angrier. "Is that some kind of threat, Colonel—" She looked for a name tag.

"No threat from me, ma'am," he said. "But if these asinine questions convince the Soviets to retaliate with an ICBM laydown, you won't have enough time left to get your notes into print!"

"I'm a television commentator," she said icily, the tone contrasting sharply with the fiery look in her eyes. Anger added color to her cheeks as she continued, "You'll need more than scare tactics to keep us from telling the truth."

"What I need is some common sense in the way you people approach this story."

Before she could respond, nearby reporters called for quiet to hear the discussion of the missile firing. She looked embarrassed and turned toward the stage, where Benes was using his hands to describe the maneuverings of the aircraft beneath the clouds.

Jack bit his lip and crossed his arms. He decided she was one of the ambitious reporters he was worried about. He also cancelled out the nice thoughts he had had about her at the airport.

"And so, Captain Benes," a questioner said, "an aircraft you were pursuing crashes, you returned from the flight with an empty pylon, and you claim you didn't shoot down the aircraft?"

"It was an empty weapon station," Benes responded.

"What?" The questioner looked confused.

"You said empty pylon. A pylon carries two missiles. I only launched one missile so only a single weapon station was empty."

"That's beside the point. I—"

"Negative, sir," Benes said. "That's an important point. Only one missile was accidentally launched, and your report should show that. And your report should also show that the low altitude maneuvering meant the missile didn't strike the airliner."

Way to hang in there, kid, Jack thought. He was pleased that Benes was handling the newsmen much better than Radisson had. Jack hoped Benes would continue to stay cool.

"That part of your story seems illogical, Captain," a man next to Braxton said. "Why in such a serious emergency would a pilot turn his aircraft away from the closest airport?"

"I wasn't in his cockpit, sir. His maneuver must've made sense to him, considering the condition of his aircraft at the time."

Another questioner followed up. "You're saying that Soviet National One was out of control, then under control, and then crashed. Is there any proof—say recorded radar images—that would verify that the aircraft did the maneuvering you say?"

Come on, Radisson, Jack urged mentally. Terminate this thing! If the President really had been involved, Jack thought, enough had been said already to "fill the square" for a press briefing.

Benes looked angry, but filtered most of the anger from his voice as he addressed the implications instead of the question.

"I've admitted I accidentally fired the missile. I have no reason to lie."

"Unless the firing was *not* an accident." Kane rose to his feet. "Unless you intentionally wanted to destroy the aircraft carrying Minister Valinen."

There was another round of murmuring among the audience. Some reporters seemed surprised at how direct Kane was. Many appeared interested in, and perhaps envious of, the insights he apparently had into issues the Air Force did not want to discuss.

"That's absurd," Benes said. "I'm a United States Air Force officer, and I—"

"That's enough," Radisson interjected. "We're not here to indulge your fantasies, Mr. Kane."

Benes looked nervously at the bank of microphones rather than at his accuser. Jack studied Benes' expression. The young pilot seemed more relieved at Radisson's intercession than angry over Kane's accusation. Suddenly Jack felt there was something Benes had not admitted.

Radisson continued, "We're about out of time. Unless someone has a question that focuses on the facts, I believe—"

"The fact is, is it not," Kane interrupted, "that your captain had a special hatred for Minister Valinen, based on personal reasons we all could appreciate?"

The quizzical look on Radisson's face suggested he had no idea what personal motivations Kane was talking about. Benes' expression, however, told Jack that the young captain knew. Jack started pushing through the people and equipment that filled the aisle between him and the stage.

"He's sworn to support and defend the Constitution," Radisson said rising from his chair. "Personal motivations are immaterial. I think you're way out of bounds, Mr. Kane."

Kane shouted, "Can't Captain Benes speak for himself and assure us he didn't squeeze the trigger because of his hatred for Valinen?"

Benes said firmly, "I did not intentionally attack the aircraft."

"You weren't trying to avenge the death of your very famous great-grandfather who may have died at the hands of Valinen's secret police in Czechoslovakia?"

Damn, Jack thought, as he neared the stage. Until that moment, he had not made the natural connection between Czechoslovakia and Benes' name.

"No!" Benes' voice was filled with anger.

"Are you denying that Eduard Benes, the last president of free Czechoslovakia, was your great-grandfather?"

"Yes."

The response was the first to catch Kane off guard.

Benes added, "President Benes was a cousin of my great-grandfather."

"I believe that's all the time we have," Radisson said, stepping back from the table.

Kane rebounded with one more question. "Can you deny you're glad Minister Valinen is dead?"

"No!" Benes stood and shouted toward Kane as if they were the only two people in the room. "I'm glad that murdering son of a bitch is finally dead, and I hope he's already burning in hell!"

"That's enough," Jack shouted as he reached the stage. "There's an official Air Force investigation in progress, and we're not going to play it out in front of cameras." He jumped to the stage and deliberately kept his back toward the cameras that turned in his direction. "Benes! Walker!" He pointed toward the backstage exit.

"Wait," Kane shouted.

Radisson also shouted at Jack, "Wait! What am I—"

"The stage is all yours." Jack glared at Radisson, then herded the two pilots away amid a roar of protests from the reporters. Once in the hallway, he told Benes to lead the way to the Command Post.

Jack wondered how soon he would get his next call from General McClintock. The general was going to be unhappy about the revelations of the last few minutes. At least, Jack thought, he could slip the President's name into his explanation of how the news conference came about.

Most people in the Command Post were clustered around two television sets. One showed Bruce Kane.

"Bratislava, Valinen, and Benes are significant names in twentieth-century Czechoslovakia," Kane said. "Four decades ago, Minister Valinen was the chief political officer in Bratislava, the third largest Czech city. Valinen earned the nickname, 'The Beast of Bratislava,' for his sadistic subjugation of the Czechoslovakian citizens of that city. In that same era, President Eduard Benes resigned after refusing to sign a Russian-dictated constitution. Benes died mysteriously a few months later—probably at the hands of Valinen's police. Now we have to ask if that death finally has been avenged by a distant relative of the Czech patriot."

Jack had even more questions than before as he turned to Benes. "You're full of surprises, Captain."

"I swear," Benes said, "on the name of my father and our fathers before him that I didn't intentionally attack that aircraft."

"We'd have been better off," Jack said, "if you'd stuck to that line without the editorializing."

"Mr. Kane asked," Benes said. "I simply told the truth."

"With these folks," Jack said, "it doesn't pay to tell everything you know. Anyway, we can't do much about that now. We need to figure out what else that guy knows that might jump up and bite us."

"I didn't have any idea you were famous," Walker added.

"I'm not," Benes said. "Many in my family have been activists against the Communist regime in Czechoslovakia. However, the subject of my namesake hasn't come up in a long time."

Jack asked, "Who here at Howell is aware of your background?"

Benes hesitated. "No one. The subject hasn't been mentioned in the three years I've been here."

Walker asked, "How'd he know that Ed fired the AIM-17?"

"That's easy enough," Jack said. "With all the radio scanners around, Kane probably found out there'd been a firing. Once he got that, he may have bought a few details from someone on the flight line."

He was more curious about how Kane had made the connection between Captain Benes and Valinen. Less than seventeen hours had passed since Benes had climbed aboard his Eagle, so Kane obviously knew how to piece things together in a hurry.

Jack saw Christine Merrill's face on one of the television sets. He moved close enough to catch her angry words.

"What we've seen here this morning," she said, "is reminiscent of the press censorship during the American invasion of Grenada in 1983—a direct conflict between the people's right to know and the military's desire to suppress the free flow of information. One senior Air Force representative was overheard questioning the President's judgment in permitting even this much of a look at what happened aboard Air Force jet fighters in the dark skies beyond the Golden Gate."

Nicely done, Jack thought sarcastically. He also thought about having to explain her comments to bureaucrats who would not be interested in his answer about how the President's judgment was "questioned." He wished she had kept her mouth shut. He wished he had kept his mouth shut.

"Obviously," Christine continued, "there were some things the Air Force would prefer to have kept covered up. We'll have more on the 'Czechoslovakian Connection' this evening on the early news."

A noisy clamor of voices from the hallway accompanied Radisson as he forced his way through the door. Looking irritated and with his hair in disarray, Radisson leaned against the heavy door for a moment while almost everyone in the Command Post returned to work. He scanned the room, then headed directly for Jack.

Jack spoke first, "Nice job of crew scheduling."

Radisson ignored the remark. Instead he asked, "What in the hell did you think you were doing out there?"

"That's my line," Jack said, vowing not to let Radisson get the initiative. "The next time you want to show how well you can walk on water, you'd damned well better know where the stepping stones are!"

"Watch your mouth, Colonel." Radisson said as he came almost toe-to-toe with Jack.

Jack crossed his arms in front and stood his ground. "General McClintock wants to know why that conference wasn't coordinated with General Raleigh. You weren't supposed to pull anything like that without notifying me."

"The President personally directed it," Radisson said. "His orders take priority over yours!"

While they argued, a young sergeant approached. "Pardon me, sir," the sergeant said, offering to Radisson a sheet of paper that had been ripped from a teletype machine.

"Stand by, Mossman," Radisson said without moving away from Jack. "Whatever you've got will keep."

"Maybe not, sir," Sergeant Mossman answered, but obediently stepped back a couple of steps.

"Give me that," Radisson said, grabbing the paper from the sergeant's outstretched hand.

"Sir," Mossman said, "Soviet warships have reached the crash site, and it looks like there's going to be trouble."

Chapter 8

LIEUTENANT PETER FALLON STOOD ON THE BRIDGE OF THE *VALIANT*, a medium endurance cutter of the U.S. Coast Guard. The *Valiant* was holding its position eighteen miles off the Point Reyes Peninsula. The wreckage of Soviet National One was on the ocean floor 470 feet below. The other ships and helicopters in the hastily created search force were closer to shore, where ocean currents might have carried debris.

One of the divers—three had been added to Fallon's crew before the *Valiant* left the dock at 4:00 a.m.—was returning to the surface after exploring the wreckage. On the fantail of the cutter, eight men were working to raise the diver the last few feet. Fallon was dividing his attention between their progress and that of a Soviet guided-missile destroyer a few miles away. He was growing more uneasy with each minute that brought the destroyer closer.

For the last three hours, he had received radio messages updating the location of two Soviet ships: the *Gnevnyy*, a destroyer of the *Kanin* class, and the *Karpaty*, a submarine rescue ship. Both ships had been steaming at sixteen knots toward the crash site. However, the last report indicated that the destroyer had increased its speed, moving several miles ahead of the slower ship.

A few minutes earlier, Fallon's cutter had been the first to make visual contact. One of his lookouts had spotted the Soviet destroyer on the western horizon, almost directly off the bow. Initially, the destroyer's course toward the crash site seemed natural and had caused no concern as Fallon's men attempted normal contacts using signal lights and flags. However, the *Gnevnyy* had ignored all signals and continued bearing down on the smaller *Valiant*.

Through binoculars Fallon studied the oncoming ship. As the distance narrowed, he could see that the Russians were maintaining speed and course. He suddenly had a frightening thought—perhaps the Soviets were not planning on a joint recovery effort. "Sound General Quarters!"

A baby-faced seaman answered, "Aye, aye, Captain!" Simultaneously he slammed his palm against a large red button on the forward panel. A Klaxon sounded its electronic warning throughout the cutter.

Fallon felt the familiar tingle that always accompanied the Klaxon's shrill scream and the sound of running feet. He studied the adversary, dark gray steel knifing through light seas. His mind computed velocity vectors, rates of change, and the rapidly diminishing separation. A collision course, no doubt, unless the *Gnevnyy* turned or the *Valiant* got underway quickly.

He shouted to the helmsman, "Prepare to make way, emergency!" Not waiting for an answer, he moved to the bridge's starboard ladder near the aft bulkhead. Below on the fantail, the eight men worked frantically. Wet from windblown spray, the seamen pulled on ropes and air hoses to raise the diver.

Cupping his hands around his mouth, he shouted "How much longer, Chief?"

"Give me a couple more minutes, Captain," Chief Petty Officer Barney Neilsen shouted without breaking his rhythm of brace and pull, brace and pull.

Fallon looked forward. The growing menace continued to churn greenish-gray sea water into angry white foam and sea spray. "You've got one minute, Chief! We've got to get underway!"

Neilsen let loose a string of salty epithets, causing the younger men around him to struggle harder.

Fallon focused his binoculars on the dark smoke that belched from the Soviet ship. Thirty minutes earlier, he had assumed the recovery would become a joint effort. His main worry had been how he might communicate to the Russian captain what the American divers had learned. Now he was concerned about the intentions of the *Gnevnyy*, and his concerns were turning to fear.

He knew that Soviet ships sometimes played "chicken" with ships of the U.S. Navy. In most cases, maneuvering at the last minute avoided a collision. Since the *Gnevnyy* was more than twice as long and nearly five times heavier than his *Valiant*, he did not want to have to depend on, or be at the mercy of, the skill of the Soviet captain to avoid a collision.

"We're out of time, Chief," he shouted.

"Fifteen more seconds, Captain!"

The ropes and air lines were taut, but Fallon saw no signs of Johnson, the twenty-year-old seaman in the diving rig. Fallon checked the destroyer's distance and the dark smoke that spewed back across the Soviet's aft deck.

"Sound the collision alarm," he shouted, knowing he had only a few more seconds to make a decision he did not want to make. "Send out a Mayday on all emergency freqs."

The warbling wail of the collision alarm added to the sense of urgency. He knew he had to act. Each second delayed for Johnson increased the danger for the other sixty-three men on the ship.

"Helmsman, stand by," he said, raising his hand. He turned and shouted over the noise of the collision warning, "We've got to move out, Chief. Secure the diver's lines!"

"Just a few more seconds, Captain," Neilsen pleaded. "Please!"

Fallon hesitated. His raised hand quivered as something appeared just below the water's surface. An instant later, the oversized mechanical head of a diver's suit bobbed above the water. Neilsen's shouts produced one last flurry of action. With robot-like arms flailing above the water, the diver was yanked backwards against the side of the cutter.

Fallon looked forward. The destroyer was terrifyingly close.

The chief's two biggest sailors lunged toward the diver while other seamen held on to keep the two men from falling overboard. Everyone on the fantail grabbed the struggling mass of sailors.

Satisfied, Neilsen shot his clenched fist toward the sullen sky and shouted "Go!"

"Go!" Fallon dropped his fist.

The ship lurched as twin propellers slashed into the green-gray sea beneath the ship. Sailors tumbled wildly over one another, but Fallon was satisfied that Johnson would not be lost. The destroyer was so close, however, that he was unsure the diver's rescue mattered.

"Five degrees port," he said, ordering a new course aimed directly at the bow of the oncoming destroyer.

Maneuverability depended on speed, so he decided to take the destroyer head-on while the cutter built up speed. Not turning away was a dangerous ploy, but he wanted to put some doubt in the mind of the Soviet captain. Both captains, however, would have to guess correctly on their final turns.

Above the roar of the cutter's engines and siren, he heard the warble of the destroyer's warning horn. He detected a decrease in the destroyer's smoke plumes, suggesting that the Soviet captain was having second thoughts about his game of chicken.

Fallon held off until the last moment. Then, bracing for the turn, he shouted, "Hard starboard, forty-five degrees."

Simultaneously the Soviet destroyer turned right.

The two ships were so close that Fallon was unsure they could avoid the collision. As soon as he could tell the ships would miss, his fear changed to anger. He stepped through the bridge's left entryway and stood glowering up at the bridge of the onrushing destroyer. As the *Gnevnyy*'s bow charged past a few feet away, he looked at the men on the fantail of his ship. Chief Neilsen stood defiantly, his upraised middle finger gesturing to the men on the Soviet ship.

"Damned right, Chief," Fallon yelled. Then, shaking his fist at the unseen Soviet captain, he shouted as loudly as he could, "You crazy, son of a bitchin' Russian!" He felt better, but only for an instant.

Then his executive officer screamed, "Holy shit!"

The frantic tone sent another surge of adrenaline through him. A blur of motion directly ahead got his attention.

A helicopter gunship had swooped from the helipad on the fantail of the Soviet destroyer. The pilot was flying right at the cutter's bridge. Fallon dropped to his knees. The seamen on the bridge scrambled in all directions as the cutter bucked crazily through the destroyer's bow wave.

The helicopter climbed a few feet just before the cutter's superstructure slid beneath the swirling rotor. The landing gear slammed into the cutter's tallest radio mast, snapping it off. Debris clattered loudly off the top of the bridge. As Fallon sheltered himself from the falling guy wires, fractured tubing, and antenna elements, he realized a radio call from an American helicopter had been interrupted.

"I say again, *Valiant*, this is Jolly One, responding!" U.S. Air Force Lieutenant Colonel "Buck" Buchanan radioed from the pilot's seat of an HH-53C Super Jolly Green Giant helicopter.

Five miles east of the Coast Guard cutter, he and his crew had been retrieving a floating cushion from the water. Answering the call for help, he pulled the large helicopter into a climbing turn toward the western horizon. In the copilot's seat to Buchanan's left, First Lieutenant Grant Smallwood continued trying to establish radio contact with the *Valiant*. Airman Tiny Murphy climbed into the jump seat just aft of the pilots. Murphy was one of the two pararescue jumpers, commonly referred to as PJs, on the crew. The other PJ and the flight mechanic were securing items in the cargo compartment.

As the helicopter gained speed and altitude, Buchanan spotted the Coast Guard cutter and the Soviet destroyer still steaming away from each other. He leveled his helicopter at one thousand feet, staying just below the ragged clouds. From that altitude he saw the intermingled wakes of the two ships. He studied the cutter for signs of fire or other damage, wondering if a collision had caused the loss of radio contact.

"Traffic, ten o'clock, nearly level," Murphy said, leaning over the copilot's shoulder and pointing to the left. "Looks like another chopper, sir."

Buchanan located the approaching helicopter, but could not identify the type, for the whirling blades, dark markings, and the angle to the craft made it difficult to pick out details against the dingy background of sea and clouds. He assumed that a civilian helicopter, perhaps carrying a news team from San Francisco, had strayed into the restricted area.

When the other helcopter moved rapidly to a position in front of the Americans, Buchanan thought, Something isn't right. He reduced power and raised the nose to slow his forward speed. When the distance separating the helicopters narrowed to less than a mile, the Soviet craft swung around to face him.

As soon as he saw the head-on profile, showing the characteristic chin turret and stubby wings of the Soviet Union's most formidable helicopter gunship, he shouted, "That's a Hind-D!"

He was shocked. Before takeoff, he had not considered adding the miniguns that were standard equipment during combat rescues. Now, he wished his bird were carrying those guns whose six rotating barrels could spit out six thousand rounds a minute.

"Maybe the helicopter's trying to keep us away from the destroyer," Smallwood said.

Buchanan doubted that. The destroyer continued moving away to the left while the gunship remained almost directly between the American helicopter and the Coast Guard cutter. However, he had no better explanation.

As he watched the ominous form hovering a few hundred yards away, his right hand took a tighter grip on the cyclic, the helicopter's "stick" that controlled pitch and roll. With his left hand, he yanked his lap belt tighter, then reached down beside his seat and grabbed the collective, the lever that was the main control for moving the helicopter up and down. Taking a deep breath, he said, "There's one way to find out if they're just out here to pass the time of day." If they weren't, Buchanan thought, he was going to have both hands full for the next few minutes.

He slipped his helicopter to the right, and the Hind-D responded, mirroring the movement.

"Son of a bitch!" Buchanan experienced a surge of exhilaration that he had not felt since he had been a combat rescue pilot in the final days of the Vietnam War. Long-dormant memories of his toughest mission near the outskirts of Hanoi flashed through his mind, mixing new anger with the overwhelming excitement. "They couldn't keep us out of North Vietnam, and I'll be damned if I'll let a friggin' helicopter stop me from answering a Mayday just off the coast of California."

Moving right and edging forward, he narrowed the distance to the cutter. The Soviet helicopter followed the sideways motion. When the Hind-D was less than a hundred yards in front of his Super Jolly Green Giant, Buchanan slowed momentarily to a near standstill. He had never tried to outmaneuver an opposing helicopter, but the situation reminded him of earlier years. In college football games he had stood as a wide receiver facing a corner back beyond the line of scrimmage. Back then his tactics had been fake once, twice, then sprint for the end zone. That seemed as good a plan as any.

"Hang on, troops," he said as he forced a quick movement to the right.

His helicopter leaped sideways and dropped a few feet to increase the acceleration. The Soviet pilot's response lagged by a few seconds, but then he forced his craft to chase. Buchanan waited until the Hind-D was accelerating sideways at a high rate and had almost caught up. Then he reversed his controls and had Murphy advance the throttles.

The Soviet helicopter flashed by as the Super Jolly Green Giant climbed and accelerated in the opposite direction. Again, the Soviet was a couple of additional seconds behind. Attempting to catch up, he made even greater corrections.

The Hind-D was moving much faster from right to left when Buchanan reversed his controls the second time and dived toward a point just below the chin turret on the Hind-D. He was gambling on the likelihood that he and the Soviet pilot shared a similar fear—flying through the whirling rotors of someone else's helicopter. With the six blades above his craft slashing a cylinder of air more than seventy feet across, his maneuvering had placed the Soviet helicopter into a dangerous position. Watching the Hind-D's dark form balloon to frightening proportions, he hoped that the Soviet pilot was good—very good.

The Soviet helicopter skidded and shuddered momentarily, reacting to the pilot's frantic efforts. Buchanan shoved the cyclic forward and jammed the collective to the floor, increasing his dive. He could see the chin turret clearly and was just starting to make out Russian lettering on the gunship when the control inputs by the Soviet pilot took effect. The oily gray underside of the Hind-D soared overhead, clearing the American helicopter by fewer than ten feet.

Buchanan turned a few degrees to the right, pointing toward the bridge of the cutter, still a couple of miles ahead. Leveling his helicopter at six hundred feet, he glanced over his shoulder. He hoped to see the Hind-D moving toward the destroyer, but he could not spot the helicopter anywhere. He tried to concentrate on how to help the cutter, but the longer the Hind-D stayed hidden, the more uncomfortable he felt. He wished he had the fighter escorts that had accompanied him on his rescues in combat.

Suddenly, the Soviet helicopter swooped in, diving from beyond Smallwood's side. Buchanan had little time to react before the Soviet pilot swung his craft around, pointing at the Super Jolly Green Giant. Buchanan started to slip his helicopter right just as he saw sparkling flashes from the chin turret contrasting with the dark and sullen background. His left hand turned the collective loose and swung up involuntarily in an attempt to shield his face.

"Look ou—" Smallwood shouted in the fraction of a second before bullets from the minigun peppered them.

The clattering roar, like large hailstones hammering a tin roof, intermingled with the sounds of pieces ripping from the American helicopter. The windshield in front of Smallwood buckled, then disintegrated as a half dozen slugs smashed through. Other bullets tore into overhead panels. A sizzling crackle accompanied the shower of sparks that cascaded through the cockpit in the milliseconds before circuit breakers popped out from various panels.

Trailing in the deadly wake of the bullets, chunks of the windshield slashed through the cockpit. Razor-like flicks of pain sliced across Buchanan's cheek and hand as he heard Smallwood cry out and slump sideways. Airman Murphy's arm swung through Buchanan's field of view as the young PJ was knocked backward by the bullets and glass.

Simultaneously, the master caution light and the warning light for the primary hydraulic servo flashed on, and the helicopter began a hard roll to the right. He shoved the cyclic against the left stop, trying in vain to counteract the roll. At the same time, his free hand shot back down to the collective—and its servo disconnect switch.

Even as the helicopter was rolling through forty-five degrees of bank, he forced himself to take one more look at the warning light. If he disconnected the wrong hydraulic system, they were dead. Primary! He jammed the servo disconnect switch forward with his thumb.

Instantly the position of the cyclic began having an effect, and the roll stopped with the aircraft almost exactly on its side and starting to fall. Buchanan felt a sensation like starting down the first dip of a roller coaster—sideways.

He glanced out his side window. At that angle the ocean looked as if it were just beyond the tips of the rotor blades. The terror made him want to pull back from the water. Nevertheless he knew he must sacrifice most of the remaining altitude to try to get the big chopper flying again.

The smell of overheated engine oil mingled with the odor of shorted electrical circuits as his eyes darted to the altimeter—passing through five hundred feet and decreasing rapidly.

The chilling warble of the fire warning horn screeched a message of additional problems. The fire light for the number one engine glowed brightly, reflecting on a hazy blue vapor of oil smoke that swirled through the cockpit.

"Give me a scan for a fire on number one," he shouted. The roar of the wind blast and the engine swallowed up his words, and he realized the intercom system was already a casualty. No one in the cargo compartment would hear any of his calls for help.

He quickly scanned the engine instruments for number one. The exhaust gas temperature was bouncing erratically and the fuel flow was nearly double that of the other engine. He pictured a severed fuel line and raw fuel gushing into the engine compartment.

Praying he was in time, Buchanan yanked the engine fire handle, thereby cutting off the fuel. If he did not regain control of the helicopter in a hurry, however, an uncontrollable engine fire was inconsequential. Millions of gallons of sea water were waiting to extinguish the fire within the next few seconds.

The collective also had switches for the throttles, and he shoved the switch forward for the other engine. To make sure he got all the remaining power, he yelled, "Give me full throttle on number two!"

A quick look to his left told him that that plea for help also would remain unanswered. Smallwood was straining against the shoulder straps. Foamy red saliva oozed from his mouth and lines of red seeped wider across his thighs, arm, and shoulder. Murphy had disappeared into the cargo compartment.

Falling toward the sea, the helicopter had dropped through two hundred feet. Buchanan knew he had almost enough forward speed to level off without "power settling," a helicopter's corkscrew version of a stall. He began easing the collective up. His hands were steady, but inside he was frantic—there was no good way to hit the water.

The altimeter continued to unwind as the helicopter partly fell/ partly flew below one hundred feet.

Clouds and sea became blurred images as the rotors blasted water from the ocean, coating the remaining sections of windshield and sending a heavy mist swirling throughout the cockpit. The moisture left a salty taste on his lips and burned across his cheek.

Besides stealing his outside references and forcing him to rely only on the flight instruments, the hundred-mile-per-hour downwash was doing something else. The steady rush of air downward was compressing, forming an invisible cushion between the whirling rotors and the ocean. This was the extra bit of lift Buchanan had counted on as he kept raising the collective and easing back the cyclic. The sink rate decreased to zero as the radar altimeter reading hit twenty-five feet, hovered there momentarily, then increased.

Staff Sergeant Wozniak, the flight mechanic, tapped Buchanan on the shoulder and shouted over the noise, "Murph's hit bad." Referring to the second PJ, he said, "Snake says Murph doesn't have a chance unless he gets to a doctor ASAP. Let's get the hell outta here, sir!"

As soon as possible might be never, Buchanan thought as he raised his helicopter above the sea spray. "See what you can do for the lieutenant."

He turned toward the coast and wondered where the Soviet helicopter was. His Super Jolly Green Giant was tough, but another attack would put his helicopter into the water. He tried to broadcast an emergency call, but the radios were dead.

He finally spotted the Hind-D flying toward the Soviet destroyer. As he continued coaxing his helicopter higher, he had a moment to assess his injuries. Though relatively unscathed, he felt for the first time the burning sensation across the back of his right hand. The accumulated sea spray had seeped through the red gash across his glove. The wet cloth and leather stuck to the cyclic momentarily as he tried to pull his hand away. He suppressed a sudden wave of nausea as he slipped off the glove revealing a wound that felt worse than it looked.

"He needs help in a hurry, too," Wozniak shouted as he forced a compress against Smallwood's chest wound. "Looks like he took a hit in a lung."

Buchanan nodded. "Get him out of the wind blast. I'll get us home."

He had done that before. Returning from Hanoi, he had fought to keep control of a damaged helicopter that had a dying mission commander strapped into the right seat. Hang in there, Grant, he pleaded silently as he watched Sergeant Wozniak and the other PJ struggle to remove the copilot's limp body from the cockpit. Buchanan fought shock and another wave of nausea. He prayed for his copilot. He prayed, also, that he would have a chance to get even.

Chapter 9

Monday Afternoon, 1:55 p.m.
Pacific Standard Time

AT HIS SAN FRANCISCO ESTATE, WHICH SERVED AS THE WESTERN WHITE House, President Marshall Cunningham stood looking out the window at the city stretched before him. A growing mixture of fog and clouds had engulfed the bay and was swallowing adjacent buildings in block-size bites of wispy white. Though Cunningham stared at the slowly changing patterns, his mind was not registering any of what he saw.

His thoughts were fixed on a teletype message that had reached him a few minutes earlier. In his fist he still held the crumpled paper. He was angered by the Soviet attack on the rescue helicopter and by the casualties—one dead and three wounded!

Finally he turned toward the others in the room. Three men were gathered around a communications suite, which had been set up in one corner of the large study. For the past few minutes these men had been working to place a call to Soviet Premier Konstantin Medvalev. Leonid Petrov, the President's interpreter, was the most animated of the three. His occasional, rapid-fire forays in Russian indicated that the connection had been made. Cunningham assumed there would be some delay in getting the premier on the line—two p.m. in San Francisco was one a.m. the following morning in Moscow.

Secretary of State Winston Shafer sat quietly in a large easy chair in front of the President's desk. John Kellogg, the White House chief of staff, was on a nearby couch. A large notebook of information was open on a coffee table in front of him.

"I wish I'd called a full alert last night," Cunningham said. "Right after I heard we'd fired the missile, I knew damned well the Russians wouldn't stand by and do nothing."

Shafer looked up from the journal in his lap. "An alert wouldn't have changed one word in that message in your hand, Marsh. Going to DEFCON Two would have readied us for fighting in Europe, but who would have thought to send armed escorts with our helicopters twenty miles off the coast of California?"

"If we'd been at DEFCON Two, there might not have been any firing at all."

"The hot-head piloting the Soviet helicopter probably didn't know our DEFCON level," Shafer said.

Cunningham added, "And you're suggesting he probably didn't care?"

"The fewer armed troops that are faced off against each other right now, the better. We must prevent uncontrolled shootings like this one from escalating into something no one can stop."

Referring to the speaker of the House, Clyde Harris of Pennsylvania, Kellogg said, "And you know, Mr. President, Harris would've had a fit last night if you'd called an alert."

"Harris yells if I do something or if I don't do anything."

Clyde Harris, with ambitions to be the next President, was the administration's most vocal critic. Kellogg was due to leave the White House in January to take over Cunningham's reelection committee.

"But as long as you play this thing conservative and presidential," Kellogg said, "you undercut his chance to paint you as reckless with the military."

"Reckless? This administration had come this far without putting a single American boy into combat anywhere on the globe. That's not reckless. Letting a young medic be killed by enemy fire eighteen miles off our shores seems to me like we weren't doing enough."

"But Mr. President," Kellogg said, "Harris is going to—"

"John," Cunningham interrupted, "I appreciate where you're coming from, but I'm not going to work this as if it were a campaign issue."

He stared out the window at the presidential helicopter, parked beyond the first low hedge.

"Politics aside, Marsh," Shafer said, tapping his pipe against his open palm, "you did what was right. Your responsibility's to prevent this crisis from escalating into a war. Now that the Soviets have answered with some shooting, restraint's even more important."

Cunningham turned from the window and held up the message about the attack. "Showing restraint with the Soviets gets results like this." He wadded the paper and threw it at a trash can.

Over the years he had multiplied a family fortune and risen to the top by taking risks when others were showing restraint. During his presidency, however, he had learned first-hand of the extensive limitations on the power of the office. He had to agree with Shafer about this being the wrong time to change the DEFCON, but he did not have to like it.

"If I were you, Marsh," Shafer said, "I'd be thinking about how to answer Premier Medvalev's charges. After the fiasco at that news conference, he's probably got more complaints for you than you have for him."

"Medvalev's bound to be getting heavy pressure from his military," Kellogg said. "Benes played right into their hands."

"I'm certain cooler heads will prevail," Shafer said.

"Don't be so sure, Winston," Cunningham said. "Most of the cooler heads were on Soviet National One."

Cunningham moved away from the window and the Christmas-season world beyond.

"Mr. President," Kellogg said, "the hawks that are left will demand that the blood debt be repaid. If Air Force One were down near Moscow and a Soviet missile had been fired, our hawks would be screaming for blood."

"The premier's coming on, sir," Petrov said with an accent more British than Russian.

Cunningham nodded but made no move toward the massive desk with its multi-keyed telephone console.

After another quick exchange of Russian phrases, Petrov looked nervously toward the President. The unwritten protocol of the hot line demanded that both leaders come online at virtually the same time. Shafer put his pipe aside, stood, and moved slowly to the desk. Cunningham removed his glasses and deliberately replaced them in a case he took from his pocket.

Petrov looked frantic.

Moving to the desk, Cunningham took on the look of a professional poker player about to deal the final hand of the night. He pushed the button that activated the console's speaker phone, then said in a crisp, clear voice, "Good morning, Mr. Premier."

A female voice on the Moscow end of the circuit repeated the greeting in Russian. Medvalev's voice responded with a couple of short phrases that Petrov translated. With great impatience, Cunningham tolerated a couple more pleasantries and comments about the early hour in Moscow.

He hated the delays caused by working through the interpreters. In lighter moments he liked to joke about Premier Medvalev speaking better English than Clyde Harris and half the members of Congress. Now Cunningham wanted to grab Medvalev by the collar of his robe and demand an apology for attacking an unarmed rescue helicopter and for the death of Airman Murphy. However, he kept his temper in check and used the interpreter's delay to formulate the proper opening.

"There's been a serious incident near the crash site," Cunningham said. "We must come to an understanding about rescue and recovery operations."

"Did our aircraft not crash in international waters?"

Cunningham grimaced as he struggled to keep his voice from showing the emotions he felt. "Yes, Mr. Premier, but since the accident occurred so close to our shores, I have ordered all American personnel to provide appropriate assistance."

"Thank you, Mr. President, but the global forces of the Soviet people are capable of performing the recovery even though the aircraft was under your control when it crashed."

"Some of your military forces have been reckless," Cunningham said, looking at his notes that were on a yellow tablet near the telephone. "One of your destroyers, the *Gnevnyy*, I believe, nearly ran over one of our rescue vessels. The destroyer's armed helicopter attacked and damaged one of our unarmed rescue helicopters." There was a long pause after Medvalev's translator converted the words into Russian.

As Cunningham awaited the response, he imagined Medvalev sitting on a large bed or at a dressing table in an ornate bedroom much fancier than even Czar Nicholas II would have contemplated. Perhaps, Cunningham thought, there was an unspoken reason for the delayed response. Medvalev's aides could be using another line to get an update on the shooting from a Command Post deep beneath a Moscow suburb.

"We have received no reports of such an incident," Medvalev said finally.

Liar, Cunningham thought. Nearly two hours had passed since the attack. He assumed that the Russians had as much information about the confrontation as he did.

"One of the medical personnel on our helicopter was killed in the attack, and three other airmen were wounded."

"Perhaps there is some confusion," Medvalev said. "Can you be certain that the bullets were fired by Soviet forces?"

"Our reports leave no doubt."

"There are rumors of others being careless and undisciplined in their use of weapons."

An obvious reference to the missile firing, Cunningham thought, but he was determined to stay with his agenda. "My reports aren't rumors, Mr. Premier. Survivors on our air rescue helicopter and observers on a Coast Guard ship all saw a Hind-D with Soviet markings fire on our helicopter."

"Perhaps there were provocations, if indeed such an incident took place."

"The provocations came from your destroyer and helicopter," Cunningham retorted impatiently.

"I am told," Medvalev said, "that your military forces were already using underwater divers."

"That's standard rescue and recovery procedure," Cunningham answered. "We'd do the same thing for an accident investigation of our own Air Force One."

"But this is not your Air Force One," Medvalev said. "Some of the Russian people think that the American military's hurry to be ahead of our recovery force is like—how do you say?—letting the weasel guard the chicken farm."

Petrov shrugged, exaggerating the confused look on his face as he translated the last phrase. Shafer also looked perplexed for an instant, then whispered the words, "Fox guarding the hen house."

"That's an incorrect assessment," Cunningham said. "Our interests are only humanitarian."

"You're expecting your divers to find survivors?"

"No, of course not," Cunningham snapped. "Just standard—"

Medvalev interrupted, "Some of my ministers believe your Air Force may be trying to remove evidence of misdeeds before Soviet forces can properly evaluate what took place."

"I've already told you we had nothing to do with the crash."

"Of course *I* believe you, Mr. President," Medvalev answered. "The Soviet people understood and supported this great historical mission of peace, which President Gorshko, Minister Valinen, and Chairman Krasnovich were embarked upon. But there have been rumors that I am sure you are aware of. It will be difficult to put those rumors aside if the flight recorders are not lifted from the water by Soviet citizens."

"It is our responsibility, Mr. Premier," Cunningham said, "to make sure our forces operate only on orders and not on rumors."

"True," Medvalev said, "but the rumors have upset all our forces. Some of my commanders are demanding quick revenge for the serious losses we have suffered."

"There are people in America who want revenge for the attack on our personnel," Cunningham said. "So you and I must agree on how the recovery is to be handled."

"I see no problem," Medvalev said. "We are quite capable of handling the recovery on our own. We have ships there already, and I have diverted a naval task force that will be there in a few hours."

"We must avoid any further confrontations between our forces until everyone's had a chance to cool off."

"If Americans do not violate the recovery area we establish, I see no likelihood of additional confrontations."

Cunnngham frowned as he realized that Medvalev was suggesting a search area that excluded Americans.

Secretary Shafer shrugged and made a "so what?" expression. He whispered, "It's their airplane and their people, and the crash site *is* in international waters."

Cunningham asked, "What about our assistance?"

"We require none," Medvalev said. "The recovery must be done under a single authority. Unfortunate accidents may happen otherwise, just as nearly happened today when the American ship moved recklessly in front of our destroyer."

"I thought you had heard no reports."

"I am told there was provocation. If the Soviet pilot fired, I must assume he was responding to dangerous and provocative actions by your crew. Soviet pilots do not fire on unarmed aircraft without provocation."

Cunningham was certain that sarcastic reference was to the F-15 and Soviet National One. He wondered what Medvalev was waiting for and why he touched on the subject only with oblique references. "Our rescue helicopter was unarmed."

"Was it marked with the Red Cross?"

"No," Cunningham said, feeling more frustrated with each counter argument. "It was a standard Super Jolly Green Giant, which I am quite sure your forces recognize as a rescue helicopter."

"Our forces know such helicopters were armed in fighting the peoples of Vietnam and Grenada and in the aggressive violation of Iranian sovereignty in 1980. We cannot assume your helicopters are always unarmed and on peaceful missions."

"This one was! I will not accept another such blatant attack on Americans in the search area."

Shafer gestured to the President that his words were sounding overly strident.

"There will be no requirements for such encounters if you keep your ships and aircraft clear while we recover our dead heroes and return them to Mother Russia."

"How big a search area do you propose?"

"We have many ships," Medvalev said. "Since there is also some uncertainty about the aircraft's location, a circle ten kilometers in all directions from your reported crash site should be sufficient."

"We'll give you five nautical miles," Cunningham responded.

Five nautical miles was not significantly less than ten kilometers. However, Cunningham did not want to seem totally compliant.

"If you keep your forces at that distance," Medvalev said, "I'm sure we can avoid further bloodshed."

As Cunningham was talking, Shafer had been writing a note in large letters. He held the piece of paper so Cunningham could read the words, "Cancel their naval exercise??? Reduce possibility of other confrontations."

"If we are to make such arrangements so close to our shores," Cunningham said, "perhaps you will also cancel your worldwide exercises and withdraw your naval forces to less provocative positions where confrontations are less likely."

There was a long pause following the translation. Cunningham was about to rephrase the comment when Medvalev finally responded.

"Will you also be withdrawing your Sixth Fleet from the Mediterranean and returning the rest of your ships to port?"

Cunningham had not expected that response. "We have already minimized our deployments for the Christmas season. We will not go beyond our normal patrol areas."

"All oceans of the world are the normal patrol area of the Soviet Navy."

Cunningham was angry at himself for agreeing to pull back from the crash site before negotiating for something in return. "Patrol wherever you choose," Cunningham said, coldly, "but your forces should understand one thing: If American forces are fired upon again, the fire will be returned."

A long pause followed.

"You must realize, Mr. President, that cancelling a worldwide exercise is not a simple matter, especially with emotions as high as today. Your offer to allow the recovery unimpeded and without harassment is a good sign. When our people have had a few days to observe your good faith and your peaceful intentions, perhaps I will be able to make additional responses in kind."

"That would serve the cause of world peace, Mr. Premier."

"All things we do serve the socialist people's desire for world peace."

Same old bullshit, Cunningham thought as he closed out the conversation with the appropriate level of decorum. When the exchanges were completed, he clicked off the telephone and turned toward Secretary Shafer. "He knows," Cunningham said almost in a whisper. "That son of a bitch knows what Benes said on TV."

"I agree," Shafer said.

"He's up to something. That young fighter pilot gave Medvalev the biggest propaganda coup of our entire administration, and he's not shoving the damned thing down our throats. That's not the Medvalev

I know." Cunningham placed a hand on the red telephone that gave immediate access to the National Military Command Center. "Maybe we need to increase the DEFCON until we figure out what he's really up to."

Shafer shook his head. "I don't think so, Marsh. Under normal circumstances, the Russian bureaucracy's decision making happens at the speed of a glacier. With half his government gone, Medvalev'll need even more time to decide how to use the admissions Benes made at the press conference. If you change the DEFCON, Medvalev will have to keep his ships deployed indefinitely."

Cunningham rotated his chair so he could look outside again. Quietly he lamented, "What a hell of a turnaround. Yesterday this looked to be the most triumphant week of the administration."

Kellogg nodded. "Having that treaty signed would sure take a lot of the steam out of the speaker's bickering on foreign policy."

"I don't think either of you should give up on that treaty," Shafer said. "I didn't hear Medvalev saying it had been a bad idea, and the treaty's biggest critic has been silenced. It seems to me that if we can stay cool, and we get by the revelation of the missile firing without too much turbulence, you might still get your treaty. Holding the line on the DEFCON seems like our contribution to keeping some life in the agreements we'd reached before the crash."

Cunningham did not look convinced. He was still angry. "I don't want Medvalev thinking it's open season on whoever his troops want to shoot at, no matter how upset the Russians are over Valinen."

"You've done the prudent thing," Shafer said. "Putting the five-mile buffer around their recovery forces should de-escalate this thing. Changing the DEFCON now is simply the wrong signal at the wrong time."

The prudent thing. Cunningham did not like being stuck with having to do "the prudent thing," especially right after the Soviets had attacked an American aircraft and killed a paramedic. He refused to be completely stymied. "I won't change the DEFCON, Winston, but I'm not sending any more unescorted helicopters anywhere near the crash scene. Where are our closest helicopter gunships?"

"I'm not sure," Shafer said, looking confused about the President's intentions.

Cunningham grabbed the red telephone and asked the same question of the duty officer who answered on the Washington, D.C., end of the hot line. Moments later, Cunningham responded to the answer to his question. "I want at least six armed and on alert with our air rescue forces at Chaney Air Force Base by tonight."

He also gave directions on keeping American aircraft and vessels out of the Soviets' area of search. When that was completed, he hung up the telephone and turned to Shafer. "The Army'll move a flight of Apache gunships from Fort Lewis, Washington, to Chaney within six hours. Under the circumstances, Winston, I can't consider anything less to be prudent."

Fewer than two hours after Lieutenant Colonel Buchanan landed his damaged helicopter at Chaney, Jack received another call from General McClintock. After discussing the attack and the casualties, the general said, "Jack, I want you at Chaney as soon as possible to interview the pilot. A helicopter will pick you up in forty-five minutes. Try to swing by the coast in time to look at the crash site before dark."

Jack checked his watch and added an extra hour to account for the flight to the coast after the helicopter arrived. "We might make it, sir, depending on the cloud cover and how quickly we can get airborne here."

"Don't get too close to the Soviets. We don't want more shooting."

"Yes, sir," Jack said. "Do we know why they opened fire?"

"General orneriness? Who knows? The initial reports said we didn't start the fight, but that's part of what you need to figure out."

"I'm sure there's equipment on the downed bird that the Soviets don't want us getting our hands on."

"Could be," McClintock said. "The Russians probably suspect we're trying to beat them to evidence of a shoot-down. Whatever the reason, this latest shooting is being taken seriously by everyone here in Washington. We're deploying one of the National Emergency Airborne Command Post aircraft to Travis within the next twelve hours, so I'll be joining you in California."

Designated as an E-4B, the National Emergency Airborne Command Post was a modified Boeing 747. The aircraft was designed to serve as the President's command post in the event of general war. Jack recognized the importance of moving it closer to the President, now that the California trip had taken on an entirely different meaning. Moving the plane from Washington to Travis Air Force Base northeast of San Francisco was a reasonable precaution in case the crisis escalated into war.

Jack was happy about that decision for two other reasons. First, General Harper's investigation team was due to land at Howell Air Force Base in less than an hour. Jack knew his task would be tougher once Radisson's mentor was on base. Having McClintock's four stars nearby could be helpful as Radisson maneuvered behind the weight of Harper's three.

Even more important to Jack, however, would be the availability of the computers on the E-4B. The computers could link him to all the data bases that were available from his computer in the Pentagon. He needed to know more about the performance characteristics of the Il-62. He also wanted to review intelligence profiles on the greater and lesser personalities on the casualty list.

He asked, "How'd General Raleigh react to the fact that Benes was on the mission with the family background he has?"

"Actually he was pretty philosophical," McClintock answered. "He said that if we had to go back four generations in everyone's background before we launched a mission, we'd have a hell of a scheduling problem whenever almost any head of state came for a visit."

After a short discussion about the press conference and Benes' credibility, McClintock said, "Public Affairs here in the Pentagon is about to announce the attack on the Jolly Green. The PA folks at Howell will make the same release within the next few minutes. That should move the attention toward Chaney and maybe help scatter some of the herd of reporters you have treed there at Howell."

"The quicker the reporters get out of our hair, sir, the quicker we can work the real problems."

After Jack hung up, he checked the scheduling board. His helicopter was due to land in forty minutes. Noticing that General Harper was due a few minutes later, he hoped he would be gone before the general arrived. He contacted Jensen and told him to be prepared to brief General Harper's team on what had been learned about the F-15s and the missiles.

Since he had not eaten in nearly twenty-four hours, he decided to pick up a sandwich at the flight line cafeteria. He got his briefcase from his room, then slipped out a side door to avoid the reporters who were gathered in and around the crew lounge.

Jack had ordered a hamburger and stood alone in the serving line, deep in thought, when a loud, challenging voice caught him by surprise. "Looks like you couldn't keep the lid on, Colonel."

He turned and saw Special Agent Thomas O'Donnell standing at the railing that separated the tables from the serving line. Jack had assumed that O'Donnell would have left the base after their early morning confrontation. Shaking his head and turning away, he tried to ignore the special agent.

"As soon as I heard Benes' name," O'Donnell continued in a voice even louder and more belligerent, "I knew there was more to the story than the Air Force was admitting."

Jack quickly scanned the cafeteria, hoping there were no newsmen around to overhear O'Donnell's charges. Fortunately, it was mid-afternoon and the place was nearly empty. He spotted O'Donnell's partner, Russell Brown, who was getting up from a table that had several beer bottles on it. Otherwise, there were only the cook, the cashier, and two small groups of fatigue-clad airmen having coffee at tables on the far side of the room.

The mention of Benes' name got Jack to wondering. Was O'Donnell the leak that put the young newsman onto the story of the Benes family? Surely not, but at this point there was no reason to trust O'Donnell to use good judgment. In any case, the man had to be quieted.

Jack said, "The general mentioned that you were disappointed with your treatment this morning."

O'Donnell looked pleased to learn that he had gotten some pressure on Jack. "I'm gonna make sure the Air Force doesn't get away with working this all independently."

Phillips smelled a strong odor of beer as he moved closer. "You just better have done a good job of fireproofing."

"What?" O'Donnell looked confused.

"You'd better be prepared to take some heat. The Air Force chief of staff may just ask your director to investigate how the rumors of an Air Force attack got passed to the media. If the chief does, he'll also suggest you're the first person who should be questioned."

O'Donnell was taken back by the threat. Brown, who had just joined them, looked worried.

"I didn't give anything to Kane," O'Donnell said in a more subdued tone. "Besides, the director knows what we lost on that plane."

"And I know a hell of a lot more about it than I'm supposed to," Jack said, "because you seem to be doing a lot of talking when you should be listening, or at least doing some professional investigating."

"That's what I'm here for," O'Donnell said, sounding much more defensive than he had been moments earlier.

"Well, mister," Jack said quietly, almost nose-to-nose with O'Donnell, "I've got time to give this to you just once, and you ought to listen right. You're looking in the wrong place. That Il-62 got in trouble on its own and crashed without any help from the U.S. Air Force. You can rant and rave all you want, Mr. O'Donnell, but that's the bottom line." O'Donnell stepped back, surprised by the intensity of the onslaught. Jack continued. "Now, you and I know there's at least half a world of people besides Captain Benes who'd like to see Valinen blown away. And if you know something about Benes that I don't, I'd be glad to listen. Otherwise America will be better served if you keep your drunken allegations to yourself."

"I'm not drunk, Colonel," O'Donnell said, standing to his full height.

"You're doing a damned good imitation," Jack said, looking also at Brown. "If there's something sinister behind the crash, start using your expertise to find out who might have sabotaged the aircraft. And the answers to that question are in Vladivostok, or maybe even in Moscow, but not in California."

He sensed that Brown agreed and that perhaps the message was even getting through to O'Donnell. Before there was a response, the cashier announced that the hamburger was ready.

"I'm on my way to Chaney Air Force Base," Jack said more to Brown than to O'Donnell. "If you do get serious and turn up some information, I'd be glad to trade notes with you later."

As he moved away to pay for his order, Brown followed. Before Brown could say anything, Jack gestured toward O'Donnell and said, "I'd expect your outfit to have better people."

"There's nobody better than Tom at sorting things out," Brown said, "when he has his mind on the job. Right now he's operating more on beer than sleep. I'd like to ask you to let me take care of getting him straightened out."

"I can't stand any more of *his* type of help."

"I'm sure he didn't leak anything about Benes or the missile to that reporter."

Jack sensed that Brown was sincere. "He's got to shut up. This place is still crawling with newsmen."

"I'll get him out of here right away."

Jack paused. He was not sold yet on O'Donnell, but respected Brown's loyalty. "Okay, but there's more to this than any of us knows. If O'Donnell's as good as you say, the sooner you can get him sobered up, the better."

"I'll take care of that, too."

"Good," Jack said, shaking hands with Brown.

On his way to the dispatcher's counter, Jack noticed considerably fewer reporters in the crew lounge than had been there earlier. Obviously Public Affairs had released the announcement about the Soviet attack on the American helicopter. A half dozen reporters were still at telephones in the lounge. In the lobby Alexander Braxton's team was taping a segment for the evening news broadcast.

Braxton was posed in front of a wall decorated with the Air Force shield and brightly colored emblems of Howell's major units. With the focus of attention on Braxton, Jack stood quietly behind the small crowd.

"Today marks the first direct exchange of fire in many years between Soviet and American forces. Back in April 1984, a Cobra helicopter of the U.S. Army strayed near the Czechoslovakian border and was fired on by Soviet MiGs. The government wants to downplay the seriousness of today's shooting and has established a five-mile buffer zone around the crash site. The—" Spotting Jack, Braxton hesitated for an instant. He covered the interruption in his concentration so smoothly that the audience hardly would notice. "—shooting obviously is an unexpected and an unwanted turn of events. Undoubtedly, President Cunningham is doing everything possible to keep this crisis from growing out of control. However, don't be surprised if you see the President's Emergency Airborne Command Post aircraft parked on the ramp at Alameda Naval Air Station. This is . . ."

Noticing that Braxton's words were more rushed than before, Jack decided to leave before the newsman finished. As Jack rounded a corner, he was disturbed by the final statement. Did Braxton have inside information when he had suggested the Airborne Command Post would be flying to Alameda? General McClintock had named Travis Air Force Base as the likely West Coast staging point, but Braxton's guess was close. Jack felt uneasy. Too many outsiders were coming up with too many pieces of the puzzle too quickly.

No one was at the dispatcher's counter, but the status boards were plain enough. His helicopter was due in a few minutes, but General Harper's plane was now scheduled to land at the same time.

Braxton came around the corner. His cameraman, with camera taping, followed closely behind. "Colonel Phillips," Braxton said, "would you be so kind as to give us a few minutes on camera?"

"Nothing on the record now," Jack said, turning his back to the cameraman.

Braxton waved his hand, and the cameraman stopped taping. Braxton also lowered his microphone to his side. Jack was surprised at how quickly Braxton acquiesced.

"A few questions off the record, then, Colonel?" Braxton smiled. "Your insights would be helpful in piecing this all together."

"I'm sorry," Jack said, "but I'm about to leave."

"Perhaps we could talk on the way to Chaney."

"We can't take civilians without special authoriza—Who said anything about Chaney?"

He was impressed with how well Braxton put information together. Braxton seemed surprised that Jack was surprised.

"No one," Braxton responded. "Actually—"

"Then why'd you say I was going to Chaney?"

"It's no mystery, Colonel. You closed the press conference in a way that identified you as a key figure in the investigation. Now the action's at Chaney." Braxton nodded toward the status board, then glanced at the rows of colorful ribbons beneath Jack's pilot wings. "And, if I may say this without sounding demeaning of your distinguished background, I learned to read aircraft flying schedules before you were born."

Jack smiled, accepting Braxton's statement though it obviously exaggerated their age difference. While the flattering words had triggered almost the same emotions as if Walter Cronkite were respectfully soliciting an interview, Jack remained on guard. Braxton had never dominated the news scene like the national network anchors, but his stands on national defense issues were widely respected by Jack and many of his colleagues in the Pentagon. He was sorry he did not have time to tap into Braxton's expertise on the Soviets.

Braxton continued, "Give me a chance to visit the survivors and get some good shots of the damaged chopper. Coverage like that could help restore a little luster to the Air Force's image."

"Authorizing civilians to fly on military aircraft takes more rank than I wear, Mr. Braxton."

"I do have a reputation for not being unsympathetic to the military."

"Sorry, sir. There's really nothing I can do." Despite his admiration for Braxton's anticommunism, the earlier argument with the newsman's associate was fresh in Jack's memory. Christine Merrill was the last person he needed looking over his shoulder as he tried to make sense out of the afternoon's shooting.

Braxton looked disappointed. "Would you be offended if I make an appeal to the higher authorities who might be able to say yes?"

"I certainly can't stop you, sir."

He was confident that even if Braxton had the connections, he did not have the time. Jack walked away, and Braxton trailed behind.

"Perhaps, then," Braxton said, "we can talk upon your return."

"Perhaps," Jack said as he walked through the door.

As he left Base Operations, his helicopter was approaching the parking ramp. Unfortunately, General Harper's aircraft was already parked, and Harper was standing near the airplane with Radisson. Jack was tempted to duck back inside and wait until the general drove away, but Harper was looking in his direction.

As the distance narrowed, Harper said, "Colonel, in fifteen minutes I want a detailed briefing to my team on everything you've learned."

"I'm sorry, General," Jack said, "but I was just leaving for—"

"That can wait," Harper said firmly. "This investigation is your number one priority, Colonel."

Jack hesitated. There were no easy ways for a colonel to say no to a three-star general. "General McClintock has ordered me to Chaney.

He wants me to get a look at the Soviet ships at the crash site before dark. That's already cutting it close, especially with the bad weather, sir."

Harper frowned and looked at his wrist watch.

Radisson said, "You've got time to fulfill General Harper's requirements and still get to the coast."

"Colonel, are you volunteering to explain things to General McClintock if I don't make it in time?" Jack spoke more for Harper's benefit than for Radisson's. Harper could lean hard, but the general would not want to explain that he had countermanded the orders of the four-star general.

Harper asked, "When will you be back?"

"Later this evening, sir," Jack said. "In the meantime Captain Randy Jensen, who checked over the Eagles and their missiles, is prepared to brief his findings to get your team started."

Harper seemed to consider the options, then said, "Okay, we'll hear from Jensen this afternoon. Have a written report of your findings ready at zero-seven-hundred hours tomorrow morning. You can brief me at zero-eight-hundred."

"Yes, sir," Jack said, feeling that he had come out of the encounter as well as he could have expected.

Chapter 10

Monday Afternoon, 3:55 p.m.
Pacific Standard Time

PULLING HIS LAP BELT TIGHT, JACK LISTENED TO THE RHYTHMIC BEAT of the rotor blades quicken, then merge into a steady roar. The helicopter lifted off the concrete and skimmed a few feet above the parking ramp. Reaching a main taxiway, the craft accelerated and climbed.

Sitting in a jump seat aft of the pilots, Jack had almost finished his hamburger when he heard a change in the noise from the engine. He realized the pilot was aborting the departure. What a time for mechanical problems, Jack thought as he looked beyond the pilot and scanned the instruments for any indication of trouble. Everything looked normal. The pilot banked left, pointing the nose toward the parking area.

The copilot pushed his earphone aside and turned around. "They want us to return to the ramp for a pickup." In response to Jack's questioning look, the copilot added, "Three civilians! We're supposed to pick up three civilian newsmen!"

Jack was instantly angry. "Pass back that I'm Phillips, Redline Alpha Three, and I want to disregard! Tell them I don't have time for the delay."

The copilot nodded and turned to his radios. Awaiting the response, the pilot kept the helicopter hovering twenty feet above the taxiway.

With so many questions still unanswered, the one thing Jack did not need was media interference with his investigation. Since General Harper was now on-station to take over, Jack was unsure if his own standing as Redline Alpha Three was still valid. However, he had not been relieved officially, and the worst that could happen was that someone would answer back that his special priority already had been rescinded.

Jack seethed inside, feeling he was getting more interference than he could stand. The December day was one of the shortest of the year. Nightfall would come quickly beneath the bad weather blanketing the coast. The flight to the crash site would take an hour, and sunset was less than an hour and a half away, so the delay was jeopardizing his mission.

After a few moments the copilot copied something on his clipboard and turned toward Jack. "Command Post says the original message was relayed from Redline Alpha One. Is three bigger than one, sir?"

"Only when you're counting," Jack said.

"What was that, sir?"

"Let's get 'em aboard!" Jack had trouble believing that he had been recalled because of the President's bidding, but he had lost the argument in any case.

The pilot landed the helicopter in front of Base Operations. Alexander Braxton, his cameraman, and Christine Merrill emerged from the building. The crew chief motioned, and all three raced forward into the downwash from the whirling blades of the helicopter.

As Braxton and the cameraman struggled with the equipment, Christine tried to keep her skirt down and her large purse under control in the swirling air. When she reached the open side door of the helicopter, she found that the floor was nearly waist-high, much too high to step aboard. For a moment the situation was stalemated as she pushed her purse inside.

Jack was tempted to ignore the problems of the news team, but as she tried to figure out how to get aboard, he yelled, "Turn around."

She looked questioningly at him. He made a circling motion with his hand, and she finally turned her back to the helicopter. He knelt, put an arm around her waist, and lifted. As she got aboard, he stood, bringing her to her feet. Their eyes met momentarily, and he said sarcastically, "Welcome aboard, ma'am." Before she could respond, he turned to help the cameraman get his equipment on board. Finally he helped Braxton up. When they were face to face, Jack shouted over the noise, "When you appeal to higher authorities, you don't mess around."

"Being personally acquainted helps," Braxton said with a pleasant smile.

As soon as the three new passengers were strapped in, the helicopter lifted off and headed toward the coast. Braxton and Jack were seated side-by-side in canvas seats behind the pilots.

"I apologize for not offering you the courtesy of an introduction earlier, Colonel. I'm Alexander C. Braxton from KASF-TV in San Francisco." He offered his hand and a warm, sincere smile. As Jack shook hands, he could not remember encountering a more charismatic person.

"And, of course," Braxton continued, motioning toward the seats behind them, "Christine Merrill is one of my station's top anchor persons and special events reporters."

"We've met," Jack answered, glancing in her direction.

"I hope you can forgive us for inviting ourselves along," Braxton said.

"Frankly I didn't think you had a chance."

"I would never claim to pull any of the President's real strings, but . . ." Braxton paused long enough to draw Jack's full attention, then continued, "whenever possible, he takes my phone calls."

Jack was surprised by the comment. He said facetiously, "I assumed the President would be a little busy this afternoon."

"Oh he is, Colonel, he is. But he also recognizes the need for some in-depth coverage of the results of the Soviet attack, especially after the bombshell revealed at the news conference."

Jack understood, but he still did not believe his mission should have been delayed to accommodate Braxton. "And you convinced him the story couldn't be told without you?"

"He is partial to the way I cover the news, and you were going in that direction." Braxton's expression suggested that he understood the unspoken concerns. He put a hand on Jack's shoulder and added, "Colonel, it's plain human nature. Suppose you had a thousand reporters challenging you every day on what a poor job you were doing as a pilot. And then I was there telling you what a hot stick I thought you were. Who would you rather swap flying stories with?"

Jack was surprised by Braxton's choice of analogies, but appreciated the point. In Washington, Jack had encountered many people who claimed personal influence far beyond what proved to be true. However, Braxton's quick results in diverting the helicopter suggested he might have even more influence than he claimed. After all, Jack thought, President Cunningham also was from San Francisco. Braxton was one of the few important personalities in the media who regularly supported the President's firm stands with the Soviets. Jack made a mental note to find out more about the background of the impressive individual seated beside him.

They had to fly nearly fifty miles beyond Chaney Air Force Base to reach the point where Soviet National One had crashed. Oakland Center cleared the helicopter into the area, but warned the pilot to remain at least five nautical miles away from the crash site.

Braxton was overjoyed when he learned of the unexpected side trip. He discussed the taping of the scene while the crew chief fitted safety harnesses on Braxton and the cameraman.

A solid overcast sealed out the sunshine from the coast and the ocean beyond. Total darkness was less than a half hour away as the helicopter flew beyond Point Reyes. Jack wondered if there was enough light for the camera. Nevertheless, he was satisfied that he himself could see whatever there was to see.

A few miles from the shore, two high-endurance cutters of the U.S. Coast Guard sailed parallel to the coast. Those ships served as a picket line, turning back smaller craft that were strung out in a disorganized armada all the way to the Golden Gate Bridge. The Soviet ships were ten miles beyond the cutters.

As the helicopter flew closer, Jack was surprised to see four Soviet ships instead of only two. The destroyer was in position to guard the approaches from the coast, and the other three ships were clustered a half mile farther west. He told the pilot to fly to the five-mile limit, but to keep a close watch for activity on the destroyer's helipad.

Turning to the cameraman, Jack shouted, "Get me some closeups if you can. I need to identify the ships."

The cameraman looked to Braxton for approval.

Braxton nodded and said, "We'll do our best, but there may not be enough light."

The crew chief completed hooking the safety harnesses worn by the newsman and his cameraman to fittings near the door. When Christine had moved to the safety of the opposite side, the crew chief slid open the door, allowing a cold, damp wind to whip through the helicopter. Stepping into the doorway, the cameraman zoomed in for a few seconds on each ship as the pilot edged closer.

Receiving a pair of binoculars from the copilot, Jack knelt by a cockpit window. He checked the destroyer first, but saw nothing significant, so he turned his attention to the group of three ships. The smallest had a remarkably high stern, which extended out over the water. That obviously was the submarine rescue ship General McClintock had mentioned. The other two ships were more than twice as long. Both appeared to be heavily loaded cargo ships. After adjusting the binoculars to a finer focus, Jack read the word "INTERLIGHTER" in large block letters just above the water line on the side of one of them.

Handing the binoculars to the copilot, Jack asked himself: How did the two merchant ships get there so quickly? Saving that question for later, he stepped into the cargo compartment to watch the taping. Accompanied by Christine's warnings to be careful, Braxton took a microphone from the cameraman and stepped closer to the large opening in the side of the helicopter. He did not show the nervousness that Jack expected. Obviously Braxton did not spend all his time behind a news desk reading a teleprompter.

Braxton shrugged, indicating he was unsure his voice would be audible over the noise of the engine and the wind. When the cameraman signaled that he was ready, Braxton gestured toward the scene behind him. "Below us in the cold waters of the Pacific, a flotilla of four Soviet ships is led by a five-thousand-ton destroyer. The *Gnevnyy* is a ship-of-the-line of the Soviet Pacific Fleet. Ladies and gentlemen, not since German U-Boats patrolled along America's eastern shores during World War II have there been warships of an unfriendly nation operating so close to our coast." He continued with his story, linking the destroyer with the afternoon's attack on the American helicopter.

Jack leaned forward to get a better look at the *Gnevnyy*, which had started a broad turn around to the south. In the approaching darkness he could not see if crewmen were around the helicopter.

Moments later, he stopped worrying about the Hind-D. A wavering electronic signal buzzed from the overhead speaker, wrenching his attention from his previous concerns. The signal meant one thing to Jack: The Soviet destroyer had activated a fire-control radar for surface-to-air missiles, and the radar had just started scanning the American helicopter.

Having experienced similar warnings many times while flying over North Vietnam, he reacted more quickly than the young, post Vietnam-era pilots. "They're painting us!" As he shouted the warning, he slapped his open palm on the pilot's shoulder, then stabbed his finger three times toward the ocean. "Get her on the deck and out of here!"

Satisfied that the pilot understood the danger, Jack whirled and yelled, "Hang on!"

In addition to their safety harnesses, Braxton and the crew chief already had firm grips on an overhead brace, and the cameraman had one arm looped around a seat support. Christine grabbed for a seat belt, but she did not get a good hold before the pilot rolled the helicopter and pushed the nose toward the ocean.

The floor tilted sideways, pitching her toward the open door just as Jack reached her. He threw one arm around her waist and tried to entangle his other hand among the nylon straps holding the canvas seats in place. His fingers missed the straps, but grabbed the top edge of one of the seat backs. Kicking with high-heeled shoes that gained no traction on the metal floor, she grabbed him around the neck as they both slid toward the gaping opening. Her notebook dropped from her hand, bounced once, and disappeared toward the ocean.

He saw that the metal clips, which attached the seats to the helicopter, had already started to spread. The seats were not designed to have nearly three hundred pounds pulling them toward the door. He clawed for a better hold because if the clips broke free, the seats would sag momentarily, then be yanked taut by the lower attachments. The grip he had would not survive a jerk like that, and for one of the few times in his life, panic nearly overwhelmed him.

He ground his boots frantically against the non-skid surface, but the floor was tilted at a sixty-degree angle, and nothing seemed to help. Throughout his flying career, he had dreamed intermittently of falling without a parachute from an airplane. His breath came in short gasps as that innate fear intensified.

The crew chief shouted through the intercom. "Roll out! Roll out!" He planted his boot between the edge of the doorway and Jack's foot, then tried to slide the door.

Jack strained to hold the top of the seat for a few more seconds. Just as the metal clips gave way, the helicopter rolled level. He fell to the floor with Christine on top of him as the crew chief shoved the door closed. Braxton and his cameraman both looked frightened, but the safety harnesses kept them secure as the helicopter continued diving.

Jack struggled up onto the canvas seats and pulled the terrified woman onto his lap. As he tried to calm down, he noticed that the noise from the threat-warning receiver ceased. That helped him relax, but he was almost choked by the death grip she had on his neck. He felt a tremble and hoped he was not the one causing the shaking.

"We're all right, ma'am," he said, realizing she had no idea why the helicopter had maneuvered so violently. "We're not going to crash."

He felt her grip loosen slightly as the helicopter pulled out of the dive. A quick look at the flight instruments verified that the pilot had leveled at two hundred feet and was racing toward the coast.

As he reassured himself they were safe, he noticed the fragrance of her expensive perfume and became suddenly aware of the warmth of her body against his. He liked the closeness and wished that they had come together under entirely different circumstances.

In a few moments her trembling subsided, and she pulled her head away from his shoulder. Even in the shadows of the dimly lit cabin, he could see that her eyes still had a look of fear. He saw a flush of color return to her cheeks as she regained her composure.

"Thank you, Colonel," she said softly, giving Jack a slight hug. There was a sultriness in her voice that had not been present during their short exchange in the briefing room or when he had seen her speaking into a television camera.

Before Jack could respond, Braxton slipped free of his safety harness and hurried to see if she had been hurt. The newsman looked shaken, but his concern for Christine's safety was apparent. She gave Jack an appreciative smile as Braxton helped her to another seat.

Jack stood, hoping to avoid the jittery feeling that would come if he took time to think about what he had just done. He patted the crew chief on the shoulder. "Thanks, Sarge."

"You had me pretty scared for a minute, Colonel." The sergeant smiled broadly.

"Never a doubt, Sarge," Jack said with a wink, but also loud enough for Braxton and Christine to hear. "I just made it look close to impress the lady."

She had been checking her skirt and stockings for damage, but her eyes flashed toward him. For an instant her reporter's instincts seemed to analyze whether that could have been true. Then she nodded slightly, giving Jack a smile like that of a woman who has just seen through a lover's teasing.

Moving up between the pilots, he saw one of the Coast Guard cutters a mile or so ahead. On the horizon a flash from a lighthouse stabbed a swath of light through the night. An irregular line of twinkling lights on small craft led past Point Reyes and in toward the Golden Gate. Most were heading in for the night, Jack thought. How long, he wondered, would the Coast Guard be able to keep the news media and the curiosity seekers out of the search area?

A few minutes later, the helicopter reached Chaney Air Force Base. Jack and his companions were met by Lieutenant Colonel Buck Buchanan, the detachment commander and the pilot on the afternoon's ill-fated rescue mission. Still dressed in his blood-spattered flight suit, he had come directly from the base hospital. His wounds were bandaged, but he was angry and determined. Airman Murphy had died before the crippled helicopter had landed. The copilot, Lieutenant Smallwood, was fighting for his life in intensive care.

"I need some time alone with Colonel Buchanan," Jack said to Braxton.

"Of course," Braxton said, "but I hope you'll let the colonel repeat some of his story in front of our camera."

Jack responded with a noncommmittal nod.

For the next ten minutes he listened to Buchanan's story and pressed for every detail. Finally satisfied, he asked, "Is there anything that happened that shouldn't be talked about in front of a camera?"

"Negative, sir," Buchanan said. "We ought to tell the American people exactly what those bastards did out there today."

Jack reasoned that the man's spontaneity and genuine grief could counter some of the negative stories resulting from the firing of the missile. Obviously Braxton was getting special treatment, so Jack decided to put Buchanan in front of the news team and its camera.

Buchanan led the party across the parking ramp to the hangar where his battle-damaged helicopter was parked. As they walked, he repeated his story of the fatal flight. Then with the shattered nose of the helicopter as a backdrop, he used his hands to represent the Russian and American helicopters in an animated description of the maneuvering. The bandages on his hand and the blood on his flight suit added a compelling immediacy to his telling of the story. Jack changed his mind. He was glad Braxton and his cameraman were there.

Standing to one side out of the view of the camera, Jack listened carefully to the retelling of the story. Christine was on the opposite side, and he was able to see her reactions to the vivid descriptions of aerial combat. As Buchanan graphically described the struggle to get the wounded copilot from the seat, she winced, then glanced toward Jack. Their eyes met momentarily and she shrugged, her expression suggesting that she was genuinely moved. Jack was pleased that she was getting a first-hand look at the reality of military service—and the "military mentality" she had held in such contempt. Perhaps her future commentaries would be less critical, he thought, still stung by her broadcast insinuating that he had intentionally questioned the judgment of the President.

Buchanan had not completed his account of the shooting when the sound of low-flying helicopters broke the evening quiet. Jack spotted two sets of landing lights, but could not identify the craft until the helicopters dropped below the towers that lighted the parking area. Immediately he recognized the distinctive markings of the presidential support unit.

Six security police vehicles sped onto the flight line to pick up Secret Service agents who quickly disembarked from the helicopters. Braxton's cameraman turned to record the frantic activity as agents hurried to establish the necessary security.

Jack had trouble accepting what he was seeing. The President just did *not* make spontaneous trips. However, the advance party meant only one thing: The President was not far behind.

Braxton joined Jack and said matter-of-factly, "The President decided to come by for a visit."

Jack had expected Braxton to be equally surprised, but realized the newsman was not. "You knew?"

"Well," Braxton said, with a knowing expression on his face, "let's just say I suggested that when American servicemen have been attacked within sight of our own shores, a personal visit seemed the presidential thing to do."

Jack could not hide his astonishment as he gained an even greater appreciation for Braxton's influence.

"Don't look so surprised, Colonel," Braxton said, smiling broadly. "I knew Marsh Cunningham before he entered California politics. When Marsh became President, he offered me a position in his cabinet until I assured him I couldn't afford the cut in pay."

Jack wondered if he were kidding about the money, but sensed that the claim was true. "I bet the Secret Service loves you for suggesting this visit."

"The Secret Service probably doesn't," Braxton said, smiling, "but a few months from now, John Kellogg and the rest of the President's reelection campaign staff will be thrilled to have this footage in the can." Then, taking on a serious tone, he said, "More important than that, the American people need to see the President here this evening. His presence will help calm a lot of fears."

As the Secret Service agents and Security Police scattered out to secure the immediate area, one contingent rushed into the hangar. They roped off the area around the damaged helicopter and directed everyone out. After being checked with hand-held metal detectors, Jack, Buchanan, and the news team were permitted into a spectator area nearby.

A few minutes later, Jack heard approaching helicopters. This time the craft came in from the east, with only their navigation lights illuminated. The helicopters maintained altitude until directly over the parking ramp. Only when they neared the ground did the pilots turn on the bright landing lights.

As soon as the first helicopter landed and the pilot cut power to the engines, the door slid open. Members of the White House press corps and reporters from the Bay Area got out of the helicopter.

"There goes the exclusive," Braxton said facetiously.

President Cunningham stepped from the second helicopter. His chief of staff, John Kellogg, a military aide, and several other members of the White House staff followed closely behind. As Cunningham drew near, he seemed to be looking for someone and brightened noticeably when he spotted Braxton. The President warmly acknowledged Braxton and Christine and encouraged them to film whatever he thought the American people needed to see.

Braxton introduced his two military companions to the President. Seeing Buchanan in his flight suit, the President turned somber, and he invited Braxton's group to join him. As they moved toward the hangar, Buchanan retold his account of the confrontation.

When the President entered the cargo compartment of the damaged helicopter, he saw a sobering mixture of hydraulic fluid and blood still smeared across a large section of the metal floor. In the cockpit, a bullet-riddled overhead panel still dangled above the bloodstained cushions of the copilot's seat. The damaged Super Jolly Green Giant made Buchanan's account of the aerial engagement easier to visualize, and Cunningham was visibly moved. A few moments later, he stepped from the helicopter with Buchanan at his side.

Cunningham turned toward the lights of the cameras, but he had difficulty forcing enough emotion from his voice to speak loudly and clearly. "As the President, I remain mindful of the enormous responsibilities that are mine. I must prevent the unnecessary escalation of any crisis into a direct Soviet-American confrontation. However, I will not accept wanton attacks on unarmed American rescue aircraft or vessels—and I made that point very clear to Premier Medvalev earlier this afternoon.

"We will not interfere in any way with the Soviet Navy's investigation of the crash and recovery of the wreckage and the remains of the deceased. I have agreed that the United States will provide only whatever recovery assistance the premier requests. This was done to prevent additional confrontations and to prove we had no ulterior motives in offering our assistance.

"At the same time, however," Cunningham added with a look of determination, "no one should misunderstand America's resolve to protect its citizens. I have ordered several of the U.S. Army's most advanced helicopter gunships to join Colonel Buchanan's rescue helicopters here at Chaney Air Force Base. In the event that his unit is required to fly additional rescue missions, his crews will have all the protection they need."

As the President, Buchanan, and Braxton walked around the helicopter's exterior, Jack trailed closely enough behind to hear Buchanan finish his description of the mission. Jack listened again for anything he might have done differently if he had been flying the helicopter—he found nothing.

The President and Braxton talked privately as they walked from the hangar to a car that would take Cunningham to the base hospital. All the reporters except Braxton and Christine got on two buses. When the buses pulled away, Braxton motioned for Jack and Christine to join the group near the President's car.

Braxton said to the President, "Colonel Phillips is the Air Force investigator we were discussing."

Before Jack could respond, Cunningham said, "Colonel, I cannot overestimate how important your investigation is. It must be completely open so that the Soviets cannot claim there's any kind of coverup."

"Yes, sir."

"If there's anything that Watergate and the Contra scandal taught us," Chief of Staff Kellogg said, "it's that the American people are less tolerant of mistakes when an attempted coverup is involved."

A strange response, Jack thought, feeling a twinge of uneasiness about the remark. He hoped that presidential politics were not replacing good judgment and common sense.

"Meanwhile," Cunningham said, "we can't afford to have the Russians acting like it's open season on Americans until there's proof we didn't shoot down half the Soviet government."

"We're doing everything we can, Mr. President," Jack said. "General Harper, the Air Force inspector general, arrived at Howell Air Force Base this afternoon to personally take charge of the investigation. The Air Force is—"

"That reminds me," Cunningham said. "I understand that Miss Merrill reported this afternoon that a high-level Air Force official was openly questioning my decision to hold the press conference. I'd like for you to get to the bottom of that, too."

"Well, sir, the—"

"Mr. President," Christine interrupted, "I'm afraid that misunderstanding is partly my fault."

What an understatement, Jack thought, but he was relieved she had spoken up.

She smiled at the President and continued, "I'm really embarrassed at all the fuss that must have caused. I overheard something that I misinterpreted as questioning your decision to hold the press conference. I must apologize for—"

"Actually," Cunningham said, smiling at her, "I've spent some time questioning that decision myself." He shrugged and looked at Braxton. "But maybe it's better to have that missile information out into the open."

Braxton nodded. "It's still pretty early to know how much that hurt or helped, Mr. President."

"The premier didn't mention the missile when we talked this afternoon," Cunningham said, "but we haven't heard the last of it. In any case, we're embarked on a policy of complete openness, and we shall continue that course until this whole, terrible incident is resolved."

"The American people must be shown very clearly," Kellogg added, "that this administration will not tolerate the coverup of a single bit of wrongdoing in this entire matter."

You've already made your point, Mr. Politician, Jack thought, disgusted. Stiffly he said, "The Air Force made a comprehensive press release following the news conference, Mr. President. The release should answer most of the questions."

"I'm talking about more than routine approaches to what obviously is not a routine situation, Colonel. I want Mr. Braxton to observe your investigation with complete access to all reports. He's served on a couple of blue-ribbon committees for my administration, and he has the background and common sense to help keep this in perspective."

Kellogg nodded his agreement.

Jack swallowed hard, unsure how to respond. He was not inclined to say no to the President, but he certainly did not have the authority to say yes on behalf of the Air Force. He strongly opposed inviting newsmen into the middle of any safety investigation, no matter how sympathetic they might be.

"Sir, I understand. I certainly—"

He was interrupted by the President's military aide, who had been quietly observing the conversation. The aide was a brigadier general in the Army, but he obviously understood the dilemma Jack faced. "Mr. President, I'll make sure that the Air Force understands your desires and that Mr. Braxton and Colonel Phillips receive the appropriate level of support."

"Thank you, John," Cunningham said, "I'm sure that the coverage by Mr. Braxton and Miss Merrill will provide the openness I want."

Although relieved by the general's intervention, Jack was uncertain how much the two reporters could be brought into the investigation. However, that would be General Harper's problem. Walking to his car, he knew one thing: the sooner he was relieved of all responsibility for the investigation, the better he would feel.

Chapter 11

Monday Evening, 6:25 p.m.
Pacific Standard Time

THE WAITING ROOM NEAR THE INTENSIVE CARE SECTION OF THE HOSPI-
tal barely accommodated the reporters, cameramen, and presidential aides. The doctors were treating Smallwood when the President
arrived, so he tried to visit quietly with the wife of the wounded
copilot. The glare of camera lights and the crush of reporters convinced Jack that there was nothing to be gained by trying to listen to
the conversation. Instead he sat on a couch at the far end of the
waiting room and started writing notes on what he had heard and seen
in the last hour. He needed to get started on his report or the deadline
set by General Harper would mean little sleep for the second night in
a row.

A few minutes later the President, a few staff members, and Mrs.
Smallwood were invited into the intensive care unit. Some reporters
hurried to telephones while others improved their notes. Christine
spotted Jack and started toward him. Before she reached him, however, she was intercepted by Bruce Kane, the reporter who had asked
the provocative questions at the press conference at Howell.

"Got any good tips for me, Chrissy?" He moved in front of her as
she tried to step around him.

She stopped and said, with an exasperated smile, "Sure. I hear the
President's making a surprise visit to Chaney Air Force Base tonight."

"Cute," he said. "I've already picked up on that one."

Jack acted as if he were absorbed in his notes, but he continued
listening. He was curious about why Kane might expect Christine to
give him information on the story, but assumed his request was just a
line to get her attention.

Kane steered her toward a window along the side of the room and
said, "But seriously, my boss has given me a green light to go with
anything I can turn up. One more scoop like this morning, and I'm
definitely on my way back East."

"We'll miss you, Brucie." She did not hide the sarcasm.

"Come on, beautiful," he said. "I hear you got a look at the Soviet ships this evening. How many were there and what are they doing?"

"Alex has the whole story on our news tonight. If you want more than that, you'll have to do your own investigating for a change." She flashed a goodbye smile and tried to move away.

He frowned and blocked her path from the window. "Well, at least let me buy you dinner."

"I'm not sure where I'll be having dinner this evening. I'm also working on—"

"It doesn't have to be tonight," he said. "After we get back into town's fine."

"I don't think so."

She was trying to avoid attracting attention, but she made a more determined effort to get around him. He remained persistent. Jack decided to help her.

"Come on," Kane said. "Really, I owe you. Dinner's the least I can do to repay you."

Jack wondered what that meant as he moved toward them. Kane sounded as if she had given him some of the information he had at the news conference, but that made no sense to Jack. He was convinced that reporters did not give tips on hot stories to the competition, and the firing of the missile was the hottest story of the day.

"No." Her answer was more determined.

"I'll put in a good word for you when I'm back East."

"I'm happy where I am," she said crisply.

"I'll—"

"No!"

Jack stepped beside Kane and said in an official sounding voice, "Ma'am, it's time to go to the vehicles. The President should be returning to the flight line shortly."

She appeared surprised for an instant, then said, "Of course, Colonel." She smiled a fake smile at Kane and took hold of Jack's arm as he started for the door.

"But—" Kane said, unsure how to respond. His expression changed as he seemed to realize he had seen Jack before. "Wait! Aren't you the—?"

Before Kane finished, they passed through a doorway and hurried along a corridor, but he caught them as they stepped outside.

"You're the colonel from Washington who broke up the news conference."

"Could be," Jack said, continuing toward the Air Force sedan that had brought him to the hospital.

"Look," Kane said, "I want to know what the Air Force is going to do about a trigger-happy pilot who shoots down the whole Russian government."

"An Air Force investigation is in progress," Jack said in his most bureaucratic tone. "I cannot comment on preliminary findings of that investigation. You can receive reports on the investigation's progress through Public Affairs at Air Force headquarters."

"Does that mean that the Air Force is going to whitewash the whole incident and let the captain get away with murder?"

After opening the door of the car for Christine, Jack turned. "Captain Benes did not shoot down Soviet National One. The missile firing was accidental. Captain Benes did not have any prior knowledge that he was to be intercepting the Soviet aircraft, which was miles off course as a result of what seems to have been a significant blunder in navigation by the Soviet crew." He slipped into the car and continued, "Before you get thrilled by the thought of how aggressively you worked another scoop out of me, be aware that the same information was released officially by the Air Force several hours ago."

He started to close the door, but Kane grabbed it.

"What evidence do you have that proves Benes wasn't out to assassinate Valinen?"

Jack pulled, but Kane held the door open. Jack leaned forward and locked the front door. Grasping the arm rest on the back door one more time, he said, "The Surgeon General has determined that holding a car door when it's slammed can be hazardous to your fingers."

He made a guttural yell as if about to deliver a karate blow and jerked on the arm rest. He moved the door only slightly, but the fake was enough to make Kane yank his hands back. Jack closed and locked the door and locked those on the other side before Kane could recover. He stood by the car shouting additional questions and threats.

Christine seemed amused by the way Jack had handled her dogged colleague. "It seems that I'm indebted to you again for coming to my rescue, Colonel."

"You were doing pretty well, but sometimes a wingman can speed up the disengagement."

"I'm always uncomfortable when I owe anyone anything, and I still haven't figured out how to repay you for saving my life."

Jack tried to interpret her tone. She sounded sincere, maybe even a little suggestive. The instincts that guided his personal life welcomed a much friendlier relationship with this beautiful woman. His military instincts, which dominated most of his actions most of the time, warned that he had been eye to eye with the *real* Christine Merrill during their short confrontation over the relationship between the military and the media. Now she probably was just being pragmatic—he was a news source she must work closely with for the next few days.

"You don't owe me anything," he said sincerely. "If you really feel obligated, I'll settle for your being even-handed when reporting on the American military from now on."

For an instant a combative sparkle flashed in her eyes. "I always—" She stopped. "I was about to be very self-righteous and very wrong."

He smiled. "I think we're making progress already."

"In San Francisco I haven't had occasion to work on many stories about military men." Her expression was friendly in marked contrast to the determination that had characterized their confrontation at the briefing. "I thought I knew a lot about the military, but I'm just realizing that almost everything I've learned, I've learned from other reporters."

"Probably there are worse sources." He paused, then added, "But none come to mind."

"Colonel Buchanan taught me more about military people in ten minutes than I've learned in ten years. I had no idea."

"If you end up getting acquainted with Captain Benes, you'll find that he's a much worthier individual than most of your colleagues will depict him as."

She nodded. "It was fun watching how you just handled Bruce." She leaned against the door and looked over Jack as if she were sizing him up. With a sly smile, she added, "I don't think he's used to coming up against a man like you either."

"Reporters and fighter pilots seldom get along well, ma'am."

"Perhaps, Colonel, your stereotype of reporters is as inaccurate as some of our stereotypes of Air Force brass are."

"Your contemporaries in Washington spend most of their time building up both stereotypes."

She smiled skeptically. "Surely it's not that bad."

"I'll give you a 'for instance.' Suppose we're working on a new aircraft or missile system we're pretty pleased with. The routine usually goes something like this." Jack began a parody of an interview, with his hand moving a make-believe microphone between the imaginary newsman and himself. "What's the system's real weakness, Colonel? Nothing, we're pretty happy with it. Then, Colonel, you're claiming it's perfect? No, I didn't say that. Then what's the thing you expect to go wrong if anything does? We don't expect anything to go wrong. But, Colonel, if it's not perfect, you must have at least one thing you're concerned about. If there were one thing I had any concerns about, it would probably have to be the navigational system." He paused, then said, before extending the make-believe microphone to her, "Now what's the headline for that story, ma'am?"

She answered with a smile. "Air Force official expresses concerns about navigational system on—"

"You got it," Jack said, then added facetiously, "Sounds like you're ready to move on to Washington."

"Not all of us believe in working that way." Christine was serious, then softened and added, "Of course, the way you and I started off this morning surely didn't increase your confidence in reporters. I really am sorry we had to meet that way." Instinctively she placed her hand on his, then pulled back self-consciously.

"I agree, ma'am," Jack said, but smiled in return. "But the way you squared things with the President for me was really Sierra Hotel."

"Sierra Hotel?" She looked puzzled.

As soon as the words were out of his mouth, he chastised himself for slipping unintentionally into fighter-pilot jargon. Sierra and Hotel were the two words in the phonetic alphabet representing the letters S and H. (The phonetic alphabet consists of twenty-six words such as Alpha, Bravo, Charlie, Delta, Echo, Foxtrot, etc., commonly used in place of letters in radio transmissions to prevent misunderstandings of similarly sounding letters.) During the Vietnam War, fighter pilots often described something that was really good with the phrase "Sierra Hotel," meaning "shit hot." He was too embarrassed to explain. "Just accept that as a fighter pilot's compliment, ma'am."

She smiled and seemed ready to press for the inside story of what Sierra Hotel represented. However, she changed the subject. "Look, if we're going to be working together, there's one problem we need to resolve."

"What's that, ma'am?"

"Every time you call me 'ma'am,' I feel about twenty years older than I like to feel." With a playful look of anger, she added, "And I can assure you, Colonel, neither of us wants me feeling that grumpy."

"Yes—" He avoided the word. "I'll buy that."

He was uncertain what to suggest. Usually when he worked officially with a female, she had a rank. If she were another colonel, they would work naturally on a first-name basis, except in front of generals or military personnel of lesser rank. Using first names with Christine would be just as awkward when he was working with her in front of other military personnel.

He asked, "How about Ms?"

She shook her head.

"Miss Merrill?"

"Only when I should be calling you Colonel Phillips."

"Oookay, lllady," he said, drawing the words out as if trying to solve a real dilemma.

Their surprisingly friendly discussion was interrupted when the President emerged from the hospital. After escorting her to her car, Jack returned to the flight line and told the crew of his helicopter that he wanted to depart for Howell in about twenty minutes. Then he went into Base Operations for copies of the messages that Buchanan had submitted describing the Soviet attack.

Waiting for the documents, he looked out the windows, which had a perfect view of the VIP parking area. He saw the President climb into his helicopter, leaving Braxton and Christine standing at the bottom of the steps. Braxton seemed to be explaining the use of an electronic pager to Christine. She nodded her understanding, and he handed the pager to her. Jack wondered why they didn't get out of the way since they were delaying the President. Braxton embraced Christine, then turned and climbed into the helicopter. The entry door closed behind him as she hurried away.

"No," Jack said as he bolted for the door. By the time he got outside, the rotors on the helicopter were turning. "Damn!" He yanked the door open angrily and walked back inside. Having Braxton thrust into the middle of the investigation was bad enough—Merrill alone would be even worse.

Buchanan joined him at the counter and said, "I hear they threatened your chopper today, too, sir."

"The *Gnevnyy* started painting us with their fire-control radar, but we got our tail out of there before they launched anything."

"If you decide you need a closer look, Colonel," Buchanan said, "give me a call. For the last couple of hours my maintenance crews have been pulling our miniguns out of storage and mounting the guns on the rest of the Jollys."

Jack understood Buchanan's anger and enthusiasm, but the guns used for self-defense during combat rescues in Vietnam were no match for the antiaircraft weapons on the Soviet ships. "A couple of Gatling guns won't do much against the SAMs on the *Gnevnyy.*"

Motioning toward a status board on the far wall that listed aircraft inbound, Buchanan pointed out that the six Apache gunships from Fort Lewis were due in an hour.

"Unless you figure a way to hang Harpoons on those Apaches," Jack said, "you're still outgunned." Those anti-ship missiles were too large to be carried by the attack helicopters. He added, "And the *Gnevnyy*'s only the beginning."

"I know, sir," Buchanan said with a look of resignation.

"I listened to everything you said this evening," Jack said, "and I still haven't figured out why you were fired on."

"I can't figure it either, sir," Buchanan said. "Perhaps he thought our refueling boom was some kind of a cannon, but I don't think so. We were clear of him and on our way toward the *Valiant* when he flew in between to attack us."

"If he'd been afraid of your refueling boom, he wouldn't have maneuvered in front of you again."

"Maybe it's as simple as another aircraft commander feeling like I feel right now." Buchanan smashed a fist against his open palm. "He knew why his ship had been sent there, and maybe he just wanted revenge."

"I've studied the Soviets for a long time. What I see them do usually makes sense to someone over there, even if it seems to make no sense at all to me. If he were acting in revenge, then the attack made sense to him. If he acted under orders, then something else is happening out there."

Buchanan nodded. "The only thing I could think of was that maybe Soviet National One carried special intelligence-gathering equipment, and they want to beat us to it."

Jack remembered the Soviet attack on Korean Air Lines Flight 007 after the Boeing 747 had overflown Kamchatka in 1983. The Soviets' most persistent justification for their role in the deaths of hundreds of innocent passengers was a claim that airliners routinely carried intelligence-gathering equipment.

"If Soviet National One carried that kind of gear," he said, "their muscling in and taking over the recovery area makes some sense. It's just too early to tell, but I intend to obey the President's directive about keeping away from the crash site. If the situation changes, though, and I need another look, I'd be proud to have you along."

Buchanan looked pleased, then excused himself to return to the hospital.

A few moments later, a clerk brought an envelope containing the copies of the messages. As Jack signed for them, Christine came inside. She caught his eye and asked, "What's next, Colonel?"

"I'm about to go back to Howell."

Christine hesitated, then said, "I thought you'd ask where Alex is."

Jack tried to look stern. "I try never to ask questions I can't stand the answer to. Anyway, I thought the President wanted Mr. Braxton to stick to me like glue."

"The President agreed to a 'suitable substitute,' and I'm her." Christine smiled warily and looked as if she expected an explosive reaction.

"The deal was that Mr. Braxton would be the President's observer."

"I told Alex you'd have trouble accepting the change."

"You've got that right, ma'am, or lady, or whatever." Braxton's national reputation and personal standing with the President would help the Air Force tolerate him as an observer. Her reputation obviously was not in the same category.

She said with a hesitant smile, "The President was sure you'd find a way to accept the change."

"I'd say the President was right." Jack gave her an exasperated grin, knowing he had never been in a position to dictate any terms of the agreement. But, he thought, he needed to get a few terms of their working relationship agreed to, right from the beginning. "Do you honor 'off the record' limitations?"

His experiences with the media representatives at the Pentagon had taught him that anything said in front of a reporter was fair game to be quoted—or misquoted—unless there was a prior agreement that the conversation was "off the record." Though reporters preferred to avoid the restriction, the compromise allowed them access to insights and background information that otherwise would be held back.

Newsmen were honor-bound not to report off-the-record conversations. However, he had seen such items in print and on television often enough to know that unprofessional reporters did not always live up to the agreements. He was confident that Braxton's desire to maintain his professional reputation of longstanding would protect such discussions. Jack was unsure about a younger reporter like Christine. He reasoned that by his making it a point right from the beginning, she was more likely to honor off-the-record agreements too. That could be helpful to both of them, especially if he needed to educate her on a subject using details that were too dangerous to have in print.

"I honor any commitment I make," she said seriously. "However, I very rarely work off the record."

"Please appreciate that my primary role is to protect the national security of the United States. And—"

"I understand that. I don't see where that's a problem."

"By following my investigation in real-time, you may see fragments of information that may suggest something entirely different from the final answer. Publicizing a wrong intermediate conclusion could be dangerous to national security."

"Obviously," she said, "the President believes that the people's right to know and the concern to avoid any coverup outweigh the risks you're worried about."

That was not the answer he wanted to hear. However, he had

learned long ago there was little to be gained in debating with reporters about the balance between the people's right to know and the
need to keep some things secret. "I'm just concerned that he may
have gotten some bad political advice."

"Our leaders keep partisan politics out of vital decisions on national
security."

Was she really that naive? he wondered. But, he thought, that's
what we'd all learned in high school civics classes. Surely she had been
a reporter long enough to know that what happened in the real world
of Washington politics did not always fit the theories.

"I believed that, too, until I was almost your age."

Her expression made him think she was about to debate the lack of
significance in the difference between their ages. Instead she asked,
"What do you mean?"

He thought briefly of the tumultuous presidential campaign of 1968.
That fall, he had just arrived as a young lieutenant at a fighter base in
Thailand. While battles were being waged in the streets of America,
he took part in another campaign. The Air Force and Navy were
being more successful than ever before in disrupting the flow of war
materials between the North Vietnamese harbor at Haiphong and the
battlefields of South Vietnam. Unless the North Vietnamese could
replace the troops and supplies lost during the Tet offensive and the
siege of the U.S. Marine base at Khe Sanh, the Communists would be
forced to reduce the fighting in South Vietnam.

In October 1968, the fliers had been optimistic about their fight—
the President pessimistic about his. Then, with only a few hours
notice, Johnson had ordered a halt in the bombing of North Vietnam
a week before the American elections. In spite of the political decision, his party still lost its contest. As a result of that decision, the
fliers lost their campaign, too, and Jack had learned a lesson about
American government he would never forget.

"We're not far enough off the record for me to go into all that. The
bottom line is that I'm a good soldier—I always have been. I obey the
rightful orders of the civilian leadership that properly is in command
of our military forces." He paused, then looked at her to make sure
she was attentive. He put a fist against his chest and said, "It's just
that I get an upset feeling right here when I have to carry out rightful
orders that I know are wrong."

"And you think putting me with you to observe your investigation
is wrong?"

"Off the record—yes."

Christine shrugged. "Alex said to tell you he was sorry he couldn't explain the change to you personally, but the President was ready to leave."

"A personal explanation wouldn't have helped much. I just don't see how this can work without Mr. Braxton's personal involvement."

"Alex had commitments in San Francisco that he couldn't break."

Jack found that hard to believe. "More important than the President's bidding? I'd think Mr. Braxton's boss could find someone else to handle those commitments."

"Alex *is* the boss." Jack looked confused, so she added, "Alex owns the station, and it's only a small part of his holdings."

"But if the President really wanted Mr. Braxton to have a role in the—"

"The President understood," she said. "Anyway, Alex left his beeper with me." She pushed aside the jacket of her suit, revealing an electronic pager attached to her belt. She pressed the test switch and produced a soft, warbling tone. "If he needs anything from me, he beeps. And, of course I can call in as soon as I learn something Alex needs to know. Alex said that was almost like having him along."

Jack started for the door and pictured making that argument to General Raleigh. "Try selling that to the chief of staff."

"What?"

"Nothing," he said, pushing the door open for her. As they stepped into a misty rain, he added with a frustrated smile, "Off the record, this is a hell of a way to run a war."

Chapter 12

Monday Evening, 7:50 p.m.
Pacific Standard Time

CAPTAIN JENSEN MET THE TWO WHEN THEIR HELICOPTER LANDED AT Howell. "I've got all your gear in the car, sir," he said as he led them to the Air Force sedan parked nearby. "General Harper wanted his team chief to stay in your bedroom in Base Operations, so I'll take you to the VOQ."

"Visiting Officer Quarters," Jack said, in response to the questioning look on Christine's face. "I need to stop at the Command Post first."

Driving to the Command-Post side of the Base Operations building, Jensen explained that he had briefed General Harper and the rest of the IG team. Since the briefing, the team's findings had simply verified things discovered in the preliminary investigation.

Jack wanted updates on two items. Hoping to get his answers without causing the newswoman to raise new questions, he asked, "Did you get the results on the nav systems?"

'I've checked and double-checked the accuracy of the INSs on both Eagles."

She inquired, "INSs?"

Jack said, "The Inertial Navigation Systems that tell the pilot where his aircraft is throughout the flight."

She wrote a note, and Jensen continued, "Colonel, if you were in Benes' F-15 and passed your INS coordinates to Ms. Merrill to join you using Walker's INS, she could be close enough to end up right on your lap." He paused, then added, "So to speak."

Jack asked, "The data are really that good?"

"Well," Jensen said with a mischievous grin, "she'd be close enough that she could hit you with her note pad."

She smiled at the captain. "We're being more civil to each other now than we were this morning."

"Good enough," Jack said to Jensen. "If you discover any surprises in the paperwork on the ordnance, you can let me know later."

"The IG's taking a close look," Jensen said, "but when the paperwork's all sorted out, it'll be clean. I called a friend at the depot and read him all the serial numbers of the local missiles. The only missile I can't account for is the one Benes fired."

Christine looked quickly at Jack and said, "Was there reason to believe that Captain Benes had fired more than one missile?"

Jack chose his words carefully. "I've seen no evidence of more than one."

He was determined to tell the truth and nothing but the truth. He did not feel obligated, however, to tell her the *whole* truth. In this case, the whole truth included O'Donnell's unsubstantiated charges about more than one missile being fired at Soviet National One.

Jack added, "Of course, the Air Force is thorough in all aircraft accident investigations, especially when an inadvertent ordnance release is involved."

"Great terminology, Colonel," she said with an impish smile as she made a note of his description of the missile firing.

Jensen parked the car. Before Jack got out, Christine asked, "What's next?"

"This evening I plan to listen to the tape of the ATC—that's air traffic control—communications during the crash," Jack said. "I've also got to finish a summary report for General Harper."

"Both sound good to me," she said. "When do we start?"

"Those aren't audience-participation events. I'll need to concentrate."

"I can be quiet," she said, running her fingers across her lips in a zipping motion. "I want to hear the tape, too. I'll only ask questions when I don't understand something."

"But," he said, not expecting to discourage her, "the tape will be mostly jargon. I'm not sure—"

"I've ridden with Alex in his little planes a hundred times. I've heard plenty of 'pilot-speak.' "

"His little planes?"

"Sure. He's a great pilot. When do we start?"

After retrieving a hangup bag she had left earlier in Base Operations, they agreed that Jensen would take her to the quarters. She was to meet Jack at his room in an hour.

Checking in with the duty officer in the Command Post, Jack was given a folder of information that had accumulated during his absence. Included was the message he had expected from the Pentagon authorizing Braxton and Christine to observe the Air Force investigation. Other items were in response to requests he had made after the morning press conference.

He sat at an empty desk and began reading. The first set of

materials had been used to brief Captain Benes and Lieutenant Walker when they had come onto alert the day before the crash. The intelligence summary included three paragraphs on the extraordinary deployment of the Soviet Navy, pointing out that the current exercise was the most extensive and realistic yet by the Soviets, whose surface Navy had been capable of little more than coastal defense before the 1970s.

The summary also included two paragraphs on the war games in progress throughout Czechoslovakia, East Germany, Hungary, and Poland. The emphasis was on winter maneuvers. However, he recognized that the Warsaw Pact had considerably more troops and armor in the field than in any exercise he could remember.

The analysis concluded with a suggestion that these war games could become known as the "spy games." Some maneuvers had not been observed previously. They seemed to reflect a new knowledge of NATO deployments gained through the major spy ring that had been broken by NATO counterintellgence in 1988. Even more disconcerting, the analysis continued, were the naval exercises conducted by the anti-submarine warfare units of the Soviet Navy. These warships and aircraft were ranging into and beyond patrol areas routinely used by the nuclear submarines (SSBNs) that carried America's sea-launched ballistic missiles. Some search patterns indicated a fresh insight into the tactics of the American SSBNs.

The naval maneuvers had ominous implications, he thought. They suggested that the U.S. Navy secrets, which had been passed for years by another spy ring, had included critical information on how to search for and find the American submarines. If true, the balance of power had shifted significantly. For years, one President after another had relied on the premise that the second-strike capabilities of the SSBNs would deter a first strike by the Soviets. The analysis concluded that if the spies had told the Russians how to locate and destroy the SSBNs, the nuclear balance had swung in favor of the Soviet Union.

Jack saw nothing in the briefing materials that contradicted anything Benes and Walker had said.

The folder also included detailed information on the Il-62 aircraft. He found a technical description of the Il-62, in general, and specific details about the aircraft that had crashed. He compared the data to things he knew about comparable commercial aircraft and found no surprises. The speeds Benes and Walker had observed during the rapid descent were almost identical to the emergency descent profile published in the flight manual for the Il-62.

The data also confirmed that Soviet National One was equipped with the most advanced navigational aids available to the Soviet Air

Force. As Jack expected, onboard equipment could receive signals from the Soviet's *GLONASS* and the American *NAVSTAR GPS,* the satellite-based navigational systems of both nations. The list of equipment left him with an earlier question for which he still had no reasonable answer: how could a pair of hand-picked navigators be seventy miles off course while using equipment that could determine the aircraft's position within feet instead of miles?

He studied copies of weather reports for the entire day of the crash. The high winds and heavy seas whipped up by the winter storm would have doomed almost any ditching attempt, especially at night. Still, if he had been flying, he would have tried to pick a heading that quartered into the head wind and with the primary swell on the ocean's surface. However, the Russian pilot had not. He had crashed with almost a full cross wind and—if Benes were to be believed—had not even bothered to turn on the landing lights to get a look at the water.

The pilot's action seemed to Jack to be those of a rookie or a flier overwhelmed by panic. He had felt panic in flight a number of times, but training and air discipline had always brought him through, and he expected the pilot of Soviet National One to be every bit as good. As he closed the folder and left the Command Post, he could not justify why the performance of the Soviet crew had not been better.

By the time he reached his room, only a few minutes remained until Christine was due to join him. As he cleaned up and put on a fresh shirt, he thought about the difference a few hours had made. Less than twenty-four hours earlier, he had watched her with great interest as she broadcast from the airport terminal. Then, he would have been very pleased by the thought of this beautiful woman coming to his room the next evening.

Now he dreaded her visit, even though the strong physical attraction had been sharpened by the few moments of close contact in the helicopter. However, he was used to giving "mission" the top priority over his personal life—several times to the detriment of relationships that afterwards he wished had continued.

Now he was on a mission that obviously had to have his top priority, and she would only be a distraction, interrupting constantly with her questions. Not only would the interruptions make it difficult to keep the two tape recordings synchronized, but he also would need to be on guard about everything he said. He would be lucky to make any progress on his report for General Harper while she was present. The more Jack thought about it, the more he became irritated at being forced to include her. He decided that he had a better chance of getting his job done if she were the one who had the distractions.

The furnishings in the room included a small refrigerator stocked with juices, soft drinks, and small bottles of wine. In addition, a selection of miniature bottles of liquor was on a cabinet near the refrigerator. He could use any of the refreshments he wanted and pay for them when he checked out.

As he looked over the bottles, he wondered if she drank. If so, perhaps a few drinks would take the edge off her abilities as a reporter. On other occasions, he had sometimes used liquor to relax a young woman. In this case, he rationalized, his intentions were more honorable, though he expected the results to be less interesting for both of them.

He picked a miniature bottle of bourbon and poured a fourth of it into a tumbler. He dumped the rest into the bathroom sink, then placed the empty bottle where Christine could see it easily in front of the full ones. After filling his glass with Coca Cola, he took a couple of sips.

He had just finished loading the tape players and synchronizing the tapes when she knocked. Opening the door, he was surprised at how different she looked in designer jeans and a silk blouse tied off at the waist. Her hair was pulled back into a ponytail, and her makeup was much more subdued. Standing in the doorway, she seemed more like a kid sister than a sophisticated television personality. As she slipped by him, the fragrance of her fresh perfume cleared his thoughts completely of the kid-sister image.

"I was stuck on a call with the studio," she said. "I hope you didn't start without me."

"I waited," he said. Raising his glass, he added, "Except for starting with the refreshments. What can I get for you?"

Christine's look seemed to question whether he was treating her visit as business or personal.

"Strictly your choice," he said. Gesturing toward the empty bottle on the cabinet, he added, "I'm just having a little bourbon." Nothing but the truth, he thought.

She chose a bottle of wine and soon was settled on the couch. He sat beside an adjacent table that held the two tape players.

"How long will this take?" she asked.

"Depends on the number of interruptions. The tapes cover an hour or so."

"Good. Alex is sending a camera crew over in the morning. At seven-thirty, we're going to tape a few spots he's planning to offer to the network for their evening news."

"Sounds like good exposure," Jack said. He was willing to encourage anything that could shorten her visit and let him get to his work.

He was also pleased that the taping might keep her busy until he had finished briefing General Harper.

"Alex gives me breaks whenever he can." Smiling, she added, "I don't suppose you'd like to be on-camera for some national exposure."

He gave her a look that said she knew better than to ask. "Let's listen to the tapes, lady."

For the next couple of hours, they worked hard. There were numerous interruptions as she asked the meanings of words and of the events documented on the tapes. In most cases, he could explain in ways favorable to the Air Force. His explanations emphasized the overall professionalism with which the two pilots had flown their mission.

Jack was pleased that he still found nothing on either tape that contradicted the reports of Benes and Walker. The only discrepancy was a difference in the logs of the two controllers. The FAA log indicated that the crash occurred at twenty-two forty-five hours, Pacific Standard Time. The Air Force log showed twenty-two forty-eight hours.

Initially he assumed the discrepancy might be due to a difference in the clocks. Yet, he thought, the accuracy of the clocks in the air traffic control centers was checked regularly. A minute of difference could be explained if one controller had rounded off the time one way while the other had rounded in the opposite direction. However, when he compared other items common to both logs, he found exact matches.

The difference of three minutes probably didn't matter, he thought. No one's chance to survive had slipped away because of three minutes of confusion. He made a note to see which log matched Benes' acknowledgment of the crash.

In the long periods of silence on the tapes, Christine organized notes for her morning presentations while he continued drafting his report. During the evening, they became more relaxed and cordial in dealing with each other, even though the relationship's formal nature kept it from a first-name-basis. Evolving almost as a game, the terms "colonel" and "lady" became substitute forms of address when first names might otherwise have been used. They discovered the terms to be quite useful across the spectrum from formal to friendly, depending upon the emphasis and tone of voice.

He had fixed a third round of drinks when Benes' voice on the tape said, "Tell Oakland I think she's going in."

She listened with rapt attention.

"Oakland, Guardian. Better scramble the Coast Guard. Looks like you've got a crash on your hands!"

As Guardian passed the estimated position of Soviet National One, she asked, "What's the bottom line? You're apparently convinced that your captain didn't shoot the aircraft down, so what caused the crash?"

Recognizing that this could be his best opportunity to get the Air Force position on national television, he stopped both tapes. "I can only speculate until the flight data recorder, the cockpit voice recorder, and other key pieces of the wreckage are recovered."

"Key pieces?"

He paused. He must choose his words carefully, to avoid telling the whole truth without actually lying. The tail and each engine were the key pieces he would want to examine. The tail was important for what it should show: a mechanical failure in the linkages to the flight controls. The engines were important for what they should *not* show: damage caused by the missile fired by Benes. However, mentioning the engines risked the possibility that her report would focus on how the missile might have caused the crash.

He said, "I'd be most interested in the tail—primarily the connections to the horizontal stab—uh, that's the horizontal stabilizer." He noticed she still seemed uncertain about the term. "You know, the flat part of the tail that looks like a small wing." She nodded and started writing again. "Once the Soviets have the recorders and the wreckage, I guess I would buy—given that I'm not familiar with the actual mechanical linkages in the flight controls of an Il-62—I'd buy it if the Soviets said that the jackscrew had stripped. That would—"

She giggled, then tried harder to control her reactions. "I'm sorry, Colonel. Drinking without eating much sometimes makes me a little giddy. Please continue."

Great, he thought with concern. He finally had the chance to offer an explanation totally independent of the missile, and she was going to have trouble getting his story straight. He pulled out the metal fragment he carried and moved it back and forth like a coin between his fingers.

"Anyway, with a stripped jackscrew that . . ." He paused when it appeared she was going to laugh again.

"Really, I'm sorry," she said, fighting to maintain composure, "but I'm still not sure what you're talking about. What's a jackscrew, and how does one go about stripping one?" She giggled.

"Think of it as a long, threaded bolt that moves back and forth through a threaded nut. The jackscrew is attached to the stabilizer. The nut's part of the structure of the tail, or vice versa. That doesn't matter. What matters is that if the threads on the jackscrew or nut strip out, which could be caused by lack of regular lubrication and by abnormal metal fatigue, the jackscrew is free to move through the nut without any control from the cockpit. Since the jackscrew normally controls the trimmed position of the horizontal stabilizer, the Soviet aircraft would have a free-floating stabilizer, free to seek its own position, based on the airflow."

Glancing at her, he noticed she had stopped writing. He decided to continue, hoping she would pick up some of his official-sounding explanation. He placed the piece of metal on the table and positioned his hands to represent the horizontal stabilizer mounted on the top of the vertical tail fin of an Il-62.

"At the speed they were flying when the threads stripped—assuming they failed—the stabilizer's center of lift would be ahead of the pivot point that still connected the stabilizer to the aircraft. That means, of course, that the front of the stabilizer would rise as far as possible, forcing the nose of the aircraft down, producing a steep dive."

He stopped and looked disappointedly at her.

She giggled, then fought to regain a straight face. "I'm sorry. I'm just having trouble picturing myself on national TV and talking about stripping jackscrews." She laughed again. "My friends would never let me hear the end of a story like that."

Jack grabbed the piece of metal and said, with a hint of sarcasm, "Maybe the words will be easier to say in the morning, lady, when you've only got the hangover."

"Really, I'm sorry," she said, reaching over and putting a hand on his arm. "Your explanation was fine. But I don't think my viewers will understand centers of lift and pivot points and horizontal stabilizers and—" She bit her lip to keep from laughing.

He held the piece of metal between his thumb and forefinger, staring at the fragment as if it could inspire a better approach.

When she noticed that what he was holding was not a coin, she asked, "What's that?"

"That's my personal attitude indicator," he said, using the name of an important instrument in an aircraft cockpit. "In an airplane, the attitude indicator lets you know when you're flying wings-level or in a dive or upside-down. This one tells me when I'm not taking life seriously enough." He flipped the metal like a coin, then snatched the spinning fragment from the air. "Or when I'm taking things too seriously." He smiled, finally having become amused at her difficulties with the words. "Well, lady, if you can't say 'stripped jackscrew,' just tell your viewers that the tail broke and the airplane fell into the ocean."

She laughed. "You don't have to make it quite that simple, Colonel. Don't you have something in between?" She was poised again, ready to write.

He spoke slowly, to allow her to copy his words. "Just say that the Air Force expects the Soviet investigation to find a failure in the linkages between the cockpit and the flight controls in the tail. That kind of failure apparently caused a dive from which the highly trained pilots were unable to recover."

She seemed to consider the words after she had written them in her notebook. "That was it? They had no chance?"

He would have agreed completely if Benes had not reported that the Il-62 had leveled off and made the low altitude turn. Again, Jack chose his words carefully. "You asked what I would buy as the bottom line, and that explanation's close. I know of two similar incidents involving large jets of the U.S. Air Force. In one, the aircraft entered a steep dive, gaining enough speed to break it into pieces about a mile above the ground."

She winced at the thought, then asked, "And the second crash?"

"That one didn't crash. There was a crusty old colonel on board." Jack paused, then added, "At least he seemed old to me at the time. Anyway, he locked his arms around the control wheel while another pilot moved the throttles, and they managed to land the plane." He tried to picture the Soviet pilots doing the same thing. Perhaps the crew could have leveled the Il-62 as Benes reported. But there was no corresponding explanation for why the aircraft plunged into the ocean minutes later. He continued, "With a failure like that, the odds are against you. It's unfortunate our pilots weren't able to help."

"Listening to this is almost enough to make me want to stop flying," she said as she put her notebook into the large purse she carried. "I've got an early call in the morning, so I think I'll finish my notes on my own."

"Wait," Jack said as he turned on the recorders. He remembered the genuine concern that had filled Benes' voice after the crash. "There are a couple of more minutes on the Air Force tape that you should hear."

The next transmission was Karl Wilson alerting the Coast Guard. His words sounded as if the crash had already taken place. Less than a minute later, the Air Force controller ordered an immediate scramble of air rescue helicopters from Chaney. Jack was getting confused about whether the crash had occurred or not. He had not yet heard Benes' troubled announcement, which he remembered clearly from listening to the tape the first time.

Another minute had passed before Benes said, "She's out of fifteen hundred feet."

Christine looked puzzled. "Haven't they already crashed?"

"Not yet. Guardian's words about having a crash on their hands made Oakland think the plane had already crashed. Captain Benes will announce the crash in—"

He froze. As he was speaking, he had heard Russian words from one of the recorders. The words were almost blocked by Karl Wilson answering a question from the Coast Guard dispatcher, but Jack was certain he had heard Russian.

She asked, "What's wrong?"

He motioned for silence as he strained to hear if more Russian words were on the tape. Moments later, however, Benes announced the crash, and Jack knew there would be no more.

After listening a few seconds longer, he stopped the tapes, then rewound the last minute of the FAA tape.

She asked, "What happened? What did you hear?"

"Someone said something in Russian."

"Why would someone suddenly talk in Russian after everything else had been in English?"

"I don't know," he said as he started the tape player. He had the same question.

The tape was silent for the first ten seconds. Then a voice from the Coast Guard asked Oakland for the number of people on board the aircraft. As Wilson responded that the flight plan indicated ninety-three, a new voice on the tape said three words of Russian. Although the words were difficult to hear, Jack caught them—*"Sluzhu Sovetskomu Soyuzu!"*—"I serve the Soviet Union!"

The words sent a chill through him, and he fought to hide his reaction.

She asked, "Who said whatever that was?"

"I don't know."

Jack shrugged to emphasize his uncertainty. He did not know, but he had a good idea. However, he did not want to steer the conversation toward all his doubts and unanswered questions. He hoped Christine would not ask if he could translate the Russian words.

"It's always amazed me," she said, "that the air traffic controllers and pilots all around the world have to speak English. That must cause confusion and probably some accidents."

"Probably," he said as he clicked off the recorder. He stretched and forced a yawn. "Well, I guess that's the end of the evening's program."

She looked at her watch and gathered her things. "You may be finished, Colonel, but I still have plenty to do."

As soon as she left, he called the duty officer at the Command Post to send someone to pick up the report for General Harper. He wanted it typed into a computer during the night so he could edit it quickly in the morning.

After making the telephone call, he replayed the Russian statement over and over again. He was more impressed each time he heard it. On many occasions he had heard the voices of men reacting under extreme stress, but this voice was different—firm and steady, without a hint of panic. He sensed in the voice a military man calmly and resolutely doing his duty.

He was still replaying the words when the messenger from the Command Post knocked at the door. After passing on the report, he contacted the front desk for a wake-up call at five-fifteen.

There were only a couple of minutes left until the late evening news, so he turned on the television to Braxton's channel. Jack hoped the report would provide another good look at the Soviet ships at the crash site. However, the scenes taped aboard the helicopter had been edited almost exclusively to those of Braxton standing in the open doorway. Only five seconds showed the four Soviet ships, and most of that segment showed only the destroyer. Jack was still curious about the other ships so he made a note to ask Christine for a copy of the rest of the footage.

Braxton's report on the President's visit to Chaney was masterful. The pictures and words were sensitive and resolute. They showed a President who was concerned for the safety of individual servicemen and women but who also knew he must keep the tragedy from escalating into war.

Braxton's summary was thick with patriotism and wrapped in the American flag. While he castigated the Soviets for the wanton attack on Buchanan's unarmed helicopter, he focused on the need to temper the desire for revenge. He closed with a call for the American people to stand behind the President's determination to resolve the crisis through quiet diplomacy.

After the report, Jack turned off the television set and stretched out on the bed. Over and over his thoughts kept returning to the words at the end of the FAA tape: "I serve the Soviet Union."

Long after he had turned off the light, he remained awake. He was still troubled by his belief that he had listened to the final, unflinching words of a pilot who was doing his duty—even if that duty demanded the cold-blooded murder of ninety-two people.

Chapter 13

JACK WAS ALREADY UP AND SHAVING BEFORE RECEIVING THE WAKE-UP call. He arrived at the Command Post at five forty-five and used most of the first hour working on his report to the Air Force Inspector General. Jack decided not to mention the Russian phrase he had heard on the FAA tape. His theories about the phrase and its implications were better discussed in person. He did not want to write them into an official record, especially if that record might have to be released to the media within the next few hours.

While Jack awaited his meeting, he reviewed the latest information on the growing crisis. Intelligence messages reported that the Soviets had forty-seven surface ships in the vicinity of San Francisco. Most were approximately 150 miles off the coast in a fleet led by the aircraft carrier *Minsk* and the battlecruiser *Kirov*. Several ships, including four Soviet merchant vessels, had gathered at the crash site. The naval force was much larger than he had expected.

He also learned that after the attack on the American air rescue helicopter, an Airborne Warning and Control System (AWACS) aircraft had launched from Tinker Air Force Base near Oklahoma City. The aircraft was similar in appearance to a Boeing 707 passenger plane, but carried a highly sophisticated radar in a saucer-shaped radome above the fuselage. The inside of the aircraft was equipped like a high-technology radar site. This AWACS now was flying a racetrack-shaped orbit thirty miles northwest of Howell Air Force Base. From that location, controllers aboard the AWACS could monitor the Soviet fleet and all aircraft approaching the coast for several hundred miles around San Francisco.

Jack also learned that the normal alert commitment of fighters at Howell had been increased. Instead of two, four armed Eagles now were poised for action on five-minute alert. The extra fighters had been put on alert to protect the AWACS aircraft if it were threatened.

When Jack went to the flight-line cafeteria for breakfast, he saw

Christine and her camera team outside. They were taping her report, using the Howell Air Force Base signs in front of Base Operations as their background.

A few minutes before eight, Jack was invited into Colonel Radisson's office in the Command Post. General Harper was seated on a large couch. Radisson sat behind his desk, and as Jack sat down, the two colonels exchanged glares of pure hatred.

After the initial, strained formalities, Harper said, "Now tell me, Colonel, what's the story on this reporter who's tagging along?"

Jack told of Braxton's influence and how the President had decided that the Air Force investigation must be open to the public. Harper was not pleased. Jack suggested that since Christine might arrive at any time, certain aspects of the report should be discussed as quickly as possible.

Harper said that he liked the quality of Jack's report, but was concerned that it did not contain any hard evidence that could clear the Air Force.

"General," Jack said, "the evidence you and General McClintock are looking for is either in the water or in Russia."

Radisson asked, "What would we expect to find in Russia?"

Harper nodded, showing that he was also interested in the answer to that question.

Jack continued, "Sir, I'm relatively certain some people in Russia knew the aircraft was going to crash before we knew. My gut feeling says we're dealing with sabotage—at the very least."

"You get a little stomach ache," Radisson said sarcastically, "and suddenly you're making wild accusations again."

Harper ignored Radisson and said, "But Colonel Phillips, the Soviets weren't flying out of some Pakistani airport where a bomb could be put on the President's airplane in a crate of mangoes. You're talking about a saboteur having to bypass security at a major airfield in either Moscow or Vladivostok."

Jack knew the next part would be even more difficult to sell. He wished that he could get rid of Radisson and talk only to Harper. However, he wondered if Harper were using Radisson's presence to provoke a level of anger just as Jack had tried to provoke Benes into a slip-up during the debriefing. He decided he did not care since he had nothing to hide. And if the general wanted to see some anger, he would oblige, especially if Radisson did not stop interrupting.

"Most likely," he said, "sabotage would've been an inside job, probably involving the crew. There's a Soviet phrase near the end of the FAA tape."

"I know," Harper said. "My team discovered that last night, but they haven't learned who said the words or what they mean."

"The phrase means two things. Translated, it means 'I serve the Soviet Union,' kind of a short version of an oath of commission and a pledge of allegiance all rolled into one. The most important thing it means, as far as this investigation's concerned, is that the radios weren't dead."

Radisson looked confused by Jack's logic.

Harper leaned forward with an expression indicating none of his investigators had yet made that point. "You're certain the transmission came from the airplane?"

"Background sounds match earlier contacts between Soviet National One and Oakland Center. Up to that point, no Russian words had been spoken on the radio. If someone at Oakland Center had tried to use Russian to make emergency contact with the crew, the words wouldn't have been 'I serve the Soviet Union.' " Jack added resolutely, "Soviet National One was the source."

Harper nodded. "Our investigation certainly takes on a different dimension if we can assume the Russian radios were still operational."

"That highlights one of the biggest unanswered questions of my investigation. Why plunge all the way to the water from more than twenty thousand feet and never utter a single Mayday, especially if you've got an operable radio tuned to the center's frequency the whole time?"

"Maybe the crew was too busy handling the emergency," Radisson said. "You should know that some pilots get a case of 'sweaty palms' when the pressure's on."

Jack glared at Radisson. "Listen to the damned tape, Colonel! You might *learn* something about keeping your shit together when you're looking death straight in the eye." He turned to Harper. "Pardon me, General, but there's not one decibel of panic in that pilot's voice."

Harper was giving his full attention. "Why not?"

"I think he knew exactly what was going to happen."

"Of course he knew," Radisson said, gesturing with his hands as if he were terribly frustrated by the answer. "What do—"

"Bob!" Harper's voice implied that he was running out of patience with his protégé.

Jack continued, "I believe the pilot knew he was going to crash before he left Vladivostok."

Harper leaned back, seeming to study the implications. Radisson exaggerated his look of disbelief and seemed to struggle to withhold his response before the general spoke. Finally Harper said, "I'd sooner accept that someone put a bomb aboard than that a pilot crashed the plane deliberately."

Jack said, "I don't know what it takes to convince a man to crash a plane or to drive a truckload of explosives into a Marine barracks in Beirut or to be a Viet Cong sapper. But that kind of thing happens."

"You're comparing apples and coconuts, Colonel," Radisson said. "There also were fanatics flying as *kamikazes* in World War II, but you're not talking war here. We're talking about peacetime and well-disciplined, professional airmen—and I mean airmen, plural. Even if one man went nuts, the other crewmen in the cockpit would stop him."

"I didn't say someone went nuts," Jack said. "I say it was pre-planned, which would have to include the cooperation of everyone in the cockpit."

"Even if that made sense," Radisson said, "the low altitude maneuvering blows any credibility this silly theory has."

Harper asked, "What do you mean by that, Bob?"

"If you were out to destroy that planeload of people," Radisson said confidently, "there'd be no reason to level off, sir." He turned to Jack and said facetiously, "Let's not crash here. Let's crash over there." His tone became decisive. "No way, Colonel!"

Jack hated to give Radisson credit, but he had pointed out two major flaws in the theory of an intentional crash. In time of war, professional soldiers accepted suicide missions, or at least the equivalent in which there was virtually no chance of survival. Jack was unsure how one could convince a dedicated Russian pilot, not to mention an entire crew, to give his life to assassinate much of the Soviet government. Jack assumed there were people who willingly would give their lives to kill Valinen. However, Jack doubted that any Valinen-haters would rise to the hand-picked unit that flew the leaders of the Soviet Union.

Radisson's argument about the final maneuvers of Soviet National One was even more convincing. If the pilot were trying to destroy the airplane, there was no need to stop the dive and fly a 270-degree turn before crashing.

Jack nodded. "It's difficult to explain why the pilot might choose one spot over another for the crash. But he never turned on the landing lights, so I don't think he was trying to ditch."

"Preposterous," Radisson said, "I can't believe you're wasting our time with this."

"Maybe, Colonel," Jack said, "you could find a more productive use of your time than interrupting my answers to the general's questions."

"Bob's raising some valid points," Harper said. "What you're suggesting is . . . well, rather difficult to believe."

Barely hiding his anger at having to put up with Radisson, Jack said, "I'm trying to interpret the facts that I see, General. I see a hand-picked crew flying well-maintained equipment and doing things that make no sense. First, I see them making a seventy-mile navigational error, probably while using our own Global Positioning System."

"Our system's better than that," Radisson said.

"That's exactly the point, Colonel," Jack said. "Our system's about seventy miles better than that, and I would expect that Soviet crew was too. For chrissakes, even *you* could beat seventy miles with a GPS."

Radisson jumped from his chair.

"Gentlemen," Harper said, "that's enough from both of you." He paused until Radisson sat down again. "How would you explain the seventy miles, Colonel Phillips?"

"The Soviets wanted an audience. If you're planning to kill half the Russian government, what better diversion than having a pair of F-15s close in trail when your bird hits the water?"

"You're suggesting they violated the ADIZ intentionally?"

"I can't think of an easier way to get a military escort, sir."

"But," Radisson said, "they had no way of knowing that one of my birds would launch a missile."

Jack was tempted to suggest that maybe the Russians knew Radisson was the commander and thought they might get lucky. Before he responded, however, there was a knock at the door. Harper's executive officer entered and said that Christine was waiting in the Command Post to join the meeting.

Harper invited the newswoman in and greeted her cordially. Almost as soon as the introductions were completed, however, the executive officer returned. He said that the networks were about to switch from their regular programs to a special report from the Russian consulate in San Francisco. Harper adjourned the meeting, and everyone went into the main Command Post.

Three television sets were on a table along one wall. Set on different channels, each showed a slightly different view of a room in the Soviet consulate. The volume was reduced on two sets. Only the narrator on the center set could be heard above the noise of the busy Command Post.

Jack was more interested in the actual announcement than the speculation, so he sat on the corner of an empty desk and waited.

Christine joined him and said, "You were hard to find this morning. What did I miss?"

He still was unwilling to share his new suspicions about the cause of the crash, so he decided to stall until the broadcast would take her attention away from the meeting with the general. "You missed the part where the three-star chewed on the colonel."

"Which colonel? You or Colonel Radisson?"

"Don't ask questions I can't stand the answer to, lady."

"You're not smiling," she said. "I'm sorry I missed it."

"You would've loved it."

"Any chance of an instant replay?"

"Not with this colonel, I hope." He smiled, then changed the subject. "How'd your taping go?"

"Fine. However, if this announcement's serious, my update may be old news before the tape gets to San Francisco."

"Any chance I can read your script?" She looked suspicious, so he added, "No censorship or trying to talk you into changing it or anything like that. My problem is that at the Pentagon, letting your boss be surprised is almost as bad as letting him be wrong." As she laughed, he continued, "So if your report's controversial and gets national coverage, I can let my boss know, and he'll let his boss know."

She pulled a folder from her purse and quickly leafed through the first few pages. She handed the papers to him and said in a tone that seemed to be a cross between facetious and flirtatious, "Any other requests, Colonel?"

He could think of a few he might make under other circumstances, but the mission-first part of him forced them from his mind. "Since you're offering, I didn't get to ask Mr. Braxton for a copy of the tape your cameraman shot last night. I need another look at the ships."

"Since you kept me from joining them, I suppose that's the least I can do for you, Colonel."

He started scanning the script, but stopped when Ambassador Sherinin came into view on the televisions. The Russian's expression was grim. He stepped behind the microphone-covered podium decorated with the hammer and sickle symbol. In lightly accented English, he read a statement.

The peoples of the Union of Soviet Socialist Republics look with extreme concern upon the unprovoked attack made by American aggressor pilots on the unarmed airliner carryng many patriots of the Soviet government. The Soviet people join the peoples of the world in condemning this reckless act of aggression and in demanding that the pilots and their conspirators be given swift punishment for their crimes.

Premier Konstantin Medvalev has this day ordered termination of diplomatic relations between the peoples of the Union of Soviet Socialist Republics and the government of the United States of America.

Exclamations of surprise and disbelief rose from the audiences in the consulate and the Command Post.

Looking shocked, Christine asked Jack, "Has there ever been a break between Russia and America? That didn't even happen during the Cuban missile crisis, did it?"

"Negative."

He glanced at the board showing the alert status of American forces as if he subconsciously expected the ambassador's words to instantly change the DEFCON status. He hoped this Soviet action would jolt the President into a quick response.

Ambassador Sherinin stepped from the podium. A moment of stunned silence prevailed. Then a roar of questions erupted from the reporters as they realized Sherinin was finished. He ignored them and disappeared through a side door.

The television pictures switched back to newsmen. The anchorman on the center set hesitated, obviously surprised by the brevity and the dramatic content of the Soviet statement. Finally he said, "We had expected strong rhetoric. Yesterday's surprise revelations about possible involvement by our Air Force in the crash almost ensured a response of outrage once Premier Medvalev decided how to react. However, Ambassador Sherinin's brief announcement goes further than anyone had predicted. Everyone here is simply stunned. It's hard to remember a precedent. Breaks between world powers normally come when the nations have gone to war—or are about to.

"What are the implications of this break? Will there be a complete exodus of Soviet diplomatic personnel? While we seek answers, here's Fred Clark in Red Square for comments on this startling development."

The picture switched to a nighttime scene in Moscow. Light snow was falling. The American newsman stood in the snow with scores of people in the background.

"Throughout this afternoon and evening," Clark said, "thousands of Russian citizens have been passing by the memorial wreaths placed beside the Kremlin wall. This appears to be a genuine outpouring of grief for the fallen leaders.

"The announcement we just heard goes beyond anything we anticipated. However, there were rumors that the U.S. Air Force is trying to determine if American F-15s fired more than one missile at Soviet National One."

"Colonel Phillips," Harper called out above the sound of the newsman.

"We looked, General," Jack said, standing in response to the Harper's call. "Nothing indicated more than one."

Harper returned his attention to the television.

Jack looked at Christine questioningly, since she had heard the subject discussed the previous evening.

"My reports didn't raise the question," she said. "Last night you sounded satisfied with paperwork on the missiles. I don't report non-stories."

Jack nodded. He wondered about O'Donnell—maybe he was still talking more than he should be.

Clark continued, "There was another new angle here this afternoon. The Kremlin announced that . . ." He paused to read the name from a piece of paper. "Colonel Nikolai Bochkov has been declared a 'Hero of the Soviet Union.' The veteran pilot was at the controls of Soviet National One. The Ministry of Defense reported that Bochkov's last words as he struggled to save the crippled jet were a declaration of his dedication to serving the Soviet Union."

Interesting, Jack thought. How had the Soviets learned of the Russian statement on the FAA tape? Perhaps they already had recovered the cockpit voice recorder. He quickly dismissed the recorder as the source of a story Clark would have heard rumored in the afternoon in Moscow. There simply was not enough time to get the recorder to a laboratory and to recover the data.

Clark concluded, "But if Premier Medvalev believes a deliberate attack downed the aircraft, it's easy to understand the break in diplomatic relations. Heroes like Colonel Bochkov stir genuine patriotism among the Russian people. That surge of patriotism may increase Medvalev's mandate for action. We can only speculate about his next move."

The anchorman at the Soviet consulate in San Francisco reappeared on the television screen. "We have just learned that several Aeroflot airliners are en route from the Soviet Union to carry diplomatic personnel and their families home from the United States. Consulate personnel expect Ambassador Sherinin to leave from San Francisco tomorrow morning without returning to Washington. We hope to have a reaction soon from the Western White House. Now here's a look at reactions of some of the Warsaw Pact allies. Of course, these pictures were taped before the stunning announcement you heard moments ago."

The next scene was captioned Prague, Czechoslovakia. The narrator explained that Czech citizens were placing wreaths and flowers around a black-draped picture of Minister Valinen.

"Right," Jack said, sarcastically. "I can imagine how broken up the people of Czechoslovakia are over Valinen's death."

Christine asked, "What do you *really* think about what we've just seen?"

"On the record or off?"

"On, of course."

"No comment. As a military officer, I have no on-the-record opinions on the diplomacy conducted between the United States and other nations." He started dividing his attention between the television sets and the script Christine had given him earlier.

She waited, then said, "Okay, Colonel. Off the record."

"Off the record, I think Premier Medvalev knows they've got us by the—that they have us on the defensive. He'll wring every drop of propaganda he can out of the missile firing. What else could he have done, short of a military attack, that would have grabbed more attention in every world capital?" He paused to give her a chance to respond. Then, he added, "Now we need to go onto a military alert—and we'd damned well better do it in a hurry."

"Wouldn't an alert give Medvalev even more headlines? He can claim the diplomatic high ground."

"Right."

"Then you're making no sense," she said. "If an alert plays into Medvalev's hands, why would President Cunningham make that kind of mistake?"

"I didn't say it was a mistake. Deterrence is played at two levels."

"I'm not sure what you mean."

"Politicians work deterrence on their level, but they'd better have the military punch ready—ask the ones who thought they were deterring Hitler. Right now, the Soviets are a hell of a lot better prepared for a fight than we are." He gestured toward the status board that showed American forces at DEFCON Four. "Until the DEFCON One light flashes on, stay a little bit—no, a whole lot—nervous."

She looked shocked. "I thought DEFCON One meant we're going to war."

"Not if the alert comes early enough." She looked unconvinced, so Jack continued. "Simple logic. If you're a Soviet, and you finally decide war's worth the risk, one of—"

"Why would I decide that? No one's going to win a nuclear war."

"Check out the massive underground facilities built for the Soviet civil defense program. Then tell me no one believes a nuclear war can be won."

"Do you think they can win, or even survive? What about the nuclear winter?"

He was pleased by her knowledgeable questions. "I didn't say your decision had to be logical to us—only to you. You may choose war for a number of reasons. *Perestroika*'s gotten away from you, and you're losing the nationalities at home. Maybe your rivals in the Politburo are ganging up on you, and you're on your way out anyway. Maybe you've learned so much about American nuclear submarines and NATO defenses from your spies that you believe the right opening strategy will win it for you."

"I suppose you can tell me what my strategy would be."

"No, but I know one thing. You'll hit with a surprise attack while we're sitting fat, dumb, and happy at DEFCON Four or Five."

"What makes you so sure?"

"Surprise has long been the most important principle in the art of war."

"Your expert opinion, Colonel?"

"I wouldn't argue hard against the statement," he said with a smile. "But those words were translated from a Soviet tactics manual. Anyway, you'd want our bombers and fighters clustered at their home bases, our warships in port, and the President at his desk." He gestured again toward the status board. "That's why, early in a crisis, I want DEFCON Two or One lit up."

"But I'll notice when you put everything on alert. Won't that scare me into attacking?"

"Depends on the timing. If you're thirty minutes from your attack, you may launch as soon as you see our DEFCON Two or One light blink on. Then you're gambling that you can deal a crippling blow before I get enough forces ready to fight. If your attack was two days away, you'll probably put your plans on hold."

She nodded. "And instead of attacking, I turn on my propaganda machine."

"Right. Screaming about how the 'reactionary imperialist circles are striving to wreck detente, to prevent disarmament, and to provoke a world war'—that's also out of the Soviet manual. When we finally come off alert, you restart the clock on your plan."

"Are you saying the Soviets are about to attack?"

"I don't know what they're up to. But I'm nervous anytime the Soviets deploy in major war games and we're home watching the NFL playoffs on TV."

"So the President's making a mistake by not putting all our forces on alert?"

He smiled and said, "We've already been through the 'colonel critiques the President' routine. I don't challenge the President's foreign policy decisions."

"But if I see the *Minsk* sail through the Golden Gate, I'll know he's waited too long."

"Better be careful," he said facetiously. "Keep thinking that logically, and they'll never let you into the Washington press corps."

As the three television sets continued showing reporters rehashing the ambassador's announcement, he studied the script of her report. She had not speculated about a second missile. Much of her story was her interpretation of the possible mechanical causes of the crash. Generally, her treatment of the issues he was concerned about was superficial, as television reports almost inevitably were. Nothing was controversial enough to warn General McClintock about.

As he turned toward the television sets, the picture on one changed so abruptly that he thought the color had failed. The new picture was a dull, gray ocean scene. The ghostly outlines of three ships were barely visible in the fog. Where the fog did not link the clouds with the ocean, the dark clouds were just above the tall antennas on the ships. The absence of color reminded him of black-and-white movies of convoys in the North Atlantic during World War II. Yet one of these ships was a modern destroyer. As he went forward and increased the volume on that set, he suddenly understood what he was seeing—but he did not want to believe it.

"Are we on? Are we transmitting yet?" An unidentified voice came from the set showing the ocean scene. "The ships . . ." The voice accompanying the picture sounded uncertain as the camera zoomed in on the destroyer that was nearly a mile away. After a pause the voice continued more confidently. "The destroyer in the distance is a warship of the Soviet Navy. The waters are just off the California coast."

"Bruce, no," Christine said quietly as she recognized Bruce Kane's voice. She put her coffee cup on the desk and clasped her hands in front of her.

"Oh, God," General Harper said. Turning toward one of the colonels on his inspection team, he added, "Some fool's in the restricted zone. Get the Air Staff on the line. The network may not be broadcasting this in Washington."

The colonel hurried to a telephone.

The camera doing the on-scene filming swung left, showing the front of the boat carrying the news team. The picture focused on the narrator standing beside the driver of the speedboat.

"Good morning, ladies and gentlemen. This is Bruce Kane broadcasting live from where Soviet National One crashed less than thirty-six hours ago. I'm on one of two small boats sent out this morning to bring on-the-scene reports of the recovery of wreckage of the Soviet jetliner."

His bright blue raincoat contrasted sharply with the dull grays of the previous scene. He gripped the windshield with one hand and his microphone with the other. Even with the boat traveling at a reduced speed, he had difficulty maintaining his balance as the boat pitched unsteadily from swell to swell.

"Please bear with us," he continued. "This is a live telecast under difficult conditions. We are approximately twenty miles west of Point Reyes. Navigation through numerous fog banks and over four-to-six-foot seas is extremely challenging. We've been in and out of fog since leaving the dock. However, our captain has done a superb job. Why am I so confident that we've reached the right spot in these vast miles of ocean? Here's your answer."

He motioned to the side with his microphone. The camera followed the motion, and the background changed to a darker gray. When the camera refocused, the new background was identifiable. It was the hull of a Soviet ship less than two hundred yards from the speedboat.

Nearly everyone in the Command Post gasped or swore. The ambitious young newsman's flair for the dramatic, Jack thought, was going to get him killed.

Kane continued, "We're approaching three large Soviet ships that are floating side-by-side. Two appear to be large merchant vessels. The third is a military ship of a rather unconventional design. Several other ships are nearby."

The cameraman tried to show all three. However, the bow of the closest ship blocked most of the view of the other two. The long bow of the center ship was still visible.

Jack watched closely and saw the outline of doors on the bow of the middle ship. He was nearly positive it was the *Ivan Rogov*, the first of the Soviet's advanced class of amphibious warfare ships. Having that ship onscene was another interesting piece of "luck," he thought. Equipped with many smaller craft, it was well suited for recovery operations in the open sea.

He remembered General McClintock's comment about how having the submarine rescue vessel *Karpaty* nearby was such a stroke of good luck. Jack was willing to accept that the Russians could be lucky. He was always suspicious, however, whenever they were lucky twice in a row.

If there had been prior knowledge of the plane crash, he thought, someone also could have chosen which ships would be nearest to the California coast at the time of the crash. That idea sent a chill through him—ships did not cross oceans overnight. If sabotage *had* caused the crash, he wondered how long ago someone had decided that Soviet National One would not reach San Francisco.

As Kane continued trying to describe ships he did not understand, the camera tilted skyward momentarily, giving Jack a glimpse of what appeared to be camouflage netting stretched between the two ships. Tough trick, he thought, especially in rough seas. He wanted to see more, but the camera scanned toward the side of the nearby ship.

Although he had not expected the Soviets to hide their actions, he was not totally surprised. Deception and camouflage were ingrained in the psyche of the Soviet military, just as air superiority was a basic tenet of the U.S. Air Force.

"General Harper," he said, "did you notice—"

Harper raised his hand for silence. "Quiet. I want to hear this."

Jack moved away from the television sets and sat on the edge of the desk beside Christine. The camouflaged netting gave him an uneasy feeling he wanted to discuss with the general. The netting seemed unnecessary—unless the Russians were trying to keep outsiders from seeing the wreckage lifted from the ocean.

He wondered if, somewhere in the Soviet Union, another Il-62 had been selected for sacrifice. He pictured a plane with engines idling, sitting on an isolated taxiway somewhere in central Russia. From a safe distance Soviet soldiers prepared to fire a missile toward the hot exhausts of the aircraft. A streaking flash and a thunderous explosion would provide wreckage for display in Moscow. Those shattered engine nacelles would support Soviet charges of American deceit and aggression.

The President must demand the acceptance of an international recovery force, he thought. Unbiased observers were vital—whether the Soviets wanted them or not.

Kane's boat kept its distance, moving parallel to the port side of the towering ship.

"We're told," Kane said, "this Russian freighter had been en route to San Francisco when Soviet National One was shot down or crashed."

"Irresponsible," Jack said in response to Kane's use of the term "shot down." He frowned in Christine's direction. She did not refute his criticism.

Smiling, Kane continued, "Unfortunately, my Russian is a little rusty, so I can't read the name of the ship for you."

The camera showed Cyrillic letters painted on the bow. The speedboat already had passed the lettering, so the angle made the two words difficult to read, but Jack was pretty sure the ship's name was *Tibor Szamueli*. He wrote that name in his notebook.

"But," Kane continued, "we are coming up on a word I can read."

The camera panned toward midships on the freighter. Well above the water line, the word "INTERLIGHTER" was painted in block letters that extended approximately 150 feet along the side of the freighter. Jack recognized it as the markings he had seen on a ship as he flew to Chaney Air Force Base the previous evening.

"In big, white letters, we see the word—" Kane stopped in response to distant popping sounds from somewhere beyond the bow of the Soviet ship. The camera panned to him briefly, then pointed toward the fog-shrouded horizon. "That sounds as if they're using small explosives for something."

A larger explosion echoed beneath the low clouds.

Although the young newsman obviously did not understand what he had heard, Jack did. He had recognized the high-pitched, humming whine that had preceded the firecracker-like noises by less than two seconds. The whine was the characteristic noise of a Gatling gun spitting out shells faster than anyone could count. The short interval between the whine and the explosions told him the gun had been fired at close range. He assumed that the Soviets had located and destroyed the other speedboat Kane had mentioned earlier.

He grabbed Christine's arm and said, "If you know how to get hold of Kane's studio, tell them to get him out of there now!"

"I realize you don't agree with Bruce and that the President's restricted entry—"

"The President and I are the least of Kane's problems." He could tell that she still did not understand. "Those people are going to blow him away. The Soviets just attacked the other boat, and Kane's next."

She hesitated, then reached for an address book in her purse. "I think I have their number."

He turned to a young captain serving as the Command Post duty controller. "Captain, get this call through as an Immediate!"

The Immediate precedence was reserved for calls that could have an immediate operational effect on tactical operations or that directly concerned the safety of rescue operations. He rationalized that getting the call through might avoid an attack on the American newsmen and preclude additional rescue or tactical operations.

Since nothing of interest was visible in the direction of the noises, the camera returned to Kane.

He gestured toward the ship behind him and continued, "As I was saying, there's the word 'Interlighter.' Apparently this freighter was coming to America to pick up a load of goods. Now it seems the cargo for the return trip will include the twisted wreckage of Soviet National One." He motioned with his microphone toward the deck railing above the lettering. "We've attracted an audience."

He continued ad libbing as the camera zoomed in on several men at the railing. They appeared to be merchant seamen, soldiers, and rescue personnel.

Jack thought that was an interesting combination. He expected the seamen, curious about the visit by the American speedboat. However, the two soldiers and their AK-47 automatic weapons were out of place on a merchant vessel. Perhaps, he thought, the soldiers had flown from a Navy ship hidden nearby in the fog.

Three men were dressed in wet suits of the type worn by scuba divers, and he also was curious about their presence. The wreckage was too deep for scuba divers, who worked much nearer the surface. Perhaps they could be helpful in attaching cradles to pieces of wreckage once large cranes raised the wreckage to the surface.

As he tried to think of other uses for them, a commotion erupted among the men at the railing. One diver climbed onto the railing, but a seaman grabbed the diver's arm. The soldiers rushed toward the struggling men. Before they reached him, the diver broke free and vaulted over the railing.

Kane was speechless as the flailing form hurtled toward the ocean. About halfway to the water, the man stabilized with his frog fins pointed downward and his face mask held high above his head.

The diver hit the water, and the rapid staccato of automatic weapons brought the cameraman's attention and the camera to the railing. The two soldiers fired several bursts downward. Then they stopped, ready to fire when the diver surfaced again. He had jumped without any breathing apparatus, so he would have to surface soon—if he had survived the jump.

"We have just witnessed a death-defying leap for freedom of at least fifty feet." Kane's voice betrayed his excitement. "A Soviet frogman is apparently trying to defect to our boat. The Soviet soldiers are trying to stop him. We can't tell if he survived the jump or the gunfire that followed."

He continued describing the scene as the speedboat angled toward the ship. The picture showed a closeup view of the water, but did not reveal the diver. One soldier fired a short burst. The camera aimed where the bullets had hit. Only the waves were visible.

Christine rejoined Jack and said that the station was going to try to contact Kane.

When the picture switched to the men along the railing, Jack saw no reaction to the previous firing. He assumed that the soldiers had missed. One soldier turned his gun in the direction of the speedboat. Almost immediately, twinkling flashes sparkled from the gun.

"Look out," he said an instant before Kane shouted the same warning.

As the sounds of the gunfire reached the speedboat, the driver slammed the throttle forward and turned away from the Soviet ship. The camera momentarily showed clouds, then pointed at the bottom of the boat.

Jack heard bullets ricocheting off the water and passing over the boat. He assumed the bullets were just warning shots to scare off the newsmen. He also heard an argument away from the microphone. Kane wanted to turn back toward the ship. The driver wanted to flee.

The camera showed the three distant ships as the speedboat continued in a wide circle. Jack wondered why those three Soviet ships, which Kane had shown earlier in his broadcast, were so far away. He decided the ships must be recovering debris that had floated toward the coast in the day and a half since the crash.

The soldiers at the railing fired at the diver again and again, but each time they were too late. Finally, only one soldier fired a short burst.

"They're out of bullets," Kane shouted. "Let's get him."

The boat surged toward the diver's last position as the camera showed an animated conversation between the two soldiers. One motioned toward the stern. The other soldier hurried away in that direction.

The roar of the engines overwhelmed Kane's attempts to describe what was happening. Only the words "There he is" could be understood. The camera showed him pointing as the speedboat plowed roughly through the uneven seas. Finally, the driver pulled the throttles to idle, and the nose of the speedboat lowered enough for the camera to show the water ahead.

Less than fifty yards away, the diver's head appeared momentarily above the water, then disappeared. Kane urged on the defector while intermingling instructions to the driver on how to maneuver the boat.

The diver surfaced again, only seconds after he had gone under.

"Hurry," Kane shouted as he motioned to the man in the water. "No bullets. *Nyet* bullets!"

The diver seemed to recognize that there had been no gunfire after the last two times he had surfaced for air. He swam toward the speedboat, varying his direction every fourth or fifth stroke to be a more elusive target.

The driver kept his speedboat away from the ship. He maneuvered so that one side was toward the diver, and the bow was pointed away for a quick escape.

Describing the diver's progress toward the boat, Kane also pointed out how significant his decision had been to come on-scene for the news report. Just as Jack began to believe that Kane might get away with grabbing the story of a lifetime that the newsman was after, the noise of a helicopter became audible in the background. The sound increased a few seconds before anyone in the boat seemed to notice.

Someone shouted, "Let's get out of here!"

Kane pointed toward the stern of the Soviet ship, and the camera followed.

A Hind-D helicopter had flown around the stern. At an altitude about halfway between the water and the railing of the ship, the helicopter raced toward the speedboat and diver.

The diver either heard the helicopter or noticed that the attention of the Americans was directed at something else. He stopped swimming and shouted.

At first his words were inaudible. Then Kane extended the microphone toward the diver.

"Zemletryasenie! Zemletryasenie!" The diver shouted and looked again toward the helicopter. *"Budet Vzryv!"* He looked once more toward the helicopter, then swam directly for the speedboat.

"Jack," General Harper said, "what's the defector shouting?"

"I'm not sure, sir. The first part sounded like 'country shock' or maybe 'field shock.' Then he said something like there's 'going to be an explosion.' That could mean—"

"They're about to get their asses blown away," Radisson interrupted.

"Seems like as good a guess as any," Jack acknowledged.

The camera showed the helicopter, which had climbed almost to the height of the deck. The pilot kept close to the ship until his helicopter was between the ship and the speedboat. Then he banked left and dropped the nose into a shallow dive. Immediately, the Hind-D's weapon operator fired the machine gun in the chin turret.

Bullets churned the water short of the swimmer, then walked a deadly path forward. The swimmer screamed, and so did Kane. The cries were drowned out by the sounds of the exploding bullets and the helicopter roaring overhead. The picture on the television jittered, then showed an out-of-focus view of the inside of the boat.

Moaning could be heard as the helicopter's noise decreased. Moments later, the engines on the speedboat roared above idle. The picture bounced crazily as the boat sped away.

Slowly the cameraman lifted the camera and focused on the scene around him. The picture shuddered as the boat smashed from wave to wave, but the damage was evident. Kane's blue raincoat was spattered with blood. Unmoving, he was slumped across one seat and hanging over the side of the boat.

"No," Christine said, then began sobbing. Jack put his arm around her.

The picture showed a jagged hole above the water line in the side of the boat. The windshield was shattered, and part of the frame had been blown away. The driver, with a bloody arm hanging limply at his side, stood at the wheel. He divided his attention between guiding his boat through the sea and watching the Soviet helicopter.

The camera swung back to the helicopter, which had swooped into position directly behind the fleeing speedboat. The camera lurched momentarily as the driver began zigzagging.

The cameraman's got balls, Jack thought, as he watched the frightening pictures. It was the most audacious display of combat photography he had ever seen.

There was little time for the speedboat's maneuvering to have any effect. Beneath the stubby wings of the helicopter, the outboard UB-32 rocket pods flashed. A pair of fifty-seven-millimeter S-5 rockets raced away from the helicopter. Heat waves similar to those rising from a desert highway on a hot afternoon blurred the helicopter's image as sixty-two more rockets roared from the pods in quick succession. The picture on the television changed to static as the high explosive rockets obliterated the speedboat.

"No!" Christine cried out, louder this time. She pushed her face against Jack's shoulder.

"Your call was too late," he said, unable to think of anything that would comfort her.

A "Please stand by" placard replaced the blank screen for a moment, then the picture switched to the anchorman at the Soviet consulate. He did little more than acknowledge that the station had lost contact with the speedboats sent to photograph the Soviet ships.

General Harper told the duty officer to get a secure line to General McClintock's office on the Command Post aircraft. Then Harper added to Radisson, "Bob, I'm not sure if this will convince the President it's time to put more forces on alert. While we're waiting to find out, I suggest you see how many Eagles you can get armed and ready."

Jack was surprised that Harper would suggest increasing the alert force while Christine was present. However, she seemed completely absorbed in shock and grief over the attack on Kane's news team.

"General," Jack said, "you need to tell General McClintock about the camouflage netting between the Soviet ships." He explained his concerns about the Soviets' extraordinary efforts to recover the wreckage without anyone else observing the pieces. As Harper entered the booth, he agreed to discuss those concerns.

For the next few minutes, Jack answered Christine's questions about the attack and whether there was even a small chance anyone survived. He offered no hope.

As they talked, he realized he was subconsciously disturbed by something he had seen or Kane had said. Something had been wrong, but he had no idea what. He sometimes had experienced similar feelings immediately after air combat. In those days, as he had evaded North Vietnamese missiles, perhaps there had been a fluctuating oil pressure reading or an exhaust gas temperature climbing toward the upper limit. As the life-or-death intensity of combat had subsided, he had been nagged subconsciously until remembering what needed to be checked.

Now, as he divided his attention between Christine and the three television sets, he had that same feeling.

In a live broadcast from his studio a few minutes later, Alexander Braxton summarized what was known about the latest attack.

"On this extraordinary morning, the Soviets have sent strong messages diplomatically and militarily. The break in diplomatic relations between the world's two superpowers is unprecedented. Premier Medvalev has protested—in the strongest diplomatic terms—the firing on Soviet National One by an American jet fighter. However, we should keep in mind what he did not do—he did not order military retaliation. Premier Medvalev's message actually may have been one of restraint.

"Contrast his restraint with the brutal attack on unarmed journalists witnessed only minutes ago. Not since Vietnam has the realism of combat been brought so vividly into American homes. Obviously, Premier Medvalev could not have known the newsmen would enter the area. This attack seems to have been directed by the local Soviet naval commander in reaction to the newsmen's violation of the restricted zone.

"One lesson is clear. Everyone should stay away from the search and recovery zone where the President has promised the Soviet Union unhampered access. And I suggest we all pray that cooler heads will prevail. If quiet diplomacy cannot calm this crisis, we could see an escalation to open combat between the Soviet Union and the United States."

Chapter 14

Tuesday Morning, 9:50 a.m.
Pacific Standard Time

MOMENTS AFTER WATCHING THE ATTACK ON KANE'S BOAT, PRESIDENT Cunningham had ordered a call to Moscow. Fifteen minutes later, Secretary of State Winston Shafer reached the President's study in the Western White House. Cunningham was still sitting behind his massive desk waiting for Premier Medvalev to answer the call. Shafer put his raincoat aside and sat in a chair near the desk.

Cunningham gestured toward three men who were busily involved at the communications suite. "The Russians are stalling, Winston! If Medvalev really wants to see how far I'll go, he's about to find out."

Shafer spoke in calmer tones. "He probably knows less about the shooting than you do. If the situation were reversed, you'd want to know what happened before trying to calm him."

"The situation isn't reversed," Cunningham said angrily as he rolled his chair forward and leaned on the desk. "It's not just the shooting. Medvalev gave damned little notice about breaking relations. I may have to take that kind of 'cooperation' from the Speaker of the House, but I'll be damned if I'll let the premier keep shooting Americans without learning he's crossed the line."

"Still," Shafer said, trying to calm Cunningham, "our embassy reports there's genuine anger among the average Russian over the possi—"

"Medvalev's not running for reelection," Cunningham said. "The 'people' can play ring-around-the-Kremlin, and Medvalev'll still do what's best for Medvalev." He stood and looked toward the men working at the communications suite. "What's happening, Leonid?"

Leonid Petrov, the President's interpreter, pushed the mouthpiece of his headset aside and said, "The premier is still unavailable, Mr. President."

"Tell whoever *is* available," Cunningham said in a deliberate tone, "that the President is about to place all American military forces on

170

full alert, and that the President had intended to offer the premier the courtesy of discussing the change before implementing it."

"Yes, Mr. President," Petrov said before speaking Russian rapidly into the headset.

Cunningham placed his hand on the red telephone connecting his office to the National Military Command Center. "Americans killed twice within twenty-four hours in our coastal waters more than justifies a military alert."

"But Marsh," Shafer said as he rose from his chair, "we don't have confirmation yet on any deaths this mo—"

"Christ, Winston," Cunningham said, yanking the receiver of the telephone from its holder, "I saw enough. I don't have to touch the corpses."

"But has Medvalev ordered a military reaction yet? His response to our missile was diplomatic, not military."

Cunningham paused to consider Shafer's argument. In the background, the words "Yes, Mr. President," were audible from the telephone in Cunningham's hand. He raised the telephone and said, "Good morning, General. Have you seen any changes in the last twenty-four hours indicating the Soviets are positioning for an attack?"

"Negative, Mr. President. Other than this morning's attack by the helicopter from the *Udaloy,* nothing's changed in the naval exercises we've watched for two weeks, sir."

"Their Strategic Rocket Forces?"

"Normal operations, sir. They're on routine alert, fighting the weather just as our crews are in Montana, Wyoming, and North Dakota."

"And no changes in the Warsaw Pact games?"

"They've quieted some, sir. It's dark in Eastern Europe now, of course. They haven't conducted operations after dark for the last six nights. In fact, about seven hours ago, there were general movements back from the exercise's most forward positions."

"What would that mean, General?"

"They may be between phases or maybe they're starting to terminate."

"How about—"

"Pardon me, Mr. President," Petrov said, "Premier Medvalev will be on in a few moments."

Cunningham nodded, then spoke into the red telephone. "General, I'm considering changing the DEFCON, but I'll hold off for now. Call immediately if the Soviets change anything significant."

He hung up the red telephone and activated the speaker-phone for the hot line. After the initial formalities, he spoke as Petrov translated. "Mr. Premier, recalling Ambassador Sherinin to Moscow increases the danger in this difficult situation."

"The attack by your fighters caused serious tumult among the people. Many demand punishment for that criminal act."

"By evening, Mr. Premier, two hundred million Americans will have watched pictures of your helicopter attacking unarmed newsmen. There will be *serious tumult* among the people here, too."

"Perhaps you should forbid your newsmen from such dangerous and provocative actions."

For once, Cunningham thought, he almost agreed with Medvalev. "In this country, Mr. Premier, we do not control newsmen."

"The Soviet people cannot be responsible for the unfortunate results of such provocations. The people say I am foolish to accept the word of the American President. How am I to answer those criticisms, Mr. President?"

Angered by Medvalev's goading, Cunningham slowly twisted his fountain pen in and out of its cap. Reluctantly he continued the ritual of words necessary before they finally would back into the real discussion. "I have ordered our forces to respect the recovery zone. Surely the captains of your powerful warships were not frightened by two civilian boats armed only with news cameras."

"Most reactionary attacks by American warships in the Persian Gulf were against Iranian speedboats like those that put our ships in peril today."

"There was no justification for firing this morning."

"The captain's first responsibility is the protection of his ship and his crew." Petrov blushed and appeared hesitant to continue. "That, Mr. President, is what your American Navy said to justify the careless killing of three hundred innocent civilians on the airliner over the Persian Gulf."

Cunningham twisted his pen so hard that it stuck in its cap. He frowned his impatience in Shafer's direction. Finally he responded in slow, resolute tones. "That was a war zone. It was dangerous for civilian airliners to fly into that zone."

"Many Soviet people believe it is dangerous for Russian airliners to fly into America. But I am trying to be a voice of reason among loud voices of unreason."

Perhaps, Cunningham thought, Medvalev finally was ready to be substantive. "I seek to hear reason, Mr. Premier, but the unreason of the new killings and the break in relations overwhelms all sounds of reason."

"The break was necessary. The people's demands for revenge could not be quieted by anything less."

"Many Americans will interpret the break as preparations for war. They will demand no less than a full military alert of American forces."

"If our diplomatic action receives a military response, you force me to choose a military response. That cycle may be without end—unless we agree to end it now."

Shafer said quietly to Cunningham. "See what he suggests."

Cunningham nodded and said, "Ordering your ambassador to return to Moscow has started the cycle."

"That action is not irreversible. Military actions could become irreversible."

"How soon would the break in diplomatic relations be reversed?"

"If our investigators find other causes for the crash, there is no need to continue protesting the unwarranted firing of the missile."

"When would Ambassador Sherinin return?"

"Within days after our people are told the cause of the crash. Of course, out of respect, no serious negotiations about a new date for the treaty signing can happen until after the mourning period."

Shafer nodded and gave Cunningham a thumbs-up signal following the mention of the treaty.

Cunningham wondered if the mourning period would stretch into months of anti-American rhetoric, allowing Medvalev to postpone the conference indefinitely. Finally he said, "Your arrangements regarding the treaty are understandable and acceptable. However, if I do not put American forces on alert today, you would need to announce within the next few days the results of your investigation and your commitment to restore diplomatic relations. Even then, I may be unable to hold off making some response for as long as your investigation takes."

"The heroic seamen of the Soviet Navy have made miraculous progress despite difficult weather and treacherous ocean currents. Much wreckage, including the flight recorders, has been located. We soon should understand the secrets the recorders contain."

Cunningham still wanted a commitment. "If the American people believe you are stalling for propaganda purposes, they will demand I take strong action. There must be no delay in resolving the crisis."

"You have my word, Mr. President. If your fighters did not cause the crash, the government of the Soviet people will announce those findings immediately."

Shafer nodded his encouragement.

Cunningham had mixed feelings. He was pleased to see some hope for a quick resolution of the diplomatic crisis. However, he was still angry because of both attacks on Americans. "I shall try to overcome the so-called voices of unreason here who demand a stronger American response. But you should not miscalculate, Mr. Premier. Too many Americans have died this week in front of Russian guns. Additional firings by your military forces will not go unopposed."

Medvalev responded before his translator had spoken half the President's message.

"I shall raise your concerns about too many American deaths with Minister Valinen—the next time I talk to him."

Cunningham clicked off the speaker-phone and said loud enough for only Shafer to understand, "You do that, Konstantin—you sarcastic son of a bitch."

Petrov pushed an earphone aside and turned toward the President to find out what was said. "I'm sorry, Mr. President. I missed that."

"Sleep well, Mr. Premier." Cunningham slid his fingers past his neck in a gesture indicating he was ready to cut off the conversation. He sat quietly until Petrov completed the closing formalities and removed his headset.

Cunningham said to Shafer, "I don't know whether he wants a quick end to the crisis or not."

"In four or five days," Shafer said, "we'll know if Ambassador Sherinin's returning right away."

"You may be right," Cunningham said. Gesturing toward the red telephone, he added, "We'll hold off on the alert, but get Alex Braxton over here. I want to know how he's reading all this."

Fifty-one hundred miles away, Premier Medvalev removed his headset. The premier was in a command center deep beneath the woods near Lytkarino, just beyond the southeast suburbs of Moscow. He sat behind a desk and electronic console on an elevated platform near the back of the largest room in the command center. Three other chairs were on each side of him, with high-ranking officials sitting in each.

Most of the front wall was covered with Plexiglas, which was lighted from behind and outlined with a map of the world. Words and symbols written in luminous markers were scattered over the map, showing the locations of major military units.

A status board, which had been added four days earlier, was centered above the map on the front wall. The word *ISKRA* was lettered on an unlit panel at the top of the board. Two countdown timers were mounted beneath the title. One timer was labeled as *Pervaya Zadacha* (First Mission) and set at 20:00. The other timer was set at 44:00 and labeled *Vtoraya Zadacha* (Second Mission). The numbers were unlit and unchanging, awaiting future events to activate them.

Medvalev sat quietly until the lights on his communications panel went out, confirming that the hot line had been disconnected. He turned to the uniformed man sitting beside him and said, "Well, Andrei, do you agree with President Cunningham that the American casualties have been excessive?"

Leaning back in his chair, Minister of Defense Valinen said, "Tonight the American President can still count his dead on his fingers." Gesturing toward the new status board on the front wall, Valinen added in a voice devoid of emotion, "When *Iskra* ignites, he will be unable to count the dead."

Medvalev nodded. "If he's still alive to do the counting."

Chapter 15

Tuesday Morning, 10:05 a.m.
Pacific Standard Time

GENERAL HARPER FINISHED HIS TELEPHONE CALL WITH GENERAL McClintock, who was flying to California on the National Emergency Airborne Command Post. Exiting the booth for the secure telephone, Harper joined Jack and Christine.

Harper said, "Colonel, you're relieved."

In more ways than one, Jack thought. "Yes, sir," he said, concealing his eagerness to leave this part of the investigation. Remaining at Howell would have meant repeated arguments with Colonel Radisson, and Jack would have won few in General Harper's presence. Jack preferred to fade into the background and work quietly behind the power of General McClintock's four stars. Also, the new orders meant he could shed the burden of dealing with Christine Merrill's questions.

"General McClintock wants you with him on the E-4B."

"At Travis, sir?"

"They'll land at Travis in an hour," Harper said, "but he doesn't think they'll stay."

Christine asked, "Why not, General?"

Harper hesitated a moment, then answered. "Travis Air Force Base is nearly fifty miles from the Western White House. Other airfields are closer."

Her instincts as a journalist helped her overcome the shock of watching Kane's death. "I understand the E-4B is the President's wartime command post. Does General McClintock believe we are about to go to war?"

Harper looked uneasy. "I can't speak for the vice chief. However, moving the E-4B even closer is a natural precaution in light of this morning's events."

Jack asked, "Is General McClintock expecting to end up at Alameda Naval Air Station?"

176

Harper nodded. "He'll pass the word as soon as the decision is made. He wants to see you at fourteen-hundred hours."

Harper took Christine to meet his executive officer who would serve as her new point of contact.

The television reports of the last few minutes had raised many new questions. Jack was particularly curious about one new issue: How did the Soviets know about the Russian statement on the FAA tape? While waiting to learn the E-4B's final destination, he called Brad Lindon, a friend who worked at the FAA's Western/Pacific Region office in Los Angeles.

Responding to a question about cooperation between the FAA and Soviet investigators, Lindon said, "We've offered to let them analyze the flight recorders on our machines in Washington."

"I suppose the break in diplomatic relations blows that," Jack said.

"They'd already refused."

Jack thought of the camouflage nets he had seen above the ships a few minutes earlier. "Do you think that's because they're trying to hide the data and the real cause from us?"

"Probably a combination of that," Lindon said, "and being afraid we might doctor the results if the data showed that your boy got the Soviet bird. In fact, they've given us the cold shoulder entirely on all the help we've offered."

"So the Soviets haven't listened to the Oakland Center tape the Air Force received?"

"We offered copies the day after the crash. Those tapes are just gathering dust in our San Francisco office. The Russians probably assume we'd doctor the tape too if we had something to hide."

Perhaps the Soviets had seen a copy of the transcript, Jack thought. "Have you released the transcript of the Oakland Center tape anywhere else?"

"Negative," Lindon said. "There's a discrepancy with the Air Force concerning the time of impact. We're keeping the annotated transcripts 'close hold' until that's straightened out. The copies sent to Howell Air Force Base are the only ones released outside the FAA so far."

Jack explained what he believed had caused the confusion over the time of the crash. As he talked, however, he was thinking about the Russian words near the end of the Oakland Center tape. Since the Soviet investigators had not heard the tape, how did they know that Colonel Bochkov's last words were of his dedication to serving the Soviet Union?

While he was on the telephone, Christine returned. She was watch-

ing the commentaries on television until her beeper sounded. When
he hung up, she was using another telephone to call Braxton's office.

Jack got her attention and said, "I've got to pick up my bags. Good
luck, lady."

Touching his hand, she smiled and said, "Good luck to you too,
Colonel."

A few minutes later, he was nearly finished packing when a knock
at the door interrupted him. Not again, he thought, as he discovered
Christine outside.

"Looks like you're stuck with me for a while longer, Colonel" she
said with a mischievous smile.

"But," Jack said, "I'm not—"

"Alex thinks the action's finished here at Howell. The real story's
with the President and his Airborne Command Post at Alameda."

"We're not sure the E-4B's going to Alameda."

"Alex is," she said matter-of-factly. "Anyway, he believes you're
the Air Force's real trouble shooter, and if I stick with you, I'll stay
closer to the real story."

He shook his head in mock disgust as he considered his reply.
There was no point in refusing, since Braxton's influence obviously
overshadowed his own. Even if she went along, she still would have to
obtain special permission to enter the President's aircraft. Not even
the President—or his political adviser John Kellogg—would compromise the plane's security by allowing anyone inside without going
through the proper security requirements.

Jack smiled wryly in defeat. "How fast can you pack? I have to be
at Alameda by two."

"I'm on my way," she said.

When they stopped at the Command Post, he confirmed that the
E-4B indeed was going to Alameda after minimum ground time at
Travis.

Driving a government sedan to Alameda, he tuned the radio to an
all-news station. Most stories rehashed the break in diplomatic relations and the deadly attack on Kane's news team. At noon, the
national news quoted a report broadcast a few minutes earlier on
Radio Moscow.

The report claimed two American speedboats had invaded the
search area, nearly ramming the merchant ship, *Tibor Szamueli*. The
Americans supposedly were attempting to lure defectors from the crew.
After provocations by the Americans, a helicopter gunship from the
destroyer *Udaloy*, acting in defense of the ships, had sunk both boats.
No Russians had been injured. No Americans had survived.

He said, "The seaman who jumped overboard must not count."

She did not answer immediately. Her face was turned toward the window, but he saw a tear on her cheek. He wondered why she was taking the attack so personally.

"In a way," she said emotionally, "I'm responsible for the death of the young man who jumped overboard, too."

He remembered how she had rebuffed Kane when he had pestered her for information about the ships. Surely she couldn't feel that her failure to answer Kane's questions had made the deaths her responsibility. He touched her shoulder. "Hey, don't blame yourself. They were grown men. Everyone knew risks were involved."

She tried to answer, but made no sound.

"Kane made his decision," he continued. "Once he visualized the Soviet Navy as his backdrop, there was no way he'd pass up his chance for the big story."

She sat quietly sobbing for a few moments, then said, "It wasn't just that. I knew he'd lose all sense of proportion. Bruce was that way. He was so ambitious."

Was she referring to more than her brush-off of Kane the previous evening? Jack wondered. Perhaps there was something more between them than she had acknowledged. He said, "I can be a pretty good listener."

Though she remained silent, she put her hand on his and kept it there a long time.

Upon reaching the E-4B, they encountered the problem he had expected. Security personnel would not let Christine on the aircraft.

She stressed the President's personal interest in her assignment, but her protests carried no weight against the computer used by the security force to determine access. The sergeant was persistent in his explanation: The E-4B was on an operational mission in direct support of the President. As long as her name was not in the computer, she was not getting onto the aircraft.

She turned to Jack. "Can you do anything?"

He could speed things up, but he wanted to talk to General McClintock without her present. "I can put a request through to the President's military aide, but that'll take time."

She asked, "How long?"

"Longer than you'll want to wait."

She considered the answer, then said, "I suppose a call from Alex to the President's press secretary would be quicker."

Jack nodded, then asked a Marine captain in charge of the security detail to get her the assistance she needed. As the captain escorted her toward a nearby building, Jack went aboard the aircraft. He was confident he could work a couple of hours without her tagging along.

As he entered the section of the aircraft outfitted for the President and his senior advisers, he was surprised to see Joanne Kingston at one of the desks. She was General McClintock's personal secretary at the Pentagon. Jack had assumed McClintock would be supported by the normal battle staff on the E-4B. However, since the vice chief of staff normally did not fly with the Airborne Command Post, bringing one or two members of his personal staff was not inappropriate.

Jack was glad to see her. Years ago he had learned that getting along with the generals' secretaries was almost as important as getting along with the generals. The secretary was the guardian of the general's schedule, and she had great influence over whose names ended up on the schedule and when. Kingston always scheduled Jack whenever he needed to see the general.

"Welcome to sunny California," he said with a smile. "I hadn't expected to see you."

"The general said I could come along or stay home and shovel snow in Arlington."

"It's nice to see a friendly face for a change."

"Then you weren't disappointed that the general cut short your visit with General Harper and Colonel Radisson."

He smiled knowing that Kingston understood. They often communicated without using specifics that could be considered inappropriate for the vice chief's personal staff. "How's the general?"

"He's taken flak over the accusations about a second missile. He thinks there's nothing more we can do on that but wait until it's old news. He's interested in your opinions on what happened."

"I can fix that."

"Give him your opinion?"

"No," he said, grinning. "Make him wish he hadn't been interested."

She laughed. "He'll be off the phone in a moment."

When he stepped to the doorway of the general's small office, McClintock motioned him inside toward the only other chair. Jack entered the small cubicle as McClintock continued listening to the voice on the telephone.

Before reaching the chair, he noticed a map beside the door. The map showed the San Francisco area, the coastline, and ocean to the northwest. Numerous pins with colored flags dotted the ocean west of Point Reyes. A note on the map said, "Radar positions, as of 2130Z."

Less than an hour old, he thought, as he subtracted eight hours to convert the time reference to local time. Scanning the map, he decided the red flags represented Soviet ships and the blue flags represented American ships. The reds outnumbered the blues, forty-seven to four. The blue flags were in a picket line about half way between the crash site and the coast.

The red flags were in three groups. Six formed a picket line on the ocean side of the American ships. Twelve more were near the crash site. The rest were deployed over an area nearly one hundred miles from the coast.

The deployments made sense to him until he noticed a stick-on note near the crash site. The note listed two sets of coordinates. The number three was beside one set, the number nine beside the other. He studied the map and noticed that the twelve flags at the crash site were actually two clusters. Three flags were at the first set of coordinates, and nine were at the second. He remembered that the pictures from Kane's boat had shown a second group of ships.

Jack checked his notes. The coordinates for the three ships were close to those reported by Captain Benes on the night of the crash. The diver from the Coast Guard cutter had seen parts of the aircraft nearly five hundred feet below the ocean's surface at that location. The other nine ships were nearly a mile west.

The location of the nine ships made no sense to Jack. Benes had said the aircraft had crashed in a steep dive, so Jack did not expect the wreckage to be widely scattered. While he was writing both sets of coordinates in his notebook, McClintock finished his telephone call.

"Well, Jack, there's one hell of a debate going on." McClintock motioned toward the map. "The Navy and a bunch of other folks want more blue flags on that map and the red ones pushed back a couple of hundred miles."

"From what I've seen so far, General," Jack said as he sat in the other chair, "the only way you'll get rid of those red flags now is to sink them."

"We won't sink much at DEFCON Four."

"Where's the rest of our Navy, sir?"

"We've got one carrier but the group off of San Diego that was about to finish an exercise. They're staying at sea, but well to the south. The submarines that already were shadowing the Soviet fleet are still tagging along out there somewhere." McClintock crumpled a piece of paper and tossed it into a trash can. He paused. "Of course, the President's right. This isn't the time to start trading shots."

Jack decided this also was not the time to debate why DEFCON Four could be more dangerous than the general and the President believed. He looked at the clusters of flags and said, "I might feel better about DEFCON Four if I knew what they're really up to out there."

"The Russians are just being Russians, Jack. They shoot first and sort out the details later."

"I'm not—"

"Just ask the folks on the Korean airliner."

"I expect them to shoot at anyone inside that five-mile circle, General. But the more I look at this whole incident, the more I find to add to my worry list."

McClintock leaned across the desk giving his full attention to Jack. "You have new ones I need to put on the chief's list?"

Jack did not have anything solid enough to bother General Raleigh with, but he was confident enough to discuss his concerns with McClintock. "Not just yet, sir, but I want you to know about them."

"Name 'em, Jack." McClintock opened a notebook.

"First of all, I guess General Harper told you about the camouflage netting I saw during Kane's broadcast."

"Right," McClintock said. "The Public Affairs people in the Pentagon have been taping every story the networks are putting on the tube, and they've got his full broadcast."

"So our intelligence people have seen the camouflage?"

"Yes, but no one's particularly upset. They figure it's probably up to protect the little boats from the weather."

"The weather?" Jack had not considered that possibility. "Hell, sir, the Soviets spend nine months of the year sailing in snow and ice. It's hard to buy that they'd mess with nets between ships on the open ocean just to get out of the rain. I think they're trying to hide something."

"But Jack, they know we've got sensors that can see through camouflage netting."

"Yes, sir, but they may figure if the weather clears, it's a lot easier for us to just watch from outside the five-mile limit. The nets will make it easier to conceal any pieces of wreckage they want to hide."

"I'll think about that some more, Jack, if the weather gets better. But from the looks of the satellite photos of the North Pacific, I don't think the weather's going to clear before Christmas."

Jack was not satisfied, but he knew that discussion was effectively over. "Are the Soviets still searching, or have they settled on these two spots?"

McClintock looked at his watch. "These groups haven't moved in the last fifteen hours."

"So, they seem to have—"

"Except for the destroyers," McClintock added. "Before that fool TV crew went in there, three destroyers were on the picket line opposite the Coast Guard. After the shooting, three more destroyers moved on line."

"Assuming the coordinates are accurate," Jack said, "I'd like to know why they've concentrated on two spots nearly a mile apart."

McClintock opened a folder on his desk. He sorted through teletype messages until he found one reporting the locations of the Soviet ships. He scanned the message a moment, then handed it to Jack. "These are the latest estimates. Intel says one set of coordinates is damn close to those reported by Benes."

Jack checked the message and found that the coordinates matched those on the note on the map.

McClintock had not written anything yet. He tapped his pen on the notebook and said, "Why are you concerned about the wreckage being scattered?"

"I'm bothered by the scattering and where it seems to be scattered, sir."

"Ever skip a flat rock on a pond, Jack? The plane could have skipped a time or two, dropping pieces each time it hit."

"It seems to me, General," Jack said, picking his words diplomatically, "that if you ditch a bird the size of an Il-62, one of three things happens. You get her in smooth and flat, or you catch a wing tip in the water and cartwheel a time or two, or you hit steeply and sink like a rock."

"And you believe—?"

"Captain Benes said the bird hit the water more than thirty degrees nose low. The wreckage didn't scatter much if his report's accurate."

"If the water's deep enou—" McClintock began, then checked himself. "But the ocean isn't even five hundred feet deep where Soviet National One crashed."

"Wreckage won't scatter fifteen hundred yards while an airplane sinks five hundred feet."

McClintock nodded. His expression indicated he still was searching for a plausible answer. Finally he said, "Maybe ocean currents? The currents in and out of the Golden Gate are among the strongest in the world."

"The bird weighed nearly a hundred tons when it hit. Besides, the storm was moving ashore, and Soviet National One was flying a course of—" Jack flipped back a couple of pages in his notebook. He moved to the map and drew an imaginary line with his finger across the crash site. "—zero-four-zero, also toward the coast. Ocean currents don't explain what has the Soviets' interest a mile back from where the bird crashed." He tapped the map at an exaggerated distance west of the crash site, then turned toward McClintock and saw the general writing in his notebook.

Without looking up, McClintock asked, "Do you have any plausible explanations that I can offer to the chief?"

"I suppose you could tell General Raleigh that if Captain Benes blew the tail off the Il-62 at thirteen thousand feet, there could be two main chunks of—" He noticed McClintock had stopped writing and was staring wide-eyed at Jack. Bad joke, he thought as he rushed into an additional explanation. "That's not what happened, but that's the most plausible explanation at the moment for why those two groups of red flags on your map are where they are."

McClintock's expression brightened. "You can prove Benes didn't hit the Soviets?"

"Not exactly," Jack said, pulling from his pocket a tape of the FAA recording. "All I've got so far's a head full of hunches and three words on this tape that'll keep you awake tonight."

As he handed the cassette to McClintock, Jack told about the Russian statement near the end of the tape.

"The more I listen to those words, General, the more I'm ready to swear the pilot was on a suicide mission. I'm just not sure how you get a professional pilot to sign up for something like that."

"There's one little war story I never got around to telling you, Jack," McClintock said as he leaned back in his chair and propped his feet up on the desk. "Back in 1962, I was a young lieutenant living the good life as a flight instructor in south Texas. All of a sudden President Kennedy announced the Russians were putting offensive missiles in Cuba. If Khrushchev didn't take them out, we'd do it for him. What kind of career opportunities do you suppose that opened for first lieutenants flying old Lockheed T-33s?"

Jack pictured the old jet trainers. They were the same design as the F-80 Shooting Star, a jet fighter used in the Korean War. "I'm afraid to guess, General. Did they put the machine guns back in the nose?"

"If we'd only had it so good," McClintock said with a weary smile. "For three days I flew back and forth along the coast from the Mexican border to Corpus Christi. Our orders were to stop any bombers we discovered trying to penetrate south Texas from Cuba."

"In an unarmed T-33?"

McClintock sat back and smiled, indicating he would let Jack answer his own question.

Finally, Jack said, "You're kidding!"

McClintock looked pleased. "We were all full of piss and vinegar back then. If the President needed us to crash a bird into an inbound bomber, we were ready." He paused, then added, "I've never been too disappointed that it didn't get down to me in my T-bird and some Ivan in his Beagle."

Jack just shook his head.

"That week we seemed on the brink of nuclear war," McClintock continued. "That's quite different, of course, than if the President were asking us to destroy a plane carrying half the Congress. So I'm not sure how that little story applies to your conclusions about the words on this tape."

"First of all," Jack said, "I doubt anyone below Valinen convinced the pilot to destroy the plane."

McClintock paused thoughtfully, then said, "Then you're thinking Medvalev? That'd put a different spin on everything if the premier was sending everyone to their deaths instead of to a treaty signing."

"Medvalev, or Valinen—assuming he sneaked off in Vladivostok and sent everyone else on their way. A plot involving the pilot makes more sense with Valinen as mastermind instead of victim."

Leaning back as if trying to sort out the ramifications, McClintock said, "Jack, you can make more out of a little bit of nothing than anyone else I've ever seen. What are the odds that you've figured out the right picture?"

"About the same as if I were sitting beneath a glass-topped table watching someone—maybe Valinen—put together a jigsaw puzzle."

"The bottoms of the pieces are all you can see," McClintock said with a smile, "and we expect you to tell us what the picture is."

Jack appreciated the general's confidence. "I may not figure out the whole picture, General, but maybe I can warn you if you need to kick over the table."

"Okay, Jack, try to identify a few more pieces. I'll try to figure out how to sell your theory to General Raleigh."

Gesturing toward the cassette that included the Russian statement, Jack said, "Your best salesman's at the end of that tape, General."

He stepped from the office, then remembered he had not mentioned Christine. He stood in the doorway and explained to General McClintock that she had come along instead of staying at Howell Air Force Base.

McClintock considered the situation, then said, "Getting her away from General Harper was probably a good move."

"That wasn't really my idea, sir," Jack said. Knowing that she would not be cleared into the sensitive sections of the aircraft, he added, "I figured I'd hide in the intel section until she gives up on learning anything here."

"Maybe not," McClintock said. "If she follows you around a day or two, Harper will have learned about everything he's going to learn."

"Yes, sir," Jack said, his expression accentuating his lack of enthusiasm for working under her scrutiny.

"I'm sure you can work around her, Jack," McClintock said with a smile. "She can probably even listen in on a few of our conversations. If you discover something hot, we can always discuss it in the intel section."

"Yes, sir." Serving as a diversion for Christine Merrill was not the role Jack wanted, but he did not have a good argument against McClintock's logic.

"Before you leave the aircraft, Jack, check out a beeper from Joanne."

Joanne Kingston had been listening to the discussion about Christine, and as Jack approached her desk for the electronic pager, she asked, "Is she the cute one who was broadcasting about unnamed Air Force officials after yesterday's news conference?"

Jack grimaced in mock disgust. "She's the one, but at least she cleared me with the President."

She smiled and nodded knowingly as if she suspected that he had ulterior motives for getting into his current dilemma. "Very clever, Colonel. Very clever."

He laughed as he clipped the pager to his belt. "Why don't you go back to Arlington and shovel some snow?"

Before going outside to see if Christine was still waiting, he wanted to check some information in the intelligence section. There, he was surprised to see Thomas O'Donnell and Russell Brown, the two national security agents he had encountered at Howell. He stared at O'Donnell and said, "Forcing your way in here must have been tougher than getting into the briefing room at Howell."

Before O'Donnell could respond, Major Lockhart, a member of the intelligence staff on the E-4B said, "They've been cleared, sir. We've worked together in Washington."

Ignoring Jack's opening remark, O'Donnell said, "We've lost some agents in Russia in the last forty-eight hours, and we thought—"

"Maybe the Soviets think your guys caused the crash," Jack said. "If you're the guy leaking the idea of a second missile, you sure as—"

"I don't leak information, Colonel."

"Someone sure as hell did, and you're the only loose cannon I've seen on the deck."

"Look, Colonel," O'Donnell said, "I know I was out of line yesterday. I'm not usually such a horse's ass, but I—Anyway, the director's already chewed my butt and told me to get normal."

Jack noticed Brown was nodding in agreement and Lockhart seemed shocked by the entire interchange. Jack extended his hand and said, "Sometimes I'm easier to get along with, too."

While they shook hands, Lockhart said, "Colonel, Mr. O'Donnell wanted to know if the code word '*Iskra*' means anything to us."

"*Iskra* translates as 'the spark,' " Jack said, trying to recall any recent appearances of the word in the messages and papers he had read on the Soviet Union. "*Iskra* was what Lenin named his newspaper back at the turn of the century. The Soviets used the same name for a series of minor satellites in the early eighties, but I doubt any are still in orbit."

O'Donnell said, "Sunday morning, one of our sources in the Ministry of Defense sent a message saying that '*Iskra* plus twenty' and '*Iskra* plus forty-four' have a special meaning."

Brown added, "Our source thought the terms were involved with the Soviets' naval exercise."

Jack asked, "That's all we've got?"

"We're lucky to have that," O'Donnell said. "Since the crash, the Soviets are so busy investigating each other we haven't heard from anyone else in the Ministry of Defense."

"The KGB's rounded up everyone at Vladivostok, too," Brown said, "so they're obviously considering sabotage."

Jack asked, "Any chance Valinen wasn't on the aircraft?"

The other three men seemed surprised by the question. Brown said, "We haven't seen evidence saying he wasn't."

O'Donnell's expression showed a fascination with Jack's new line of reasoning. "What's making you think he wasn't aboard?"

"I could just say general principles," Jack said, "since he's the slipperiest man in the Kremlin." He told of the Russian statement at the end of the FAA tape.

O'Donnell looked skeptical. "What does that have to do with Valinen?"

"The pilot worked for Valinen," Jack said, "and I think the pilot knew what was going on."

"But," Brown said, "that would be suicide."

"That's crazy," O'Donnell added.

"I know." Jack shrugged and added, "I can't fit everything together yet, but—"

"Colonel," O'Donnell interrupted, "you don't have to keep trying to convince me your pilot didn't blow Soviet National One out of the sky."

"If Benes had," Jack said firmly, "I'd have fewer unanswered questions. But there's one skill I've learned in twenty years of yankin' and bankin' and that's how to read what's in the voice of another pilot.''

O'Donnell seemed more interested in listening than challenging.

Jack continued, ''I once 'heard' a Laotian airplane get shot down. When I say 'heard,' I mean that all I could hear were the voices of other Laotian pilots. I didn't understand Laotian, but I knew damned well something serious had happened. The pitch of the voices and the speed of the words increased about fifty percent, communicating almost as much as the words themselves. I've also heard pilots heading for Route Package Six—that was the operational name for the heavily defended area around Hanoi—and some of those guys sounded no different than if they were driving to the store to get a loaf of bread. Those voices changed once MiGs, SAMs, and flak filled the sky, and things got out of hand. Nevertheless, while the mission was going according to plan, the words of those fighter pilots were calm and professional—just like the last words of the pilot on Soviet National One. My gut feeling says his mission was going according to plan.''

''We've considered sabotage all along,'' O'Donnell said, ''but that's one hell of an angle.''

Brown added, ''How would Valinen, or anyone else, have talked him into it? I mean, it's not like asking the pilot to take a stroll in the park.''

''Somebody had to make a damned convincing argument to the whole crew,'' Jack said. ''I don't believe anyone outside the Ministry of Defense could have sold them all on crashing with Valinen on board. Do we know why Soviet National One was scheduled through Vladivostok instead of on a nonstop polar route?''

Brown suggested, ''Fuel?''

''With a normal passenger load,'' Jack said, ''the Il-62 should go nearly six thousand miles.''

O'Donnell said, ''You're suggesting the stop at Vladivostok was because someone wanted off before the plane left Russia?''

Jack nodded.

''But if Valinen got off,'' Brown said, ''all the doves on board would have known. Once they got to San Francisco—'' Brown stopped. The rest of the comment made no sense if Valinen knew the aircraft would not reach San Francisco.

Jack asked, ''Can we find out if an aircraft left Vladivostok for Moscow after Soviet National One departed for San Francisco?''

''We know that already,'' Brown said. ''The backup aircraft returned to Moscow.''

Jack chided himself for not thinking about the aircraft that would have backed up Soviet National One.

O'Donnell still looked skeptical. "Even if Valinen got off, why not just leave a bomb on board instead of ordering a pilot to fly all the way over here and then dive into the ocean."

"I give up," Jack said, looking toward O'Donnell as if he now should answer his own question.

O'Donnell laughed defensively. "Don't look at me. It's your theory."

"I know," Jack said, "but that's one of the answers I don't have. Why not do it the easy way? Why risk his assassination plot by making five men play *kamikaze?*"

Brown said, "It sounds like you've shot down your own theory."

"I think you'll have trouble selling this one, Colonel," Lockhart said.

"I know, Major. I've already had trouble." Jack paused, then added, "But gentlemen, I still think that's the way it happened."

He and O'Donnell agreed to continue their individual investigations and to share their findings. Before leaving, O'Donnell gave Jack a business card listing the telephone number of an answering service that could reach either agent.

After they left, Jack opened his notebook to the list of items he wanted to investigate using the Pentagon's computers. Major Lockhart volunteered the assistance of his staff, so Jack divided his list.

"First of all, I'll want to see files that show any Soviet redeployments of large units within the last seventy-two hours."

Lockhart wrote a note on a clipboard. He told a sergeant at a nearby computer terminal to locate the files.

"While I'm looking that over, Major," Jack said, "pull together everything we have on Soviet National One's passengers and on Politburo members who skipped the trip. In particular, I want info on the power struggles—who was winning, and who was about to lose. Get me printouts of the unclassified information. You can store the classified files online for my review. I need the same type of summary on the Soviet fleet between here and Hawaii. I want the name of every ship, including those merchant marine ships that got to the crash site so quickly. Be sure the printouts include the unclassified descriptions of the capabilities of the individual ships."

"You may need a wheelbarrow, sir," Lockhart said.

"You have to collect a lot of answers," Jack said, smiling, "when you're not sure what the questions are. I'd also like—By the way, what ever happened to the Russian sub that was in trouble before all this started?"

"They must have solved her problems," Lockhart said. "Last I heard, the Navy was still tracking her near San Diego."

"I wonder what we'd find in the captain's log on that sub."

"Do you mean about San Diego?"

"I mean about what put the sub 'struggling' on the surface off San Francisco five days ago, and who pulled the 'Oral Roberts.' "

"The what?" Lockhart looked confused. A sergeant at a nearby console laughed.

"Someone miraculously healed that sub just in time to release the *Gnevnyy* and the *Karpaty* to head for the coast." Jack paused. "See if the Navy knows when the Soviets fixed the sub and what direction the two surface ships headed when they left."

Lockhart added that request to his list.

"Finally, I'd like anything you can find on a Mr. Alexander C. Braxton and a Miss Christine Merrill. They're both with KASF-TV in San Francisco."

Lockhart wrote the names. "Is this the Braxton who's the expert on the Russians?"

"The same."

"I can't think of anything in the computers that covers news personalities. In fact, I don't think that kind of information is allowed. His station should have a biography available."

"I don't want to call them. If you can't find anything in the computers, send someone to a local library. I'm sure all the libraries in this area have a file on him. Anyway, run their names through the normal security check process, and let me know if there's anything derogatory."

"On Alexander Braxton, sir? The Russians would be thrilled if there was something bad on him."

"I doubt you'll turn up anything," Jack said, "but I'm working with those two, and I'd like to know more about them."

Jack sat at one of the available consoles and reviewed the recent movements of the armed forces of the Soviet Union. Most of the message traffic involved units already participating in the war games in Europe and at sea. One major movement seemed related to the crash. The large fleet of Soviet ships between Hawaii and California had turned toward San Francisco an hour and a half after the crash.

He also looked for redeployments whose timing seemed related to Benes' news conference and Sherinin's announcement of the break in diplomatic relations. There had been none. He had not expected to see much movement, since many Soviet units already were on a near-war footing as part of the exercises.

Jack called up a display of the world showing locations of warships of the Soviet Navy. Seeing the names and numbers translated from columns of data into clusters of tiny red markers was more disconcerting than he had expected. In eighteen months of sitting through briefings almost daily at the Pentagon, he had never seen anything that compared to the movements of Soviet ships during the last month.

He mentally checked each area where nuclear submarines of the U.S. Navy were on patrol with Trident missiles. The display on his console showed several red markers in or near each patrol area. He decided that if this were a combat simulation at the war college, this was one scenario where he would want to lead the Red Team.

He selected a file that listed the crew and passengers believed to have been aboard Soviet National One. He studied the short biography accompanying each name marked as a member of the Politburo. Most were old men. Most had served, or claimed to have served, in the Great Patriotic War. Most had been members of the Communist Party of the Soviet Union for more than forty years.

He tried to imagine how, if O'Donnell's angry revelation were to be believed, one of those old men on the Politburo had been an American agent for many, if not all, of those forty years. Jack wondered how anyone could maintain cover that long and get that high in the government. He smiled in admiration since that was comparable to being a seven-term member of the Senate and keeping Communist loyalties secret for all those years. He studied each name two more times before quitting. He had no idea which man O'Donnell had referred to.

Major Lockhart brought several computer printouts. Looking pleased with his results, he offered the papers and said, "We've even got info on Mr. Braxton and Miss Merrill."

"Really?"

"We fudged a little, sir. Naturally, there were no listings in any of our files. One of my sharp sergeants hooked a portable PC to a modem and linked through the telephone land-lines to a couple of the commercial databases. This is just the beginning, at least on Braxton. His name appears more on the financial pages than on the television listings."

"This is plenty," Jack said as he scanned the information. He already had more than he had expected or needed.

"We put in a couple of more requests," Lockhart said as he turned toward the compartment of the aircraft that included the high-speed printers. "Anyway, the printouts on the ships and the passengers are almost ready."

Jack checked the time. More than two hours had passed since he had left Christine with the Marine guard. The printouts would give him enough to study for the evening. Once he had them, he would go outside and look for her.

While he waited, he scanned the page and a half of information on her. The source, less than a year old, was a publication on outstanding women in California. As a fine arts and communications major, she had been educated in New England with postgraduate study in Europe. Upon returning to America in the early 1980s, she had broken into television doing features on public television. She had joined KASF-TV five years ago.

The article included a long list of accomplishments, both as a news reporter and on behalf of the Chase Foundation, a philanthropic organization in San Francisco. Jack noticed no mention of a husband or children.

Before he finished reading, Lockhart returned with a thick folder of printouts. Jack slipped the information on Braxton and Christine in with the printouts on the Soviet leaders. While he did not plan to share any of the printouts, he certainly did not want to reveal to either of them that he had checked their backgrounds.

He went to McClintock's office to mention the term *Iskra,* but the general was not there. Jack wrote a brief note describing what he had learned from O'Donnell about *Iskra* plus twenty and *Iskra* plus forty-four. He put the note in an envelope marked for classified information and handed the envelope to Kingston. "Tell the general I found a piece of the puzzle they'd knocked off on the floor, and I got a peek at the picture side."

"What?" She looked confused. "I don't understand."

He winked at her and said as he walked out, "General McClintock will."

Chapter 16

Tuesday Afternoon, 4:20 p.m.
Pacific Standard Time

OUTSIDE THE E-4B, JACK SAW SEVERAL REPORTERS TAPING STORIES using the impressive aircraft as the backdrop. Christine, Braxton, and a cameraman were in the area roped-off for news personnel. He watched until they were finished, then moved to join them.

Christine saw him approaching. "I was beginning to think you'd given me the slip, Colonel."

"Did my best," he said, "but I finally gave up. Is security going to let you on board?"

"They're working on my papers now."

"Unfortunately," Braxton said, "I had already left a meeting with President Cunningham when I learned Chris had a problem. If I'd known earlier, I'd have straightened out the misunderstanding and brought her papers with me."

Jack was surprised by Braxton's comment about the meeting, but before he could respond, Christine said, "What's next, Colonel?"

"I'm planning to check into a room and stretch out on a bed for a while."

"Great," she said enthusiastically. When he looked confused by her reaction, she added, "Not great that you're going to bed, but great because I can go to San Francisco with Alex and pick up some fresh things to wear."

Braxton nodded. "Making Chris stay on the road while I went home was terribly unfair. Unfortunately, a couple of business deals have been stirring for weeks, and I couldn't let them slide."

"But," she said to Jack, "I don't want to miss anything important."

"I'm just going to look over data from the computers."

Braxton asked, "Have you turned up something new?"

"Negative," Jack said. "I'm just getting a refresher on the casualties. I want to look at who's left in the Kremlin who might have benefited from the crash."

Braxton's expression brightened. "Sounds like you're investigating

193

some linkages besides those connecting the cockpit to the control surfaces."

"I still have a few unanswered questions."

"I've been thinking, too," Braxton said with a conspiratorial smile, "trying to decide who would've been first in line to put Valinen into a watery grave."

"I didn't say that's what I'm thinking," Jack said, concerned about future quotes attributed to "a high-ranking Air Force official."

"I'd consider it a privilege to discuss some of my ideas with you." Braxton put his arm around Christine's shoulder and said, "Chris hasn't stopped talking about you." She looked embarrassed so he added, "I mean about what a good grasp you have of everything that's happened."

Jack was flattered by their interest. He was even more eager to hear Braxton's views on the sudden break in diplomatic relations. "I'd like to share some of your opinions, sir."

"How about the three of us having dinner," Braxton said, "if you don't mind waiting until a decent hour?"

Jack quickly considered pros and cons. There was more to be gained by spending an evening with Braxton than by sitting in the hotel room. Though he hesitated to admit it, he wondered what Christine was like in a social setting, far removed from helicopters, command posts, and news cameras.

He pulled his jacket aside to show the pager. "As long as this beeper doesn't sound off, I can be at dinner whenever it works for you."

"I must be at the station during our evening news, but Chris and I can fly back afterward." He gestured toward a company helicopter parked near the tower. Jack shook his head, smiling at the fact that Braxton had been cleared to land at the important military airfield while the E-4B was there. Braxton added, "The President's staff is very helpful."

He suggested a hotel a few miles away, near the Oakland airport. Jack agreed to check in and reserve a room for Christine. They planned for dinner around eight.

Jack got the rental car he had left at Alameda the night of the crash, then drove to the hotel. Once in his room, he propped a couple of pillows against the headboard and settled onto the bed with his open briefcase beside him. He began with printouts describing the Soviet ships in the recovery force. The summary showed forty-three warships on the surface and four ships of the Soviet Merchant Marine. Six submarines of the Soviet Navy were known to be patrolling near the fleet.

The printouts included a page of information on the *Minsk*, which served as the flagship. The *Minsk* was the second of the *Kiev* class of warships. It was designated by the Soviets as *takticheskoye avionosnyy kreyser,* or tactical aircraft-carrying cruiser. He thought that the thirty-seven-thousand-ton warship—with its handful of helicopters and thirteen *Forger* vertical takeoff-and-landing fighters—was out of place so far away from Soviet waters. The *Minsk* was armed with SS-N-12 cruise missiles, giving it a powerful anti-ship capability, but it did not carry enough fighters to defend itself against a determined attack. So, he assumed the Soviets would not risk the *Minsk* in any serious fighting so close to American shores.

The cruiser *Kirov* was the other major ship in the fleet. The first nuclear-powered warship built by the Soviets, the *Kirov* displaced twenty-eight thousand tons when loaded. With the exception of aircraft carriers, the cruisers of the *Kirov* class were the largest warships built by any nation since World War II.

As he expected, the fleet included smaller cruisers and several destroyers, but he was surprised by the number of ships whose main purpose was amphibious warfare. These included the *Ivan Rogov,* which he had identified in the pictures taken from Kane's boat, and her sister ship, the *Aleksandr Nikolayev.* He assumed that amphibious training must have been part of the exercises before the fleet was diverted. He thought, however, the Soviets could have practiced on beaches much closer to home. The mid-Pacific offered no islands that would welcome a practice invasion by the Russians.

He was even more intrigued by the twelve ships over the crash site. Eight were warships. Besides the *Ivan Rogov* and the destroyer he had seen during Kane's broadcast, there were the *Karpaty,* the *El'Brus,* and four BDKs.

The BDKs, short for *Bol'shoy Desantnyy Korabl',* were large landing ships with bow and stern doors for loading and unloading at sea. Depending upon what landing craft were on board, the BDKs could be helpful in recovering floating debris.

The other two ships were submarine salvage and rescue ships. The *Karpaty* was notable for the lifting device on its stern, which was rated at six hundred tons. The *El'Brus* was one of the largest submarine salvage and rescue ships in the world. Both ships were appropriate for a crash of this significance. But was it fate that had put them over the wreckage the day after a crash thousands of miles from the Russian coast? Jack's instincts responded with a resounding No!

The data on Soviet ships also included information on the four ships of the Soviet Merchant Marine. Those ships were thought to have been en route from the port of Nakhodka near Vladivostok. Their destinations were San Francisco and Los Angeles. The four were two pairs of sister ships that had been built in Finland for the Russians.

The *Tibor Szamueli* and the *Julius Fucik* were based on an American design. They carried large barges that permitted quick loading and offloading. The open stern with its large elevator allowed the barges to be floated aboard, then raised to one of three storage decks. The design was well adapted for amphibious warfare. The ships did not need piers and could offload twenty-five thousand tons of cargo in thirteen hours.

Such ships, he thought, were well designed for carrying cargo to third world nations not having good harbors or docks. All the same, the ports of Los Angeles and San Francisco had no shortage of docks. On first look, that was even harder to explain than having the *Karpaty* and *El'Brus* nearby. He made a note to find out more about the cargo and destinations of these two ships.

The other two merchant vessels were heavy-lift ships of the *Stakhanovets Kotov* class. These ships were extremely versatile. The large ramps on both the stern and bow permitted vehicles to be driven aboard from a dock. In addition, cargo could be lifted on and off with 350-ton gantry cranes or could be floated aboard through the stern gate. The floodable well deck was large enough to carry two *Osa II*-class missile boats in the docking well.

He leaned back and closed his eyes, trying to imagine a plausible reason to bring all those ships together. The pragmatic side of him still believed that a bomb was the smart way to sabotage the aircraft. But he sensed that something else was happening. In his years of trying to interpret Soviet actions, he had learned that whatever he was seeing made perfect—though perhaps diabolical—sense to someone in the Soviet Union. He was convinced of one thing: He still had not seen the key piece that would tell him what picture was on the puzzle.

Setting aside the information on the ships, he picked up the printouts on the people. As he opened the folder, he noticed the information on Christine and Braxton protruding beyond the edge of the other printouts.

Jack wanted to review their biographies before dinner. He reread the page on Christine and found nothing he had missed earlier. Meanwhile, Braxton's biographical sketch appeared to be from an American Who's Who type of publication. Jack was surprised that Braxton's prominence as a newscaster received less emphasis than his role as a philanthropist and businessman.

Braxton was born as Aleksandr Classon Webern in 1936 in Vienna. He came to the United States as a penniless orphan in 1952. He earned undergraduate and graduate degrees at Stanford. His reputation as an outdoorsman included being an experienced mountaineer, yachtsman, skydiver, glider pilot, golfer, and fisherman.

The article referred to extensive holdings in real estate and in more than a dozen corporations, including his television complex in San Francisco. The summary estimated the worth of his holdings at more than six hundred million dollars. Jack reread the figure to make sure he had not misread the amount. No wonder, he thought, Braxton got his telephone calls returned by the White House. He was curious about who benefited more from this relationship—the President of the United States or the wealthy entrepreneur?

As the head of the Braxton and Sylvia Chase Foundation, Alexander Braxton had contributed millions of dollars to charities and other worthy causes in California. Jack wondered who Braxton Chase and Sylvia Chase were. Another page indicated that the Chases had adopted Braxton not long after he had come to America. The name "Alexander C. Braxton" had been a stage name that Aleksandr Classon Webern later made official.

Quite a rags-to-riches story, Jack thought, even for someone with Braxton's obvious personality and intelligence.

After tucking the biographies in with other papers, he reviewed the data on the Soviet leaders. He read assessments from various intelligence organizations. The assessments, all of which were written before the crash, focused on intrigues—real and imagined—behind the walls of the Kremlin.

The analysts generally agreed that Valinen had been on the edge of losing to an alliance of five other members of the Central Committee. Premier Medvalev apparently had remained neutral as the infighting increased during the late summer and early fall. Most analysts cited the recent decision to sign the Pan-Pacific treaty as evidence that the premier finally had sided with the alliance and Valinen had lost. Medvalev's public declaration that Valinen would go to San Francisco seemed aimed at further undercutting his standing in the regime.

Jack looked over the ninety-three names on the passenger and crew lists for Soviet National One. The five names mentioned as being aligned against Valinen were on the lists. Chairman Krasnovich, the head of the KGB, was also listed among the passengers.

Jack put the papers aside and closed his eyes. Long ago he had learned a key lesson about evaluating Soviet power struggles. Always keep an eye on the leaders of the big three: the military, the KGB, and the CPSU, the Communist Party of the Soviet Union. Before the crash, those leaders had been Valinen, Krasnovich, and Medvalev. Jack wondered if they still were.

Normally the man who headed the party was all-powerful. He

served as premier and sometimes also took the presidency. The party leader often played the military against the KGB, thereby discouraging any lasting alliances between their leaders. No matter how badly he managed the Soviet government, the head of the CPSU remained in control unless the military and KGB joined against him. Then, Jack thought, all bets were off.

What if both Valinen and Krasnovich had not rejoined Soviet National One in Vladivostok? If one man could slip away without American intelligence knowing, why not two? His eyes popped open— Why not ninety?

He considered the implications, then rejected the idea of the airplane being empty. Valinen would have left the doves aboard, thereby ending one power struggle, but perhaps beginning another.

Jack's mind drifted between the collection of people on the passenger list and the interesting collection of ships that had gathered at the crash site. He was dreaming about buzzing the flight deck of the *Minsk* in an F-15 when the telephone awakened him. Braxton was calling from Christine's room. They would be ready to meet Jack in the restaurant in fifteen minutes.

As Braxton and Christine walked into the restaurant, Jack was impressed again by how attractive the newswoman was. Wearing an expensive stole over a black dress that was slit provocatively up one thigh, her appearance clashed once again with his image of her as a workaholic reporter.

Braxton offered a warm greeting, then added, "After the burden we've been to you, Colonel, I bet you really missed having either of us around for the last couple of hours."

Jack glanced approvingly at Christine and said, "Not until now, sir."

Dangling diamond earrings glistened in subdued lighting, framing her face radiantly as she gave Jack a sparkling smile. "Alex insisted that I get out of my reporter's uniform and try to get back into the spirit of the season."

"I'd say Mr. Braxton gives good advice," Jack said even while a small voice inside warned against lowering all his defenses.

Braxton had arranged for a private booth and a seven-course meal. Before sitting down, Christine unfastened the catch on her stole. Jack touched her neck lightly as he lifted the stole from her shoulders. He discovered that her back was bare nearly to the waist. Deciding that he liked the dress even better than when he first saw it, he quietly cursed the timing that seemed always to put his military life in conflict with his personal life. He wished that he and Christine had come together under entirely different circumstances. He also wished that, at least for this evening, Braxton were on another planet.

Throughout dinner the trio's conversation covered a wide variety of subjects unrelated to the current crisis. The programs of the Chase Foundation came up several times, reflecting Braxton's pride in the philanthropic side of his life. In most cases he emphasized Christine's personal leadership in foundation-funded projects that benefited the less fortunate. The newsman sounded, Jack thought, more like a proud spouse or father, than like the man who oversaw the distribution of the foundation's millions of dollars.

She seemed modestly embarrassed by some of Braxton's praise, but was particularly vibrant and passionate in discussing her work with disabled children. Jack enjoyed watching how animated she became and how much more genuine she really was than his recollections of her making insinuations about a darker side of the Air Force. As the evening passed, Jack became more impressed and intrigued by his host and hostess.

When nearly finished with dessert, Braxton said, "Colonel, how about if we talk off the record for the rest of the evening?"

"Sounds great, sir," Jack said, pleased that he might be able to have a more free-wheeling exchange with this expert on the Soviets.

"I'm uneasy about the President's decision not to put our own forces on full alert," Braxton said. "That's taking a big gamble on Medvalev's good will and common sense."

"I share your concerns," Jack said. "I was saying just this morning how uncomfortable I am with us deployed like it's business-as-usual while the Soviet Navy's spread across the oceans as never before."

"An excellent point," Braxton said. "I suppose your bosses are pushing hard to change the DEFCON."

Jack thought about mentioning General McClintock's earlier comments favoring diplomacy. However, Jack did not share such confidences with outsiders, so he put a different slant on his answer. "Time's the critical factor. The longer the Soviets keep us hung out to dry over the missile, the more nervous everyone will be with remaining at DEFCON Four."

"Secretary Shafer tells me he's confident Medvalev will end the crisis within a couple of days. The President expects Ambassador Sherinin back in Washington before the new year."

"I wouldn't bet the rent money on it," Jack said. "Kane's broadcast showed that the Soviets are using camouflage netting to hide their recovery efforts. That tells me the Soviets aren't planning to kiss and make up right away." He wished he could get another look at the netting.

Braxton appeared surprised by this conclusion. "The President didn't mention any concerns about camouflage."

"The weather's preventing anyone from getting good pictures of what the Soviets are doing. Could you get me a tape of Kane's broadcast?" Jack thought that perhaps Braxton could get a copy sooner than Lockhart could get one from the Pentagon.

"Kane wasn't from my station, of course," Braxton said, "but I'll see what I can do about getting a copy passed to Chris."

"There's something in those pictures I missed," Jack said. He still had the feeling that had nagged him since watching the broadcast. "I still think the Russians are doing more out there than just picking up the pieces."

Braxton asked, "Meaning?"

"Meaning their attempts to keep us from seeing the wreckage or the data in the flight recorders. The Soviets could be dummying up phony wreckage right now to prove that Captain Benes put the missile up the tailpipe."

Braxton nodded. "A little *imitatsiya*," he said, using the Russian word for deception.

"And *desinformatsiya*," Jack said. "This wouldn't be the first time they've tried both on us. I'm wondering if the whole crash doesn't involve a lot of *imitatsiya*."

"Your earlier comments convinced me that you suspected sabotage, Colonel."

"Perhaps even more than that. We're still off the record, right?" After waiting until Braxton nodded in agreement, Jack said, "I've got a couple of ideas to run by you. First, do you think there's a chance that Minister Valinen got off the plane at Vladivostok?"

Both reporters looked interested. Braxton asked, "Did he? I mean, have you seen anything indicating he did?"

"No, but I doubt there's hard evidence he went down with the plane."

Braxton paused as if giving serious thought to the possibility. "You do ask stimulating questions, Colonel. You're making me wish we were doing this on the record. What makes you think he wasn't aboard?"

"The passenger list includes everyone who was trying to force him out. If he were about to lose, this was his chance to eliminate his opposition."

"An interesting thought," Braxton said in the tone of a professor about to redirect the thoughts of a student who had tried hard but missed. He removed his glasses and wiped the lenses. "However, predictions of Valinen being about to lose to that 'gang of five' were simply the wishful thinking of our more liberal Kremlin-watchers. Certainly Soviet foreign policy is becoming less 'hawkish.' In my opinion, however, his five detractors were the ones losing ground, in spite of his failure to prevent the Pan-Pacific treaty. If anyone could have gotten off in Vladivostok, they're the ones who would have sent Valinen on his way with a bomb."

"But," Christine asked, "wouldn't Valinen have stopped the plane right there?"

"Of course, Chris," Braxton said. "Actually, President Gorshko would have straightened things out if anyone had tried to stay behind." Turning to Jack, he added, "I guess that's my answer to your question. I wouldn't argue against sabotage, but the crowd of people wanting to blow away Valinen is infinitely bigger the number of people wanting to kill all the other passengers." He paused, then added with a smile, "And you're ignoring the person with the most to lose if Valinen got rid of the pack of dogs nipping at his heels."

"Medvalev," Jack said. "I'd say that's a definite—"

A beeper interrupted. Feeling a shiver of anticipation, Jack pulled his jacket aside, then was relieved to discover that his pager had not sounded.

Braxton and Christine also checked their pagers and found that the call had come on Braxton's.

"I hope I'll be right back," he said as he stood. "I'm surprised I've had this much time to myself. Before I leave, Colonel, let me suggest you consider two questions: Who put all the key names on the passenger list, and who benefited most from the elimination of everyone on that list—including Andrei Valinen?" He paused, then added with a broad smile, "And if your answer to both doesn't begin with M and end in V, Colonel, you've got a scoop."

Jack had expected Braxton to be fascinated by the possibility that Valinen had escaped, but the newsman's assessment was equally fascinating. Now, he thought, he would have to rethink all the possibilities with Medvalev and not Valinen being the instigator. Medvalev certainly was the big winner—assuming Valinen had stayed on the airplane.

A few moments later, the maitre d' brought a note to Christine.

She scanned the note, then read it aloud. "He says, 'Sorry, but duty calls. I have to fly back immediately.' " She paused, then continued. " 'I've covered the dinner, but please don't cut the evening short on my account. The band in the penthouse lounge is pleasant. Have a drink for me. Alex.' "

Though Jack had gotten what he had wished for, his instincts immediately were in conflict.

He certainly liked the possibility of having some time to get better acquainted with Christine—as long as his pager stayed silent. Yet the part of him that seemed always to be on guard was shouting, Why did Braxton seem to be playing matchmaker? Maybe, Jack thought with amusement, Braxton finally realized that Christine had only learned what Jack had chosen for her to learn. Perhaps the veteran newsman thought the colonel would be less on guard in a romantic setting than in the professional atmosphere that thus far had existed with Christine? And what about her? Was this a scheme she and Braxton had carefully worked out on their trip to San Francisco?

Jack eyed the lovely woman across the table and disliked his suspicions and their implications about her. She was rereading the note, obviously waiting for him to respond first to the suggestion. He knew one thing—he was not ready to go back to an empty hotel room. Besides, he rationalized, no woman—not even this one—could get him to say something he did not want to say.

"Well, lady, do you feel like having a drink?"

She looked at her watch. "I'm not sure. This has been such a trying day."

"A nightcap might help."

She looked uncertain as she put the note into her purse.

He pulled the shell fragment from his pocket. "Let's flip for it. Heads we call it a night. Tails we go have a drink." He ceremoniously flipped the piece of metal into the air, caught it, then slapped it onto the back of his other hand. He revealed the fragment just long enough for her to get a look, then declared, "Tails, I guess we go have a drink."

"Wait a minute, Colonel," she said, grabbing his hand. "What was that?"

"Tails," he said with a straight face.

She pulled his hand away, looked at the piece of metal, then looked at him. "That's not tails. That's that thing—"

"Does that look like heads to you?"

"Of course not, but it doesn't look like tails either."

Feigning surprise, he picked up the piece of metal, studied both sides, then said disappointedly, "Well, it could have been heads. We can call it a night, if that's what you want?" He fixed her with a gaze that said that was not what he wanted.

"I didn't say that," she said firmly as she slid from the booth.

The penthouse lounge included a dance floor, live music, and a view across the bay toward the lights of San Francisco. On the Tuesday night before Christmas, they had their choice of several candle-lit tables near the floor-to-ceiling windows. While waiting for the waitress to deliver their drinks, he said, "That's a beautiful dress, and it's very attractive on you."

"Thank you, Colonel. It was a birthday present from Alex. It's one of his favorites."

"I can understand why he likes it," he said, suspecting that her answer was meant as a message about the personal relationship she shared with Braxton. Yet he was confused. Braxton's note seemed to imply the lack of a romantic attachment. Perhaps, he thought, she was more devoted to maintaining a relationship than the multimillionaire was. Jack steered the conversation to safer subjects.

She pointed out various sets of lights on the far shore giving a verbal tour of points of interest in the San Francisco skyline. After a lull, she took a sip of her drink and looked across the bay. "Is there a Mrs. Phillips back East?"

The question surprised him, but pleased him. "If you mean one waiting for me to get home and put up the Christmas tree, the answer's no."

"I'm surprised," she said in a way that did not tell him if she were serious or joking. "I'd think such a dashing colonel would have women lined up wanting him to play Santa."

"The only dashing I do is up and down the halls of the Pentagon— about fourteen hours a day, or maybe thirteen and a half if you average in Saturdays and Sundays."

"You haven't been at the Pentagon forever. Surely, there's been a Mrs. Phillips or two in the past.

"Is this interview on the record or off?"

She leaned forward and rested her chin lightly on her hands. Light from the flickering candle reflected in her eyes and from the polish on her fingernails. "Your choice, Colonel."

"I just wanted to make sure," he said with a look of mock concern. "If all my buddies were going to hear about the life and loves of Jack Phillips, I'd need to make it sound more exciting."

"You don't need to worry, Colonel. Your secrets are safe with me."

"Just one Mrs. Phillips. We spent seven years together, or maybe I should say apart. Between the war and alerts and deployments and training, there wasn't time left for us."

"And no one special since her?"

"You ask a lot of questions."

"I'm used to being on the job fourteen hours a day, too."

"There've been one or two special ladies," he said. "Unfortunately the only one I could've spent the rest of my life with wasn't sure she could spend the rest of hers with just one man."

"I suppose fighter pilots and liberated women don't always make a good match."

"You got that right, lady. She did say she might look me up again when I'm sixty, so I took the job in the Pentagon, which is making me grow old fast." He paused to finish his drink, then said, "The real mystery is why you aren't married."

"Alex keeps me about as busy as your generals keep you." She added with a smile, "Maybe I'm also like you, Colonel, married to my job."

He wondered how much Braxton had to do with her being single. "In five years in San Francisco, you haven't come across any guys who make you want to spend less time working?"

"In my business, I meet handsome and successful men by the hundreds. Few are available, and some who are available would have no interest in spending the rest of their lives with me."

That comment stopped him for a moment, but then he realized what she meant. "Well, some pilots don't want to fly the F-15, and I don't understand them either."

"I'm not sure whether to feel insulted or flattered. Is that another one of those fighter pilot compliments?"

"Most definitely, lady."

In the background, the band started a medley of slow, romantic songs, so he said, "I don't suppose your boss would mind my asking his number-one reporter to dance."

"I determine the names on my dance card," she said, extending her hand to him.

When they reached the dance floor, he put his hand lightly on her waist. She stepped forward as if he were pulling her into a tight embrace, then rested her cheek against his shoulder. He pressed her firmly against him as they began moving with the music.

He was pleased at how comfortable she felt following him flawlessly as they danced. The rigid images in his mind of reporter and colonel faded, swept aside by the clean smell of her hair and the fragrance of a perfume he had never encountered before.

The longer he held her, the more he sensed that she was both close and distant at the same time. He raised his hand and sensed a slight shiver run through her as his fingertips began exploring the softness of her bare back. She cuddled closely but did not speak for a long time. Finally, she breathed what seemed like a sigh of frustration.

He asked, "Is something wrong?"

She pulled away and said, "Would you mind terribly if we leave?"

He wondered for an instant if she were about to invite him to her room, but he sensed she was not. "Your choice." He gave her hand a reassuring squeeze, then added, "I'm not in any hurry for the evening to be over."

"I'm truly sorry," she said, then led him to the table to get her purse and stole.

So am I, Jack thought.

As they walked silently to the elevator, he wondered what in the hell was going on. Was she just a tease? He didn't think so. Had her boss pressured her to go farther than she wanted to go? He couldn't be sure.

In the privacy of the elevator Christine looked up at him with the hint of tears in her eyes. "I thought a few drinks might help, but I can't get Bruce Kane and the rest of those men off my mind."

Once again, Jack began to see her differently. He remembered how upset she had been in the car on the way to Alameda. He put his arm around her, wanting somehow to ease her pain. "Is there anything I can do to help?"

"No," she said, placing a hand on the back of his neck and kissing him quickly on the cheek. "I've enjoyed your company. Really, I have, but this should be such a joyous season, and it won't be for any of those families. Right now, I just need to cry, and that's something I need to do alone."

Chapter 17

Wednesday Morning, 6:50 a.m.
Pacific Standard Time

JACK WOKE EARLY AND LOOKED AT THE EMPTY PLACE BESIDE HIM IN the bed. For a moment he pictured Christine sleeping peacefully, her auburn hair offering an inviting contrast to the plain white of the pillow. He remembered her perfume and the warmth when she had pressed firmly against him as they danced. Disappointed in the way the evening had ended, he sat up on the edge of the bed. How, he wondered, could his instincts and timing always work so well in his military life and so poorly with someone like Christine? Perhaps, he thought as he turned on the television set, he was better off sticking to what he did well.

The picture showed a studio decorated for the holidays, but the mood of the host was somber. The news anchor was in a three-way hookup with a senator in Austin and a congressman in Miami. They were comparing the week's events with those of the Cuban missile crisis a generation earlier, so he went into the bathroom to shower and shave.

The news segment at seven was devoted to the break in diplomatic relations, and he sat on the edge of the bed to watch. As the narrator talked, a montage showed the exodus of Soviet diplomats and their families. People and their possessions were being loaded aboard airplanes at Kennedy in New York and Dulles in Washington. One sequence showed fearful dogs and cats riding in shipping cases up a conveyor belt into an airliner at Dulles. Jack recognized the pair of stately dogs in the two biggest containers. The dogs were prized Russian wolfhounds belonging to the Soviet ambassador.

As the Aeroflot jetliners moved along snow-packed taxiways and disappeared into cloudy skies that promised more snow, Jack's thoughts remained on the wolfhounds. He had seen the show dogs numerous times on television in Washington. Ambassador Sherinin usually was nearby, accepting a championship ribbon or extolling the virtues of the dogs and their Russian heritage. Jack had concluded long ago that

206

Sherinin was more passionate about owning those dogs than a good Socialist was supposed to be about material possessions.

Sherinin's obsession, however, was not what concerned Jack as the television commentator introduced a reporter in the lobby of the headquarters of the State Department. Jack wondered how long Public Health would keep the dogs in quarantine when the dogs returned to the United States. Would days or weeks have to pass before the dogs would be free to return to the ambassador's residence? Seeing the wolfhounds made Jack almost certain of one thing: Ambassador Sherinin was not planning to return within the next few days as the President hoped.

After Jack dressed and packed his bags, he met Christine for breakfast. Her manner was soft and friendly as during the previous evening, but her appearance had reverted back to professional reporter. Her business suit was expensive and nicely tailored, but with padded shoulders that made him think about defensive linemen instead of the feminine body concealed beneath. A silk blouse was held together at the neck by a delicately crafted pin that he guessed had cost more than his entire uniform. Though he told her truthfully that he thought she looked nice, he wished it was still last night and she was still wearing the black dress.

When she learned he planned to check out of the hotel and keep his luggage in the car, she decided to do the same. By the time they arrived at the E-4B, it was nearly ten o'clock.

He suggested that he try to arrange an off-camera interview with General McClintock. She agreed and he went into the aircraft while she filled out the forms for her security badge. His maneuver gave him the chance to see McClintock before she joined them.

When he reached the area that included McClintock's office, Joanne Kingston greeted him. She said that the general's schedule was being kept open so that he would be available to react to new events. Therefore, Christine should be able to see him with the understanding that he could be called away at any moment.

While writing Christine's name onto the schedule, Kingston told Jack that things had been quiet during the night. However, General Raleigh had called a few minutes earlier, and McClintock currently was on the telephone with General Harper at Howell Air Force Base. Moments later, McClintock finished the telephone conversation, and Jack entered the small office.

"Problems, sir?" Jack asked as he noticed McClintock's expression.

McClintock nodded in disgust. "We've got another flap going on over at Howell. Colonel Radisson and General Harper have—" McClintock paused, then showed a hint of an exasperated smile. "I'm not even going to tell you. You'd get too much perverse enjoyment out of their troubles."

Jack knew four-star generals did not discuss with colonels the problems of three-star generals. He was curious, however, about what new problem Radisson might have brought upon himself. Since the subject obviously was closed, he mentioned the proposed interview with Christine.

McClintock agreed to the interview. He also summarized what he knew of activities overnight. Other than the beginning of the airlift of Soviet diplomats and their families, the news was that there was no news. According to reports from units that were using radar to monitor ship movements at the crash site, the recovery operation continued as before. Some debris and body parts had started washing up on the beaches, but he doubted that the pieces would help the investigation.

When Christine arrived, McClintock welcomed her warmly. After a few pleasantries Jack excused himself.

In the intelligence section he asked Major Lockhart for copies of the recent message traffic. While a sergeant collected messages received since the previous afternoon, Jack made additional requests. He wanted pictures of the ships at the crash site, including a copy of Kane's broadcast. He also wanted specifics on the four cargo ships at the site: their ports of departure, destinations, and cargo, and whether the ships had been inspected anywhere since leaving the Soviet Union. Finally, he asked Lockhart to find out where the FAA was gathering debris that had washed ashore.

Lockhart already knew that the debris was in a hangar at San Francisco International Airport. He added that a press conference was scheduled at one-thirty to show the parts of the Il-62 that had been picked up so far. Jack nodded glumly. The wreckage he needed to see would not be floating.

As Lockhart started looking for more information on the ships, the sergeant provided two folders of messages. Jack sat at a computer console as he scanned them and confirmed what McClintock had said—not much was happening. The lack of activity mystified Jack, especially considering that the Soviets had broken diplomatic relations barely twenty-four hours earlier. He expected the Soviets to follow the diplomatic action with movements of troops, ships, and aircraft, preparing for the possibility that the crisis would escalate into war. He expected stacks of messages reporting precautionary movements, but there were no such reports.

One thing he saw in the messages was truly remarkable: the efficiency of the airlift of Soviet diplomats, their families, and other Soviet citizens. Although the break had been announced just the previous morning, only two of the Aeroflot airliners were still in the United States. All the others had already flown all the way from the Soviet Union, loaded their passengers, and departed. Jack checked his watch. Fewer than forty-eight hours had passed since Kane's dramatic revelation that the Air Force had fired a missile at Soviet National One. Even if the Soviets had decided immediately to break relations, the airlift had been carried out with unbelievable swiftness. The Soviets were acting, he reflected, as if the President had given them until sundown to get out of town.

With an unsettling sense of dread, he wondered if the decision to withdraw diplomatic personnel had been made even before Soviet National One had left Moscow. He realized if somehow that were true, he had been focusing on the wrong parts of the mystery for the last two-and-a-half days. If fighting within the Soviet government had caused the crash, there was no justification for recalling the ambassador or for being in such a hurry.

He checked a message that discussed the two remaining Aeroflot airliners. One was due to leave San Francisco within half an hour. The other had been delayed by weather and maintenance problems at Dulles.

His thoughts were interrupted by a telephone call from Thomas O'Donnell, who said he was on his way to a meeting in San Francisco. The agent wanted a meeting later in the day to compare notes. Jack told of his intention to look over the debris at the airport, so they agreed to meet at the hangar. They decided to meet during the FAA's news conference so they could talk while Christine was occupied with the briefing.

Major Lockhart returned with little to show for his efforts. American radars were monitoring the movements of the Soviet ships. However, good pictures of the activities at the crash site were unavailable because low clouds and fog continued to blanket the recovery area. Jack was disappointed since he had hoped to verify what the Russians were doing beneath the camouflage nets. At the very least he had hoped there would be photographic evidence of how extensively the Soviets were using camouflage.

Lockhart did have information on the Soviet merchant ships. Those four ships had started at the port of Nakhodka on the Sea of Japan, about sixty miles east of Vladivostok. Their departure dates were within four days of each other, and none had stopped en route. Maritime records indicated that the *Tibor Szamueli* had been headed for Los Angeles while the destinations of the other three were San Francisco or Oakland. Lockhart had requested copies of any photographs taken of the ships during their voyages across the Pacific. His contacts in Navy Intelligence had agreed to forward close-ups taken from patrol planes as the Russian ships had approached the coast of North America.

Jack tried to think of other things to look at or to call up from the computer. Nothing else came to mind. His inability to think of anything else reminded him again that the situation seemed incredibly stable for the middle of a crisis. The Soviets should have been pressing for advantages in a dozen different trouble spots. Yet, the Russians were quiet—deceptively quiet—and he was uncertain why.

At a little after one, Jack parked his rental car near the FAA hangar. The press conference was scheduled in an adjacent office area, so Christine went to the offices while he entered the hangar.

The cavernous building was nearly empty, dwarfing the small amount of debris collected from the beaches and pulled from the coastal waters off Point Reyes. Ropes hanging between portable stanchions divided much of the floor into large rectangles. As he had expected, there was little of significance: seat cushions, panels from inside the aircraft, life preservers, and trays from the galley. The people studying the debris nearly outnumbered the items being studied.

One corner of the hangar was sectioned off by portable walls. A hand-lettered sign marked with the word "Morgue" hung above a sheet that served as the makeshift entrance. Jack saw Thomas O'Donnell and Russell Brown standing nearby. Even before Jack got close, he could see that O'Donnell was excited.

"Colonel," he said, gesturing toward the morgue, "you'll never guess who's in there."

Since all consular officials apparently had flown out of San Francisco earlier in the day, Jack had no idea about who was arranging for the return of the human remains. Before he could respond, O'Donnell said, "Solomenkov!"

Jack was stunned. There had been no indication that the KGB's number two man—perhaps even now the head of the KGB—was coming to handle the job personally.

He spoke quietly to avoid being overheard from the morgue side of the wall. "Why's he here? No one gave me a hint that he was inbound."

O'Donnell seemed confused by Jack's response.

Brown gestured toward the debris on the hangar floor. "Solomenkov, or should I say what's left of him, got here the same way as the rest of this stuff."

"That can't be. I saw him on television with Premier Medvalev in Moscow, waving goodbye to Soviet National One. There must be a mistake."

"If there's a mistake," O'Donnell said confidently, "I'd say Solomenkov's the one who made it. The bastard's still wearing the leg brace we fitted him with eight years ago."

"Was he your spy who died?" Then Jack realized that Solomenkov would not qualify as the Politburo member O'Donnell had referred to as an American spy.

"Hell, no," O'Donnell said. "We held him almost a year and a half, but he was pure-blood KGB all the way. One of our agents had put a bullet through his knee during a shootout in West Germany."

"Too bad someone didn't put the bullet through his head," Brown said. "That would have saved a lot of people a lot of grief over the last few years. The Soviets really wanted him back and finally offered to trade some of our people that we really wanted back."

"I spent three months on the interrogation team," O'Donnell said, "and that was when the medics were patching him up. I've handled that brace a dozen times." He paused, then added, "We didn't let him have it all the time."

"You're certain it's Solomenkov?" Jack was still having trouble accepting that the man would have been left behind in Moscow, then be on the aircraft when it crashed. "After a crash like that one, you can't have much to work with."

"Come and see for yourself," O'Donnell said as he pushed aside the suspended sheet that served as the door.

Stepping past him, Jack entered the area where the human remains had been gathered. There were three rows of gurneys. Each gurney was covered with a white sheet and about half were empty. There was little difference between the gurneys that were empty and those with parts of bodies.

O'Donnell continued, "There's enough of the leg to show the scar from the bullet wound to the knee."

Deciding he did not need to see the pieces of bodies in this accident investigation, Jack stopped abruptly. Brown, who was following closely, bumped him. "Actually," Jack said, "my contract with the pilots' union says the government has to pay me extra if I have to look at remains of crash victims."

"What?" Brown looked confused.

"That means," Jack said as he turned and walked out of the morgue, "I'll take your word for it."

"I thought you flyboys were tough," O'Donnell said, chuckling as he and Brown followed Jack toward an unoccupied area of the hangar.

Jack ignored the comment. "If I accept that you're right about the brace being Solomenkov's, he must have flown to Vladivostok on the backup aircraft."

"His name wasn't on the passenger lists Customs and State were using in San Francisco," Brown said. "I saw the lists. If Solomenkov's name had been there, I'd remember."

Jack agreed since he had studied the list as well. "Do you know when your agent at Vladivostok was picked up?"

"Early Monday morning," O'Donnell said. "The KGB grabbed everyone who even came close while Soviet National One was on the ground."

Jack asked, "Was that Monday our time or their time?"

"Our time," O'Donnell said.

Brown looked puzzled. "Why do you ask, Colonel?"

"Makes a big difference. The bird crashed late Sunday evening, San Francisco time. Vladivostok's on the other side of the international date line, so that was mid-afternoon on Monday in Vladivostok."

Brown looked mystified. "If you were rounding up troops in Vladivostok on Monday morning, you were ahead of the crash."

"I'll make a check on the timing," O'Donnell said with a look of concern. "When someone mentioned Monday morning, I'd naturally assumed that the roundup began after the crash, not right after takeoff."

"But if someone had suspected sabotage that early," Brown said, "they should've recalled the aircraft right away."

Jack shook his head and said, "That depends on who was doing the suspecting and who was doing the sabotaging. We need to sort out all those possibilities."

O'Donnell raised his eyebrows. "Where do we start?"

"We need to get a handle on who was really on the plane," Jack said. "As far as Solomenkov is concerned, I'd bet we're talking about substitution, not addition. If you couldn't get a report saying he'd gotten on, you couldn't get any reports saying if anyone had gotten off."

"Krasnovich?"

"If I were the head of the KGB," Jack said, "and I knew President Gorshko wouldn't leave without me or my deputy, I know who I'd have meet me in Vladivostok."

"And this is on top of your theory about Valinen getting off," O'Donnell said. "So far we haven't tracked down anything that indicates he wasn't on the plane. But if Valinen and Krasnovich jumped ship and left their main critics on board, the whole picture changes."

"If those two stayed behind," Brown said, "the delegation changes from hawks and doves to a bunch of pigeons."

O'Donnell sighed, seeming to try to grasp the enormity of the possibilities. "Interesting, but none of that answers the question about why not just put a bomb on board and let the airplane disappear in the middle of the ocean."

"And even if Valinen decided to use the flight crew to wipe out his enemies," Brown said, "why not just let the U.S. haul in the wreckage? I see no justification for shootouts at the crash site."

"I still don't have solid answers," Jack said, "but when I look at the ships in the recovery force, my instincts say that the Soviets wanted the pilot to fly all the way to San Francisco before nose-diving into the ocean."

O'Donnell asked, "Why?"

"Damned if I know why," Jack said.

"I mean what makes you think Valinen wanted the crash near the coast?"

"There are too many specialized ships—ships that can do special things in the open sea—for them to have gotten there by coincidence," Jack said. "And since the airplane seems to have been flown to that point by a pilot who intended to crash there, I have to believe those ships were put near San Francisco expecting a crash and ready to rush in to pick up the pieces."

"Even if Valinen's pulling all the strings," O'Donnell said, "I still don't see what he gains by ordering the pilot to crash near our coast."

At that moment an FAA official and a few dozen reporters and cameramen came into the hangar. The official led the group to the first roped-off area, which included pieces of paneling that had been part of the aircraft.

The two agents wanted to avoid Christine, so Jack went to intercept her before she began looking for him. As he approached, the pager Braxton had given her started beeping so she went to an office to use the telephone. He continued to watch and listen, even though he remained convinced that the parts of the aircraft he wanted to see were still on the ocean floor or beneath canvas covers on the windswept deck of a Soviet ship.

Minutes later, he felt a hand on his shoulder. Turning, he saw Christine's excited face.

"Let's go," she whispered urgently. He hesitated, and she grabbed his arm and whispered louder, "Now, Colonel!"

He followed her toward the doors of the hangar, and when they were far enough from the other reporters so that no one would hear, she said, "Alex told me there'll be an important announcement at the Western White House within an hour. We need to get there right away."

Chapter **18**

Wednesday Afternoon, 2:50 p.m.
Pacific Standard Time

AFTER CLEARING SECURITY AT THE WESTERN WHITE HOUSE, JACK followed Christine into the briefing room that had been set up for the press conference. The network anchors and many members of the Washington press corps milled around near a podium marked with the presidential seal. Jack stayed in the back while Christine hurried over to Braxton.

Her boss explained what he wanted her to do, and when he was finished, she gave him a hug, then joined the rest of the crew from the studio.

Walking over to Jack, Braxton said with a smile, "You see, Colonel, not everyone hates a newsman."

"I thought maybe you'd given her a Christmas bonus."

"Better than that. I told her the President was about to announce the end of the crisis, and I wanted her to do the story."

Jack was surprised. "How did the President pull that off?"

"In this case," Braxton said, "the credit may all belong to Premier Medvalev and his sailors. Apparently the Soviets have recovered enough of the wreckage to verify that the missile didn't hit the plane."

Great news, Jack thought, even as another voice told him, the timing's awfully strange. Six hours earlier, the Soviets were rushing to pull their diplomats out of the country. Now Medvalev was saying everything was okay. That made sense only if the Soviet divers had located all four engines and determined that none had been hit by the American missile.

He was curious about why Braxton would give Christine the opportunity to report the most significant event in a week of stunning happenings. "Doesn't the boss keep the exposure of the big stories for himself? That's the way everything works in Washington."

"In this story," Braxton said, "we have to give the Russians credit for being extraordinarily reasonable for a change. If I can't do a little Russian-bashing, I'd rather let someone else handle the item."

214

Jack was reminded of his suspicions that Kane had gotten at least part of the story on the missile from Christine. Since she worked for Braxton, Jack said, "I suppose stories like 'trigger-happy American pilots' attacking an unarmed plane aren't the kind you'd take the lead on, either."

Braxton studied Jack's expression for a moment, as if questioning whether Jack was implying that the newsman had passed that story to Kane. Jack looked casual, concealing the fact that he wondered if Braxton actually had.

"That was Kane's type of story. This one's more Christine's type. She's destined to do big things in this business."

"She seems very talented."

"Superb, in spite of our slowness in recognizing it. Christine was an undiscovered gem languishing as our art expert and women's-features flunky. One week she'd work her way through 'Self-Defense for the Woman of the Eighties in Five Easy Lessons.' The next week, she'd be judging finger-painting contests at a suburban grade school. About four years ago, my personnel director suggested her for a Special Assistant position I'd created. She'd always looked good on camera, but her first serious assignment was a feature on the Strategic Arms Limitation Talks. On our plane to Geneva, I assumed I'd have to explain that SALT wasn't something in the shaker next to the pepper." Braxton laughed and added, "I believe I got in about the first thirty seconds of that conversation, and she got in the next thirty minutes."

Jack smiled picturing a younger, even more outspoken, Christine Merrill explaining a few things about international relations to Braxton.

"I learned very quickly that she was a woman of the world—in the most refined sense, of course." Braxton smiled as he continued, "And a woman, incidently, whose tastes are also refined—and expensive. Must be old money in her family back East. Anyway, I'm glad she got most of her traveling out of the way before I started paying her expenses."

Although Jack was eager to learn more about the beautiful reporter, he was unsure why Braxton was choosing to tell so much about her. "That much traveling?"

"I would bet, Colonel," Braxton said with a mischievous grin, "Christine probably has more time in the Kremlin than you do."

Jack could not disguise his surprise. "If she has *any*, that's more than I have."

Braxton laughed. "I've taken unfair advantage of you, Colonel, as your expression shows. Her visits were to the State Museums of the Moscow Kremlin. By the time I met her, she was a noted expert on eighteenth- and nineteenth-century European art. She's probably visited every major art museum in Europe."

"Western *and* Eastern Europe?"

"Well, she hasn't seen every little museum in European Russia, but I think she's covered all the main ones in Moscow and Leningrad."

Jack was angry because no one had told him right from the beginning about her travel behind the Iron Curtain. Had anyone conducted a background check before granting her access to the investigation? He hated political decisions that paid no attention to standard safeguards. He also wondered how much Russian she understood. Maybe, he thought, she had not asked what the Soviet pilot had said because she already understood that *"Sluzhu Sovetskomu Soyuzu"* meant, "I serve the Soviet Union."

"She never mentioned that she had so much exposure to the U.S.S.R."

Braxton smiled as if Jack had just made an important discovery. "Sometimes reporters don't tell everything they know when they're trying to get a story."

Jack chose not to confess that colonels didn't always tell everything they knew, either.

As they talked, the turmoil he felt inside did not subside. Though he did not go by-the-book on everything, security was one place where he stayed very close. The thought that he unknowingly might have been teamed with a security risk angered him. Then he slowly came to the conclusion that his anger would have been different if the suspicion had been about Braxton instead of Christine. He realized that his strongest disappointment was the possibility that *she* could be a security risk. Almost immediately, he was angry at himself for even suspecting her of any wrongdoing without any real evidence. After all, travel to Moscow had become less of a reason for suspicion in the days of *Glasnost*. His growing interest in her was adding a complication he did not need—at least until the crisis was resolved.

A member of the President's staff distributed handouts to the reporters. After Christine read hers, she got two more copies and brought them over. "Colonel," she said, smiling as she handed him one of the releases, "you're a lot smarter than I gave you credit for when we first met."

"No doubt," Jack said. He was unsure what had inspired her comment, but he vividly remembered her reaction to him at the first press conference.

After giving the second copy to Braxton, she hurried to her seat near the podium.

Braxton scanned the paper, then said, "This is better news than I expected."

The release covered the conclusions of the Soviet government about the crash of Soviet National One. Just as Jack started to read, someone announced the arrival of the President.

Marshall Cunningham looked tired but was smiling broadly as he stepped into the glare of the floodlights and walked to the podium. After everyone was seated, he began.

"I am pleased to announce that the prayers of people all across America, and throughout the world, have been answered. Yesterday there were serious misunderstandings about the unfortunate crash of Soviet National One and the tragic loss of nearly one hundred Soviet citizens. Soviet-American relations had taken a serious turn that seemed irreversible.

"Yet this afternoon I can announce, unequivocally, that the crisis is over. The Soviet investigators have concluded that Soviet National One crashed as a result of mechanical failure and not because of any actions by the armed forces of the United States of America.

"The Soviets have determined that there were failures in the mechanical linkages to the control surfaces in the tail of Soviet National One. These failures caused an uncontrollable dive from which the crew was unable to recover before the aircraft struck the Pacific Ocean."

Jack could not disagree with the conclusions, but the words sounded unexpectedly familiar. The description seemed strangely like that he had offered to Christine a couple of nights earlier.

Cunningham continued, "The details of the Soviet statement are provided in the press release given to you a few minutes ago. Because of our rush to have this press conference and get the good news out to everyone as quickly as possible, we haven't assembled any technical experts who can comment beyond the details provided on the release."

Braxton nudged Jack and whispered, "Would you like for me to volunteer your expertise?"

"Not on your life!"

"So," the President continued, gesturing toward his press secretary, "I'm afraid you'll have to give Bob some time to get those answers, if you need to know more about horizontal stabilizers, centers of lift, and jackscrews."

These words jolted Jack more than anything else he had heard in the last few hours, and he quickly looked at the press release in his hand. As he studied each line, the phrasing seemed *too* familiar. The jackscrew was a long, threaded bolt; threads on the jackscrew had stripped away; metal fatigue; lack of lubrication; free-floating stabilizer; uncontrollable dive. The statement read like a dictation of a summary of his speculations on the crash that had been translated into Russian, then back into English.

Had Christine not been as drunk and giddy as she had seemed when he had talked to her about the causes of the crash? Even that made no sense. He was sure she had not made notes when he had given his detailed explanation. Even if she had written what he said, his words should have ended up in her newscast, not in the statement from the Soviet government.

He pictured the scene that night in his room. Suddenly, he thought, maybe the room was bugged! He had not selected the room—someone else had. Certainly if someone was trying to determine what he had learned, that person could have hidden a recorder or a transmitter in the room while Jack was at the Command Post.

Or, he thought as he studied the beautiful newswoman, she might have carried a recorder and made a secret, verbatim record of what he said. But why? If she had wanted to make a recording, all she had to do was ask.

Perhaps he was making too much out of nothing. After all, if the wreckage revealed a stripped jackscrew, what other conclusions could the Soviet experts have reached? He had almost convinced himself to accept the statement when he realized something was missing. He reread the entire statement. Nothing was said about examining the wreckage of the engines! Regardless of what they learned about the jackscrew, the Soviets should not have backed down without knowing for sure that the missile had not blown apart one of the engines. He certainly wouldn't have, he thought, if he were wearing the insignia of a Soviet colonel.

The President was already taking questions.

"What's the future, Mr. President, of the Pan-Pacific treaty? Will plans for the treaty be revived?"

"I'm confident once again that the treaty will become a reality. With the Soviet government and its people just starting a period of mourning, however, this is not the time for formal discussions. Secretary Shafer has received every assurance in private that the Soviet premier still supports the treaty. The Soviets have asked for our forbearance for the next thirty days, and naturally we will give them that during their period of sorrow."

"Mr. President," a woman near Christine asked, "considering the months required for our own National Transportation Safety Board to complete investigations, haven't the Soviets reached their conclusions in a remarkably short time?"

Jack nodded his agreement. He did not believe the Soviets could have data from the flight recorders already. Where, he wondered, had they even taken the recorders to have their contents interpreted so quickly?

"Frankly," Cunningham said, "Premier Medvalev came forward with results sooner than I had dared hope. Much of the credit belongs to Secretary of State Shafer. His quiet, patient diplomacy convinced Soviet leaders that the crisis had to be defused at the earliest possible moment. Obviously their investigation will continue for many more weeks. As the handout explains, their review of the flight recorders and the controls led to the preliminary conclusions we all prayed for." He started to take the next question, but paused and added, "Our decision honoring the Soviet request for unlimited access to the crash site, while restricting our own access, contributed to the quick resolution."

Jack noticed that John Kellogg was nodding vigorously in a front corner of the room. Jack hoped the news conference was not going to become the kickoff for the President's reelection campaign.

Christine was the next questioner. "Mr. President, when will the Soviet Navy withdraw to normal operating areas?"

"We expect good news within the next few days about the end of the Soviet's massive naval exercise. Again, Christine, I credit the quiet diplomacy of Secretary Shafer for establishing the momentum that has reduced tensions between the United States and the Soviet Union."

A male reporter asked, "How about our own military forces? Have you ordered them off alert?"

"Few redeployments are necessary. We've had an AWACS—that's an airborne warning and control system aircraft—orbiting over northern California. The AWACS has been keeping an eye on the Soviet fleet west of San Francisco. Once the aircraft carrier *Minsk* sails out to sea, the AWACS will return to Oklahoma City. Naturally we hope the crews will be home before Christmas. And"—the President paused as if reviewing other changes of the last few days—"we sent some Army helicopters to Chaney Air Force Base. They'll be going home soon."

"Yes, Mr. President," the reporter said, following up his previous question, "but I was considering our overall forces. Didn't they go on an increased state of alert this week?"

"I considered declaring a full alert after the unfortunate deaths of some of our citizens at the crash site. However, common sense and reason prevailed. I made a conscious decision not to change the DEFCON status. And, whenever possible, we always try to let our service men and women share the holiday season with their families.

Today's step away from a superpower confrontation will permit the Department of Defense to be more generous with time off than otherwise would have been possible."

Many hands were still raised, but Cunningham brought the session to a close. "Speaking of time off with families, I'm sure many of you would like to file your stories and be on your way home for the holidays. I know I have grandchildren that were promised more of my attention than they've received in the last few days."

After the President had left, Jack returned his attention to the press release. Braxton waited a few moments, and when Jack did not look up from the paper, he said, "Colonel, I thought you'd be overjoyed, but once again you don't seem to share the President's enthusiasm or his point of view."

Jack took a deep breath. "Just seems too good to be true."

"Maybe you do things differently in the Pentagon, Colonel," Braxton said, "but in San Francisco we try to avoid kicking a gift horse in the mouth."

Jack smiled at the misuse of the aphorism. "First of all, Mr. Braxton, conflict-of-interest rules never allow us to accept gift horses. Second, I don't buy the part about the flight recorders. The Soviets have been at the crash site for only forty-eight hours."

"That's not enough time?"

"Roger that. Say you run an airliner into the weeds off the end of a runway in the heart of America, and all you have to do is unbolt the black boxes from an airplane that's still in one piece. By the time you get the flight recorders to Washington and the NTSB plays them back and interprets the data, you won't beat forty-eight hours by much."

Braxton nodded in agreement.

Jack added, "Medvalev's boys had to find the wreckage, and that was after telling us to take our help and shove it."

He paused. For the first time in his investigation, he wondered how the Soviets had located the wreckage so quickly. Perhaps the *Gnevnyy*'s sonar had helped, and the position of the Coast Guard cutter *Valiant* would have been a good place to start. But within a matter of hours the Soviets had placed three ships over the coordinates that Benes had recorded the night of the crash. That information was available from the FAA and the Air Force, but the Soviets had never asked for the information—at least, not formally. Strange, he thought.

Braxton said, "I suppose that once the divers found the cockpit, getting the black boxes out of the wreckage wasn't easy."

"Right," Jack said. "The airplane's in maybe five hundred feet of water and pretty badly smashed. And once you recover the recorders, they're still fifty-one hundred miles from Moscow."

"And I've still got to get them dried out, unsmashed, and interpreted." Braxton clasped his hands and leaned his chin forward as if considering Jack's argument. "Colonel, you've convinced me, and I'm sure the President would find your argument persuasive. I'm not sure what we tell him after that."

"What do you mean?"

"Do we advise him to tell the Soviets to continue the crisis because we don't believe Premier Medvalev's rationale for stopping?"

As much as Jack hated to agree, Braxton's question was appropriate. Barely twenty-four hours ago, Jack had insisted that the Soviets were trying to frame the Americans for the loss of the Il-62. Obviously his suspicions had been incorrect. Seldom, Jack thought, had he been so wrong about anything in his entire career. He did not mind being wrong as much as he minded not knowing why he had been wrong.

Jack shrugged since he had no better answer, so Braxton continued, "Their answer wasn't meant to fool experts like you, although Premier Medvalev may have hoped it would. I'd say his answer was targeted to one audience and one audience only: the average Boris-on-the-street in Moscow. I imagine Medvalev's hoping his smartest colonels aren't asking the same questions our smartest colonels are asking."

"I suppose by dramatically declaring that there's evidence of mechanical failure," Jack said, "you might stop your countrymen from asking about sabotage once they stop blaming the Americans."

"Exactly," Braxton said.

That could explain the sudden turnaround, Jack thought reluctantly. "I'd still like to see the recorders and learn what they really say."

"Colonel, Colonel, Colonel," Braxton said. He smiled as he placed his hand on Jack's shoulder, "Aren't you ever off duty?"

"Not entirely," Jack said.

"Look, Christmas is upon us. You and Christine haven't had a chance to catch your breath or to enjoy yourselves this entire week. I know a restaurant downtown you'd both enjoy. Quiet atmosphere, superb cuisine. My treat. I'll make a call."

Jack was unsure how to interpret this offer. Perhaps Braxton was suggesting a threesome again for dinner, but he sensed that Braxton was not planning to join them. Although Jack had been convinced that the relationship between Braxton and Christine was more than business, now he was less certain.

"Sir, I appreciate your generosity, but Christine may have other plans."

"Until the announcement we just heard, her plans were to be

working for me, doing what she's been doing for the last three days. My offer's also a thank-you bonus for her as well as showing my appreciation for your professional performance over those same three days."

"Thank you," Jack said, impressed by how genuine Braxton's words seemed. "But I can't accept gift horses *or* gift dinners. I already need to return the favor for the dinner you hosted last night."

"Next time I'm in Washington, it can be your treat. However, the cost this evening is inconsequential. The restaurant's in a building I used to own. The owner of the restaurant owes me more favors than I'll ever collect. I just have to make one call."

"I certainly would like to take Christine out to dinner, but I'm a little old-fashioned about paying my own way."

"Colonel, if you go on your own to the place I have in mind, you—How can I put this delicately? I have some appreciation for what a colonel makes each month. Frankly, you can't afford the place without your friends suspecting you've been embezzling funds from the procurement budget."

"Frankly, I'd feel more comfortable picking someplace I can afford."

The response sounded more combative than he had intended, but he did not like being reminded how little government service paid in comparison to Braxton's millions. He had decided long ago that if a woman could not be comfortable with his salary, they probably weren't very well matched anyway.

"Your choice, of course, but Christine loves the place."

Christine joined them and asked, "Christine loves what?"

"I was just telling Colonel Phillips that I'd like to treat you both to dinner at your favorite restaurant, but he's reluctant to accept the offer."

Christine looked unsure how to interpret Jack's refusal.

"What I told your boss," Jack said, "is that I think he's an unconscionable slave driver, and if he'd agree to free you for the evening, I'd be glad to take you to the place of your choice—provided of course General McClintock doesn't want me to look into anything else."

She appeared much more pleased with that interpretation. Jack thought her smile was particularly genuine when she said, "I'd love to, but this story's going to require follow-up at the studio. Can you hold off for a late dinner?"

"Follow-up," Braxton said as he took away the papers she was holding. "Follow-up is what I overpay the regular news team for. I don't want to see you around the studio for at least twenty-four hours."

Christine grabbed Jack's hand and pulled him forward. "Let's get out of here before he changes his mind."

"Sure," Jack said, eager to leave everything else behind for a few hours. "I will need to find someplace to call General McClintock."

"I'll get you to a phone."

As Jack and Christine hurried away arm-in-arm, Braxton called after them. "My original offer's still open. I'll make that call, just in case you decide later you want to check out the restaurant."

Shaking his head, Jack smiled. "Your boss doesn't give up easily, does he?"

"Alex is spoiled," she said, snuggling against his arm. "He usually gets what he wants."

Chapter 19

Wednesday Afternoon, 4:10 p.m.
Pacific Standard Time

FOLLOWING CHRISTINE'S DIRECTIONS, JACK DROVE TOWARD THE HEART of the city, maneuvering slowly through streets crowded with Christmas shoppers and with the traffic of the afternoon rush hour.

"Mr. Braxton was sure singing your praises today," he said.

"Sometimes he acts as if I were his favorite daughter."

"If I hadn't already seen you, I'd have thought he was trying hard to marry off his ugliest one. I was about to ask how big a dowry he was offering."

Christine laughed, then said, "Alex worries that he keeps me too busy with work. He seems to push the hardest when he's got a handsome stranger in town."

"Is that a 'reporter's' compliment?"

She tried to look noncommittal. "Could be, Colonel."

"That's not the hardest I've been pushed by someone trying to convince me how charming a certain lady could be." He paused, as if seriously trying to remember. "Twice, I think. Once by a guy who thought I could be the answer to his alimony problem, and the other time was outside a strip bar in the Philippines."

She hit him on the arm, then said with a coy smile, "Alex gets enthusiastic, but he knows he doesn't need to get extreme."

"You've got that right, lady."

She smiled again and looked out ahead of the car. "Follow that Mercedes."

A Mercedes was signalling for a turn into the parking entrance of what appeared to be a high-rise office building. Once inside, Jack watched as a husky attendant greeted the other driver and activated an electrically operated gate. The Mercedes drove through, and Jack eased his rental car forward. Through the windshield, the attendant looked at him as sternly as the Marine guard had at Alameda on the night of the crash.

Just before the attendant looked through the side window, Jack asked, "You're sure this is where you want to go?"

She smiled but did not answer.

"Can I help—" the attendant said solemnly before noticing her. Then he brightened and said, "Miss Merrill! Good afternoon!"

He stepped quickly into the cubicle containing the controls for the gate. Jack expected the gate to slide open. Instead, the attendant returned carrying a single long-stemmed, red rose.

"Pardon me, sir," the attendant said as he extended the rose across to her. "I hope you're having a most pleasant holiday season, Miss Merrill."

"Thank you, Ramon."

He smiled and opened the gate.

"We park on the next level," she said as Jack guided the car onto the ramp.

"Is Ramon just after a big tip for Christmas, or is he one of your more ardent admirers?"

She raised the rose seductively to her face as if the flower had been a gift from Jack. "The flowers are one of Alex's ideas."

Jack was confused.

She placed the rose near his nose and said, "Alex used to own the building. He thought flowers each day were a nice touch for the ladies living here."

Trying to imagine the cost of that many fresh flowers for a year, Jack just shook his head.

"Don't look so concerned," she said, pulling the rose back. "One of the companies he owns is California's largest wholesaler and importer of exotic flowers. Roses are some of the least expensive flowers he deals with." She pointed toward a parking place marked for guests, then said flirtatiously, "Since Ramon didn't scare you off, I'll show you a few of Alex's other touches."

They rode a high-speed elevator to the eighteenth floor. Unlocking the door to her condominium, she said, "This is the best unit on the floor and one of the best in the building."

When he walked in, he was unable to imagine how any of the others could be nicer. She pressed a switch near the door and a series of shell-shaped sconces filled the living room with gentle light. She turned her head slightly to watch his face.

With the perceptions of an experienced observer, he slowly scanned the large living room and adjacent patios beyond the two outside walls. Those walls were mostly glass, with floor-to-ceiling draperies pulled to the side. On the east, the windows and enclosed patio offered a view of San Francisco and the bay. The north patio was an open balcony with a view of the Golden Gate Bridge and the Marin Peninsula.

The furnishings and paintings were as impressive as the view. The hardwood floor was covered in the center by a white woven rug. A couch and chairs of black leather were grouped around the rug and a green glass table. A cut-crystal vase was on the table as if waiting to receive a single rose. Matching couches and large decorator pillows faced a fireplace on the wall near the entry. A black cabinet of oak veneer with ebonized wood and bronze mounts stood along the other wall. An impressionist painting shared the same wall.

He felt a bit overwhelmed, wondering if he made enough in a year to pay for the furnishings of that single room. When he noticed that she seemed to be waiting for his response, he asked, "Any units like this vacant? Congress promised to increase my housing allowance a couple of dollars next month."

"If you're really interested, I can ask the manager."

"As long as I can get in a car pool to the Pentagon." Then he gave a more serious look of approval. "Lovely. This is all very nice."

"Thank you." She looked pleased as she placed the rose in the vase. Gesturing toward a designer telephone, she said, "There's the phone I promised."

She hung his coat in a guest closet, then hurried around, taking care of things neglected because of her absence. As he picked up the telephone, she disappeared into a hallway that apparently led to the bedrooms.

He dialed General McClintock's number. Joanne Kingston said that the general was just leaving to check into the VIP quarters on base, and she went to try to catch him.

While Jack waited, he looked over the delicate items in the black cabinet. They were a mixture of bronze figures, porcelain baskets, and colorful bowls with enamel decorations. Reflecting the tastes and interests of his hostess, all items looked old and very expensive.

He shook his head in awe of his surroundings. He doubted that the pay of an entire Air Force career would match the cost of the condominium. He assumed that unless she had inherited considerable wealth, the name on the deed was probably Braxton and not Merrill. Yet, if this were an expensive love nest maintained by Braxton, Jack could not understand why the newsman had made it so convenient for her to bring him home. He was certain that if she were his mistress, he would not share her with anyone.

Moments later McClintock came on the line and said, "General Raleigh told me to get some sleep in a real bed for a change." From the time the E-4B had left Washington, D.C., McClintock had remained on board, sleeping occasionally in one of the bunks available to the crew for long airborne missions. "I imagine you can use some rest, too, Jack."

"I'm fine, sir, but I'm uncomfortable with the Russian announcement on the crash."

There was a short silence, then McClintock asked, "Anything we can talk about on this line?"

"First of all, sir, I don't believe the Soviets could have gotten any data from the flight recorders yet. I doubt they'd have the right equipment on the *Minsk* even if the black boxes have been recovered."

McClintock hesitated again, then said, "But you have no way of knowing what they have on the *Minsk*. You can't be positive they didn't get the recorders interpreted somehow."

Jack wished they were talking on a secure line. He sensed he was making an argument that the general was not prepared to spend much time on. He wanted to discuss the possibility his room had been bugged when he had discussed the crash with Christine. Instead he said, "Some things about that announcement give me a bad feeling. I'm not sure this is really winding down."

"Get some rest, Jack. Maybe you'll feel better about it tomorrow, especially if the Soviets start pulling back their ships."

"It's not a matter of getting rest, sir. I just—"

"Jack, what I'm trying to keep from dumping on you is that the chief is a little embarrassed. General Raleigh was pretty vigorous making your case about the camouflage nets being meant to hide evidence that could prove Benes didn't hit the aircraft. Frankly, Jack, today's announcement made the chief look foolish."

"Yes, sir." Jack did not know what else to say. McClintock's words burned like a laser through the self-confidence that Jack seldom questioned—or had questioned by others. Growing older had tempered the arrogance that had made him such a good fighter pilot, but Jack still hated being wrong. Whenever he was wrong, he became his own worst critic, questioning his actions until he knew why he had failed. That self-analysis had kept him from repeating mistakes that could have killed him in a high-performance jet fighter. At the moment, a wave of caution swept over him. He did not want to damage the careers of others because of his mistakes.

"The chief would go back in there fighting if we had facts," McClintock said, "but I can't suggest that he hoist the red flag again just because you think the Soviet announcement sounds too good to be true."

"I understand, sir," Jack said, with a tone of resignation, then added, "but that's how it sounds."

"Jack," McClintock said with an exasperated laugh, "take two shots of scotch and call me in the morning if you don't feel better."

"Yes, sir." Jack assumed the discussion was over.

Instead of saying goodbye, McClintock added, "Look, Jack, I'll have Major Lockhart's people in Intel keep a good watch on things just in case. We'll call you on your beeper if Lockhart starts seeing something."

"Thanks, sir."

Jack hung up and walked to a window overlooking the city. Though he stared beyond at the streams of red and white lights of the evening commuters, his thoughts turned inward. He felt guilty for causing embarrassment to the chief of staff. Perhaps, he thought, it was time to pull his enthusiasm back out of afterburner instead of letting his instincts propel him too far ahead. If the Soviets were starting something new, Lockhart's people should see the indications.

After a few moments he sensed rather than heard Christine's presence. Turning, he saw her standing quietly behind him. Her appearance had changed, and he liked the transformation. The jacket of her suit had been left behind, revealing the soft lines of her tailored silk blouse. She had removed the jeweled pin that had held the neckline closed. She also had released her hair from the strict confines that had made her look professional—but less feminine. Now restrained only by a diamond-studded clip on one side, her auburn hair cascaded down onto her shoulders.

"Great view," he said, keeping his eyes on her but motioning toward the scene beyond the windows. "If I'd known reporters were paid this well, I'd have defected years ago and joined the media."

"It helps when you have a boss with more money than he can spend in a lifetime."

"I'd better stay with the Air Force," Jack said. "I'd never find a boss willing to pay me so well for my services." He realized immediately that the word "services" seemed a reference to sexual favors. Though that was close to what he had been thinking, he had not intended to say it. Studying her expression, he could not tell if she were offended or if she had even noticed the dual meaning. He hastily added, "What I mean is, like being a pilot—" Was she suppressing a grin or was she about to launch into a feminist lecture? "Or, being a troubleshooter, or being whatever it is no one's willing to pay me very much for." He paused with a pleading look on his face. "Help me make this right."

She finally smiled, much to his relief, and said, "I thought I'd enjoy watching you struggle for a while, Colonel." She turned away and looked out the window toward the lights twinkling from the cities of the East Bay. "Many of our professional contacts, and almost everyone I bring here, assume I earn my success by being Alex's mistress."

"That's not what I was meaning to suggest," he said seriously. Then in a more playful tone he added, "But I assume he finds your legs much more attractive than mine."

She turned to face him and asked, "Is that another of those 'fighter pilot compliments'? "

"Definitely."

She did not seem displeased. "Anyway, I keep my job because I'm a good reporter, so I ignore the innuendos. But"—she paused for effect—"I wanted you to understand things between Alex and me are purely business. Working for Alex isn't the only job opportunity I have."

"Mr. Braxton tells me you used to be a mean judge of fingerpainting and that Bruce Lee couldn't have put a hand on you."

She laughed, obviously pleased that he had accepted her explanation. "The news director wanted a feature on the self-defense courses for women. I'd had some training in college, so I was volunteered for the one-week, all-expenses-paid course at Mac's Gym."

"I guess I'd better stay on my best behavior."

"I've got a few moves that would get your attention."

"No doubt," he said with a grin.

She responded to his playful tone as if it were a challenge. Turning to face him, she said, "Suppose you were someone who wanted to be friendlier than I wanted and were getting threateningly obnoxious."

Deciding to play along, he faced her. "This isn't going to hurt, is it?"

She smiled as she took a well-balanced, fighting stance. She glanced at her feet and said, "High heels and tight skirts don't make this any easier."

He followed her gaze and noticed that the skirt seemed to be limiting the width of her stance.

"Sometimes a woman has to improvise," she said. She took hold of both sides of her skirt and quickly raised the hem above mid-thigh. "Then I—"

Instead of finishing the sentence, she snapped her right leg up in a karate kick that drove the pointed toe of her shoe to within a couple of inches of his groin.

The seductive move with her skirt had distracted him, and his reflexes responded a fraction of a second later than if he had stayed alert. Both hands rose in a blocking maneuver, but he would have been too late.

She stepped back, allowing her skirt to slide partway back toward her knees. "Get your attention, Colonel?"

"Definitely. Do you ever misjudge?"

"I thought you didn't like questions you couldn't stand the answer to."

He grimaced and said, "I'm starting to wonder if I would've been better off letting Ramon scare me away."

"I don't think so," she said with confidence. "Anyway, distractions are only the first rule they taught us for self-defense. Here, grab my right arm just above the elbow."

"Wait a minute," he said, raising both hands and stepping back. He gestured toward the large floor pillows near the fireplace and said, "I'd rather do this over there, just in case I suddenly find myself on the floor studying your ceiling."

"Don't be such a baby, Colonel," she said, following him toward the fireplace.

He pulled several pillows together and made a comical scene of ensuring that his landing place would be soft enough. Then he turned his back to the pillows and said, "Okay, where were we?"

She shook her head and gave him a "you're too much" look. "First, take hold of my right arm, then put your right hand behind my waist as if you're about to pull me close."

He hesitated and looked toward her skirt, which was still higher than normal. "This isn't the old 'knee in the groin' trick, is it?"

She pulled the hem of her skirt lower and said, "I promise not to hurt you."

Jack tentatively took her arm and put his hand on her waist.

"The first thing we're going to do is—"

As she spoke, he sniffed twice in quick succession and drew his head back as if starting to sneeze. He closed his eyes and turned his face away from hers.

Instead of sneezing, however, he twisted sideways, slipped his arm around her waist, and moved his right foot quickly across in front of hers. Before she could react, he swept her up over his hip and into the air. She shrieked as her feet swung high above his head and she started falling. Instead of driving her hard against the floor as he would have in unarmed combat, he kept hold of her arm and belt, breaking her fall as she landed on the pillows. They ended in a position close to an embrace with him above her. Her shocked expression gave way to a series of giggles.

"At my school, lady," he said, "they taught that surprise is even more important than distraction."

She asked, "Do you ever miss?"

"Well, I don't think I'd try that with a woman who outweighed me."

She smiled seductively. "How hungry are you, Colonel?"

"Are you ready to go to dinner?" He started to rise, but she had a firm grip on his necktie and kept him close to her.

"Would you be disappointed," she said, pausing to take a deep breath, "if we didn't go out." Using the necktie, she pulled his face to hers, meeting his lips openly and eagerly.

After a series of long, lingering kisses, he moved his lips lightly against her ear and asked, "No more kicking?"

"Or screaming," she said in a sultry tone. As he settled onto the pillows and pulled her onto him, she added, "Well, maybe a little screaming."

Braxton was right, Jack thought. He should spend more time off duty. A few minutes later, he carried her into the bedroom.

Much later, he retrieved their luggage from the car and put the bags in the bedroom. Then he found Christine in the kitchen, busily working at a counter near the stove. She was wearing a short robe of black satin and a pair of high-heeled dressing slippers. Her hair was pulled back into a ponytail, held in place by a black lacy bow. Since she had obviously dressed for his approval, he stood for a few moments in the doorway waiting for her to discover him admiring her.

She was totally absorbed in chopping something he could not see so he moved quietly across the tile floor. When his shadow crossed the counter, she turned. "I'm afraid there's no seven-course meal this evening. I just haven't been around to do any shopping."

He put his arms around her waist and pulled her to him for a gentle kiss. "Your hospitality's already won the Phillips seal of approval whether I get fed anything or not."

She smiled, then turned back to chopping olives. He kept his hands on her waist and stood closely behind, looking over her shoulder. On the counter he also saw an unopened bottle of wine, a cup with chopped capers, and a glass cannister holding uncooked vermicelli. A pot of boiling water and a pan with a red sauce were on the stove.

"If nothing else,' she said, "you should enjoy the wine. Fiano di Avellino has been my favorite white wine since my first trip to visit the museums in Rome."

He reached over and turned the bottle to see the label. "Mastroberardino. I've visited their vineyards near Naples."

She stopped momentarily and turned her head enough for him to see the exaggerated look of concern on her face.

"Is that just a coincidence, or could I have named any wine and you'd have claimed being there to stomp the grapes?"

"I didn't stomp any grapes, but most fighter pilots my age have spent a part of their lives pounding the ramp at Aviano, and—"

She stopped chopping momentarily and asked, "Pounding the ramp at Aviano?"

"Killing time on the parking ramp at Aviano, an air base in northern Italy. Anyway, most of us managed to work in some R and R down around Naples."

"Then you're probably familiar with the *vermicelli a la puttanesca* I'm fixing. I like it because it's tasty and takes so little time to throw together."

Jack started snickering and immediately tried to cover his laugh by clearing his throat. "I've always heard it was quick and easy."

He tried to force a straight face but could not totally suppress a grin as she turned with a very quizzical look.

"What's so funny, Colonel?"

"Who said anything was funny?" His grin broadened.

"You'd better tell me," she said, pushing him away playfully. "I had to find out from Captain Jensen what Sierra Hotel meant, but I'm not going to wait that long to find out what you're laughing about."

He feigned seriousness. "You really don't know what *a la puttanesca* means?"

She looked surprised to find out that his laughter was caused by the name of the dish she had chosen. She raised the knife as if seriously threatening him and said, "I do not know, and if you don't tell me in a hurry, this may be one of the shortest romances in history."

He grabbed her wrists. Holding her knife hand to the side against the counter, he forced the other around behind her, drawing Christine close to him. She did not resist except with her eyes, which seemed to say that the answer had better be forthcoming.

"Well, I'm not sure you'll find *puttana* in any of the phrase books, but it translates to, shall we say, 'lady of the night.' So *a la puttanesca* means—"

"You're kidding?" She blushed an embarrassed smile and acted like she wanted to pull away.

"Because so many of the 'ladies' around Naples found it such a quick and easy meal to fix between tricks, the name stuck." He kissed her on the forehead as he released her.

She tried unsuccessfully to look serious. "There's just no imagining what I may learn hanging around you, Colonel."

Putting the knife aside, she started mixing the capers and the olives into the sauce. He put his arms around her again and snuggled against her back. He started kissing, then nibbling the top of one of her ears.

She made a little noise of approval and wiggled slowly against him. Her breathing deepened as she continued stirring the sauce. Then she turned slightly away from his lips and said, "If you don't stop that, I may burn the sauce."

He moved his mouth to the ribbon in her hair and caught one end between his teeth. At the same time, he dropped a hand to the side of her leg just below the hem of the short robe. As he pulled on the ribbon, he also raised his fingertips along the side of her bare thigh and hip, dragging one fingernail lightly on her smooth skin. The ribbon came loose, freeing her hair just as his hand encountered the feeling of lace lingerie.

She exaggerated the shivery feeling the fingernail had caused and pulled away to reach for the cannister of dry vermicelli. "Why don't you open the wine, Colonel, because if you don't let me concentrate, I may even burn the water."

A clock had chimed ten by the time they finished eating. She poured the rest of the wine and led him onto the enclosed patio where they settled into a love seat that offered an unobstructed view.

Gesturing toward the panorama before them, he said, "I can't imagine being able to afford a place like this with a view like that."

"Working for Alex has brought more than a few fringe benefits."

"He indicated you'd started out with money of your own."

She looked to see if he was serious. "I don't know why he'd say something like that. He knows better."

"Maybe he didn't want me to think he'd provided this place as part of an arrangement."

"In a way," she said, "he did, but not as part of *that* kind of an arrangement. When I became his understudy, he decided that my apartment didn't have the right image, so he made an offer I couldn't refuse. This building had been part of his inheritance, so he gave me a price corresponding to what this unit cost new, before twenty-five years worth of inflation."

"That sounds like the deal of the century."

"Better than that. He lent me the money at no interest, permitting me to buy the unit outright. His only stipulation was that whenever I got better job offers, I had to give him the opportunity to outbid whoever was trying to hire me."

"I suppose you might call that golden handcuffs," he said. "I guess there's no chance you'll be taking a job back East anytime soon." He wanted to find a way of spending more time with Christine after he had to return to the Pentagon.

"I don't like the thought of having to give up this place, but . . ." She paused as if trying to decide whether to say more. "Well, maybe I could tell you if you can keep a secret."

"I've held on to one or two in my career."

She still seemed hesitant. "I guess it isn't like insider trading, or anything like that to tell you. Anyway, everyone in the business knows Alex has been moving into cash for the last six weeks." She laughed and said, "That's got a few liberal commentators scared half to death."

"Why would they care if Mr. Braxton starts gathering his nickels into one pile?"

"Everyone believes Alex is about to lead a takeover bid for one of the networks. Some of the Ivy Leaguers, who've never delivered a straight story on a conservative issue in their lives, are very concerned about Alex becoming their boss. Anyway, he closed deals on his last four big commercial properties this week, so he can finally make his move. When he does, he's promised to promote me into an executive position back East."

"New York?"

"Right, but I could justify a few trips to Washington."

"Sounds great," he said as he pulled her closer for a kiss. Then he added, "Speaking of traveling, Mr. Braxton says you've been holding out on me." She looked confused, unsure of what he was referring to. "Sounds like you might be more of an expert on the Russians than I am."

"That was a long time ago, when I was younger and wilder and more adventurous."

He recoiled in an exaggerated gesture of shock. "You were wilder and more adventurous?" She tried to hit him in mock anger, but he grabbed her wrist and stopped her. "I'm not complaining, lady," he said as he kissed her playfully on the neck.

"If you're interested in Eastern European art, you have to go to Russia," she said. "The Russians carried off almost everything that wasn't destroyed in World War II. Oh, but the works the Russians have collected in the State Museums of the Moscow Kremlin are exquisite."

Jack liked the enthusiasm in her voice. He was in a quandary over what to ask next. Part of him wanted to encourage her to tell more about the subject that held so much interest for her. However, the on-duty part of him still had a question he needed the answer to. "I suppose you speak Russian."

"Not enough to count."

"You haven't been there recently?"

She looked confused. "I guess you only heard the 'wilder and more adventurous' part when I said it had been a long time ago."

"Pilots do filter out extra information and focus on what they find the most interesting." He wanted to conceal his concern about her travel in Communist countries and the closeness she had had to the investigation, so he did not press further. Her answers seemed innocent enough, but he also recognized that they had been vague—perhaps as intentionally vague as some of the answers he had given to her over the last couple of days.

"I wish I could take you there sometime," she said.

"Don't hold your breath while I'm getting a visa and passport," he replied. His security clearances and the access he had had to the highest levels of classified information would restrict him from travel to Communist countries for several years.

She sounded melancholy as she snuggled closer and said, "It's such a paradox. Collections with so many objects depicting Jesus, the Virgin Mary, and the saints are housed right at the focus of a government that's so intolerant of religion." Her voice almost cracked as she added, "So much of this tragedy doesn't make any sense to me."

He wondered what had caused the change of tone.

She remained quiet for a long time, seemingly lost in the view beyond the windows. Then she slid forward onto the edge of the seat, facing away from him. "Is your offer to be a good listener still open?"

"Roger that." He put his hands on her neck and began to lightly attack the tenseness he felt there.

She gave an approving sigh, then began swaying slightly in response to the rhythm of his massaging fingers. "Do you remember my discussion with Bruce Kane at Chaney?"

"I sure do."

"He was pestering me for more because I'd given him his other big story."

"The firing of the missile?"

She nodded.

"Where'd you get that kind of information?"

She stiffened. "Sorry, but we don't identify sources." She paused, then added, "I assume the original information came from an aviation buff. He probably had a scanner covering the frequency we listened to on the tape in your room."

He agreed that the source could be someone who enjoyed eavesdropping on the conversations of fliers. However, any real aviation enthusiast who had listened to the drama unfold through the words of Captain Benes surely would have shared the story immediately. So why had the story taken more than twelve hours to break into the news? He doubted that she knew, and he was not sure she would tell him if she did.

He also was curious about why she had involved Kane in the first place, so he said, "Why didn't you use the information yourself? That was one hell of a story."

"I wasn't burying the story. But . . ." She hesitated as if trying to find the right words. "That's kind of our policy."

"Mr. Braxton and I talked a little about that." That was true, he thought, although Braxton had not admitted as much as she just had.

She looked over her shoulder and brightened at the mention of a discussion with Braxton. "It doesn't happen often, but sometimes there are stories that Alex would prefer we don't take the lead on." She loosened the belt of her robe, allowing the black satin to slide down on her arms and back, out of his way. Only the straps of her lacy teddy remained on her shoulders.

Jack's fingers started massaging more of her bare skin as he asked, "Politics?"

"He does prefer to defend, rather than attack, the current administration. Mainly, he likes to stay on the patriotic side of an issue. He lived under Communism when he was younger, you know."

"I guess I didn't know that." He remembered that the biographical sketch had listed Braxton's birthplace as Vienna in the mid-1930s. Jack had overlooked the possibility that during the ten years after World War II—when Austria was occupied by the forces of France, Great Britain, Russia, and the United States—Braxton could have lived in the Russian zone of occupation.

"Oh, Alex was famous," she said with obvious admiration. "He wasn't quite sixteen when he escaped by flying a rickety little airplane from the Russian zone to the American zone. He never forgot what it's like to live under Russian domination, so he's always had little use for the people who want to apologize for the Communists."

Jack suddenly had a greater appreciation for Braxton. No wonder the man was so willing to take stands that clashed with his more liberal colleagues in the media. "Does he ever get anything in return for the hot stories he lets someone else take credit for?"

"He's stayed popular with the President and his press secretary."

"I'd assumed that," Jack said with a smile. "I mean, do other reporters give him stories that are too patriotic for them?"

"Not really. Alex has so much experience and so many contacts that he seldom gets beaten to that type of story—not on the West Coast anyway." She paused, then said, "I suppose giving away stories earned some good will that kept a few people from ridiculing him over the Woodson thing."

"Woodson?"

"He worked for Alex until the FBI swooped in one day and arrested Woodson as a Russian spy. Alex was extremely embarrassed."

"When did that happen?"

"It's been maybe four years."

"I don't recall that case." Jack was not surprised that he did not recognize the name. There had been too much espionage in the last decade for him to remember names of all the spies.

"I think Woodson had been passing information he'd gathered in Silicon Valley. You know, the technical details of computers and hardware for satellites. There were more than a few snickers about how Alex could be such a Russian-hater and not recognize a Russian-lover right next to him."

Jack was curious to learn more about the Woodson case.

"Anyway," she said, turning so that he could no longer reach her back, "none of that makes me feel less guilty about Bruce Kane and the others who died yesterday morning."

"I told you before, what happened to them isn't your fault." He pulled her toward him. She resisted at first, but he remained determined to comfort her.

"But if I hadn't given Bruce his first spectacular, he wouldn't have been out there trying for his second. He was so ambitious, and I knew that."

"No," Jack said, grasping her firmly to make sure he had her attention. "He'd have been out there trying for his first if you hadn't already given him one. I'm a good judge of men, and Kane was the type who was going to take the risks. Soviet ships right on his doorstep were like magnets. And if he hadn't gone out there yesterday morning, another news crew would have been out there by yesterday afternoon."

She finally snuggled against him, holding on tightly and letting her robe slip away as he kissed her. They cuddled for a long time without saying anything as the fog moved in over the bay. Like snow covering a frozen pond, the fog added its own shimmering reflections of the lights of the holiday decorations, the city, and the bridges.

"I was trying to imagine sunrise here on Christmas morning," he said. "Not quite like watching the sun rise over Lake Tahoe, with the lake frosty and the mountains covered with snow, but this has got to be the next best thing."

She snuggled closer and kissed him lightly on the neck. "The quality of the view depends a lot upon the quality of the company with whom you share it."

Chapter 20

Thursday Morning, 3:25 a.m.
Pacific Standard Time

IN THE EARLY MORNING HOURS, JACK STIRRED FROM A TROUBLED SLEEP. In an instant he was completely awake and sat up on the edge of the bed. In the darkened bedroom it took a few moments, and the faint fragrance of Christine's perfume, for him to figure out where he was.

He saw her sleeping beside him so he sat quietly for a moment, hoping not to disturb her. He had been dreaming about their playful games of surprise and distraction a few hours earlier in the living room. Now, the words "surprise" and "distraction" rebounded through his head. A quote from the tactics manual of the Soviet Army flashed into the middle of his thoughts: *Achieving surprise involves misleading the enemy, exploiting his unpreparedness. . . .*

He thought of the terms *Iskra* plus twenty and *Iskra* plus forty-four—perhaps one represented the timing of a distraction and the other, the timing of a surprise. He felt very uneasy again about whether or not the crisis was over.

Going quietly into the living room, he dialed the number of the Intel section on the E-4B. The duty officer who answered assured him that nothing of significance had happened since the President's announcement.

As Jack hung up the telephone, he thought again about causing the Air Force chief of staff to be embarrassed. Jack seldom doubted his judgment because his judgment was seldom wrong. Yet the events of the afternoon said he had been wrong, so far wrong that his Air Force career probably never would recover. After all, he hadn't just embarrassed himself. But then, he never did anything halfway. Maybe General McClintock was right about needing rest.

Jack stood by the windows for a few moments. The clouds had merged with the fog, eliminating the view of anything beyond the patio. As he turned away from the dull white of the nighttime clouds and headed for the bedroom, he wondered if the Soviets were being just as effective in obscuring their real intentions from everyone's view.

Or, was his imagination posing more danger to world peace than the Soviets were? He hated it when his common sense and his gut feelings did not agree.

The next time he woke, it was both to thoughts of having embarrassed the chief of staff and to the aroma of fresh coffee. Before he got out of bed, Christine brought in a tray with coffee and hot cinnamon rolls. She was wearing a dressing gown of flowing white silk and enough lace to make it tantalizing as well as elegant. Her fresh, no-makeup look was accented with a hint of lipstick.

Jack smiled, noticing a sprinkling of freckles that had not been apparent before. *"Dobroye utro."*

She looked surprised. Then as she sat on the edge of the bed, she said, "Good morning to you, too."

"Well, you do remember a little bit of Russian."

"Of course," she said as she poured the coffee. "I've heard that phrase many times." She kissed him, then added, "But that's the first time I've heard it from a man in my bed."

She fluffed up a couple of pillows and slipped into the bed beside him.

"General McClintock thinks I've been working too hard."

"I agree with that," she said lightly. "Maybe you can take some vacation or leave or whatever it is you call time off. That might be fun." As she spoke, she drew one foot up along her other leg, causing the gown to fall provocatively away from her legs.

"I've been thinking about that." Though his eyes followed her sensual movement, his tone reflected his preoccupation instead of the anticipation of spending a few days off-duty with her.

"Well," she said, looking a little disappointed and embarrassed, "I didn't mean to suggest that—"

She reached for her gown and started to cover up as if the earlier movement had unintentionally revealed more than intended. He grabbed her wrist and pushed back across her thigh until she stopped resisting and let the silk fall away behind her again. He pulled her closer and began rhythmically stroking her thigh. "I'd love to spend some time with you. And I certainly may have a lot more free time in the future than I'd expected." He tried to make the last part sound more like a joke than it was.

"What do you mean?"

"I've screwed up pretty royally and caused General Raleigh a great deal of embarrassment." Jack paused, then forced a grin. "If you were holding any stock in Jack Phillips' career, you should have sold it all last week."

She kissed his cheek. "I haven't lost confidence in you yet."

He shook his head in mock seriousness. "You must not be as smart a reporter, or woman, as I've been giving you credit for."

"Maybe I'm smarter," she said confidently. "Why don't you come to work with me this morning? After the noon news, I could probably slip away for the rest of the day, assuming the war's over."

"I'll need to check in with the general, but I have a feeling I'm more welcome with you than with him." He finished a cinnamon roll, then added, "I thought your boss ordered you to stay away for twenty-four hours."

After putting her plate on the nightstand, she slid over and slipped her arms around him. "I don't have to be there right this minute."

Later they showered, and he dressed in a civilian suit instead of his uniform. He was ready several minutes ahead of Christine, so he went into the living room and phoned McClintock's office. Neither McClintock nor Kingston was available. The sergeant who answered, however, had a message from Major Lockhart: Thomas O'Donnell was on his way to the E-4B and hoped to meet the colonel there. Jack checked his watch and decided he could fit in a quick trip to Alameda so he told the sergeant to pass that message to Lockhart.

He considered changing into his uniform. Since he would be on board only for a short time and not on-duty as a member of the crew, he decided to remain in civilian clothing.

A few minutes later, Christine was ready. On the way to the elevator, he told her of his new plans, and they agreed that he would join her for lunch after the noon newscast.

Jack followed her through the parking area to a light blue Mercedes near his rental car. He asked facetiously, "Company car?"

"Not quite," she said, "although working for the company pays for it." As she slipped into the driver's seat and Jack closed the door, her beeper sounded. "Great timing," she said sarcastically.

Jack asked, "Do you need to go back and call?"

She gestured toward the cellular telephone in the car, then said, "No. I'll call on the way." She disappeared down the ramp as Jack started his car.

Outside McClintock's office, Kingston greeted Jack with unexpected news. "You just missed the general. His helicopter left for Howell a few minutes ago."

"Howell?" Jack remembered McClintock's reference the previous morning to a problem. With the crisis apparently over, the general was no longer tied to the E-4B, but what could require his personal attention at Howell? "He's not going just to offer season's greetings, is he?"

Her expression told Jack the visit was not a joking matter. "There's a big flap over Colonel Radisson putting extra fighters and crews on alert. Medvalev accused the President of breaking a commitment by responding militarily while he himself was rushing to end the crisis. Radisson's action almost scuttled the President's announcement yesterday afternoon."

"I remember hearing General Harper tell Radisson that he should get more planes ready. The general was assuming the DEFCON was going to change momentarily." He shrugged in disbelief. "Surely that wasn't the source of an argument between the premier and the President."

"That must be it," Kingston said. "General Harper's acknowledged making the suggestion. I think General McClintock's less concerned about the airplanes than he is by the fact that a commander can't make a tactical decision without the Soviet premier hearing about it."

"How'd the word leak out?"

"That's what General McClintock wants to learn this morning. He hopes that someone just did a little bragging to a reporter about the base responding to the attack on the speedboats. However, he's afraid there may be a real security leak, so he put an OSI team into Howell yesterday morning." The Air Force Office of Special Investigations was responsible for investigating charges of possible espionage.

Jack sighed and slumped down into a chair near her desk. When she said "reporter," his mind raced ahead of her words. He remembered Christine being nearby when General Harper had suggested the alert. She had seemed so concerned about the attack on her colleagues, however, that Jack was unsure she had heard the general's suggestion. Jack suddenly had a very bad feeling. He hoped a young fighter pilot or a sergeant out on the flight line would quickly acknowledge leaking the story unintentionally.

He asked, "Did news stories mention the increased alert?"

"Not that I know of."

"If someone had bragged to a reporter," he said, deciding that the information must have leaked another way, "the alert should have appeared on the news instead of being questioned by the Soviet premier."

"That makes sense," she said, then answered a call on the telephone.

As he walked to the intelligence section, his mind pieced together things he did not want to deal with. He remembered the Soviet statement on the cause of the crash and how closely that statement had matched words he had used that evening in his room. And he still did not know how the Soviets had learned of Colonel Bochkov's final words before the crash. And O'Donnell did not seem to be the source of the Soviets knowing there had been a question about more than one missile.

Though part of him fought to deny it, there was one common link between those three items and the suggestion that more F-15s be put onto alert: *All had been dicussed in Christine's presence, and she had not acknowledged the importance of any of them.*

He wondered about her. She had seemed open and honest both in their discussions and when she had made love. He had been confident that her lovemaking had not been mere recreation, that she really seemed to care about him. Now he was less certain. Could she have been so treacherous as to lead him on solely to gain information for the Soviets? Seduction was a tactic the Soviets used. Jack did not want to believe, however, that seduction was simply a tactic to her.

He usually was an accurate judge of character. Until the last few minutes, he had been very comfortable with her and she seemed comfortable with him. Yet if she knew of his suspicions, she would be terribly insulted and hurt—assuming of course that she was not spying for the Soviet government. In the past, his sense of duty had helped ruin his marriage. He did not want that sense of duty to mistakenly destroy his chances with Christine. Since receiving General McClintock's gentle reprimand on the telephone, he remained confused about the instincts he had always trusted so implicitly.

Jack looked troubled as he spotted O'Donnell, Brown, and Lockhart.

"Well," O'Donnell said enthusiastically, "we think we've confirmed what it was all about."

"I'm glad someone knows," Jack said, wishing he could have had a couple of minutes in private with Lockhart before talking with the two agents.

"You were pretty much on target," Brown said.

O'Donnell added, "We intercepted a message about four hours ago. Someone in Moscow repeated 'The Beast lives' three times before the transmission was cut off."

"That has to refer to the Beast of Bratislava," Brown said. "You were right on, Colonel, when you guessed Valinen had sent his competition off with a one-way ticket."

"And you were also right about the timing of the roundup in Vladivostok," O'Donnell said. "In all the uproar after the crash, no one had picked up on the fact that Monday morning over there came before Sunday night over here."

Jack did not comment. He was thinking of the implications of Valinen being alive and an instigator rather than a victim of the crash.

"You don't seem overjoyed, Colonel," O'Donnell said. "I figured you'd gloat a little. Hell, you had that answer before the rest of us even thought of the question."

"I'd rather have been wrong," Jack said.

Brown asked, "So where does that leave us?"

"Valinen's been pulling our strings for the last three days," Jack said, "and we've gone through a donkey dance that makes less sense than a budget drill at the Pentagon. And we still don't know if Valinen was acting with or without Medvalev's blessing."

O'Donnell's enthusiasm had disappeared. "So even though Medvalev's not blaming us anymore, you don't think it's over?"

Jack shook his head. He had a new question that he did not want to forget about. He asked O'Donnell, "Do you have any staff in this area that can research into local records?"

"San Francisco records?"

"Right."

"We've got people."

Jack took a pen and paper and wrote the unit number and building name of Christine's condominium. Handing over the paper, he asked, "Could you find out the sales history on this unit over the last ten years?"

O'Donnell nodded. "Is this part of the answer?"

"I hope not," Jack said, not wanting to get into his new questions about Christine. "Have we heard any more on *Iskra* plus twenty or *Iskra* plus forty-four?"

O'Donnell shook his head. "That may have been a false alarm. The *Iskra* thing supposedly had something to do with their naval exercises. Now our analysts expect those exercises to end within the next day or two."

"We haven't picked up anything on *Iskra* either, sir," Lockhart said. "I don't know if this will help, Colonel, but I've gotten some of the other information you requested. First, the Navy sent an answer to your questions about the Victor II–class sub that was disabled and the two ships that provided emergency assistance." He looked at his clipboard and read the message.

The Victor II-class SSN got under way at 0602Z, on a course of 167 degrees. The two accompanying ships, *Karpaty* and *Gnevnyy,* were not tracked immediately. However, both ships were taken under surveillance at 0827Z and tracked en route toward San Francisco. Extrapolations of surface speed and course indicate that *Karpaty* and *Gnevnyy* departed the SSN's position some time between 0600Z and 0617Z. Departure course estimated at 037 degrees, which matches course maintained all the way to aircraft crash site, where *Gnevnyy* confronted *Valiant* approximately fourteen hours after leaving the submarine.

Brown asked, "What does the submarine have to do with anything, Colonel?"

Jack had already subtracted eight hours to convert the times in the message from Zulu, or Greenwich Mean Time, to the corresponding times at San Francisco and the crash site. "I'd say the message means the Soviet Navy has some ship captains who are psychic or that Soviet National One was late. The ships turned toward the crash site thirty minutes before the crash. I'll need a copy of that message to give to General McClintock."

"Yes, sir," Lockhart said.

"We do know the aircraft was late taking off from Vladivostok," Brown said. "So you're suggesting that the ships turned at a pre-planned time that was supposed to have been a few minutes after the crash."

"Not only at a pre-planned time," Jack said, "but someone also knew the direction, which means the crash was planned to be near San Francisco."

"And *that* someone obviously was Valinen," O'Donnell said, "since we're talking ships of the Soviet Navy."

"I still wonder whether he had Medvalev's blessing."

"If Medvalev knew the plane was going to crash," O'Donnell said, "we've got an entirely diff—Jesus. The whole treaty-signing thing could have been a farce right from the beginning."

Jack continued, "The locations of the ships tell us a lot. The crash wasn't a spur-of-the-moment decision where Valinen says to Bochkov, 'I think I'll get off here in Vladivostok. Would you mind crashing just before you get to San Francisco?' Moving ships takes a lot longer than pre-positioning a wing of jet fighters. At seventeen knots, the *Karpaty* needed nearly two weeks to sail from Vladivostok to join the nuclear submarine that claimed to be in trouble. Whatever's happening, the plans had to be put together several weeks, if not months, ago."

"And if you're Medvalev," Brown said, "you can agree to on-site inspections and anything else the Americans want since the treaty's never going to be signed."

Jack nodded.

"Speaking of Vladivostok," Lockhart said, "we've learned more about the four merchant ships at the crash site. As I learned earlier, their official point of departure is the civilian port at Nakhodka. However, your questions caused a couple of my friends in Navy Intel to do more digging. They were surprised to discover that all four ships had been in the military port at Vladivostok in the two weeks before they were at Nakhodka. It's even possible that those ships took on their loads in Vladivostok and the loading activities at the civilian port may have been faked."

"Have you gotten pictures yet?"

"Some are due this afternoon, Colonel. Patrol planes out of the

Navy base at Adak got pictures of three of the four ships sailing south of the Aleutians."

"Good work," Jack said. "There's another question I need to follow up. Do you have direct contact with the operations staff on the AWACS?"

"Yes, sir," Lockhart said. He gestured toward a young sergeant at a communications console. Sergeant Ervin can put you through. Do you want to go unclassified or secure?"

"Secure," Jack said as he moved toward the console.

"Sir," Ervin said, "would you like to write your request?"

"Negative, Sergeant. You contact them, and I'll talk."

Ervin rotated a wafer switch on the control head of one of the radios. Then he flipped the switch for the speaker and said into his microphone. "Skybird, this is Regal Fox with a request, over."

"Go, Fox. This is Skybird."

Ervin passed a hand-held microphone to the colonel.

"Roger," Jack said. "Request to know if your records show any Soviet air traffic from the naval task force you have under surveillance to any destinations outside the task force."

"Copied your request, Regal Fox. Stand by." A minute passed before a crackle of static announced his return. "Regal Fox, this is Skybird."

Jack keyed the microphone and said, "Go."

"Roger, Fox. The answer to your request is negative. No flights left the fleet from the carrier *Minsk* or from any other ship. Can we be of further assistance?"

"Negative, Skybird. You've been very helpful." Jack handed the microphone to Ervin and said to the others, "Yesterday, less than seventy-two hours after the crash, the Russians announced that the flight recorders confirmed that the crash was an accident. They didn't use the FAA's equipment to interpret the recorders, and they didn't fly the recorders from the *Minsk* to Moscow. Although this fleet miraculously seems to have every kind of ship the Soviets could possibly need, I don't buy that the *Minsk* was carrying the special equipment needed to disassemble a smashed recorder and reproduce the information contained inside."

"So," O'Donnell said, "they were lying in their announcement."

"Through their teeth."

Brown asked, "Why lie about something like that?"

Jack shrugged. "None of this seems to make sense. Valinen decides to get rid of his competition, but waits until they're twenty miles off our coast to kill them. Furthermore, we know Bochkov crashed where he was supposed to, because the recovery ships started toward the site before the crash."

"Presumably Valinen wanted to blame the Americans," O'Donnell said. "That would play better with the people in Russia."

"Agreed," Jack said, "but why take us off the hook a couple of days later? Out of the goodness of his black heart?"

O'Donnell responded, "No way!"

"Actually, Medvalev brought the crisis to a close," Brown said. "Maybe he wasn't in on it from the beginning, and he just discovered what happened. He might've been afraid of a shooting war if he let the Soviet military keep thinking the American F-15 was responsible."

"I hope the answer's that simple," Jack said.

That explanation was the most plausible of all he had considered. A part of him shouted to accept it, be glad the crisis was finished, and take a few days off. A quieter voice deep within still whispered that he had been on the right path all along even though he could not yet see where that path was leading.

He sat on the edge of a desk and said, "Maybe all we're seeing's a power struggle, but let me tell a little story. Once when I was young, a carnival came to town. One of the games of chance—and I use that term loosely—had maybe a hundred little plastic ducks floating around in a trough. Each duck had a number or a message on the bottom. The big prize was a hundred dollars, and you got the hundred by selecting ducks until you built up a score of fifteen.

"My buddy, Verne, put down a couple of bucks and pointed at a duck bouncing in the water. The carny grabbed the duck, took a look at the bottom, and seemed worried. He dropped the duck into the back part of the trough, which was out of our view, and announced that my lucky friend had gotten a ten on the first try.

"Verne put down a couple of more bucks and made another choice. 'Three,' said the carny, who was two points away from losing big. We were already starting to count Verne's winnings and wishing he'd hurry and finish so we could have a try. Then, what do you suppose happened?"

Brown said, "Verne had a run of bad luck?"

"Bad, with a capital B. Verne picked his next duck and looked at the bottom. The duck was worth an eighth of a point. The next duck was no points but had a 'double the bet' message instead. After picking several more ducks out of the water, Verne had put down nearly all his money. He didn't even have fourteen points yet, and the next duck was going to cost him forty dollars back when forty dollars was real money."

"If the first two ducks were a setup," Brown said, "why didn't Verne look for himself?"

"The news was so good at that point that none of us thought about needing to verify it."

"And," O'Donnell said, "that's your point?"

"Exactly," Jack said. "I feel like the Russians didn't even look at the bottom of our first two ducks and gave us a score of thirteen— maybe even fourteen. No one wants to question them because we're overjoyed at how good our score is."

O'Donnell asked, "What are the Russians getting out of all this?"

"I don't know yet," Jack said, "but for one thing, they have us playing their game by their rules, and we can't believe we're having so much luck."

"And," Brown said, "you're afraid we're about to have a run of bad luck."

Jack nodded. "Deception and surprise are how the Soviets play the game. I think we've been seeing the deception. We damned well better figure out what Valinen's planning for the surprise before he shows us."

"I think we'd better get started trying to find out what Medvalev knows," O'Donnell said.

As soon as the two agents left, Jack asked Lockhart, "Did you get anything on the security checks of Mr. Braxton and Miss Merrill?"

"Yes, sir," Lockhart said as he stepped to his desk and picked up a folder. "I've also got printouts here on what a business tycoon Mr. Braxton is. I'd thought he was just a newsman, but if we ever need another E-4B, Braxton's got enough money to buy us a fleet of them."

Old news, Jack thought, as he took the folder and stuck it in his briefcase. "Thanks, but about the security information?"

"Yes, sir. They checked fine. The Defense Investigative Service had run background checks on both of them a couple of years ago when they were invited to a media orientation sponsored by the Department of Defense. I think they'd traveled overseas quite a bit, but nothing got flagged as being of concern."

Great news, Jack thought, relieved that the standard security checks had not denied Christine classified access because of her travel to Russia. He would feel better, though, once the information leak at Howell was identified as someone else.

He reviewed the messages that had come in since the previous day. The most significant thing about the messages was that there were no significant messages. How, he wondered, could the Soviets break diplomatic relations one day, rescind the break the next day, and not move a single major unit of their Army, Navy, or Air Force in response to either diplomatic action? His instincts said that the Soviets should have done some additional posturing for war the first day and backed off on the second.

As he closed the message folder, he could think of only two explanations: Either nothing appeared to be happening because nothing really was happening, or the Soviets had been trying very hard not to scare the Americans into putting more forces on alert. What bothered him was if the second explanation was correct, he still didn't have enough evidence to convince anyone that it even mattered.

Satisfied that he could learn nothing more at the E-4B, he left to meet Christine for lunch.

It was nearly eleven at night, and Andrei Valinen was dozing in the large leather chair in which he had spent much of the last three days. Since returning to Moscow on Monday morning, he had remained almost continuously in the command center beneath Lytkarino. The large chair on Valinen's left was empty. Premier Medvalev had gone to the sleeping quarters nearly two hours earlier. Valinen had stayed, wanting to be present when a long-awaited message arrived from the *Minsk*.

A three-star general entered from the communications center. He awakened Valinen, then said, *"Minsk* has signalled."

Valinen was instantly alert. He took a piece of paper offered by the general and quickly scanned the message. The words stated that the admiral expected to complete the recovery in fifteen hours, but Valinen understood the hidden meaning—preparations were almost complete. In fifteen hours, the escorts would be ready to leave the crash site.

He looked at the clock, quickly computing times and offsets. It was almost noon in San Francisco—the timing would work out favorably. He got up, went to a small safe in a corner of the room, and turned the dial through a combination known only to him. Removing an audio tape that Premier Medvalev had recorded the previous afternoon, Valinen checked that the seal was still in place, then handed the tape to the general. He nodded toward the clock that showed the local time in Moscow to be ten-fifty and said, "You will begin the broadcast at four minutes to one."

The general took a deep breath as he accepted the tape. "Yes, Comrade Minister. I will have all forces standing by."

The minister of defense nodded, knowing that the general was one of the few who understood the tape's significance.

Valinen returned to his chair and sat quietly absorbed in his thoughts. He glanced at the unlighted *Iskra* timers. They would remain still for barely two more hours. Though he appeared calm, he could hardly contain the excitement he felt. Some of the uncertainty was over. Finally the schedule was set.

Chapter 21

Thursday Morning, 11:50 a.m.
Pacific Standard Time

WHEN JACK REACHED THE TELEVISION STUDIO, CHRISTINE WAS IN A dressing room with her hairstylist preparing for the noon broadcast. Braxton greeted Jack and led him into a control room overlooking the set. Before returning to the set, the newsman mentioned that the President was expecting another announcement from the Soviets. By mid-afternoon he expected Medvalev to call an end to the worldwide naval exercise. Jack was pleased. If the Soviets withdrew to normal operating areas, he would be more willing to believe that the crisis was over.

After the opening ritual of the newscast, the male and female co-anchors exchanged a brief preview of the top stories of the day. Then they turned to Christine, who discussed the aborted conference and the failure to get signatures on the Pan-Paclfic treaty. She reported that the Japanese had offered to host a new conference in late January. The State Department believed the Japanese suggestion would be accepted by both the United States and the Soviet Union. At the end of her report, the anchorman asked her when she expected an official announcement of the new date and location.

Jack assumed that everything on the subject at this point was just media speculation, and he watched her with more personal than professional interest. He smiled in amusement at how demure she was in the studio compared to how uninhibited and sensual she had been with him. He was anticipating how pleasurable the next few hours would be when suddenly the wall he was leaning against began to shudder. The motion reminded him of the feeling when he eased the speed brake out on an F-15 at a very low airspeed. Then the building started swaying as the shuddering increased.

He looked around the studio. Things had started moving; people had stopped. The conversation between Christine and the anchorman was forgotten as both looked around, sizing up the severity of the earthquake. Off camera, Braxton was holding onto a post that sup-

249

ported the ceiling. The newsman looked frightened, so Jack decided he should be more concerned, too. Before he could react, the shuddering gave way to a double jolt, then quit. The building and the overhead lights continued to sway, but with decreasing magnitude.

The lead cameraman focused on the anchorman, who smiled nervously and said, "San Francisco has just experienced an earthquake—and we've felt it right here in the studio. This shaker seemed bigger than the one we experienced on December second. Let's hope this one qualifies as the big quake that's been predicted for California before the end of this year. In any case, we'll have more details on the location and magnitude of this tremor later in the broadcast. Now. . . ."

Jack stopped listening and concentrated for a moment. Though there had been no emphasis by the anchorman, the word "tremor" seemed to jump out. *The last time Jack had heard the word, it had been shouted in Russian.*

He remembered Kane's fateful broadcast. With microphone extended, Kane had been leaning over the side of his speedboat. The Russian frogman was swimming frantically from the Soviet ship. The Hind-D was swooping in from behind. The frogman had yelled, *"Zemletryasenie!"*—a word that was forgotten in the carnage that followed. Jack remembered translating the word as "country shock" or "field shock" for General Harper. Yet translations of "country tremor" or "field tremor" or "earth tremor" would have been as accurate. Jack realized *Zemletryasenie* could have been the frogman's attempt to say "earthquake."

His mind was racing as he slipped out the back door of the control room and into the office area that supported the news department. Suddenly he wanted to know a lot more about earthquakes and whether quakes could be initiated as a military weapon. He knew only one thing about man's ability to cause earthquakes: underground detonations of nuclear weapons on test ranges in Nevada had been measured at greater than 5.0 on the Richter scale and usually shook buildings in Las Vegas, nearly a hundred miles away. Jack tried to reassure himself, however, that being able to shake buildings in Las Vegas did not equate directly to a weapon Valinen would find of interest.

He also wanted to know more about the spot where the Soviet pilot had chosen to crash. Did the crash site have any connection with the web of geological faults interlaced beneath the area around San Francisco?

He saw Braxton coming out of another door and hurried over to him. The older man appeared pale, so Jack asked, "Are you okay, sir?"

"Sure," Braxton said, forcing a smile. "Those damned quakes always get to me. You'd think after all these years I'd be used to them."

"I doubt I ever would be," Jack said. "Say, do you know where the San Andreas fault runs in this part of the state?"

Braxton seemed surprised by the question. "That little shaker probably wasn't on the San Andreas." When he noticed Jack was still waiting, he added, "The fault passes about five miles from here, between us and the ocean."

Jack asked, "Doesn't the fault go out to sea along here somewhere?"

"Why would you want to know that?"

Before Jack could answer, Christine joined them and said, "You can't say my stories don't shake things up."

She looked brightly at her new lover for a reaction to her joke, but when he did not respond, she asked, "What's wrong?"

"Nothing," Jack said, wishing she had stayed busy somewhere else for a few more minutes. "Mr. Braxton and I are a bit edgy about earthquakes."

"To answer your question," Braxton said, "the San Andreas fault hugs the coast."

Christine recognized the deadly serious look on Jack's face and said, "If you're really interested, I'm sure we have maps in our files."

Jack hesitated. He was already feeling ridiculous for mentioning his interest. However, he still pictured the Russian frogman struggling in the waves. Jack could find no other explanation for *"Zemletryasenie!"* He decided to see what he could learn without revealing exactly why he was asking. "I don't want to make a big deal of it, but I would like to see a map."

She led the way to an adjacent room containing files and research materials. As the two men followed, Jack said, "Sir, I don't think you need to waste your time on this."

"I just hope we can put your mind at ease," Braxton said reassuringly, "so you can enjoy the holidays like everyone else in America."

Christine selected a topographic map of northern California and spread the map on a table. Pointing to a pair of long, narrow lakes stretching along the San Francisco peninsula, she said, "These two lakes show exactly where the fault is."

Jack asked, "Where does the fault go under the ocean?"

"That's obvious here," Braxton said as he took an expensive fountain pen from his pocket. The line defined by the two lakes crossed into the water on the ocean side of San Francisco. He placed the pen on the lakes, then slid it straight across the coastline. The pen crossed outside the Golden Gate and over the part of the ocean leading into

San Francisco Bay. Almost immediately, the pen encountered land again where the Point Reyes Peninsula touched the mainland. "Right here, the San Andreas fault almost separates Point Reyes from the coast. Tomales Bay is over the fault." Braxton picked up the pen and sat on the edge of the table watching Jack's single-minded interest in the map. "Oh, I see what's bothering you, Colonel. But the plane crash was nearly twenty-five miles west of the fault."

Steeling himself to betray no emotion, Jack bent over the map and studied the imaginary line traced by the movement of the pen. He pictured where the crash had occurred and saw from the map that Braxton's estimate was accurate. Jack would have been convinced except for the word *"Zemletryasenie"* that continued to echo through his mind. Jack stepped back and said, "It's pretty obvious that the crash and the San Andreas aren't related."

As Braxton folded the map and handed it to Christine, he eyed the colonel curiously for a moment before saying, "How about lunch? Our executive dining room isn't as good as the restaurant I suggested for last night, but it's quite passable."

Before Christine shut the file drawer, Jack asked, "Would you have any maps showing all the faults in the area?"

"Colonel," Braxton said in a tone that seemed to be a cross between amusement and exasperation, "I'd hate to try to get away from you in a dog fight. We have two or three different maps of the Bay Area that should answer all your questions, whatever they are."

He searched the files for a few moments, selected three maps, and spread them on the table. "All three of these tell the same story. The Hayward fault is second in prominence to the San Andreas, and the Hayward's even farther from the crash." Braxton's eyes gleamed above a broad smile.

Jack picked the map showing the most detail. He saw names of other faults—Pleasanton, Calaveras, San Gregorio, Green Valley. All ran almost parallel to the San Andreas. He had expected to see faults stretching from the coast toward the point where Soviet National One had crashed. None did.

After a few moments Braxton placed his hand on Jack's shoulder and said, "Lunch, Colonel?"

Jack accepted reluctantly and went with the two to the executive dining room in the station's penthouse. He tried to join in the conversation during the meal, but he remained preoccupied. He was trying to fit everything he had learned in the last three days into a scenario that depended on the location of the crash.

Earlier, he had dreamed of being in the cockpit with a confused and panicky crew trying to save a crippled aircraft. This time he pictured a calm crew that knew exactly where it was, even when seventy-two miles left of the track filed on the ICAO flight plan. He pictured descending from forty-one thousand feet on a profile that was computed to end nearly sixty miles short of the airport. He would follow the clearances received from the controller at Oakland Center until the navigator declared that it was time to steepen the dive.

This time he regarded the navigator and his equipment with more respect than had been justified by the reported navigational error. Receiving signals from the satellite navigational systems of both countries, the navigator knew the aircraft's position and altitude within a matter of feet, not miles. Even traveling at nine-tenths of the speed of sound, his speed data was more accurate than the speedometer on an automobile doing twenty miles per hour. With that kind of data available, the navigator should be able to guide to a specific point anywhere in the world—with almost no error.

So, on the navigator's call, Jack would extend the speed brakes and increase the rate of descent. Plummeting toward his target, he would be concerned about not going so fast that the aircraft started breaking apart.

Except for the distraction of staring death in the eye all the way to the water, he thought, hitting the aim point should have been "a piece of cake." Yet something had gone wrong. The pilot had leveled off, turned 270 degrees, and crashed almost under the original flight path. It was as if he had overshot his target and decided to make another try.

Excessive tail winds during descent could explain the overshoot. Even if spies in America were passing weather data to Vladivostok or if Colonel Bochkov could have tapped into the data streams from American weather satellites, he still lacked accurate information on low altitude winds off the coast. The storm was growing in intensity by the hour. The only accurate readings of those winds would come from aircraft flying through the area, and late at night in that weather, no one else had any reason to be flying at low altitude that far off the coast.

In any case, the F-15 pilots had reported northwesterly winds of nearly thirty knots. Therefore as Bochkov dropped through a wind shear that pushed his aircraft forward an extra half-mile every minute, he may have realized he was overshooting his target. The natural response would be to reduce the descent rate, circle around, and crash beneath the original flight path.

Yet the winds would produce an error of only one or two miles at the most. An error that large could be critical in attacking a target. However, a difference of a mile or two was unimportant in destroying an aircraft that was diving into an angry ocean. How could he convince anyone that the low-altitude maneuver was due to the pilot needing to be more accurate in crashing the aircraft? He had reached another dead end unless he could think of a scenario in which the last mile or two was critical.

He was stuck once again between instinct and common sense. He could not justify why Bochkov would have tried so hard to hit a specific point. Yet his instincts said that Bochkov had.

When the meal was nearly finished, he said, "At the risk of seeming to beat a horse that you've already told me is dead, do you know of any earthquake experts in the area?"

Braxton smiled and shook his head. Jack was not sure if that meant no or just indicated amusement. "Most of the seismology experts are at Cal Tech in Pasadena or at the earthquake center run by the U.S. Geological Service at Golden, Colorado."

Christine asked, "How about UC Berkeley?"

"Since today's the last Thursday afternoon before Christmas," Braxton said, "the campus probably resembles a ghost town."

She nodded, paused in thought, then said, "How about that cute little man you talked to in that series on earthquakes a couple of years ago? Wasn't his name Williams or something like that?"

Braxton looked as if he were trying to remember. Finally he said, "You mean the old professor—an octogenarian at least. He'd have been a good choice if he still were lucid. Actually, though, I think I saw an obituary on him last year."

"How sad," she said. "He was such an interesting little man."

Braxton stood and said, "I've got a string of meetings all afternoon. Chris, maybe you could get Colonel Phillips a phone number for *The Daily Planet.*" She looked confused. Before she could respond, he added with a smile, "I think Superman was the last person who had to save us from an earthquake."

She laughed and Jack grinned. He said, "I suppose I deserve that."

"You do have an active imagination, Colonel," Braxton said. "I'm sure Chris can keep that imagination busy. Perhaps a personally guided tour of our complex. Our broadcasting facility is the finest on the West Coast."

After he left, the other two remained at the table.

"I don't have time for the tour," Jack said, "but I would like to see that tape your cameraman took on the flight to Chaney."

"I checked on that for you yesterday, and there's a problem. We have the part Alex used on his broadcast that night, but the raw tape was chewed up in the processing machine."

That seemed too convenient. Earlier doubts about her vague answers and the unexplained leaks of information again overwhelmed his personal feelings. In a slightly accusatory tone he asked, "Do accidents like that happen very often?"

She looked at him as if bothered by the tone and responded, "A little more frequently than missiles are fired accidentally at Soviet airliners, but not much more often, Colonel." Her emphasis on the word "colonel" was stiffer, and less playful, than usual.

Sounding more neutral than before, he asked, "How about a copy of Kane's transmissions from the boat? Mr. Braxton said he'd try to get a copy."

"Alex mentioned this morning that the tape should be available before the weekend." Sounding more conciliatory, she added, "If you really need to see it sooner, I could make a call."

"Tomorrow's probably fine," he said. He did not want to reveal that he thought the pictures might still be significant.

As they walked silently to the elevator, his mind raced through things that he still should check. Now, more than ever, he wanted to see pictures of the merchant ships at the crash site. Perhaps the government copy of Kane's broadcast had arrived on an airplane that had escaped the snows of Washington, D.C., earlier in the morning. If Bochkov had a reason for crashing at a specific point, Jack believed the cargo on those ships was somehow related. Surely those four specialized merchant ships had not come to the crash site at the same time through simple coincidence.

He remembered the second part of the message shouted by the Soviet frogman, just before the helicopter attacked. The young Russian had said that there was going to be an explosion. Suddenly Jack had an unsettling thought. Perhaps instead of warning of the imminent attack by the Hind-D, as Radisson had suggested, the frogman was referring to explosives he was helping offload.

Jack quickly tried to picture what Valinen could accomplish with explosives. The frogman had talked of earthquakes and explosions, but the ships were twenty miles from the nearest fault that showed on any of the maps. Earthquakes and explosions made no sense unless . . . He thought of his earlier analogy of Las Vegas and the nuclear weapons tests. Could they have been unloading a nuclear weapon? He recoiled at that thought. Almost immediately, however, he could not explain the need for four ships to deliver a nuclear weapon.

As they got off the elevator near her office, he said, "I have to go to Alameda this afternoon."

"If you can wait a little while," she said eagerly, "I could go with you. There are a couple of things I have to finish before I leave."

"You probably can't even get on the aircraft anymore."

She looked surprised, and a bit hurt as well by his flat tone.

He continued, "The President's authorization allowed you to observe the Air Force investigation of the missile firing. Now that the Soviets say the crash was an accident, and the crisis is over, security will have removed your name from the computer."

She looked disappointed, then said with a grin, "I could wait outside and flirt with the Marines, Colonel." Her emphasis on the word "colonel" was both teasing and seductive. "They didn't mind putting up with me before."

For a moment he considered going into her office for a more private farewell. Instead he pulled her firmly to him and gave her a quick kiss. "Save your flirting for later when I get back to your place, lady."

Premier Medvalev had returned to the command center, so there was more activity than normal for a few minutes before one a.m. He was wearing an expensive robe of heavy brocade with a fur collar. Looking uncharacteristically nervous, he sat quietly, drinking from a large mug of warm milk.

To the premier's right, Andrei Valinen sat listening to a headset. The minister of defense looked tired but his eyes betrayed the excitement within. He was taking in everything that was happening, though mostly he was watching the clock that showed the local time in Moscow. As the second hand reached the top for the fifty-fifth time since midnight, he said into his microphone, "Problems?"

In the communications center on the next level above, a general responded, "We are ready, Comrade Minister."

Valinen turned to Medvalev and said, "All is prepared."

The premier leaned back in his chair. He took a long sip of milk. He seemed to be weighing the decision though both men already understood: The point of no return had come and gone four days earlier. He nodded. Though he did not speak, Medvalev's silent message to Valinen was that the plan had better work.

"Go with the schedule," Valinen said into the microphone. Leaning back with his arms crossed over his chest, he watched the clock.

At exactly four minutes to one, the premier's voice filled the command center, coming through the speakers on an all-forces broadcast. The recorded message emphasized the glorious accomplishments in the ongoing worldwide exercises.

As the words of praise for Soviet military strength droned on, most people in the command center listened with polite attention. Medvalev sat back with his eyes closed. Valinen leaned onto the desk and absentmindedly tapped a pencil against a notebook that contained classified war plans. Finally, when less than thirty seconds remained until one, he reached forward to a guarded switch, which had been installed the previous week. He snapped the cover aside, exposing the toggle switch beneath.

The second hand approached twelve, as Medvalev's message was reaching its climax. "At this time, I declare a successful end to the current exercises at sea and on land. The next will come in July when the Soviet Navy will resume worldwide exercises under the code name *Iskra*."

As Valinen watched the others in the command center, he switched the toggle. On the front wall, the panel labeled *Iskra* illuminated, and the two timers activated, beginning their countdowns from 20:00 and 44:00. Hearing *Iskra* gave him a chill, though most people in the room reacted to the announcement of the exercise being over instead of to the special word. In addition to the two leaders at the desk, only three others in the room understood the real significance of the message. They exchanged nervous glances as the recording continued for a few more paragraphs of obligatory pronouncements.

At the end of the message, Medvalev stood and nodded toward Valinen before leaving for the sleeping quarters.

Valinen settled back and watched as more and more people noticed the timers. Let them be curious, he thought. They would have to wait until the first timers reached zero to learn more about the real meaning of *Iskra*. He yawned and tried to get more comfortable in the big chair. If he did not get some sleep, these twenty hours would seem like the longest of his life.

The traffic on the bridge was heavy, and it was just after two when Jack reached the E-4B. He went into the intelligence section after learning that General McClintock had not returned from Howell.

Lockhart greeted him with pictures taken from the patrol planes of the U.S. Navy. "Not that they're going to be much help, Colonel, but we've got pictures of three of the merchant ships."

Jack studied the pictures. Each ship was plowing through heavy seas in the North Pacific. The *Tibor Szamueli* and her sister ship had a full complement of barges on the upper cargo deck. Canvas covers, which were heavily encrusted with ice, protected the cargo from the winter weather and from the view of the cameras. The pictures of the *Stakhanovets Yermolenko* were similar. All three ships were heavily loaded, but nothing identified the cargo hidden beneath the covers.

"Supposedly the cargo's lumber," Lockhart said, "but we're still a little uncertain on that. Shipping lumber from Siberia doesn't make much sense. Meanwhile, the Navy says all four ships traveled at nearly top speed for the first three-quarters of the trip, then slowed the last few days."

Jack thought about that for a moment. "I'd say the Soviets wanted the ships here on time, but not so early that we might invite ourselves to inspect their cargo."

"What do you think the cargo could be, sir?"

"I need a few more answers before I make any open guesses."

After his experience with Braxton on the subject of earthquakes, Jack preferred to do the rest of his research quietly. He sat at a computer console and checked the unclassified databases for information on earthquake research. As he read through abstracts of articles on the research, he found that most focused on trying to predict earthquakes. Considerable research had been done in Russia and China. Research was being done in the United States but apparently was limited by inadequate funding. None of the titles of articles listed in the unclassified databases indicated any research on using earthquakes as weapons.

Most names of American experts were associated with the seismological laboratory at the California Institute of Technology in Pasadena. Jack wrote four names in case he needed to talk to one of the scientists. He also noticed that the databases listed articles and papers written in the 1930s through the 1980s by a Dr. William Whitney of the University of California at Berkeley. As Jack wrote a note, he wondered if Whitney was the old man Christine had remembered.

Jack found an article declaring that a major quake on the San Andreas fault was almost inevitable within twenty-five years. He was about halfway through the article when Major Lockhart rushed in from another section of the airplane.

"They just said it," Lockhart announced excitedly. "The Premier himself just used the word '*Iskra!*' "

Jack felt a shiver at the mention of the word. He looked at his watch, then asked, "When? How?"

"Within the last hour," Lockhart said. "We just got word a couple of minutes ago. The premier transmitted a congratulatory message to all Soviet forces worldwide. The message, with the obligatory amount of Sovietese, announced the end of the naval exercise and the Warsaw Pact games. The premier declared those exercises a success and announced that even more extensive exercises will start in July. The July exercises are code-named *Iskra*."

Jack was surprised. "I'd think the Soviets would hide the word a little better than that, especially if *Iskra* has any real significance."

"That might depend on its purpose, Colonel. The numbers associated with *Iskra*—the twenty and the forty-four—suggest that it's a timing signal. That means everyone involved needs to start counting at the same reference time."

"Valinen could have just sent the word and the reference time to the units that needed it."

Lockhart thought for a moment, then said, "A special message is likely to make us more curious than just inserting the word like a throw-away at the end of the premier's congratulations, especially if they don't suspect we're looking for *Iskra*. In any case, it's an efficient way to pass the word. All Soviet units world-wide had been told to listen-up for the broadcast, so the message shouldn't have missed anyone who needed to hear it."

The phrasing gave Jack a chilling thought. "Maybe everyone needed to hear it because every military unit has a mission at *Iskra* plus twenty or *Iskra* plus forty-four, or both. We damned well better get to figuring out if the twenty represents seconds, minutes, hours, or days! I doubt we're talking seconds—there's just not enough difference between zero, twenty, and forty-four. We could be talking minutes."

"The difference between twenty and forty-four minutes," Lockhart said, "is close to the flight time for an ICBM from Russia to America."

Jack looked at his watch and jumped up from the console. "We need to find out exactly when *Iskra* was broadcast and if Soviet forces have responded significantly, assuming we've already lost at least twenty minutes since the broadcast."

"Our people in the comm section can find out when the message was broadcast, and my people are monitoring overall Soviet activities."

As they hurried to the communications section on the E-4B, Jack asked, "Do we have a tape of the actual announcement?"

"Negative, sir, but I'm sure the comm section can connect you with people in Washington who could play a copy."

"Let's do it."

While Lockhart checked for any significant events that might have occurred since the announcement, Jack talked to analysts in the intelligence center in the Pentagon. He learned that the broadcast had started just over thirty minutes earlier at thirteen-fifty-six hours, Pacific Standard Time. Since the alert status was still DEFCON Four, Jack relaxed slightly. He was pretty sure *Iskra* plus twenty did not represent minutes—unless the length of the premier's speech meant that twenty minutes had not passed yet since the mention of *Iskra*. The analyst in the Pentagon started the tape of the broadcast, and Jack started the timer on his wrist watch.

The first three minutes of the premier's words were the heavy style of rhetoric Jack found so boring in Communist speeches and publications. Finally, Medvalev talked of ending the highly successful demonstration of the power of the Soviet military. When he said *Iskra*, Jack stopped the timer on his watch. Four minutes and one second had elapsed—*Iskra* had been spoken at fourteen hundred hours in California.

When the tape was finished, he asked, "Do we have any idea why the premier picked zero-one hundred hours to make his announcement?"

The analyst said, "Negative. The announcement probably was a tape, but so far we don't see any significance to the time chosen. Medvalev had pledged to cool the crisis as quickly as possible, so he may have speeded up the announcement as a favor to the President."

Right, Jack thought facetiously. In his opinion, Premier Medvalev was as ruthless as Minister Valinen, only in a more diplomatically acceptable sort of way. Medvalev did few favors for anyone besides Medvalev. As Jack hung up the telephone, Lockhart returned.

"Sir," Lockhart said as they walked to the intelligence section, "everything's quiet. One Soviet fleet in the South Atlantic seems to have turned for home already, but nothing strategic seems to have happened twenty minutes after the announcement."

Jack saw that nearly forty minutes had passed since the term *Iskra* had been used. "Have someone keep an eye on things for the next fifteen minutes, and be sure that O'Donnell knows when the clock started on *Iskra*."

"Yes, sir."

"Also I've got the name of a professor who was with UC Berkeley. See if you can get a current address on him." As Lockhart took the name and started to leave, Jack added, "And do a little quick, but quiet, asking if the Soviets have done any research involving the use of earthquakes as a weapon."

Lockhart stopped abruptly. "Are you serious, sir?"

"The last time I said I was, they laughed me out of San Francisco, so I won't admit to anything at the moment. However, if anyone knows of such research, we need to talk."

Jack checked with Joanne Kingston to see when McClintock was due to return. She said that the general was still busy at Howell, and he expected to fly to the Western White House before coming to Alameda. In any case, she did not expect him at the E-4B for at least two hours.

Jack went back to the article he had been reading on the San Andreas fault. The article, written in the previous year, indicated that the strain on the northern part of the fault was greater than when the 1906 earthquake and fire had devastated San Francisco. As bad as that sounded, there was even more concern about the strain on the southern part of the fault, near Los Angeles. Seismologists agreed that a cataclysmic quake was likely within twenty-five years. And that quake, he thought, was almost ready to happen without any help from Valinen.

In a few minutes, Lockhart returned and said, "It's been nearly an hour, sir, and everything's still quiet. So far there's nothing on Soviet research involving using earthquakes as weapons, although the analyst who might know more is on Christmas leave."

Jack thought about trying to locate the analyst, but was unsure the questions and answers could be discussed on an unclassified telephone. The man could be reached later, if necessary.

"I did get an address for your Professor Whitney. He's alive, all right. We called three or four places. He's a recluse with an unlisted phone number, so no one was sure he'd accept visitors."

Jack took the address, which indicated that Whitney's home was only a few miles away. Jack decided he could get there and back before General McClintock returned. If Whitney refused to see him, perhaps Braxton could intervene with the professor since they were acquainted.

Before leaving the E-4B, however, Jack wanted to check one more thing. He was interested in where the Soviet fleets would be at twenty and forty-four hours after *Iskra*—just in case those numbers represented hours. When he asked for the information, Lockhart led Jack to the status room.

Jack studied the markings on a map of the world that covered one wall. The locations were current for noon. The Soviet ships had moved little since he had checked their locations the previous day. He assumed that the fleets could steam toward their ports in Russia at fifteen to twenty knots. In twenty hours, the positions would change by three hundred to four hundred nautical miles. Forty-four hours could put the ships 660 to 880 nautical miles closer to home.

He looked at the location of each fleet and mentally projected the fleet toward its home port. Initially, nothing was obvious. He considered all of the fleets at twenty hours—still nothing of interest. He considered each fleet at forty-four hours. Still nothing—suddenly, a realization jolted him harder than the mid-day earthquake. In forty-four hours Soviet fleets would be in every open-ocean area patrolled by the U.S. Navy submarines carrying *Trident* missiles.

Normal protocols prohibited the close shadowing of the ballistic missile submarines of the other superpower. Yet, in forty-four hours, presumably innocent movements would put Soviet fleets in the best positions possible to defeat retaliatory strikes by American submarines. A surprise first-strike would destroy most American ICBMs in their silos—unless President Cunningham ordered a counterstrike before the Soviet warheads arrived. If the Soviets could also destroy most of the missile boats, they might escape with little direct retaliation.

He turned to Lockhart. "Do you have any contacts you can trust in Navy Intel?"

The major seemed confused for a moment by the way the question was phrased. Then he said, "Yes, sir."

Jack led him into one of the booths for secure telephones so that no one could overhear their conversation. "Watch the Soviet fleets for the next hour or two, or until all start moving, if that happens sooner. Project them forward at their initial speeds to likely locations on Saturday morning at ten-hundred hours. Compare what you find to the normal patrol areas of the Navy's ballistic missile boats. If you get some close matches, call your friends in the Navy and tell them to do the same thing. Under no circumstances, however, link Saturday morning with *Iskra!*"

"What do I tell them if they ask why I'm concerned?"

"Once they look themselves, they'll understand. Tell them you just got lucky, but tell them to keep their suspicions very 'close hold.' "

Lockhart gave him a look of admiration. "You're really on to something, aren't you, Colonel?"

"I hope not, Major," Jack said. As he started walking away, he stopped and added, "But smart money wouldn't bet against it!"

Intent on his new discovery as he hurried down the stairs from the E-4B, he was startled by the honking of a car horn. He looked toward the sound and saw a car belonging to the guards. A Marine captain got out and opened the back door. In a moment, Jack was surprised to see Christine get out of the car.

The captain saluted as Jack approached. "Good afternoon, Colonel. You have a visitor, sir."

Jack returned the salute, even though he was not in uniform. Christine rushed up, put her arm around Jack, and kissed him. He blushed and the Marine grinned.

As Jack tried to pull back from her embrace, he said, "I haven't explained to her yet about the Air Force rules on the public display of affection."

She looked up at Jack, then glanced flirtatiously at the Marine. "It's all right, Captain. I'm not in the Air Force."

The Marine's smile broadened as he stepped back and saluted. "You have a good day and a Merry Christmas, Colonel. Miss Merrill."

She maintained a firm grip on Jack, nuzzling a breast firmly against his arm. "We will, Captain. We will."

Though he liked the physical closeness and the fresh fragrance of her perfume in contrast to the smells of a busy flight line, he was unsure whether to be pleased or not by her sudden appearance. The clean security report on her helped, but he had wanted to do his investigating alone until he learned more from General McClintock about the problem at Howell. Yet she also had met Dr. Whitney, and the old recluse might be more willing to open his door to her than to Braxton.

If she really were a spy—and there wasn't any real evidence that said she was—he wanted her to keep thinking she had not been discovered. If they learned more than he could trust her with, he would stop her from telling anyone else before he got the word to General McClintock.

He said, "I guess I just can't keep you away from those handsome Marines, lady."

She smiled in response. "I have some flirting left over, Colonel. When I told Alex you were still on the chase, he told me to stick as close to you as I could." To emphasize that point, she pulled herself even tighter against his arm.

"I wouldn't want you to disobey your boss," he said with a smile, "but I'd assumed he'd think I was wasting my time."

"He probably does," she said. "However, he said that if you're still worried, there may be a story there yet."

"Maybe," he said as they started toward his car. An hour had passed since the *Iskra* announcement. In nineteen hours, he thought, a great many people would know if there was more to the story.

Chapter 22

Thursday Afternoon, 3:15 p.m.
Iskra plus 1:15

AS THEY APPROACHED THE EXIT FROM THE NAVAL AIR STATION, CHRIStine cuddled close to Jack and asked, "Are we on our way home?"

"I've got an errand to run first." Pulling out the note with Whitney's address, he asked, "Can you show me how to get here?"

"I can get you into the neighborhood, but we may have to scout around a little. What are you expecting to find there?"

"I think your little professor lives there. Was his name Whitney?"

"Right. I think that's him. What do you expect to learn from him?"

"You'll see," he said.

Though she tried to engage him in conversation as he followed her directions to the freeway, his thoughts were racing through other subjects. He was trying to link the things he had learned in the last few hours with everything that had happened in the last four days. His mind was filled with new questions he was not ready to share with her.

After a few minutes, he felt her move away and realized she had just said, "I didn't intend to be a burden to you."

He looked at her and though he had said nothing, her expression reminded him of a child who had been chastised severely. She avoided his glance, looking beyond the windshield instead.

"Hey," he said, reaching over to grab her hand, "sometimes I get very preoccupied, and I'm not used to having to think that that may matter to someone else."

She did not look totally convinced. "When Alex told me to catch up with you, I thought you'd be pleased."

He did not want to reveal his concerns about the leaks of information. "I'll be even more pleased when we can get back to your place." She still hesitated when he tried to pull her back to him. "You'll like my great powers of preoccupation better when I'm totally preoccupied with you."

She seemed satisfied that he was not rejecting her, so she slid next

264

to him and kissed him on the neck. He put his arm around her and kept her close even though his mind returned to trying to solve what the Soviets were doing.

Following Christine's directions, Jack located the street where Dr. Whitney lived. In an earlier time the neighborhood had been characterized by closely-packed Victorian homes with views of San Francisco Bay. Now Jack saw dilapidated houses, rusted cars, and the unkept yards of slum dwellers who seemed to have little view of the past or the future.

He located the address on a large house that looked as run down as the rest. There was no place to park nearby, so he finally squeezed the rental sedan between a couple of old cars near the middle of the next block.

When he knocked on the door, there was no immediate response. In a few moments he felt that someone was moving slowly through the house, and he knocked again. A voice responded through a speaker above the door: "Who's there?"

Christine identified herself and said she was looking for Dr. Whitney.

"I do not give interviews anymore."

Jack studied the voice. Even through the scratchy speaker, the words sounded firm and determined, much more so than he had expected from a man in his late eighties or early nineties.

"I'm not here with any cameras," she said. Her voice had the confidence and persistence of a person who did not always get permission the first time she asked. "I do have with me a colonel from the United States Air Force."

"I especially do not give information to the military!"

Jack was surprised by the vehemence of the answer. He had assumed that the anti-military sentiment on the Berkeley campus had centered primarily within the social sciences and liberal arts. He had not expected such a bias in a professor of the hard sciences.

Christine looked a little frustrated and whispered to Jack, "It would be a lot easier if I could do this in person instead of through that damned little speaker."

Jack agreed. He knew she was much more effective in person.

"I need your help, Dr. Whitney," she said. "I'm sure you're aware of the predictions that California will have a major earthquake before the end of this year. After the tremor we had today, a lot of our viewers are nervous and worried. Please, I would take only a few minutes of your time."

"They do not need to worry."

She gave Jack an exasperated look indicating she was unsure what to try next. "But Dr. Whitney, the Russians repeated their prediction just last week."

"Humbug," the voice answered.

Jack could not hide how much her mention of the Russians surprised him. He whispered loudly, "The Russians predicted a major quake here by the end of the year?"

"That's old news," she whispered. "They made that prediction a couple of weeks before Thanksgiving."

Jack leaned against the wall as he tried to remember the date the Soviets had agreed to on-site inspections of Kamchatka, thereby opening the way for the signing of the treaty. The date of that agreement must have been within two or three days of when the Russians had announced their prediction of an earthquake. He did not like the timing, but knew he would have trouble convincing others that anything more than unrelated coincidence was involved.

"Dr. Whitney, this is Colonel Jack Phillips. We need to talk about any experiments the Russian military may be attempting involving earthquakes."

Christine looked shocked. "You never—"

"Ssshh," he said, putting a finger on his lips for silence. He did not want to miss a response from Whitney. She complied, but looked almost overwhelmed. Was she surprised because of what he said or because he had learned one of her secrets? Jack wished he knew.

Finally, Whitney answered, "Please wait."

"You didn't tell me," she whispered.

"I didn't know," Jack whispered back. "I'm still guessing."

In a few moments, a small observation window opened in the center of the door. Dr. Whitney's eyes peered over the lower frame of the opening.

Christine smiled and introduced herself again. Jack nodded and held his military identification card so that Whitney could read the information.

Looking toward her, Whitney said, "Now if I agree to talk, my words must be, as you say, 'off the record.' "

She glanced at Jack, then said, "I will not attribute anything directly to you, if you don't want to be quoted. However, I hope you'll allow me to use some of your information. Your rebuttal of the Soviet prediction would calm people's fears about an imminent earthquake."

Whitney seemed to accept her terms as he shifted his position behind the door so he could see Jack better. "And you, Colonel, have information about Russian experiments?"

"I have seen indicators that are difficult to explain unless the Russian military is trying to manipulate earthquakes. I need to know if they're experimenting."

Whitney's answer was more to himself and inaudible to Jack. However, the old man nodded, closed the small window, and unlocked the locks.

The scene inside the house contrasted dramatically with the dreary setting outside. The living room was immaculately clean and filled with antique furniture, reminding Jack of early memories of his grandmother's home.

Dr. Whitney was a short, neatly dressed man with close-cropped white hair. With his bow tie and sweater he seemed ready to step to the front of a crowded lecture hall. Jack wondered if the old man dressed each day as if he were still a professor at the university.

After resetting the locks and the door alarm, Whitney offered tea to his guests. As he led them toward the kitchen, he apologized because it was the housekeeper's day off. He located the tea and some cookies, and Christine took over just as if she were a granddaughter who had come for a visit. Despite his concerns, Jack couldn't help admiring her and how easily she adapted to any situation. While the tea was brewing, Whitney continued to tell of the house and its contents. His father had had the house built more than one hundred years earlier. Whitney had been born in the house eighty-eight years ago. He talked about how the neighborhood had deteriorated in only the last few years.

Listening quietly and letting Christine carry their side of the conversation, Jack wondered if a "few years" meant five or thirty-five to the spry old professor.

When the tea was ready, Whitney led them to the parlor. After a few more minutes of discussion about the furnishings, he turned abruptly to Jack and asked, "Young man, just what causes your concerns about earthquake experiments conducted by the Soviet military?"

"Minister of Defense Valinen has ordered some strange deployments of ships within the last two weeks," Jack said, "and there are things we still can't explain about the Soviet plane crash."

"Crash?"

"Yes," Jack said. He wondered why the old man's response had sounded like a question.

"What plane crash?"

"Last Sunday night," Christine said. "The crash that killed much of the Soviet government."

"Good riddance," Whitney said with more conviction than Jack expected.

He was surprised that the professor was unaware of the biggest news story of the year. Whitney seemed too sharp in recounting details about the house to have a memory problem. "The plane crash has been discussed all week on television."

"There is too much filth broadcast on television, so I do not own one anymore. When you get my age, young man, you do not have enough time left to waste on that trash."

Christine blushed.

Jack tried to suppress a smile as he asked, "Newspapers?"

"I gave up newspapers years ago. Besides, in this neighborhood, it is dangerous to go outside for a paper." Whitney paused and added with a sheepish grin, "My housekeeper does bring me the sports pages."

Jack smiled. He assumed that Whitney had gained a love of sports in the days of Ty Cobb, Babe Ruth, and Lou Gehrig.

"Anyway," Jack said, "there are questions about whether the crash could have been deliberate. I need to know if the plane crashed near an important fault."

"Was the crash on land or in the water?"

"In the ocean, not far from San Francisco."

Whitney paled a bit and put down his unfinished cup of tea. "The subject would be easier to discuss in the 'earthquake room.' That is what most of my visitors call it." He stood and walked slowly toward the back part of the house. He pushed aside one of a pair of sliding double doors and allowed his visitors to step through into the room beyond.

Jack's gaze roamed from one side of the room to the other, then back. He felt as if he had just stepped through a time warp and moved forward a century beyond the parlor.

Most of the wall space was covered with maps, charts, yellowed newspaper clippings, and pictures of the destruction caused by earthquakes. Two teletype machines stood along one wall. Three desks, two with computer consoles, were against another wall. Two high-speed printers were on a table next to one of the computer desks. A large couch and a well-worn easy chair were in the center of the room. They were on opposite sides of a large coffee table piled high with scientific journals.

In response to the stunned expressions of his visitors, Whitney smiled and said, "Some of my former students provided the equipment." When he saw that they still did not seem to understand the significance of his influence, he added, "They now run the Seismological Laboratory at the California Institute of Technology and the National Earthquake Information Service at Golden, Colorado. Sometimes they humor me with a request for my comments on seismograph readings."

Jack recognized those as words of a man who did his bragging with understatements.

As Whitney spoke, one of the printers clattered to life. The print head spewed words, dots, and lines across rapidly moving paper. He walked to the printer and studied the two new pages of data for a moment. "They automatically send me excerpts from the seismograph readings when the tracings exceed a certain limit. This one is a small earthquake off the coast of Chile."

Before his visitors could get a good look, he pulled on the long strip of pages to get to an earlier printout. Then he continued, "Here's the reading from the shaker you felt this morning. Not enough to scare anyone. We get one or two of those a month somewhere in northern California." Motioning toward the expensive ring Christine was wearing, he added with a smile, "We'd cause almost as much shaking if the stone fell out of Miss Merrill's ring."

Jack agreed with the professor about the minor nature of the morning's earthquake. Then why, he asked himself, had Braxton looked so frightened?

Whitney scanned the printouts on the two teletypes for new information from the earthquake-monitoring centers. Finding none, he turned to Jack and said with a smile, "With this as my window on the world, I have little need of television and newspapers, except for the baseball and basketball scores."

Jack nodded his agreement as Christine moved to the only object in the room that seemed out of place with the modern technology.

"What an exquisite piece of art," she said as she bent down for a closer look at what appeared to be an ornamental container. The object was mounted on the center of an octagonal base of hardwood with a metal toad sitting on each corner of the base. Eight golden dragons, one facing down over each toad, clung to the side of the container.

"I call that my Chinese seismometer," Whitney said with noticeable pride. "My father brought it from China in 1890."

Whitney told how his model was based on a design of an earthquake detector invented more than two thousand years ago. The mouth of each dragon contained bronze balls and a mechanism that would release a ball in response to a tremor in a certain direction. The noise of the ball falling into the open mouth of the toad below would alert the watchmen. The number of balls released, and the location of the dragon, or dragons, that released the balls indicated both the severity and the direction of the quake.

"I imagine some of the toads got a mouthful during the San Francisco quake in 1906," Jack said.

Whitney looked a little chagrined. "My father said that the whole thing was knocked over. The Chinese obviously did not design the detector to perform near the epicenter of a magnitude 8.3 quake."

As Christine continued to discuss the artistic details of the earthquake detector, Jack went to the side wall and scanned the articles and pictures. Some showed damage as recent as the Nimitz Freeway collapse in the Bay-area quake of 1989. Other clippings were aged and brittle. Many had paragraphs or phrases underlined. With a growing sense of morbid fascination, Jack read highlights from one article after another.

Shaking hurled people against the ceilings of their homes.

The ground rolled in waves that were three feet from crest to trough.

Overturned cooking stoves set off a firestorm that consumed 300,000 buildings—and 140,000 people.

The San Francico quake, centered on the San Andreas fault, shook an area of 375,000 square miles. The fire burned for three days, destroying five square miles in the center of the city.

Had the Lower Van Norman Dam, which was close to collapse when the earthquake ended, actually failed, the 1971 San Fernando quake could have become the deadliest in U.S. history. Eighty thousand people lived in the area below the dam.

Almost a year later, Tangshan, which had housed one million people, looked like a desert. An estimated 800,000 people died in the earthquake.

He reread the death toll to make sure that his mind had not added one or two zeros. He was used to working with big numbers on Pentagon budgets, but he could not comprehend nearly a million people dying in a single act of nature. What do you do, he wondered, on the day after a million people die?

Perhaps, he thought, the Tangshan quake had been part myth and part folklore, handed down from ancient Chinese history, so he scanned the article for a date. The first paragraph provided the startling answer: the magnitude 8.2 earthquake had occurred in *July 1976*.

As he thought over the sampling of statistics and observations, he understood more than ever before what a fearsome weapon a quake could be. Nevertheless, he wondered if a quake could be caused by anything less than a nuclear weapon.

Whitney came over and said, "But, Colonel, we're here to discuss your concerns about a plane crash and not to admire the intelligence of ancient Chinese scientists."

"Sir, my first question is about California's system of earthquake faults. Are there any places that the Russians might believe are particularly vulnerable?"

"Do you mean," Whitney said as he went to the wall that had maps attached above, "if a military man wanted to use an earthquake to attack us, where would he try?"

"Right."

"Fortunately," Whitney said, "earthquakes and weather are so powerful that man cannot expect to harness them for use as a weapon. But"—he paused and stared at Jack—"that does not mean that some military men will not try."

He pulled down a large map of California, and the two visitors moved close enough to see the details as he took a small pointer from his pocket.

"Of course, young lady," he said, looking at her, "this is completely off the record." He waited until she nodded a reluctant response. "Potentially, the most vulnerable point in the entire system is right here."

He placed the tip of the pointer west of Point Reyes where Soviet National One had crashed four nights earlier.

"Damn!" Jack shivered as if someone had just jumped out to scare him.

Christine grabbed his arm and said, "Oh my God!"

Whitney seemed surprised by the reaction. "Not to worry, young lady," he said as if he were calming a student who was concerned about an upcoming examination. "Tons and tons of explosives would be needed to have any impact at all."

Jack leaned against the back of the couch and closed his eyes, trying to bring earlier images into focus. Something had nagged him since watching Bruce Kane's broadcast from the crash site. He pictured the heavily loaded freighter riding low in the water as he had seen it through binoculars on the flight to Chaney. The waves had been lapping at the bottom of the word, "INTERLIGHTER." Yet the *Tibor Szamueli* had been riding much higher the next day when the ship had served as the backdrop for Kane's dramatic broadcast. Now he finally understood—the Soviets had been *unloading* the *Tibor Szamueli*.

The purpose of the camouflage nets was also obvious. The Soviets were not trying to conceal the damaged pieces of Soviet National One; they were hiding the activities of the small boats and barges that were offloading cargo. No wonder the commander of the task force had ordered the brutal destruction of the speedboats. He did not know what the intruders had seen, and he could not risk letting them take their pictures back to shore.

Yet, Jack asked himself, could the Soviets have done any significant offloading in only fifteen hours in the open ocean? His answer came when he recalled a sentence in the computerized description of the ship. In under thirteen hours, the barges could offload twenty-five thousand tons without using piers. That meant that the Soviets could have offloaded fifty thousand tons of explosives just from the *Tibor Szamueli* and her sister ship, the *Julius Fucik*. By comparison, the explosive force of each atomic bomb dropped on Hiroshima and Nagasaki in World War II had been equivalent to twenty thousand tons of TNT.

He wanted to compare the videotapes shot by Braxton's cameraman en route to Chaney with the pictures relayed to the station on Kane's ill-fated broadcast. Those two tapes could prove that the ships were being unloaded at sea. Once again he cursed the lack of tangible proof to back up his gut feelings.

"Is it possible," he asked, realizing that the position of the Soviet ships almost demanded a positive answer, "that the Russians would be aware of this vulnerability?"

"Dr. Vasily Kutakhov and I discussed the confluence of faults many times. You see, we had hypothesized—"

Christine cried, "You—you've discussed this with a Russian, and you make this interview 'off the record' for me?"

"My dear," Whitney answered icily, "Dr. Kutakhov was a scientist."

"But—" she said.

Jack wanted to silence her before she got them thrown out, so he interrupted, "Did you and Dr. Kutakhov work together, sir?"

Whitney looked warily at Christine, then said, "We first met at a scientific conference in Moscow in 1971. Of course we had read each other's publications for many years before. As I started to say, beneath the ocean floor off Point Reyes is what Vasily and I hypothesized was the 'keystone' of the San Andreas fault."

Whitney explained the theory of continental drift and how earthquakes resulted from the shifts of huge masses of earth, referred to as "plates." In simple terms, the San Andreas fault indicated the shear zone, or interface, where two of these huge plates rubbed against each other, moving slowly in opposite directions.

He showed on the map where the fault could be traced from Mexico to Cape Mendocino in northern California. On the west side of the fault, the huge mass of the Pacific plate was moving northwest, while the North American plate was moving southeast on the opposite side of the fault. The two plates moved past each other at a rate of two inches per year.

If the plates could move freely, he explained, the two inches per year would cause problems only for people who built fences, foundations, or roads across the fault. However, friction between the materials on each side of the fault tended to hold both plates together. When enough strain built up, the plates would break free, jumping forward to a new position of equilibrium. When the friction was small and the plates moved frequently, minor quakes could be a reassuring indication that the strain was safely relieved. If the strains kept increasing for years without relief, a cataclysmic earthquake could result when the plates finally broke free.

"So," Christine said, "we should be thankful for small quakes like the one today."

Whitney nodded and said, "If you could regularly relieve the faults of their built-up stress, you would never have the 'big one,' theoretically at least."

"You're suggesting," Jack said, "that 150 million years from now Los Angeles would be across the bay from Oakland, but no one would've been upset by the ride."

Whitney smiled. "I will remember that the next time I explain the concept."

Christine asked, "Can we do things to make the small earthquakes happen instead of the big ones?"

"By all means," Whitney said. "The U.S. Army learned how, quite by accident, in the 1960s."

He explained that there had been a need to dispose of large amounts of liquid toxic waste that was a byproduct of manufacturing chemical weapons. The Army drilled a well more than two miles deep in a remote part of the Rocky Mountain Arsenal near Denver, Colorado. Then the Army pumped the liquid waste under high pressure into the well. A series of small earthquakes began within a month. In four years, there were more than a thousand small quakes in an area that had been without seismic activity in the previous eighty years. After the pumping was stopped, the earthquakes stopped.

Whitney concluded that the high pressure fluid had lubricated old faults that were still under some strain. In this case the release of the strain on inactive faults caused small earthquakes that probably never would have happened.

"However," Whitney said, "I'm sure you're more interested in preventing larger quakes, and that was the central focus of outstanding research by Dr. Kutakhov. You understand, of course, the Soviet Union was the first country to make a serious effort to predict earthquakes."

Both Christine and Jack admitted that they were unaware, so Whitney told of two earthquakes in Russia in the late 1940s that killed more than thirty thousand people. The second quake spurred the government to embark on a massive program to gather data on the geology of the region. After accumulating detailed data for more than fifteen years, the Russians presented some revolutionary findings at an international scientific conference in Moscow. The conference provided Whitney and Kutakhov their first opportunity to meet. They had shared lengthy discussions at many international conferences in the following years.

"Five years ago," Whitney said, "Vasily decided to . . ." He paused and turned once again to Christine. "This part must be off the record."

"Surely," she protested, "nothing we discuss could possibly affect—"

"They might do things to his family."

She reluctantly agreed.

"Vasily had hypothesized that if the U.S. Army could release strain on faults by using high pressure fluids, the same results might be produced quicker, and more predictably, by using carefully placed explosive charges. So five years ago, he began a series of five field tests in Central Russia. He placed the explosives several hundred feet below ground. His first four tests were remarkably successful."

"And the fifth?" Jack sensed that Whitney was becoming more uneasy as he told each new part of the story.

"After the first four, the next step was to test the effects of setting off the explosives under water." Whitney paused. "The weight of the water increased the effectiveness of the explosives much more than Vasily had anticipated."

"And?"

"Test five set off a 5.7 magnitude quake and killed 470 people." He seemed to turn inward to his own thoughts, then added in a quiet, but resolute, voice, "Four hundred seventy-one if you count Vasily."

Christine asked, "Dr. Kutakhov died in the quake?"

"That would have been better. Test five got the attention of the Soviet Supreme High Command. Vasily was summoned to Moscow, expecting to have to account for the deaths, but he found that Minister Valinen did not care that people had died. Valinen took great personal interest in Vasily's work until two years ago, when Vasily was placed in a mental institution. He had not been completely cooperative, and—" Whitney stopped, obviously troubled by the thought that came next.

Christine started to say something, but Jack motioned for her to wait.

Finally, Whitney continued, "I am a scientist. I spoke the truth freely—freely to other scientists and to the reporters, also. I expressed Vasily's concerns that his work was being subverted for dangerous purposes." His voice trailed off.

"I don't understand," Jack said.

"A few days after my last interview, Vasily was arrested and put into a hospital."

Jack tried to remember any mention in the last two years of the

Soviets attempting to use earthquakes as weapons. He was sure he would have heard rumors if there had been a claim made by two such distinguished scientists. He wanted to comfort the old man, who obviously felt responsible for the imprisonment of his colleague, so Jack said, "Perhaps the timing was just a coincidence. The Russian government probably never even heard of your statements."

Whitney directed his response to Christine. "The interview was for that program you mentioned earlier. I understand almost everyone in northern California watched."

Christine hesitated, then said, "You must mean Mr. Braxton's series, called *The Earthquake in Your Future*. Colonel Phillips is still right," she said, placing a reassuring hand on Whitney's arm. "We gathered so much material for the series that we only used short excerpts from many of the interviews. I don't remember the broadcast including anything about Dr. Kutakhov since we had no pictures of his work."

"Perhaps," Whitney said. "I just know he was imprisoned soon after."

Jack made a mental note to see if the transcript of the program might have been stored into one of the on-line computer databases. If Braxton had not used the comments about Kutakhov, Jack might be able to relieve Whitney's guilt. Yet Jack wondered why Braxton would have passed up the opportunity to accuse the Russians if Whitney's story had seemed credible. Jack wanted to know more about what the Soviets had learned from their experiments, so he asked, "Were there other tests after the five you mentioned?"

"In the year between test five and Vasily's being hospitalized, he tried to refine the process. He hoped for the precision that someday would permit the use of his procedures in the heavily populated areas where the most lives could be saved. He discovered that by packing bags of heavy scrap ore above the explosives, he could use less explosives and thereby have a greater margin of error in the placement of the explosives."

"But does that also mean that you could get a larger earthquake by using the ore and not decreasing the amount of explosives."

"Near the cities, Colonel," Whitney said, "you do not want the larger earthquakes."

"I understand, but you are saying that placing ore over the same amount of explosives causes a bigger quake."

"Very definitely, since the ore helps contain the explosion and direct more force downward toward the fault you are trying to relieve. But in any case, Vasily never did solve a timing problem for the larger blasts that Valinen wanted."

"Does that mean Valinen wouldn't be able to cause the large quakes he would need for a weapon?"

"The bigger quakes are more difficult. The explosives must all go off at the same time, or the first explosions may destroy the detonating mechanisms on the rest. The detonators must all be wired, and an electronic signal is sent through the wires."

"Something," Christine said, "like the plunger used to set off dynamite in the old western movies?"

Whitney nodded.

Though Christine's was the obvious analogy, Jack preferred to compare the wiring to the wire-guided antitank missiles. Until striking its target, one of those missiles depended upon guidance from someone at the other end of the wire who was watching the target. One of the best defenses against the missile was to attack the man at the other end of the wire. If Valinen had dumped shiploads of explosives off California, his plan apparently depended upon someone at the end of the wire—and perhaps that person could be attacked before setting off the explosives.

"So," he said, "they must have someone nearby, or could the explosives be set off electronically by a remote transmitter?"

Whitney considered the question for a moment. "Possibly, but wires of equal length assure that all the detonators receive the signal at the same time. If you wanted to minimize your risks of failure, you would use the wires."

Christine asked, "Isn't that dangerous to those who set off the explosives?"

"Vasily did not consider that a severe problem. The explosives would be several hundred feet below the surface of the sea or lake. In his tests, he used enough wire to offset the boat to the side. After the initial turbulence in the water, the boat was no longer in danger. Of course, his goals were not as ambitious as Mr. Valinen's."

Jack asked, "Did Dr. Kutakhov conduct any tests using the larger explosions?"

"Vasily kept stalling, claiming he needed to complete all smaller scale tests first." Whitney paused, then added emotionally, "Don't you see? Vasily was doing this work in the hope of *saving* lives, not killing people. Nothing was done on a really large scale before he was imprisoned."

Jack was slightly relieved. Valinen was cunning and daring, but considering the stakes involved, even the Beast was unlikely to base his opening move on an untested theory as radical as this one. And yet too many indicators pointed to some variant of Kutakhov's tests being prepared in the waters off Point Reyes.

He asked, "Have the Russians done any testing without Dr. Kutakhov?"

Whitney shrugged and gestured with his hands, indicating that he was uncertain. "My colleagues at Cal Tech mentioned that the Iranian government had claimed the Russians had something to do with their quake back in August."

Now that the Iranians had been mentioned, Jack vaguely remembered such an accusation a few months earlier. But no one had taken the Iranians seriously.

Whitney continued, "The quake's epicenter was in the Caspian Sea, about fourteen miles off the Iranian coast. The magnitude was 6.6. However, the region is not heavily populated, so the death toll was less than five thousand."

Jack mentally pictured a map of the Caspian Sea, which the Soviets considered their private lake. Most of the shoreline belonged to the Soviet Union, with only the southern end bounded by Iran. With the exception of a fishing boat or two, there would be little Iranian activity to interfere with Soviet ships fourteen miles off their coast.

"After I heard the rumors," Whitney continued, "I looked at the records of other quakes near the Russian border after Vasily had been taken off the project." He paused and wiped his forehead with a handkerchief. "Last January a 5.9 quake was centered in the Black Sea, seventeen miles off the coast of Eastern Turkey."

"But," Christine said, "if the Russians had tested this twice on other nations, wouldn't someone have seen them?"

Perhaps someone had, Jack thought, but the viewers did not recognize or understand what they saw. He made a mental note to see if either area had been photographed around the time of the quakes. Perhaps there were pictures of Soviet ships near the epicenters in the days before the quakes.

"My dear young lady," Whitney said in a professorial tone, "these regions of Turkey and Iran are not well connected with the outside world. You are probably too young to remember this, but in 1968 northeastern Iran experienced a devastating quake that killed twelve thousand people. Although the quake was only a few hundred miles from the capital, the Iranian government was unaware of the disaster until we told them what we had seen on our seismographs. Who can say if these two quakes were acts of nature or of man? The focus afterward is always on the death and destruction, not on a boat that sails away in the darkness."

She seemed to consider his answer, then asked, "What about that deadly quake in Armenia just before Christmas in 1988?"

Whitney looked frustrated. "Probably it was purely coincidence that the Armenians had been marching in the streets against their masters in Moscow.''

Jack's concern was growing. If indeed there had been successful tests in January and again in August, Valinen could now be ready for an operational test. "If the Russians were to try the same thing off Point Reyes, what would you expect to see them doing?''

"As I said before, tons of explosives would be required. Generally, they would dump the explosives between the narrow canyon walls of a trench in the ocean floor eighteen miles west of Point Reyes. Vasily and I—''

"Pardon me, sir,'' Jack said, "but how about the ore? They can't just dump a bunch of heavy rocks on top of all the cables, can they?''

"Vasily used heavy bags made from a coarse material filled with maybe two hundred pounds of ore. Using a heavy crane and cargo nets, he found he could lower many bags together and manipulate the final placement with divers or small submarines.''

Jack nodded his understanding, both of the method and of why specific Soviet ships had been included in the small fleet at the crash site.

Whitney continued, "Anyway, Vasily and I believe the trench west of Point Reyes is a surface indication of a subsurface lateral fault that intersects the San Andreas at the mouth of San Francisco Bay.''

"I've never heard of such a fault,'' Christine said. "Wouldn't everyone be talking about that fault if it's so important?'' She nodded toward Jack and added, "We looked at maps earlier today, and there were no faults near the crash site.''

"Much remains unknown about these deep faults,'' Whitney said. "A quake in 1987 made seismologists aware of an unknown fault beneath downtown Los Angeles. Unless we have deep core samples, we generally cannot confirm the existence of such faults until the faults choose to make themselves known to us. This one near Point Reyes has no record of being active.''

"If there's never been a quake on the fault,'' Jack asked, "why did you immediately pick it as the most vulnerable spot in the system?''

Whitney went to the chalkboard and made a rough sketch of the coastline of California. To represent the San Andreas fault, he added a red line almost parallel to the coast. Then he put the red chalk at the mouth of San Francisco Bay and drew another line that angled away from the Golden Gate. The result was a wedge, outlined in red, that pointed at San Francisco.

"We believe the Pacific plate is actually two pieces, separated by this unconfirmed lateral fault.'' Whitney pointed at the red line that angled out from San Francisco Bay. "For the recent geological past—

say fifty million years at least—both pieces have moved as one, with the last great movement being the San Francisco quake of 1906. Since then, this upper wedge," he said as he used the side of the red chalk to fill in the pointed area between the two fault lines, "has made itself a bit more comfortable with the North American plate that is moving the other way. Thus for more than eighty years, much of the strain has been building on this one!"

He pounded against the new fault line, shattering the chalk the second time it hit the board. He chuckled and his cheeks reddened. "I have not done that in ages. When I was teaching, I used to do that about three times a day." As Jack retrieved the largest pieces, Whitney laughed again and added, "It was a good way to wake up sleeping students."

Jack doubted that many students had slept in the old professor's classes.

Whitney took the remaining stub of chalk and drew an X on the new fault not far from San Francisco. His manner returned to extreme seriousness, and he said, "A twenty-foot shift in the San Andreas caused the 1906 quake, and by nearly twenty years ago, there was already more strain on the fault again than had been there in 1906. If you separate the two segments of the Pacific plate right here, I would expect the lower part to shift more than twenty feet." He paused, then added, "A jump like that should unload the strain along the San Andreas fault all the way to Mexico."

"You're suggesting," Christine asked, "a double earthquake in both San Francisco and Los Angeles at the same time?"

Whitney sighed and put the chalk in the chalk tray. "If it were only that simple, young lady. I'm suggesting a near-simultaneous series of quakes that would be like having an 'epicenter,' if I may misuse the term, that is five hundred miles long. That should, of course, unload every other associated fault from San Francisco on south."

Jack asked, "A single quake could be that far-reaching?"

"In 1872 the Owens Valley fault on the other side of the Sierra Nevada mountains slipped. Its movement terrorized people, driving many from their homes in a region stretching from the Oregon border down to San Diego. Few people in California would not feel the one we are hypothesizing."

Christine asked, "What would the magnitude be?"

"Possibly greater than any we have ever measured."

Jack's mind had already been struggling with estimating the loss of life. He also wondered how many of California's military bases would be operational after such a quake. "What would be the most devastating results, Dr. Whitney?"

"At this moment, Colonel, nearly twenty million people live near the San Andreas fault. Consider a quake fifty times—perhaps even one hundred times—more powerful than the World Series quake we experienced in 1989. This one will roar for maybe three minutes, not fade away in a mere fifteen seconds."

Christine looked horrified at the thought. "How could anything remain standing after something like that?"

He gestured toward the walls that were covered with pictures of damage from previous quakes throughout the world. "Pick a picture, any picture. Use the books and the files. Pick a thousand pictures. They would be only a small sample."

He lowered himself into the easy chair and became more philosophical. "As a people, we have lulled ourselves into the attitude that we will somehow be spared the big ones, that they come to the less fortunate, the less developed—the Irans, the Turkeys. We don't house our people anymore in unreinforced concrete apartments. But we do build housing developments right across the fault lines and on land fill that will liquify just as the ground in Mexico City did.

"And we are not like Tokyo in 1923 with people cooking dinner each evening on a hundred thousand open stoves in houses with paper walls and straw tatami mats. But our cities of plastics and other chemical conveniences are far from fireproof. Our broken water mains will do no more to put out the firestorms than the broken water lines did in San Francisco in 1906.

"Of course, in the days that follow, the confusion will be like nothing ever seen. One study suggests that ruptured chemical storage tanks in Los Angeles will release a toxic cloud requiring the evacuation of more than one million people from its path."

"That would be pure chaos," Christine said, "especially if some of the freeways collapse."

Jack's mind rushed ahead thinking of the confusion at the national level if the President, Vice President, and key advisers were among the victims of such a quake. Valinen would have produced a crisis like none that had been faced before.

"The first few days will be pure chaos," Whitney said, "and we haven't even mentioned tsunamis."

Jack had been too busy contemplating damage throughout California to even consider the sea waves such a large earthquake would cause. He knew little of these seismic waves other than that there was utter devastation when the giant waves came ashore.

Whitney continued, "I would expect varying amounts of destruction along the Pacific coast of North America. Meanwhile, within five hours, Hawaii would take a more direct hit from the tsunami."

"Hawaii?" Christine seemed surprised. "But Hawaii's two thousand miles away."

"My dear," Whitney said, "when Krakatoa exploded in 1883, some energy of the tsunami was measured in the English Channel."

Jack was impressed, considering that the waves' energy would have had to cross the Indian Ocean, pass around Africa, and travel up through the Atlantic. He wanted to be sure Christine understood the significance, so he told her, "Krakatoa was an island in Indonesia."

"I know, Colonel." She gave him an "I'm not some empty-headed bimbo" look.

"In the deep oceans, the waves travel at five hundred miles an hour," Whitney said.

Jack pictured the Soviet fleet trying to survive as the wave overtook the ships. Surely the Soviets would have considered the tsunami before bringing such a large fleet into the area. Or, was the fleet expendable? He did not think so.

"There's a Soviet fleet west of San Francisco," he said. "Wouldn't their ships be destroyed in such a large quake?"

"Not in deep water, Colonel." Jack looked confused, so Whitney continued, "That's a common misconception. Everyone pictures tsunamis swamping ships at sea." He raised one hand a couple of feet above the other. "In deep water, the waves are this high, hardly enough to disturb the borscht in the wardrooms."

Jack found that difficult to believe, but was sure Whitney knew his subject.

Whitney continued, "The wavelengths on a tsunami can be—" When his guests looked confused, he rephrased. "That is, the crest of succeeding tsunami waves can be more than a hundred miles apart." He started to get up from his chair. "I could show you on the chalk board."

Jack put a hand on Whitney's shoulder. "That won't be necessary, sir."

Whitney continued, "The killer waves do not appear until the tsunami moves into shallower water. This tsunami would most likely be between fifty and a hundred feet high when the first wave hits the northeastern beaches of the Hawaiian Islands."

Jack pictured the full force of a one-hundred-foot wave crashing across the Kaneohe Marine Corps Air Station on the northeast shore of Oahu.

Christine asked what would have been Jack's next question. "What about places like Pearl Harbor?"

"We can only guess," Whitney said as he seemed to be picturing the possibilities. "Just before a tsunami strikes, water rushes away from the coastline. Since Pearl Harbor is connected to the sea only by a narrow channel, much of the water could be sucked from the harbor just before the first wave rushes in. The ships might ride out the tsunami just fine, or the surging waves within the harbor might destroy every ship and all the port facilities.''

With four hours of warning that a tsunami was coming from California, Jack thought, perhaps the ships could sail from port and ride out the waves on the open ocean. He listened with interest as Whitney told of a tsunami in 1946 that killed more than 150 Hawaiians after an earthquake in Alaska. Whitney explained that the waves were *only* thirty- to fifty-five-feet high as they pounded Hawaii. He emphasized that in Alaska, one of the waves had destroyed a radio antenna located more than one hundred feet above normal sea level.

Jack was concerned by Whitney's references to more than one wave. "How long does a tsunami last? How many waves are we talking about?"

"How many aftershocks would you expect from the largest earthquake in recorded history, Colonel?" Whitney smiled, and the twinkle in his eye suggested that he enjoyed knowing more about the subject than his companion with the military background. "I've been unfair to answer your question with a question, but the answer is open-ended. The 1946 Alaska quake was a 7.2 on the Richter scale. The tsunamis from that earthquake pounded Hawaii for more than two hours. Now if you get an 8.5, or maybe a 9.0, just off the Golden Gate, how many aftershocks of at least 7.2 do you suppose there will be in the next few days? I remember one quake that had 125 aftershocks of at least 4.0 magnitude within forty-eight hours." Whitney paused, then added quietly, "There would be more tsunamis than anyone will count."

As he told of waves that destroyed buildings more than one thousand feet from the shore, Jack became increasingly uneasy about their implications. He wished he knew more about the contingency plans locked in the safes on board the flagship of the Soviet fleet. The main airfields he could think of in Hawaii—Honolulu International, Navy Barber's Point, Hilo, and Kaneohe—were barely above sea level. If the port facilities and airfields throughout Hawaii were devastated, the Islands would be more open to invasion than after the Japanese attack on Pearl Harbor in 1941. Suddenly the inclusion of so many amphibious warships in the fleet off San Francisco made much more sense to him. Their objective was Hawaii!

"I understand, Colonel," Whitney said, "that you military men like to talk in terms of the bottom line. Here is what I would call the bottom line. If you break loose that fault this afternoon, in a year people all over America will pause at the same hour for a minute of silent prayer for the uncounted dead—then those in California will go back to clearing rubble from the streets."

Jack wondered just how much Whitney was exaggerating. Jack also pictured the nation trying to clean up the devastation that would come on Saturday if Valinen followed the quake with a nuclear strike.

He asked to use the telephone, then went into the parlor and called General McClintock's office.

"I'm sorry, Colonel Phillips," Joanne Kingston said, "but the general's still off station."

"Can you contact him for me?"

"Not right away. He and General Harper flew to San Francisco to brief the President's staff on the problem at Howell. I'd thought he'd be back by now, but the helicopter's still on the ground at the Western White House."

Jack checked his watch. He would have to fight the rush hour traffic, but he should be able to reach Alameda almost as quickly as the general could fly from San Francisco.

"If his aide checks in, tell him there's something I must discuss with the general as soon as I can get to him."

"I made reservations for dinner before General Harper returns to Howell, and already they're going to be late. Can I put you down for nineteen-thirty?"

"Negative," Jack said. "This one can't wait. I should be there in twenty minutes."

"Since General McClintock is running late, he may just go straight to dinner from the helicopter pad."

Obviously she was just trying to protect the general's schedule. He had seen her do the same thing with other people a hundred times. "You've got to stop them, Joanne. This isn't something we can discuss in a restaurant."

"I don't think you're invited."

"If you can't stop them, the restaurant's where I'll have to be."

"I have a feeling that General Harper will bring up your recent track record when I tell them they're being delayed at your request."

Jack knew she was referring to his earlier assessment of the camouflage netting and the resulting embarrassment to the chief of staff. He also knew that this was her way of saying that General Harper already had made a special point of mentioning Jack's error to General McClintock.

"Just tell General McClintock I hope I'm wrong twice in a row, but I'm afraid this time I'm right."

"You're starting to scare me, Colonel," Kingston said.

"That makes two of us."

Chapter **23**

Thursday Evening, 5:35 p.m.
Iskra plus 3:35

BY THE TIME THE TWO VISITORS LEFT DR. WHITNEY'S HOUSE, LOW clouds and a heavy mist made the neighborhood even darker and drearier than it otherwise would have been. Some streetlights were not illuminated, the victims of neighborhood vandals.

Jack's survival instincts took over, and he wished the car were closer. "Situational awareness" was the term the fighter pilots of the electronic age used for being alert and wary. Learning to stay aware of the situation around him had been his main defense against someone surprising him with a missile up a tailpipe of his supersonic fighter. On the darkened street, his eyes and ears took the place of the radar and the threat-warning receivers he relied on in the aircraft.

Before stepping from the porch, he looked along the street and at everyone he could see. Several people were on the opposite side of the street, standing next to a car beneath a light at the end of the block. He assumed that someone was making a deal for drugs or sex. He saw no one on the route between the house and his car.

As they hurried toward the car, Christine was totally engrossed in what they had learned from Whitney. She talked excitedly, but Jack barely listened, concentrating instead on the people at the corner. Six similarly dressed teenagers, four boys and two girls, were gathered around the passenger side of a late-model Cadillac. One boy periodically looked up and scanned the area around the intersection, but the group's interest remained focused on the people in the Cadillac.

Since his rental car was parked in the next block, Jack had to cross one street at the corner. As he stepped into that street, he saw two men in the next block walking slowly toward him. They had come from the darkness beyond a van parked in a driveway.

For an instant he considered turning and crossing the other street toward the Cadillac. However, he was certain that the common colors intermingled in the jackets, caps, and scarves of the teenagers were the mark of a local street gang. He decided it was a greater risk to attract the attention of a gang in search of more drug money than to pass two men who might just be coming home from work.

Jack slowed so he and Christine would pass the men as close to the light as possible. He also slipped away from the hold she had on his arm and held her wrist in a way that allowed him to free his hand immediately.

She stopped in mid-sentence, then asked, "What's wrong?"

"Just keep talking," he said, giving a reassuring squeeze, "and walk like you're the toughest Amazon that ever took that karate course at Mac's gym."

She gave him a look suggesting she did not like his analogy. However, seeing how serious he was, she looked around and saw the teenagers. "The gang near the car?"

"And the two guys ahead of us."

"Okay," she said, starting an innocuous conversation about the antiques in Whitney's house.

He tried to appear casual as the distance to the two men decreased. They appeared absorbed in their own conversation, but he sensed from their clothing that the two were as out of place in the neighborhood as he and Christine were. He would have felt more comfortable if he could see their hands, which were in the pockets of their jackets. He stepped ahead of Christine so he could stay between her and the men as they passed. Enough light filtered through the trees for him to see their faces—one seemed familiar.

Suddenly the taller man hissed, "Now!" Both men stopped and yanked their hands from their pockets. Two pistols were visible in light from a nearby porch. The leader growled, "Keep quiet and do what we say!"

Jack stopped, and Christine gasped as she bumped into him.

The leader continued, "Shut up and keep your hands where we can see them."

That command was louder than the first, but Jack doubted that the gang at the corner had heard the voice above the noise of the idling Cadillac.

He raised his hands and said, "My money's in the wallet in my back left pocket."

Keeping out of Jack's reach, the smaller man moved around to the side and grabbed Christine's arm. With a grip that made her cry out, he pulled her away. Jack had forced himself to stay calm, but he reacted instinctively when she gasped. He pivoted and took a half step toward her attacker.

The leader raised his pistol toward Jack's face and said, "Freeze, man, or you're going to die right here!"

At the same time, the other man released his hold on Christine's arm. He grabbed the collar of her coat and pulled her face toward the barrel of his pistol.

Jack stopped in mid-motion.

"I'm all right," she said quickly. Her voice was a little shaky and was distorted by the pressure against her throat, but she sounded less panicky than he expected.

"Do exactly what we say, and you may get out of this alive."

Jack nodded. He got one more good look at the taller man and remembered—he was one of the KGB agents among the Soviet officials at the airport on the night of the crash. Many thoughts flashed through Jack's mind. In spite of the gun, the thought that dominated was the question: How did they know where we'd be?

Lockhart had known that Jack was going to see Dr. Whitney, but there was no reason to suspect treachery from the major. Then there was Christine—again. She had invited herself along, and he had let her be right in the middle. Had she led the KGB to Alameda, then arranged for them to follow? Was she, even now, just playing along with them? He hoped there was another answer, but nothing came to mind before the gunman's next command.

"You're going with us," the leader said as he stepped to the side and lowered the gun toward Jack's chest. The leader nodded toward the man who held Christine.

The smaller man kept the pistol pointed at her face as he deliberately moved his other hand across her breast. After a moment's hesitation, he grasped her wrist again and moved around behind her. Putting the gun against her back, he prodded her toward the van.

The leader moved carefully behind Jack and said, "Follow them."

Jack hesitated, not moving until he was jabbed in the middle of the back.

He had learned long ago that only three rules of unarmed combat mattered when confronted by a man with a gun. The first rule was to surrender your money and come away a winner by not getting shot.

That rule applied to muggings, but the KGB's presence meant this was no mugging. He had no idea how they knew he had just discovered the final pieces of the mystery, but these men obviously were there to stop that information from reaching the President. In spite of what the man behind him had said, Jack was sure that no amount of cooperation would keep them alive. Their best chance was to stand and fight while still in a public place.

He walked slowly, causing the gunman to prod him continually.

Ahead, Christine said, "No, please don't do this." Her voice sounded more frightened than before.

Jack's second rule of unarmed combat was that if you were going to get killed anyway, forget the first rule and try to disarm the gunman.

He had been through scores of training drills with someone else holding a wooden gun in the middle of his back. The objective had been to pivot quickly, block the gunman's arm aside before he could say "bang," then take the wooden gun away.

Rule three was the most important: Be certain about the location of the gun before making your move.

A favorite trick of instructors and students alike was to press two pointed fingers against the back and hold the wooden gun in the other hand. Then as the unwary student whirled and blocked away the empty hand, he was greeted with a grin and a very quiet "Bang!"

Jack had to make sure the pressure he felt was the gun, but he was uncertain how he could in the darkness.

Approaching the van, Christine pleaded in a voice that was louder and sounded more frantic.

Her captor had intertwined his fingers into her hair, forcing his hand against the bare skin of her neck. Her protests seemed to add to his enthusiasm. As the two reached the van, he released her hair and spun her around. He grabbed the front of her coat and pressed his hand between her breasts, pinning her against the front door of the van. With his gun hand, he struggled with the handle of the van's sliding door.

"No!" Her voice was louder than before. "Please! I don't want to be raped!"

Struggling against his hold, she banged her head noisily against the window, then slumped along the side of the van. Her captor was not strong enough to keep her standing, but his hold on her coat eased her fall.

Adrenaline surged through Jack. He rushed forward, kneeling to see if she were hurt. He was uncertain, but sensed she was faking.

"Get back," the leader yelled. When Jack stopped and raised his hands, the leader shouted at his accomplice, "Eddie, get her into the van." While giving the order, he jabbed the pistol into the middle of Jack's back and grabbed his shoulder. "Get up slowly."

"Okay. Take it easy," Jack said as he straightened up. A sense of relief swept over him—he knew which hand held the gun.

Once he was upright, he felt the grip on his shoulder loosen. At that instant he spun, driving his raised forearm against the gunman's arm. The gun swung sideways, firing almost simultaneously. Jack felt a searing pain just below his shoulder blade, but the injury did not stop him as he continued pivoting. Swinging his arm beneath his attacker's, he drove forward with his shoulder, forcing the gun upward.

The gunman responded with a surprised grunt as Jack got an armlock on the arm with the gun. Grabbing the barrel, he rotated it toward the face of the other man. Jack had all the leverage, and the man could no longer maintain his hold on the gun. Only the man's finger remained within the trigger guard.

The look of surprise on the man's face gave way to a look of panic.

Jack let out a guttural yell as he jerked the pistol toward the man—and against the man's trigger finger.

The muzzle flash etched into Jack's mind the image of the face as the bullet tore into the flesh of the man's cheek. For an instant afterward, Jack could see only the image of the flash in the darkness that followed. He felt a splattering of blood and flesh across his face as the man went limp.

The other gunman was trying to lift Christine into the opening in the side of the van. As he turned toward the sound of the struggle behind him, she kicked upward, driving her foot into his groin. He screamed, slumped into the open door of the van, and tried to pull his pistol from the waistband of his jeans.

Jack yanked the other gun free of the dead man's hand and fired twice into the chest of the man trying to rise from the floor of the van.

Back at the corner, the Cadillac roared away, leaving the six teen-agers crouching beneath the light. At several houses along the street, porch lights flashed on.

Jack paused a moment, sickened by the sticky feeling of the other man's blood on his hands and forehead. He was shaking and had trouble catching his breath. This was not the first time he had killed, but he had never killed someone a half step away.

Christine struggled to her feet and rushed to him. She buried her face against his chest and held him in what seemed to be a death grip. A stinging pain flashed through him as she pressed against the wound on his back. The pain seemed to clear his mind and to replace strength into his knees, which for a moment had threatened to collapse. He kissed her on the forehead and said, "We've got to get out of here!"

"Shouldn't we wait for the police?"

"There may be others trying to stop us," he said, moving toward his car. He glimpsed at his watch: *Barely sixteen hours remained to head off the attack.* "We don't have time to get involved in an investigation."

Across the street in a driveway, a man in a dark sedan had been watching. "Damn," he said aloud as he watched the two rush to their car. He had assumed Phillips would give them problems, but the colonel had been successful beyond all expectations. Now he regretted his earlier decision not to bring a gun.

He placed a call on his cellular telephone. When the police dispatcher answered, the caller said in a voice disguised as an older adult, "There's just been a shooting here on the street, and the killer's about to get away." He gave a phony name and the address of a nearby house that had been converted to an apartment.

The dispatcher asked, "Can you describe the alleged assailant?"

"He's white, maybe six feet tall. He came running down the street and grabbed a woman. She screamed. Two men tried to help and this crazy man shot 'em both. He just now forced the woman into his car."

"Can you describe the car?"

"Describe? Oh yes. I can even see the license number, if that will help."

The caller looked at a note pad on which the license number of Jack's rental car was already written.

By the time Jack turned his car around, the gang members were approaching tentatively along the middle of the street. When his lights illuminated the teenagers, he saw that one boy held a pistol, pointed upward. Two others held knives at their side, but Jack saw no other guns. He stopped the car as the gang spread out, blocking the street.

"Hey, man," the boy with the gun said, "what's goin' down?"

"It's not your fight, my man."

"You're on my ground." He glanced confidently toward his friends. He strutted forward a couple of steps but stopped abruptly when Jack extended his gun from the window. He pointed the pistol just above the gang leader. Most of the others backed toward the side of the street.

"Let it go," Jack said, slowly tilting his gun higher. "Those men back there were outsiders."

"But," the gang leader said, seemingly torn between saving face and saving his life, "this is still my ground, and—"

Jack squeezed the trigger, sending a bullet well above the startled teenager. The gang members dived toward the sides of the street as he jammed the accelerator to the floor.

He raced three blocks up Whitney's street before turning toward the hills to mislead the police in case someone reported the direction he had fled. Speeding up a quiet residential street, they had a chance to assess their condition for the first time since the fight.

"My God," she said. "There's blood all over you."

For an instant he wondered if the wound on his back had been worse than he thought. When she pulled a handkerchief from her purse and started cleaning the blood from his face, he realized she had not noticed his wound. He shifted, sliding his back against the seat of the car. The stinging was less than when she had pressed against the wound. He forced his hand beneath his coat and felt his shirt. Very little blood had seeped down his back. The man's grip had slowed him enough to keep him from getting clear of the bullet's path. Meanwhile, the heat of the bullet racing along his skin apparently had cauterized the wound.

"Are you hurt, Chris? That guy didn't hurt you, did he?"

"I'm okay, but I'm wearing a six hundred-dollar-suit and a pair of stockings that will never be the same." She paused, then added in a voice filled with concern and sadness, "Maybe nothing will ever be the same."

Hearing fear in her voice, he wanted to take her in his arms and assure her that everything would be all right. Yet he still was unsure whether to trust her. Had she somehow led the KGB there? Were her words of concern all part of a magnificent performance by a spy who already had known everything Dr. Whitney had revealed? God, he thought to himself, if she's working for the Russians, she's really good. He had to find out for sure and hoped he could stand the answer.

"You're a mess," she said. "I need water."

Sliding across to her door, she lowered the window enough to dampen her handkerchief with rain beading on the windshield.

While she was distracted, he took hold of the pistol he had dropped into his lap after firing above the gang leader. He explored with his fingertips until he found the catch that held the ammunition clip in the butt of the gun.

She talked soothingly as she dabbed the side of his face. When they got to the next street light, she checked her work, then leaned over and kissed him on the cheek. He pushed the catch on the pistol and felt the clip spring out against the palm of his hand. Almost there, he thought, but one bullet remained in the chamber. As she was getting more water on her handkerchief, he placed the clip under the front of his seat. Then he pushed the barrel of the gun beneath his leg and grasped the back of the slide.

She was about to return from her side of the car, so he asked, "Can you read any of the street signs?"

"I don't know this area at all," she said, "so I doubt the names will help." All the same, she studied the intersection ahead for signs.

He cleared his throat as he pulled the slide back. The noise masked the metallic click as the ejector sent the bullet flying from the pistol. The shell bounced harmlessly off his ankle and disappeared on the floor.

She did not recognize the street name, so she slid toward him.

"Let me get this thing out of the way," he said, lifting the pistol from beneath his legs. He pushed the butt of the gun between the console and the front corner of his seat, so she could easily reach it. With the butt down, one could not tell by looking that the gun was not loaded.

The gang members and a few residents from nearby houses gathered near the van. Others watched from front porches and second-story windows. The observer in the dark sedan opened a small, rectangular box on the seat beside him. The box contained a pair of black gloves. He put on the gloves very carefully, then got out of the car.

Pulling up the collar on his coat, he pushed through the crowd. "Make way please. I'm a doctor."

He stopped at the body on the sidewalk. Someone pointed a flashlight at the man's head and the large pool of blood beneath. The back side of the head was deformed and a large chunk of the skull was missing. Though there were no indications of life, the observer put his gloved fingers against the side of the neck a few seconds. "This one's gone." His tone was crisp and professional.

The second man was lying on the floor of the van with his legs hanging out the door. His breathing was shallow, almost imperceptible. Every few seconds a trickle of foamy blood oozed from one of the chest wounds.

"This one doesn't look good either," the observer said, bending over and reaching toward the man's neck.

The light from the flashlight played across the man's face. His eyes were open, and he tried to form words as he seemed to recognize the face above his. The light focused on the gloved hand and the man's neck. The observer stepped over the victim, blocking most of the light, but the holder of the flashlight repositioned himself to keep the man's neck illuminated.

The observer asked, "Does anyone have a watch with a second hand?" Two people in the crowd volunteered. Turning toward the man with the flashlight, the observer said, "I need you to count seconds for me. First, tell me where the second hand is now."

The flashlight was aimed at a wristwatch, and someone said, "Forty-two. Forty-three."

"Good. Tell me when the second hand gets to zero, then I'll need you to count off the time for fifteen seconds."

Just as a magician guides his audience to an inconsequential prop, the observer made an obvious effort to look toward the wristwatch. At the same time he carefully bent his little finger in toward the palm of his right hand. The motion extended a hypodermic needle an inch from a protective tube in a seam on the index finger of the glove.

He glanced toward the shooting victim as the man with the flashlight called out that there were ten more seconds to go. There was enough light in the van to see the main blood vessel along the side of the injured man's neck. The observer had no trouble slipping the tip of the needle beneath the skin.

"Five. Four . . ."

As the man with the flashlight counted to zero, the observer pumped twice with his thumb. Two doses of a drug, which would disrupt the electrical impulses of the heart, surged from the needle. The man lying in the van shuddered slightly.

The man with the flashlight restarted the count to fifteen.

The observer slowly extended his little finger, and the needle returned into its protective tube. When the count reached fifteen, the observer shook his head. "There's nothing we can do for this one either. Has anyone checked for identification? I'll need to see the ID for my records." No one had, so he pulled the man's wallet from a pocket.

Everyone gathered closer as the light shined on the wallet. The observer seemed to study the driver's license for a moment before widening the part of the wallet that held the cash. He raised the money high enough to flash a corner of each bill. A murmur went through the crowd as several twenties and three hundreds were visible in the shimmering light. Then he pushed the cash into the wallet.

"I'll leave this right here so the police can find it," he said, placing the wallet near the man's head on the floor of the van.

Quickly kneeling near the other body, the observer repeated the routine, finally leaving the wallet on the dead man's chest. As the observer stood, the sound of approaching sirens was audible. "There's nothing else I can do," he said, stepping away from the corpse. He looked toward the other body in the van. The wallet already had disappeared. The observer walked away, assuming that the identification for his second accomplice would soon be gone. He was almost to Dr. Whitney's house when the first police car rushed by.

Jack discovered that the winding streets of the neighborhood were even more confusing in the dark than in the daytime. The lights of the city reflected off the low clouds and wet streets, making it impossible for him to maintain his sense of direction. One promising street curved toward the Berkeley Hills instead of toward the freeway. Getting increasingly impatient, he had to backtrack nearly a mile. He would not feel safe until he got through the gate at Alameda and onto federal property.

Finally he reached a main residential street. He turned onto the street, then saw he had crossed in front of a police car. Half a block ahead, the police car was speeding in the opposite direction on the main street. Jack completed the turn and tried to look unconcerned as the police car raced past. Christine turned and watched the car. Jack assumed no one could be looking for them yet, but he still watched the mirror.

Ten seconds passed before he saw the brake lights on the police car glow brightly. The car fishtailed as the policeman slowed on the wet pavement. Jack floored his accelerator. The police car nearly hit an oncoming truck as the policeman yanked the cruiser around in a sliding turn.

Christine grabbed Jack by the arm and asked, "Shouldn't we stop?"

"Probably," he said, accelerating through a light that was changing from yellow to red.

He had put four blocks between him and the pursuing police car when he spotted the elevated freeway passing over the street a few blocks ahead. As he got closer, however, he discovered that there were no entrance ramps. Several blocks beyond the overpass, he turned onto a heavily traveled street parallel to the freeway. He maneuvered from lane to lane through the traffic, but his frequent checks of the rearview mirror showed that he was losing ground to the police car.

"I'll try the radio," she said, tuning an all-news station, "but it's probably too early to hear anything about the shootings."

"In that neighborhood," he said, picturing momentarily the face of the first man shot, "the police should suspect drugs were involved. How in the hell did they get onto us so quickly?"

A few blocks later, signs indicated that the next cross street had access to the freeway. He also saw the flashing lights of another police car far ahead in the oncoming traffic, but he knew he could reach the intersection ahead of both pursuers.

Once he turned, his relief was short-lived. The entrances to the freeway were two blocks away, but each had a half block of rush-hour traffic jockeying for position. He accelerated past the lines of cars and turned onto the next road paralleling the freeway.

Racing along the street, he considered stopping somewhere to let Christine out. He did not want to endanger her in a high-speed chase that might end in gunfire, but he was still uncertain about her motives. If she were a spy, she could immediately telephone in a report that he had learned about the importance of the crash site. She could also call in more agents to stop him before he reached McClintock. Even if she were just the journalist she claimed to be, her instincts as a reporter might take over. He had just handed her the biggest story of her career. However, broadcasting the story would panic millions of people in California and tip off the Soviets, perhaps forcing them to accelerate their timetable.

He assumed she would take the story first to her mentor. Braxton, at least, would have the sense and the connections to take the story to the President before revealing it to the people. Braxton's influence could be helpful. Braxton . . .

Jack shuddered as he thought of the tycoon's inordinate influence and pictured the frightened expression on his face during the small earthquake. Braxton—skydiver, yachtsman, glider pilot, adventurer, and veteran of more than three decades of San Francisco earthquakes—could not have been frightened by such a small shaker, unless . . . *unless he knew the timetable and had thought for just an instant that his masters had ensured surprise by surprising even him and the rest of their spies in the United States!*

Jack tried to think of anything that would automatically erase this suspicion. Nothing came immediately to mind. Now he was sorry he had not read all of Lockhart's material on Braxton.

In the next few minutes his route crisscrossed the freeway several times. Each time he saw an on-ramp toward Alameda, the lines were too long or the police were too close for him to use the ramp. After taking advantage of a couple of yellow lights to get beyond heavily traveled cross streets, he had increased the lead on his closest pursuer to more than three blocks. He had to assume more police cars were closing in on the area, though, and he had to do something to escape the net.

He rounded a corner and passed under the freeway almost immediately. On the opposite side of the street, two lines of traffic led onto the on-ramps. The nearer line was longer, mainly because of three semi trucks lined up nose-to-tail. As he accelerated by the trucks, he realized that they would hide his car from view if he could get into the other line beside them.

The traffic light ahead had just changed to green, releasing more cars and trucks toward the lines to the on-ramps. He hit the brakes hard and swerved toward the low median. Christine screamed as the car bounced over the median and accelerated across the other traffic lanes. Then he hit the brakes, steering to let the skid swing the back of the car around. He managed to miss the rear of the last car in the longer line and slip in just ahead of another truck. The angry trucker hit his brakes and sounded a long blast on his air horn. Jack stayed off his brakes until he was beside the trailer of a truck in the other line.

The sound of the air horn drowned out the sound of sirens as two police cars rounded the corner and roared out onto the road Jack had just left. He hoped he had not left enough dust or tire smoke to attract their attention. Still angry, the trucker stopped just short of Jack's back bumper. There was no way the police could see his car even if they looked at the traffic on the on-ramps.

The sounds of sirens diminished as the cars continued through the next intersection. By the time his line had edged forward enough for Jack to pass the trucks, the police cars had disappeared. Finally, he thought, we can get moving.

"I don't think you want to do this," she said.

Startled by her concern, he sized up the situation ahead. They were almost to the freeway, but the overcast seemed lower. A half a mile ahead, the steady streams of tail lights were being swallowed by the low clouds. Obviously the freeway was leading away from the bay.

He asked, "Do you know where we are?"

"Not exactly, but we're going the wrong way."

He had not seen any freeway signs before he had forced his way into the line of traffic. All the same, even if the maneuver cost them a few more minutes, at least he had shaken the police who had nearly caught him. "Don't worry. Maybe we can make a U-turn across the median. If not, I'll go an interchange or two, then turn toward Alameda."

"I think we're almost at the tunnel."

"Tunnel?"

"The tunnel through the Berkeley Hills that takes commuters into Contra Costa county."

He looked around for an alternative. Traffic was oozing forward, slowly but steadily blending into the homebound rush on the last Thursday before Christmas. The trucker was still right on his rear bumper leaving no way to backtrack.

He reached over and patted her arm, "Well, with a hundred feet of visibility and a million other cars, the police are going to have a hell of a time finding us for the next few minutes."

Jack checked his watch: six-fifteen, Iskra *plus four-fifteen*. He had to get to a telephone.

He hoped to find a shopping center where he could hide his car among the Christmas shopping hordes, but the tunnel seemed like some gateway from the city to the country. On the eastern slope of the hills there were no large towns at the exits nearest the tunnel, so he continued within the safety and obscurity of the heavy traffic.

The chase had left him feeling as if every policeman in northern California must be looking for his car. Fortunately the weather was in his favor. Though higher than on the Bay side of the hills, the clouds would hinder any helicopter pilots who might try to join the search.

He took an off-ramp to a small town along the freeway. Spotting a telephone booth at the corner of a grocery store, he pulled into the parking lot in front of a line of stores and shops.

Christine also wanted to make a call, but he told her to stay in the car and watch for police. He kissed her, then went to the booth, and dialed General McClintock's number. When he identified himself, Joanne Kingston cried, "Where have you been, Colonel Phillips? I told the general you'd be here when he landed." She hesitated, then added, "For that matter, where are you now?"

"I'll tell you the whole story sometime when we both have a cold drink in our hands. Right now I've got to talk to the general."

"He's just getting airborne at the Western White House and won't be in the office for at least twenty minutes. Do you want to try a phone patch?"

That wouldn't work, he thought. A phone patch to an airborne aircraft used radio communications that were more easily monitored than the regular telephones.

"Negative. Tell the general I'm convinced there's still a serious problem, and I finally know most of what's going on."

"Something's sure going on somewhere." She paused, then continued. "Well, no one told me I couldn't tell you. Security was just here. Some off-base police had called and asked who you were and if we knew where you were."

"That was fast," he said, checking his watch.

His experiences during crises had taught him that getting the right information together could be painfully slow. Yet less than an hour had passed since the shootout with the KGB agents. He had not figured out how the policemen in the first police car had identified his car so quickly, and he was amazed that the police already had connected him with that car.

She continued, "The captain from security was pretty excited. He said your name had come up in connection with a murder."

"I thought I'd get to tell what happened before anyone even connected me."

"The general will want to know."

Jack told her about being attacked after leaving Whitney's house and how he had chosen to try to get to Alameda instead of being delayed by a police investigation. As soon as he mentioned Christine's name, Kingston interrupted.

"She's the woman you put on the general's calendar yesterday?"

"Sure. She's the—"

"Is she right there?"

"Not right here. She's in the car."

"Security's concerned about her."

"I don't think I want to hear this," he said, unable to mask his disappointment.

"What?"

"I'm sorry. Go ahead."

"There was a question on the authorization papers she had yesterday. Since the papers were signed off by the White House staff, our security people initially cleared up their question by phone. However, after sending her papers over for a visual check this afternoon, security just learned that she'd given us a clever forgery."

"Damn," he said. Kingston's words sliced deeper than any of the facts he had learned so far. Turning toward his car, he saw Christine still waiting quietly for him. He hoped she had not discovered that the clip in the pistol was missing. He also hoped she was not carrying a weapon of her own.

"It's really strange," Kingston said. "The version she used to get on the airplane was virtually the same as the official papers."

"Isn't that what forgeries are all about?"

"You're missing the point, Colonel. She'd been authorized officially to do exactly what the forged papers let her do. If you have the real papers, why use false ones?"

He had no answer.

"Anyway, Colonel, you be careful around her."

"At the moment, I'm having to be careful around everyone." He finished telling her what had happened prior to reaching the telephone booth. He tried to avoid saying anything that the KGB did not already know, just in case the call was somehow monitored. He did not mention his new concerns about Braxton. That was something he would not discuss on an unclassified line.

Finally he added, "I'll find a way to Alameda—or at least to a military jurisdiction with a classified telephone. Meanwhile, I need Major Lockhart in intel to start working two things. First, have him do a computer search for the text of a television program called *The Earthquake in Your Future*. It was a series on some of Braxton's newscasts about two years ago. If Lockhart locates the text, I need to know what references were made to the work of a Dr. Vasily Kutakhov of the Soviet Union. And second, have Lockhart give you the folder of things he's gathering for me. The folder includes Dr. Whitney's address and other information on a subject that General McClintock needs to get smart on. If something happens to me, tell the general he has to see Dr. Whitney."

"Don't talk about something happening to you, Colonel."

"I'll probably end up in somebody's jail, so have the Security Police follow this case with the local police. If security hears that someone's caught me, get the general on a helicopter with the best legal people you can round up and send them to that jail. General McClintock and I have to talk—no matter what!"

He hung up and tried to decide on his next move. He was uncertain whether he still should try to get to the E-4B. Alameda Naval Air Station was on an island with only three or four roads connecting it with Oakland. Since the police had already linked him to his car, the shootings, and the E-4B, they could be watching the roads that led to the island.

Then, he considered going to Howell Air Force Base. However, at almost a hundred miles away, Howell was too far to risk. The thought of being placed in confinement by Colonel Radisson flashed through his mind. He would not give Radisson that satisfaction—unless that became the only option.

Travis Air Force Base was closer, but still nearly forty miles away— Suddenly he thought of O'Donnell. Perhaps there was a "safe house" nearby. Surrendering to O'Donnell's people would ensure that national security interests took precedence over the local investigations.

He pulled out O'Donnell's business card and dialed the number. A receptionist said she would try to locate him. As Jack waited, he glanced toward the car—it was empty. Where was she? Frantically, he looked around the parking lot.

"God—" he exclaimed when he spotted her entering a telephone booth at a service station across the street. He did not want her contacting anyone—colleagues or comrades—and telling what she had learned from Dr. Whitney. Jack had wanted so desperately to convince himself she was not a spy, but the forged clearances made believing in her much more difficult. He was about to run over to stop her when O'Donnell gave a greeting.

"I've run into a little trouble. Have you folks got any clout with the local police?"

"What's the problem? Someone got you in the brig?" There was the hint of a chuckle in O'Donnell's voice.

"I know most of the answers you and I are looking for. The KGB's trying like hell to keep me from getting the story to anyone who can do something."

O'Donnell's joking attitude changed immediately. "Where are you?"

Jack briefly described the shootings, then told of the car chase and where he was calling from. He also revealed the controversy about the forged documents and the fact that Christine was still with him.

O'Donnell asked, "Does she know yet that you're working with us?"

"I don't know anymore who knows what," Jack said. "I've never told her about you and Russell."

"At this point," O'Donnell said, "I'd rather have her where we can keep an eye on her than out there somewhere keeping tabs on us. If you can get to us, we'll claim we're old war buddies."

"Roger that."

"I'll put you on hold while I see what I can do."

"I don't have much time."

Leaning against the wall, Jack looked around. Christine was still in the other telephone booth. As he turned in the opposite direction, he discovered a new problem. A police car had entered the parking lot and was driving toward him.

He felt a surge of panic and fought the impulse to turn away. Instead, he acted as if he were in an animated conversation and could not care less about the approaching police car. The car stopped in the loading zone in front of the drug store that was next door. Both officers left the car and went inside.

O'Donnell came on the line and gave instructions: freeway to an exit a few more miles east; south on a secondary highway for three and a half miles; finally, up a dirt road on the right for three-quarters of a mile to the top of a hill.

Christine was still in her telephone booth as Jack hurried to the car. He checked the pistol and found it undisturbed. The ammunition clip was still under the front edge of his seat. He retrieved the loose bullet from the floor and loaded that cartridge into the clip as he drove across the street. She opened the door of the booth as he parked alongside.

He got out and hurried around the car. Before she had a chance to greet him, he asked, "What are you doing?"

She looked shocked by his tone. "Alex paged me while I was waiting, so I came over here—"

Damn, he thought. Both could be spies, and he did not want her reporting to Braxton what Whitney had revealed. Jack nodded toward the police car and said, "I told you to stay in the car and keep your eyes open."

"Well, I had to use the phone!" With a flash of anger in her expression, she added, "What did you expect me to do? Run over and yell, 'Police! Police!' "

He blushed, not having a good answer for her response. He also noticed that she did not seem to be talking to anyone on the telephone. "Are you finished? We need to get out of here before the police come out."

"I'm waiting for a message from Alex about an assignment this evening. They're having trouble contacting him."

"What have you told anyone so far?"

"Nothing."

"Nothing at all?"

"Just where I'm calling from. They needed to know so—"

"If you're going with me, get in the car!" he shouted as he yanked open the door on her side, then rushed to the driver's side.

She stepped from the booth but still held the telephone.

He looked toward the police car and saw both officers rushing from the drug store. One was holding a two-way radio next to his ear. The other officer pointed across the street at them.

"They're onto us!" Jack jumped into the car and released the brake.

She hesitated until he gunned the accelerator to prod her along. Then she dropped the telephone and jumped into the car.

Before her door was closed, the car bolted over the curbing and into the lane leading to the freeway.

She obviously was surprised and frightened.

He was torn between comforting her and yelling at her. If she had been a young lieutenant or captain, he would have given her a chewing out that she would have remembered the rest of her life.

"I'm sorry," he said, putting his hand on her arm.

She fought back tears. Finally she took his hand and squeezed. Looking back, she wiped her cheek and said, "They're not far behind."

He wondered if the tears were fake or real. "Better buckle in tight. I'm not sure I can outrun them this time."

He told her the name of the exit to watch for and asked her to tune a news station on the radio again. She found a station that had just started an on-the-scene report.

. . .attention now is on this two-story residence ablaze less than a block from where two bodies still lay on the sidewalk. Neighbors have identified the house as belonging to Dr. William Whitney. Unconfirmed reports say there are one or more bodies inside the burning house. Firemen are still too busy trying to keep the flames from spreading to search for victims. Witnesses report several shots were fired by the man who sped away in a late model sedan. Police here at the scene refuse to speculate whether the fire and the killings are related.

Jack turned toward his companion and saw the shocked dismay that no doubt was showing on his face as well.

"Dr. Whitney!" she cried. "Why would anyone have wanted to hurt that dear old man?"

Thank you, Dave, for that report from the scene. This is Bill Dressler back in Action News Central. Within the last few moments, this strange story has taken yet another twist. Police dispatchers have just ordered units to a location in the Berkeley Hills east of Oakland. Apparently Christine Merrill called in moments ago pleading for help.

"I did not!" Her reaction was so spontaneous and so genuine that Jack believed her. She continued, "How—how can they have everything so screwed up?"

"Reporters don't have to be accurate—they just have to beat the competition."

She flashed him an angry glance, but she could not argue in this instance.

He continued, "Imagine how you'd be feeling right now if I were a deranged killer, and we'd just heard how you'd called in pleading for help." He shook his head in disgust. "That's what I don't like about how your colleagues play the game."

The man who supposedly killed the two men on the street kidnapped Miss Merrill during his escape. Although the initial report was treated with some skepticism, Miss Merrill's television station has confirmed that she had gone on assignment this afternoon to the home of the professor, the same home that now is in flames.

He was beginning to understand. The thought that the KGB had attacked Whitney made him feel sick and angry, but he kept aggressively attacking the traffic ahead. Christine looked bewildered and started to comment. Jack motioned for silence as the reporter continued.

Action News Central has learned that the auto license number of the getaway car matches a car rented four days ago at San Francisco International Airport. That car was rented in the name of an Air Force officer attending the aborted peace treaty signing.

Unofficial reports at Oakland Police Headquarters indicate the police now believe they may, indeed, be in pursuit of a crazed killer as an earlier report had claimed. In any case, the man is now considered to be armed and extremely dangerous.

Christine looked ahead and called out that they were approaching their exit. Jack still had his car in the left lane. The road was less crowded than before, but he had to decide quickly: either decelerate and exit behind the traffic in the right two lanes, or accelerate past them and do a high-speed crossover to the exit ramp.

Just as he was deciding, he saw the flashing blue-and-white lights of at least two police cars approaching from the opposite direction.

"You're going to miss the exit!" she shouted as the car shot ahead.
"We'll make it."

There was little margin for error. The heavy traffic had dried the
rain on the freeway, but he was unsure how slick the off-ramp might
be. Zooming in front of the car in the next lane, he switched off his
headlights. She screamed when they went out, but the other headlights gave him enough of a view of the road, the shoulder, and the
exit ramp. Other drivers slammed on their brakes as he roared across
the outside lanes.

He hit his brakes as soon as possible, but he could not avoid
crossing the buildup of asphalt serving as a low median where the exit
lane edged away. The car bounced through the air and landed on the
off-ramp. Muscling the steering wheel, he hit the accelerator again.
Although he kept the car from sliding beyond the shoulder, he lost
more speed than he had planned.

Shutting off the headlights did not fool the police completely, since
his brake lights and the spray of gravel gave away his position as soon
as his car landed on the off-ramp. However, there were enough other
brake lights from surprised drivers in the other cars to confuse the
pursuing policemen for a few moments. As a result, the police car slid
to a stop beyond the exit and had to back up.

Leaving the freeway, he checked his odometer. He was looking for
an unmarked dirt road that led off through a stand of trees on the
right side. O'Donnell had said that the road was exactly three and a
half miles from the freeway.

The two-lane road seemed deserted, and he was quickly back to full
speed. Checking the rearview mirror, he saw that he had doubled his
lead. Now, however, there were at least three sets of flashing lights in
pursuit. Even in the darkness, he could see that the terrain to the
right was rolling hills with scattered stands of trees. Unless he increased the lead, the police would see his car turn off the highway.

Three miles from the freeway, he told Christine to help find the
side road. Beyond the next rise, a mile or so ahead, he also saw the
images of lights shimmering off the clouds above the road. Just as his
headlights lit a pair of small reflectors marking a culvert across the
right ditch, the flashing lights of another police car appeared above
the rise ahead.

He delayed as much as he dared, then pushed the brakes just short
of causing a skid. When he was almost at the culvert, he locked the
brakes causing the rear of the car to slide left. The car swung perpendicular to the road and shuddered to a stop. Rocking violently to the
left, the car froze for an instant, then settled solidly on all four tires.
His headlights showed that the culvert and the dirt road beyond were

directly ahead, blocked only by a gate made of three strands of barbed wire. He stomped the accelerator and aimed for a wooden post that was suspended from the wire in the middle of the dirt road. Grabbing Christine's collar, he shoved her below the level of the dashboard.

As the car crashed into the gate, the wire strained, then slashed back in wild swirls as each strand snapped. The upper strand, and most of the post, bounced above the fenders and scraped gashes into the paint on the hood of the car.

He flinched and closed his eyes as the post smashed the windshield, then bounced over the top of the car. When he opened his eyes, he saw spider-web cracks radiating out across the windshield from where the post had hit, but the car was clear of the fence and accelerating away from the road.

She grabbed the dashboard and pulled herself above it. Seeing that the car was still on a road, she turned to him and shouted, "Where in the hell did you learn to drive? Pilot training?"

"You got it, lady!"

Racing toward the top of the hill, he looked in the rearview mirror and saw the pursuing cars on the highway skidding to stops.

Her voice startled him. "What's that?"

He glanced at her and saw she was pointing ahead. His headlights were reflecting off a blurry image beyond the hilltop. He eased off the accelerator and switched the headlights to bright.

A much brighter light responded.

"Damn," he shouted as he jammed on the brakes and tried to shield his eyes from the blinding light.

Ahead, a hovering helicopter rose just above the top of the hill.

As his car came to a stop across the dirt road, he was in a near panic. He assumed the police had gotten ahead of him again, cutting him off just short of O'Donnell's safe house. Jack looked toward the highway and saw the police cars turning onto the dirt road. He would never get by them.

He glanced at the helicopter. The nose was low as the pilot started moving forward.

Perhaps, Jack decided, he could fake a run toward the highway and get the helicopter to block his path. Then he could try to get beyond the hill top and within sight of O'Donnell's people.

He shifted gears and rotated the steering wheel for a reverse U-turn. As he looked toward the helicopter, which was swinging around beside his car, he let the car accelerate backward an instant too long. The right rear wheel dropped off into the muddy ditch beside the road. He shifted out of reverse and desperately tried to accelerate forward. Spraying a rooster tail of mud and stones into the darkness, the spinning tire edged the car ahead, but would not rise from the ditch.

Still just a few feet off the ground, the helicopter moved in front and to the left of the car. When the pilot shut off the spotlight, Jack saw a man waving wildly from the open door of the cargo compartment. It was Russell Brown, O'Donnell's partner.

Jack shut off his headlights and pushed the car door against the blast of the rotor downwash. "Come on," he shouted to Christine as he grabbed his briefcase.

The copter landed immediately.

Hurrying from the car, he grabbed her arm, pulling her into the swirling wind, water, and grass. When he reached the helicopter, he threw his briefcase to Brown, then swept Christine off the ground. He shoved her onto the vibrating floor of the helicopter, then dived inside.

The helicopter rose and banked left, causing them to slide away from the open door. As Brown struggled to get the door closed, Jack pulled her onto a row of canvas seats.

The helicopter swooped away from the approaching police cars and climbed toward the low clouds covering the valley east of the hills. Once Brown got the door closed, he welcomed them aboard. "We were passing through the area and heard you needed a ride, Colonel."

Chapter 24

Thursday Night, 7:40 p.m.
Iskra plus 5:40

THE HELICOPTER ZIGZAGGED FOR NEARLY AN HOUR. JACK ASSUMED most of the turns and altitude changes were to ensure that the police and the FAA—and perhaps even the KGB—could not track them. He and Brown avoided talking about anything substantive in front of Christine.

The more time Jack had to recover from the shock of the shootings and the escape, the more he rebounded. The exhilaration he had always felt in combat was combining with a renewed faith in his judgment. Though he had been wrong about the purpose of the camouflage netting on the ships, he had been *less wrong* than anyone else. The Russians *were* hiding something, and he was the one person who had recognized that. He had been wrong only in assuming they were hiding the wreckage instead of the explosives.

Finally he sensed that the helicopter made a rapid descent, then raced along at low altitude, making several turns. He could barely see out one small window, and occasionally lights on the ground rushed by. The helicopter hovered for a few seconds, and he expected another descent. Almost immediately he felt the helicopter's skids settle onto the ground, and the engine wound down. He was surprised, because he had seen no air field or helipad lights. The pilot seemed to have landed at a clandestine site that had not been lighted for their arrival.

Brown turned the cabin lights on bright, and the side door slid open a couple feet.

O'Donnell came aboard. "Jack, you old son of a gun, it's good to see you again."

Jack was not prepared for the heartiness of the welcome, and he stammered a quick thank you for the helicopter ride.

Before he could say more, O'Donnell overacted his response to Christine. "And what a pretty thing you are. I'm even happier to see you than seeing old Jack. I'm Buzz O'Donnell at your service."

305

She quickly introduced herself and looked quizzically at Jack.

"Same old Buzz," he said, smiling and shaking his head.

"What kind of a host am I being? Let's get you on into the house, darlin'. You too, Jack."

O'Donnell jumped to the ground and reached to assist Christine. As Jack waited, he could see almost nothing in the darkness beyond the lighted cabin of the helicopter. The only light outside seemed to come from the cabin, the helicopter's navigational lights, and some cockpit lights reflected off the windows. Once he hopped to the ground and the door was closed, there was barely enough light to see to take hold of Christine's hand.

"I've got a van over here," O'Donnell said.

As soon as he spoke, the van's headlights flashed on, effectively destroying the bit of adjustment Jack's eyes had made to the darkness. Almost immediately the driver switched to the parking lights. A few seconds later, the newcomers were in the back of a windowless van without having seen any of the surroundings. The van moved along unlighted roads for the next few minutes, and O'Donnell chattered continually with Christine. Finally the van entered a garage that was connected to a house. Walking into the large, country-style kitchen, Jack guessed the building was an old ranch house, perhaps in the Napa wine country. Then he realized he could hear the distant sound of surf and decided that the house was nearer the coast.

"If you'll pardon my saying so," O'Donnell said, "you two look like you've had better days. First thing we're going to do is let you get cleaned up."

He was right about how they looked after the fight on the street and the struggle to get aboard the helicopter.

"I need to get a call through to a general at Alameda," Jack said.

"From what I've been hearing about you on the radio, Jack," O'Donnell said, "you may not want to rush that. From the sounds of things, you've made the 'Ten Most Wanted' list in just one afternoon."

Jack remembered the radio report he had heard earlier and wondered if the agent had heard something worse. Jack started to protest about needing to talk to the general right away, but O'Donnell's look was saying "cooperate."

He continued, "You can decide how to handle your surrender a little later. I'm sure Miss Merrill would like to get into some fresh clothes."

"Surrender?" Jack assumed that O'Donnell was trying to get Christine out of the way before any substantive discussions. Also, it might be helpful for her to think that the KGB had been successful in distancing Jack from the people who normally would believe him.

"Well, I know I'm not General Raleigh's favorite colonel, and right now General McClintock probably isn't thinking very highly of me either."

As O'Donnell ushered them toward the stairway, he said, "I think we can find you a change of clothes upstairs. And I'll bet you're both hungry. We'll do something about that, too."

The two newcomers were led to separate suites and told to use anything they needed. Assuming that O'Donnell would return once Christine was settled in, Jack started reading the new printouts about Braxton.

Some stories were from databases of recent news in the world of finance. These focused on the sale of several major properties in California and speculated that Braxton and some unnamed financiers were preparing a takeover bid for one of the major networks. That fit what Christine had said, but Jack was skeptical. Braxton had begun his current selloff in the last half of November—shortly after Premier Medvalev had agreed to the Pan-Pacific treaty. Getting rid of his California properties certainly did not prove that Braxton was in on the plot, but the *coincidence* reinforced Jack's suspicions.

He also found an interesting excerpt from a biographical listing of the one hundred wealthiest people in America. According to the article, Braxton—Aleksandr Classon Webern at that time—was not quite sixteen the late spring of 1952 when he had piloted a small airplane in a daring escape from the Russian zone in Austria. He supposedly had evaded MiG-15 fighters by flying low through the mountains. Evading MiGs while flying a light airplane was much more believable, Jack thought, if the fighter pilots had been told to let young Webern escape.

In any case, the young escapee rapidly attained almost folk-hero status among anti-Communists and was an honored celebrity at the Republican Presidential Convention in Chicago. There he was befriended by Braxton Chase, an influential delegate and a wealthy real-estate developer from San Francisco. The young Austrian was invited into the Chase household in the months that followed and was raised much as if he were the Chases' own son. Webern had adapted quickly to his new surroundings and opportunities, and within a decade had become a key member of the broadcasting part of Chase's financial empire.

Twelve years ago Braxton Chase and his wife Sylvia had died in a plane crash in the California mountains. The Chase holdings of nearly three hundred million dollars were divided equally between Alexander C. Braxton and a philanthropic foundation. In the intervening years Braxton had more than quadrupled his inheritance. As Jack tossed the papers on the bed, he saw Braxton from an entirely different perspective.

He found the closets and chest of drawers to be stocked with clothing in various sizes. He assumed they were in a safe house kept ready for defectors or special government witnesses. He picked a blue jump suit that resembled a flying suit, then went into the bathroom for a shower.

Once he was undressed, he checked the wound on his back. The bullet had barely hit him so the injury looked more like a bad rope burn than a bullet wound.

As he stepped from the shower, he heard a knock at the door. After the second knock, O'Donnell called Jack's name. He wrapped a towel around his waist and opened the door.

O'Donnell led two other men into the room. One carried a raised pistol. The other man, an electronics expert named Dennis Ford, wore a headset attached to a small electronic device he held ahead of him. He also carried a portable radio that was broadcasting a news report. Before Jack could ask what was happening, O'Donnell signaled for silence.

Ford used the device to scan the room, paying special attention to the briefcase and discarded clothing on the bed. After checking the bathroom, he returned to the bedroom. Turning off the portable radio, he said, "It's not in here."

Jack asked, "What are you talking about?"

O'Donnell frowned. "One of you brought a transmitter with you."

"What?"

Betrayal, anger, embarrassment, sadness—the series of emotions rippled through Jack as he settled onto the bed. The implications of Christine carrying a transmitter were almost too overwhelming to accept. Now he understood why his adversaries seemed to stay one step ahead and why Braxton had tried so hard to interest him in the woman. He was embarrassed that she had seemed so genuine and he had been fooled so badly. He had tried so hard to accept her as being what she said she was. Now he was completely uncertain about what had been truth and what had been lies.

"We didn't believe you were carrying the transmitter, Colonel," O'Donnell said, "but you were easier to check first."

"Christine's performance seemed solid this afternoon. She provided a diversion that helped us get away from the gunmen."

"In this business," O'Donnell said, "the best ones are the ones you never suspect."

Remembering the circumstances that had inserted her into the middle of his investigation, Jack said sarcastically, "Score one for the President's desire to keep the people informed." Then he added with a tone of resignation, "How do you know there's a transmitter?"

"We know," Ford said. "It's powerful and seems to be voice-activated."

Jack asked, "Transmits everything said near it?"

"It's not exactly like being on 'Candid Camera,' Colonel," O'Donnell said, "but I hope you haven't done anything with the lady that you didn't want recorded for posterity."

"That's not my biggest worry," Jack said as he thought of the afternoon's conversations with Dr. Whitney. "No wonder the KGB had to eliminate Dr. Whitney! Have you heard? Did the old man die in the fire?"

O'Donnell nodded. "The firemen found one body. Badly burned, but they made a tentative ID."

Infuriated, Jack wanted to avenge the death of the spry old man, but recognized that his death was only one of many yet to come if the Soviet plan were not stopped. "What happens when you find the transmitter?"

"We shut the son of a bitch down, of course," O'Donnell said.

"Can we wait?"

O'Donnell looked at Ford for an answer.

"Not long. The signal's intermittent, of course, but the longer the transmitter's here, the better chance they have of pinpointing our location."

"But as long as no one talks near the transmitter," Jack said, "it's not sending out a signal, right?"

"Right," Ford said. "Extends the battery life that way."

Jack pounded one fist against his other hand. "Because of that transmitter, I've spent the afternoon like a fox in front of the hounds— and I'd like to return the favor. Maybe if we send our own messages, we could make some difference in how this all turns out."

O'Donnell asked, "What do you want to say, Colonel?"

"Damned if I know," Jack said. "For the last four days, I've been operating without a script and making up things as I go. First, I need to find out what kind of ordnance General McClintock thinks he can send against the ships the Soviets leave behind."

"We could put the transmitter into a soundproof box," O'Donnell said, "except for when we want to broadcast our own messages. If we do that right, they'll think the transmissions stopped because no one's around."

"I could add extra insulation to one of the boxes used for chemical shipments," Ford said. "This all assumes, of course, you can get the transmitter away from her before she broadcasts a warning."

"That might be tough," O'Donnell said, "if she's wearing the transmitter."

"We could put her to sleep quietly," the man with the pistol said.

Jack was unsure if that meant temporarily or permanently, but he did not like either option. "The transmitter's probably in her purse. Let's see if we can get it easily before we resort to something like that."

"But we'll have to confront her," O'Donnell said. "I've got to get her isolated and under guard. Besides, there are things I want to show you, and I damned sure want to know everything you've learned."

"Get the right people together," Jack said, "and I'll fill you in until she joins us."

"I'll have them downstairs in five minutes," O'Donnell said, then gesturing toward his electronics expert, he added, "Dennis will check her room after she leaves to join us. She'd be a fool, though, if she didn't bring the transmitter to the rest of the discussions. I think you need to figure out a quiet way to separate her from her purse."

Jack frowned and nodded. "If you have any maps that show the ocean floor in the vicinity of the crash, bring one to the meeting."

O'Donnell smiled and said, "This week we happen to have one or two of those."

After Jack dressed, he joined O'Donnell, Brown, and two other men in a family room next to the kitchen. Though the room was well away from Christine's room—and the transmitter—a loud radio provided background noise. O'Donnell spread out a map on a coffee table, and everyone sat on surrounding couches.

Jack asked O'Donnell, "How much has Major Lockhart told you this afternoon?"

"Just that the *Iskra* clock had started and that you're thinking about some weird combination of nuclear strikes and earthquakes."

Brown gestured toward O'Donnell, then smiled and said, "We don't call him 'Doubting Thomas' for nothing. Your work's cut out for you if you expect to make a believer out of Tom."

"You're about to witness a conversion," Jack said confidently as he oriented the map so O'Donnell would have a good view. Pointing to contour lines on the ocean floor, Jack said, "See this canyon? That was Colonel Bochkov's aim point for Soviet National One, but he missed. Even by circling and trying a second time, he still missed—but not by much."

"If he missed," O'Donnell said, "what makes you think that was his target, or that he even had a specific target in the first place."

"The Soviet ships told me the canyon was the target, and Dr. Whitney told me why. In less than eighteen hours after the crash, the Soviet Navy put the *Karpaty* and two heavily loaded cargo ships over that canyon, even though Soviet National One crashed almost a mile farther northeast. I got a good look at the *Tibor Szamueli* late Monday afternoon and again Tuesday morning when Kane was broadcasting pictures. The *Tibor* was riding much higher in the water the second time I saw her than the first time—much of its cargo had already been offloaded."

"Dumping cargo makes no sense," O'Donnell said emphatically. "Even if the Soviets picked up the whole airplane, they'd have, what, seventy tons of pieces."

"The Soviets never intended to pick up the wreckage, or much of it anyway."

"Well, if they didn't," O'Donnell said, shaking his head, "they sure put on a good show to make us think that's what they were doing."

Jack smiled but did not answer. Instead he let his silence cause O'Donnell to rethink his words.

Brown smiled and said, "Tom, I think you just pulled your first duck from the water, and the colonel says there's a ten on the bottom."

Looking embarrassed, O'Donnell said, "That makes no sense for them to come all the way and not bother with the wreckage. Why in the hell would they do that?"

"I believe that for three days," Jack said, "the Soviets have been packing that canyon with four shiploads of explosives and bags of scrap ore, and tomorrow morning at—"

O'Donnell interrupted, exchanging a nervous glance with Brown. "What's this about bags of ore?"

"The bags cover the explosives and direct the explosion downward."

"We had some people doing a mission today out near the Coast Guard cutters," O'Donnell said. "Our guys picked up something that we couldn't explain until now. I'll show you later."

Jack nodded. "Anyway *Iskra* plus twenty is ten-hundred hours tomorrow morning, and I think someone's going to throw a switch to detonate every ounce of those explosives. And twenty-four hours later at *Iskra* plus forty-four, Valinen's scheduled a red force laydown on all our strategic forces."

Red force was the common term for Soviet military forces aligned against the American blue forces in war scenarios.

"That's—I mean—Not even Valinen—" O'Donnell stood and started pacing. "Valinen's diabolical and ambitious. I mean, I can accept that he could kill his enemies on the Politburo without a single concern for the other ninety who would die at the same time." He paused as if searching for words. "But he's too smart to think he could win a—"

He was interrupted as Dennis Ford opened the sliding door that led to the kitchen. "Miss Merrill's coming down."

O'Donnell nodded his understanding and went to turn off the radio.

"We'll discuss the rest of this later," he said to Jack as the others in the room started to leave.

"I've got some studying to do," Brown said as he folded the map and put it under his arm.

After everyone but Jack and O'Donnell left, Jack opened his brief-case and placed it on the coffee table. He did not like the sneaky role he would have to play, but he would do whatever was required to get Christine away from her purse. He kept telling himself, "Pay attention to the evidence. In this case, you have to consider her guilty unless she proves herself innocent."

As O'Donnell ushered her to the couch, he said, "The news reports say you had an exciting afternoon, Miss Merrill. I hope you weren't hurt."

She glanced toward Jack, seemingly unsure why their host was still bothering with social amenities. Jack moved to join her as she explained that some of the stories on the radio had been incorrect.

As she sat, she placed her purse on the floor beneath the edge of the coffee table. Jack sat beside her. While her attention was on O'Donnell, the colonel used his foot to push the purse farther under the table.

A voice behind him said, "Dinner's ready anytime."

He turned and saw Ford standing beside the door. His announcement meant the transmitter was not in Christine's bedroom.

Jack sighed and took a deep breath. "I'm starved," he said, grabbing her hand as he stood. He said to O'Donnell, "I assume my briefcase will be okay here."

"Safe as in your mother's arms."

She had barely gotten to her feet before Jack was pulling her toward the kitchen.

"But wait," she said as she slowed to get her purse. "I—"

As she extended his arm, the wound on his back stretched. He grimaced, exaggerating the effect of the pain. Surprised by his reaction to such a minor tug, she asked, "What did I do?"

"Nothing," he said, taking another step toward the kitchen. He raised his arm and tried to see around his side. "I'm not bleeding again, am I?"

"Where?" She hurried around behind him. "What's wrong?"

"I'm not quite as fast as when I was a kid." He put his arm around her and guided her into the kitchen. "I didn't quite get out of the way of the first bullet this afternoon."

"You've got to see a doctor."

"The bullet barely touched me."

She turned toward O'Donnell. "Is there a town nearby with a doctor?"

"We can get medical attention if he needs any," O'Donnell said, closing the door behind them. "I think food will do him more good than anything else right now."

She kept fussing about the untended wound, but seemed satisfied after confirming that no blood was seeping through his jump suit.

A couple of minutes after they started eating, Ford opened the door. He held a box in front of him. The box was one of the insulated containers used to cushion sensitive chemicals during transportation. He nodded toward O'Donnell, then left with the box. Another man and a woman took his place at the door.

O'Donnell stood and said, "Miss Merrill, I'm placing you in confinement for possible violation of the espionage sections of the United States Code and other pertinent statutes of the United States government."

She was too shocked to speak. When she saw that O'Donnell was serious, she said, "That's preposterous. I don't understand." She looked expectantly toward Jack and realized he was not going to intervene. Studying his expression for a moment, she said softly, "You knew he was going to do this?"

"There have been leaks of information for the past several days." He was outraged because she had been carrying the transmitter, but instinctively he reached for her hand. He stopped in mid-motion and put his hand on the edge of the table instead. He still hoped there was a different answer, but did not want to confirm to her that the transmitter had been found in her purse. "I had hoped the information wasn't going out through you."

"Well, it wasn't!" Her denial was as vigorous as her response in the car to the radio report saying she had asked for help against him.

"Then help us find who was leaking the information."

"How can I? I don't know what you're talking about."

"If you tell us who was getting the information," O'Donnell said, "your cooperation will be considered in your favor."

Christine was staring so hard at Jack that O'Donnell and his people might as well not have been in the room. "I—I could be reporting this story right now. Instead I stayed so I'd be there to tell your side when the police caught you. I've done more to help you than for any man in my life—and you didn't even care!" Then she slapped him.

He could have blocked her arm but did not because he felt so guilty for not taking her side. O'Donnell grabbed her wrist. The two guards moved to help, but she did not resist as O'Donnell pulled her to her feet.

"If I didn't care," Jack said as he stood, "this would have been a hell of a lot easier. I'll come and talk to you later."

O'Donnell looked dubious. "We'll have to see."

Jack faced him defiantly, then said, "I will see her." He paused, and there was a temporary standoff. "There are questions that only she may have the answers to."

O'Donnell relented, nodding his agreement.

Jack pressed the issue. "She stays here, right!"

"Right." Then O'Donnell motioned for the two guards to take her away.

Jack took hold of her arm. "I have to square things with General McClintock, but I'll come and see you as soon as I can."

She said nothing as she looked at him with eyes more frightened than angry.

After she and her guards had disappeared, Jack looked around the room. "Fuck it all," he said as he kicked a chair, sending it clattering against the table.

"Life's full of shit, Colonel," O'Donnell said. He put his hand on Jack's shoulder and added, "You've just got to play the cards you're dealt."

As angry as he was over her apparent betrayal, at the same time he felt as if he were betraying her. He shrugged off O'Donnell's hand and gave him an exasperated look.

"Well," O'Donnell said, clearing his throat before he continued, "that's what the director told me this week after the woman I loved ended up on the bottom of the ocean on Sunday night."

Jack was shocked. Then he remembered Brown's apology on O'Donnell's behalf after they had forced their way into Jack's debriefing of the F-15 pilots. "I had no idea. I . . ."

His voice trailed off. If he were facing a Mrs. O'Donnell, he could have forced his way through words of condolence on behalf of the government of the United States of America. He had already done that with the widows of fighter pilots more times than he cared to remember. But he could not come up with the right words for another man. In his view of the world, women weren't supposed to die first.

"I know." O'Donnell shook his head quickly as if throwing aside memories once again, then said, "You ready to get your ass in gear, Colonel? The Soviet Navy's got its ass in gear."

"What do you mean?"

"The *Minsk* pulled out late this afternoon with most of her escorts and all the garbage ships. Four destroyers and that submarine rescue ship, the *Karpaty*, are still at the crash site."

"I suppose you're about to tell me that the *Minsk* is headed toward Hawaii."

"I wasn't," O'Donnell said with a questioning look, "but she is.

That is, she's headed more in that direction than toward Vladivostok. After the announcement of the ending of the exercise, we'd assumed Vladivostok would be her destination."

"I've got to get a secure line to General McClintock."

"I've already gotten a message to him that he'll be hearing from you shortly. There's something you should see before you talk to the general."

He led Jack outside and they got into a golf cart parked near the door. O'Donnell drove nearly a half mile toward a barnlike building and the sound of the pounding surf. The building, which was dark and looked deserted, was located on the edge of a natural inlet, protected from the ocean by a seawall.

O'Donnell drove the golf cart into a dimly lit room that appeared to be a stable. Then he led Jack through a door into a smaller room, making sure the door was closed after them. As soon as he opened the next door, light flooded into the small room.

A large room beyond was a combination industrial machine shop and indoor dock. Overhead cranes were capable of moving large loads from the dock to the water. The lifting cradle for the largest crane was attached to a small submarine of the type used for ocean research or deep-water recoveries.

A number of men, including Russell Brown, were working on and around the submarine. Brown left the workers and joined the newcomers.

"We call her *Snoopy I*," O'Donnell said, gesturing toward the submarine. "We finally got her trucked up here last night from San Diego."

Brown joined them and said to O'Donnell, "The modules we picked up this afternoon are installed. I'm ready whenever you give the word."

"We've been planning on sending Russ and a driver to check over any pieces the Soviets leave behind. However," O'Donnell said, "picking up tons of high explosives is more then we bargained for."

Jack studied the various appendages that extended beyond the body of the small submarine. "Is that thing equipped to cut underwater cables?"

O'Donnell looked questioningly at Brown.

"We didn't set up the minisub that way," Brown said, "but we might be able to rig something using the remote manipulator arm."

Jack explained the likelihood that the explosives were wired by cable to controls on one of the surface ships.

Brown looked dubious. "What happens if cutting those cables sets off the explosion?"

"Surf's up," Jack said.

O'Donnell added with a smile, "And you and *Snoopy I* are going to catch the ultimate wave."

Brown looked less amused. "As long as those destroyers stay there, I'll never get close enough to cut anything anyway. The one thing we're not rigged for is silent running."

"I have a feeling the *Karpaty* will be by itself at ten o'clock tomorrow," Jack said. "The Soviets have done some testing, but I doubt they'll risk four destroyers above ground zero."

"We'll need at least six hours," Brown said.

Jack was disappointed. "I'm not sure we'll have that much time."

"We can be out of here in fifteen minutes, but *Snoopy I* isn't one of your jets. She can only give us five knots underwater."

"Can't you transport the sub a little closer with a helicopter? At night the Soviets might think you were just flying out to support the Coast Guard. That could put you six or seven miles from the *Karpaty*."

"If we had a day or two, we might rig some kind of harness to carry it," O'Donnell said, "but that little sucker's pretty heavy. I don't think we could come up with anything safe in the next few hours. Anyway six hours puts us in the target area with thirty to forty-five minutes to spare."

"If you can find the right spot," Jack said, assuming that navigation of the small submersible was difficult without assistance from support ships on the surface.

O'Donnell smiled and said, "Acoustic transponder beacons. We put five in the water this afternoon."

"And," Brown said, "we just checked out the updated interrogator that we brought back from Stockton and installed on *Snoopy I*. Give me a set of coordinates, Colonel, and I can navigate to them."

O'Donnell moved to a nearby workbench and picked up something resembling a large trash bag. "Our guys picked this up when they were putting out the beacons. We were confused because the bag seems to be made from some high-tech materials and the residue inside suggests it had contained gravel."

Jack studied the bag. The material was lightweight and pliable, but very strong. The bag had been stretched to hold a full load, but a cut that ran almost the length of one side had allowed the contents to spill. Small chips of rock and a paste of wet dust were stuck in the inside corners. "Looks like they ran the ore through a crusher, then heat-sealed the bags like a bag of salt for a water softener."

"Even if the material is strong enough to hold four or five hundred pounds," O'Donnell said, "you're still talking about four or five bags per ton of ore. That's a helluva lot of bags in a ship load."

"Valinen started trying this out as a weapon nearly a year ago. He's had a lot of time to fill a lot of bags." Jack put the bag aside, then looked toward the submarine. "How about air cover? Have you got anything lined up?"

"We'd assumed," Brown said, "we'd be going in after all the Soviets had sailed away."

"We've got the helicopter and a couple of light planes on a small strip over by Napa," O'Donnell said. "No real firepower, though."

"I was thinking more in terms of a diversion," Jack said. "Get 'em looking up instead of down. And assuming the Soviets don't leave any real warships behind, maybe I'll do a little 'trolling' if Brown can't get the cables cut."

O'Donnell asked, "Trolling?"

"The President told the premier we'd fire back in self-defense. So if I happen to fly close enough to draw fire, that'll give someone the right to blow their boat out of the water."

Brown looked surprised. "You really want to try that?"

"I've done it before," Jack said with a smile. "Anyway, that's a backup plan. My first choice is for you to get out there and cut the cables, Russ, and I'll try to keep them looking up instead of down."

Brown frowned and crossed his arms. "Sounds like I'd better figure out how to attach something to the manipulator arm so I can do some cable cutting."

As he started to leave, Jack gestured toward the high-tech wetsuit the agent was wearing and asked, "Can you get one of those outfits in my size?"

"No problem," Brown said.

Turning to O'Donnell, Jack said, "I'd also like to have a flak vest that'll fit under my jump suit, some size-eleven jump boots, and a pistol. And I'll need a parachute and a checklist or some flight manuals on whatever kind of aircraft you have."

"No problem on those things either," O'Donnell said. "But after hearing what some of the East Bay cops said about your driving, Colonel, I hadn't pictured you as so cautious."

"Superstitious, maybe," Jack said as he pulled the shell fragment from his pocket and held it between his fingers. "I had a good friend once. If he'd have worn a flak vest, he'd have carried this little piece of shrapnel in his pocket all these years instead of me carrying it in mine." Jack dropped the fragment into his palm and looked at the piece of metal. Then he took a deep breath, pushed the fragment into his pocket, and said, "Gentlemen, I'm overdue to receive a chewing-out."

Returning to the house, he told O'Donnell, "You need to have your analysts dig up everything on who was to receive the cargo from the

Tibor Szamueli, the *Julius Fucik*, and the two *Stakhanovets Kotov*–class freighters that came to the crash site."

"I'm not sure what to tell my people to look for," O'Donnell said. "We don't have much time."

"Those four ships were all phonies. Their captains never expected to enter port in California. However, the Soviets would have ensured that normal paperwork at the ports showed some company was expecting each ship. I want to know who those companies are, and the layer above them, and the layer above them, ad infinitum. If you find the name Alexander C. Braxton anywhere in that hierarchy, for any or all of those ships, I want to know about it."

"You think he was Christine's contact?" Before Jack could decide how to answer, O'Donnell continued. "Since she worked for him, I suppose that's a logical connection, but Alexander Braxton? That's like accusing Babe Ruth or Will Rogers."

"You said it earlier. In your business, the best ones are the ones you never suspect."

"But why Braxton? He's got a half-billion-dollar stake in American capitalism."

"Why? I can't tell you why any of those people ever go over. I do know that two or three times when I was getting close, he skillfully led me away from the answer. As far as money goes, if you take a look, you may discover he's moved most of his stake into Swiss bank accounts in the last six weeks. He sure as hell doesn't own much California real estate anymore." He added sadly, "As you said, Braxton was Christine's boss, and he opened a lot of doors for her."

Minutes later, he sat in a booth for a secure telephone as McClintock said, "When are you coming in, Jack?"

"I need a few more hours, General."

"Jack, the chief's not happy, not happy at all with the press you've gotten in the last few hours. General Raleigh wants this whole mess brought to a close—fast." Jack was unable to choose words that would not be profane or insubordinate or both. When the colonel did not respond immediately, McClintock continued, "He thinks the quicker you and Miss Merrill reappear, the better. He's waiting for my advice on how to get things under control. What do you suggest I tell him?"

"With all due respect, sir," Jack said, "I suggest you tell him that he's got you working the wrong damned problem and that he ought to be getting the President and the Vice President out of California, and he should be ordering you to get the E-4B in the air with a full battle staff—because you damned well may need that battle staff in the next thirty-six hours, sir!"

"Jesus, Jack!"

"We've only got about fourteen hours, sir, and if we don't do something, there're going to be major changes in the world as you and I know it."

"Okay, Jack. Let me have it from the top."

Jack repeated the story Dr. Whitney had told about the work of Dr. Kutakhov. Jack discussed the recent earthquakes in Iran and Turkey that could have been linked to the Soviets. He told of his suspicions that the entire recovery effort had been cover for the real mission, which was to offload the explosives from the merchant ships.

McClintok interrupted and told someone in his office to get everything they could locate on Kutakhov and on activities offshore before and after those two quakes. He also asked for a check on the availability of photo reconnaissance aircraft.

Jack told of the KGB involvement in the killings that followed his visit with Dr. Whitney, indicating someone was following the investigation closely. When he told of the transmitter discovered in Christine's handbag, McClintock said, "Damn it! That confirms she's breached the security of the E-4B. She probably transmitted everything during the interview right here in this office."

"This won't make you feel any better," Jack said, "but she's not the biggest problem. I'm almost convinced Alexander Braxton is the master spy."

"I hope to hell you're wrong about that." McClintock paused, then added, "He's got more access to President Cunningham than the chairman of the joint chiefs has."

"I'm not ready to make accusations yet," Jack said, "and I wouldn't want anyone to spook him. In any case, we're certain about Christine carrying the transmitter. She's probably had it in the Western White House, and when she rode with the President at Chaney. She was also in the Command Post when General Harper talked to Colonel Radisson about putting more F-15s on alert. So, if you—"

"That tells us how the information leaked at Howell," McClintock said. "At least she was on the E-4B during a quiet day, and we certainly didn't discuss any classified information."

"That was one critical question I have, General. Is there any possibility you mentioned the term *Iskra* to her?"

The general paused for a moment, then answered, "Negative. I remember getting your note about being on the lookout for the term. However, I hadn't seen anything else on it before I talked to her and until I read a note from Major Lockhart a half hour ago. What's your reading of its significance, Jack?"

"I believe the use of the term *Iskra* initiated the countdown of the operation Valinen's running against us. Two critical events are to happen at *Iskra* plus twenty hours and *Iskra* plus forty-four hours. The premier's announcement spoke the term precisely at fourteen-hundred hours this afternoon, California time. So, I'm looking for something at ten-hundred hours tomorrow and again on Saturday morning?"

"Just what are you looking for, Jack?"

"My guess is that tomorrow morning's the *distraction*. The Soviets on the *Karpaty* will detonate between fifty and a hundred thousand tons of explosives on the lateral fault that runs beneath the crash site. Then the Soviets'll give us twenty-four more hours to get focused on picking up the pieces all over California before Valinen launches the *surprise*, a nuclear first strike. General, you can get an update from Major Lockhart, but on Saturday morning I believe you will find Soviet fleets passing through the patrol areas for our *Trident* boats. The Warsaw Pact will have moved very little from their war-games deployments, so I'd expect them to roll into Western Europe at the same time. You'll see an invasion of Hawaii as soon as the ships with the *Minsk* get within range."

McClintock waited a few moments to respond. "That's pretty damned ambitious, even for Valinen. If I accept that he's planning to devastate California tomorrow, top-level people are going to question whether that alone gives the Soviets enough leverage to risk a first strike. You're the guy who's got this all together in his head. Talk to me, Jack."

"I'd ask the nay-sayers why we spent the last hundred billion dollars we spent on strategic forces if we're sure the Russians are never going to try. We sure as hell don't buy the missiles and bombers because we're expecting to strike first! We spent the money because we're a-hundred-billion-dollars-worth-of-worried that one morning a Valinen is going to decide that a first strike is finally worth the gamble." He paused, then added, "If people'll take off their blinders and look around, they'll see we're not talking about the setup being just the death and destruction in California. If we take a first strike against the Peacekeeper and Minuteman bases, and Valinen also catches our bombers at DEFCON Four, our second-strike threat is pretty much down to the subs. With the secrets and technology the Soviets have bought and stolen in the last decade, maybe this is the year Valinen thinks he finally can beat the boats, too."

After pausing several moments, McClintock said, "It isn't quite the same as the Egyptians and Syrians attacking the Israelis on Yom Kippur in 1973, but few dates on the calendar are better than Christmas week for attacking the United States."

"And if the people at State think this is all a bunch of coincidences, ask them who picked the date and location for the signing of the treaty."

"Medvalev offered to send his people to San Francisco the week before Christmas, and Secretary Shafer jumped on the offer like a rooster on a June bug."

"That schedule ensured the President would be home in San Francisco right before the holidays, and there hasn't been any secret about the Vice-President spending Christmas at his wife's family home in Beverly Hills."

"Actually," McClintock said, "the Vice-President and his family are away from Los Angeles until Christmas eve."

Jack was surprised. "Maybe Valinen missed something. Where's the Vice-President going to be, General?"

"You're going to love this, Jack. He's at Wrightwood."

"I'm not sure where—"

"Wrightwood's in the mountains east of LA. If we had maps in front of us, I believe we'd find Wrightwood almost on top of the San Andreas fault."

"For chrissakes," Jack said, his growing frustration showing in his voice, "the President and the Vice-President are both sitting close enough that they could each throw a friggin' rock across the fault. If there's a big quake in the morning, by noon we could be without a President and a Vice-President and only twenty-two hours from a nuclear attack."

"Maybe, Jack, but the Soviets can't be certain both the President and the Vice-President would be killed in the quake."

"Yes, sir," Jack said. "I agree. That's why I'd make sure the AWACS keeps an eye on those four destroyers off Point Reyes. I expect those ships to leave the coast sometime during the night. After the quake, those destroyers will steam toward San Francisco to offer 'humanitarian assistance.' Unless you can assure me that none of those ships are carrying *Spetsnaz* teams, I can tell you what form that assistance will take in the confusion following the quake."

The *Spetsnaz* were Soviet special forces. Instead of having distinctive insignia and uniforms, such as those of the Green Berets in the U.S. Army, the *Spetsnaz* blended in with regular troops. Thus, these specially trained units were difficult to identify until they emerged at the beginning of a war to cause as much damage and confusion as possible behind enemy lines.

He was most concerned about their mission referred to as "decapitation" —cutting off the head of the enemy government. Some *Spetsnaz* units were trained to carry out assassinations. By eliminating American decision-makers, the Soviets might forestall the decisions necessary for an American counterattack in the first few hours of a nuclear war.

"You know I can't pin down the location of the *Spetsnaz* for you," McClintock said. "I guess you're saying that's a major item I need to add to my worry list."

"Yes, sir." Jack had wanted to emphasize the danger. The resulting chaos could make protecting the President and Vice-President almost impossible even if they survived the quake. "Do the Soviets have any ships close enough to Los Angeles to send someone in after the Vice-President?"

"The Soviet Navy had a couple of destroyers off Nicaragua over the weekend," McClintock said. "Last I heard, both ships had steamed north after the crash and were three or four hundred miles south of San Diego."

"I'd recommend that the Navy make sure those destroyers don't try to send any 'humanitarian assistance' to the Vice-President at Wrightwood."

"There's one other problem," McClintock said. "We'd already put out orders to send the AWACS crew home for Christmas. When the *Minsk* gets another fifty miles farther from the coast, the AWACS is going to leave orbit and head for Tinker. Stand by a moment, Jack."

McClintock spoke to someone else in his office: "Get a secure line to the commander of the 552nd Airborne Warning and Control Wing in Oklahoma City. Tell him I want the AWACS we've got orbiting in northern California to start to Tinker as ordered. When the aircraft commander gets over the Sierra, I want him to declare an emergency for an engine problem and divert into Travis."

Jack heard another voice ask the general, "Sir, do you want the crew to go into crew rest?"

"Negative! I want the crew hanging around the aircraft like they're still eager to get home for Christmas." McClintock paused, then said, "Back to you, Jack. You were saying?"

"Okay, General, you're twenty-two hours from taking a first strike when someone chases down Congressman Harris and calls him 'Mr. President.' Christ, General, the speaker brags about having been a card-carrying liberal for thirty years. In twenty-two hours, no one could teach him it's okay to touch the red telephone, let alone pick it up and say, 'Launch a counterstrike.' "

McClintock did not refute the assessment. He paused again, and Jack could hear the general talking to someone else. After a few moments McClintock said, "Major Lockhart heard you were on the line and sent me four items he thought you'd be interested in. The first one's a message." McClintock did not say anything as he read the message. Jack heard a low whistle and the rustling of papers, but still McClintock did not speak. Finally McClintock said, "If I keep getting stuff like this coming in out of left field, I may yet convince the chief to keep you out of Leavenworth. The first message reports an incident in Pasadena. A couple of high-voltage lines were knocked down earlier this evening. Some group calling itself 'The People's Movement for Freedom and Justice in Central America' says they're protesting Cal Tech's support to the Department of Defense.''

"Right," Jack said facetiously, knowing the excuse was phony. "Does the message say anything about the status of the seismographs at Cal Tech?"

"The seismology lab's on backup power. The big computers will be down for twenty-four to thirty-six hours, depending upon when main power is restored and how much damage any power surges caused.''

"All Valinen needs is fifteen hours to keep us from using Cal Tech to pinpoint the location of the initial shock. Of course there's still the center at Golden."

"Not for the next few hours, Jack. The second message says the National Earthquake Center at Golden has power problems, too. The message assumes their power failure was caused by the ice and heavy snow from the blizzard that's over Colorado and most of the rest of the Rocky Mountains. In any case, until the snows and winds die down, Golden's in the same shape as Cal Tech."

"There are other monitoring stations, but getting rid of these two may be enough."

"Lockhart has two notes for you," McClintock said. "The first one says he located the script on the television series on earthquakes. He said there were quotes from Dr. Whitney, but no quotes from, or even any mention of, Dr. Kutakhov. What does that mean to you, Jack?"

"The series was broadcast a couple of years ago by Alexander Braxton. Dr. Whitney made comments about Dr. Kutakhov in the interviews for the program. Those comments got back to the Soviet government and resulted in Kutakhov's imprisonment. Since those comments weren't broadcast, they must have been passed by Braxton —or someone on his staff." He added the last phrase since he realized that Christine had observed some of the interviews. If she were the only spy, she could have passed the information on Kutakhov. If she had, Jack thought, her performance earlier in the afternoon at Dr. Whitney's had been masterful.

"This whole thing about Braxton is harder to sell than running into the Western White House and yelling 'the Russians are coming.' "

"In his case, they've been here—for nearly forty years!"

"I still hope you're wrong on that one," McClintock said. "Here's the other note from Major Lockhart. It says, 'A clerk called with the following information: The last sale was five years ago in April. The purchaser was Merrill. The price was 1.4 million dollars. No mortgage was involved, so the title is currently clear.' "

"That makes it sound like spying pays a lot better than it used to," Jack said, "but I've never known the Soviets to pay that kind of money for information. Someone's sure been lying to somebody."

"I'll leave that one to you to figure out," McClintock said. "Anyway, we're keeping the chief waiting. I'm afraid that without pictures or some other hard evidence, this whole story's going to be a damned hard sell to him or anyone else."

"I know some folks who are going to try to get a look, but they won't have much time."

"I suppose you'll have a hand in that."

"Well, sir, I'm—"

"Wait, Jack. Don't even tell me—yet. The chief can't order me to order you to stop something I don't know anything about."

Jack appreciated the general's attitude. For the last few hours, Jack had wrestled with what he would do if his superiors ordered him to cease all activities and surrender to the police. He had never willfully disobeyed an order in his life, but he had also sworn an oath to defend the country against all enemies. Unless he started seeing hard evidence that proved his theory was wrong, he knew he would not turn back, no matter what the personal consequences.

"If we get a look at the explosives," he said, "and can't deactivate them, someone on our side has got to pull the trigger before the captain of the *Karpaty* does. I recommend, General, that you have birds airborne prepared to launch a preemptive strike against the *Karpaty* at zero-nine-forty-five hours in the morning. The airplanes should be armed with Harpoons, or something else that will hit fast, without warning."

"That's not going to be easy to sell over at the Western White House. That crowd's so euphoric because the Soviets are going home, nothing we say's likely to faze them."

"Then, General," Jack said facetiously, "it sounds like you and the chief are about to get a chance to earn your Christmas bonus."

"Right," McClintock said sarcastically. "Merry Christmas to you, too, Jack."

Chapter 25

AFTER FINISHING HIS CONVERSATION WITH GENERAL MCCLINTOCK, Jack decided that he needed to use the transmitter soon. If it remained silent much longer, the agents monitoring it would be convinced it had been discovered. O'Donnell agreed to join him shortly in the kitchen.

Jack got a soft drink from the refrigerator and had just poured the drink into a glass when O'Donnell came in. Jack crushed the can in his hand, then threw the crumpled metal into the trash basket across the room. "We've *got* to get Braxton."

Traitors were the anathema of the "duty, honor, country" life Jack had led for more than twenty years. When spies were discovered—at least spies like Braxton—they should be dealt with. The military part of him also knew that Christine's involvement with the KGB could not be excused. However, he rationalized that she might never have been involved without some influence from Braxton. That made Jack want Braxton even more.

"I can't argue with that," O'Donnell said.

"We've still got a hell of a problem ahead of us," Jack said, "but he's priority number two, just behind getting those cables cut in time."

O'Donnell studied Jack for a moment, then said, "You're getting kind of emotionally involved aren't you, Colonel?"

"Damn right! That's the big difference between me and the airplanes I fly."

"Just don't lose sight of the big picture, friend."

Jack nodded his understanding of the unsaid warning that went with the words. "But I'm betting Braxton's at the middle of that picture. I figure he's *Iskra*'s on-scene commander in California. If so, we need to start thinking like he's thinking."

"If he's their main trouble-shooter," O'Donnell said, "then I'd say his number one trouble's not knowing what you're up to."

"He must know by now what I learned from Whitney, so his big worry is that I'll get to someone important—no offense, Buzz—who believes me before ten-hundred hours tomorrow."

O'Donnell took a mock bow for his earlier performance, then said, "If I'm Braxton and I think you're about to reach someone, I may put in a vote to move up the *Iskra* timetable."

"That's got me worried too. Our little charade in front of the transmitter needs to convince him I'm not confident enough to go forward yet."

"The two big things we've got going for us are that he doesn't know his transmitter's compromised, and he doesn't know we know when the time runs out on the *Iskra* clock."

"And there's one more," Jack said with emphasis. "He still thinks he's clean as far as we're concerned."

"That should work to our advantage."

"Damn right! It might even get him to the airport at Napa tomorrow."

O'Donnell shook his head. "No way. Braxton's got to have an escape route set up already. I mean, he's the one guy who knows not to be in California—on the ground anyway—tomorrow morning. Plus he sure isn't planning to hang around for the nukes at *Iskra* plus forty-four."

"Agreed, but I think I could get him to change his plans."

O'Donnell brightened. "I could have thirty men there waiting. Braxton'd be a hell of a catch."

Jack's response was much more subdued. "Think it through, man. You jump him at the airport, and you're probably going to get the big one before ten o'clock."

"We could take him before he knows we're there."

"If you're Braxton, you're not going to come there without a transmitter, and you've probably got someone staked out watching you from a distance. If I'm Braxton, I'm going to leave orders behind that say, 'If someone grabs me, tell Valinen to get the show on the road.' "

O'Donnell nodded but looked puzzled. "What's the use of luring him to Napa if I can't grab him?"

"If Braxton comes to the Airport in the morning, it's because he wants to go along on my excursion out to the Soviet ships."

"Ooooh, no," O'Donnell said. "That's not an option we'd even consider."

"I learned a long time ago," Jack said, "if you keep the enemy out in front where you can see him, he can't sneak up on your six o'clock. Besides, it's better if he's the one who tells the captain on the *Karpaty* that I'm coming out to nose around."

O'Donnell looked confused. "You lost me, Colonel."

"If he decides to go along," Jack said, "he'll make a call tonight to tell his comrades on the *Karpaty* when to expect us. Then I don't spook them when I show up. And they'll still keep an eye on me while Russ is at work, so I still accomplish my mission."

O'Donnell hesitated, still unconvinced. "I'd still say the safest way out is not telling him you're flying from Napa in the morning."

Jack leaned back and finished his soft drink. Grinning broadly, he said, "Tom, if I believed in taking the safest way out, I wouldn't have flown a hundred-plus missions over North Vietnam. Hell, if safety were all that mattered, I'd have gone to Canada."

"And you really think all we have to do is tell him and he'll come running?"

"I don't know for sure," Jack said. "But I do know one thing. If we don't make the invitation sound tempting enough, Braxton gets away— and I'll take some big risks to keep that from happening."

O'Donnell looked stumped for a good response. Finally he said, "The people monitoring Christine's transmitter could just send the police to the airport to pick you up."

"What's your setup at the airport? Will you know in advance if the police show before daylight?"

"We can have people at the airport who'd know."

"That'll work," Jack said. "If the police are watching, we'll skip the stop at Napa and fly to the *Karpaty* in the chopper."

"You sure as hell don't want to take his transmitter along with you."

Jack paused to think that over. If Braxton stayed fooled until Brown cut the cables, it wouldn't hurt to have that message coming back into the KGB monitoring site. However, if Brown failed and Jack had to improvise, the transmitter and Braxton could be in the way.

"Could we jam it?"

"Maybe," O'Donnell said. "Dennis Ford already knows what frequency Merrill's works on. Braxton's would probably be similar."

"We could turn a jammer on when I start the engine, and they'll assume the aircraft is causing the interference."

O'Donnell nodded and appeared to be looking for other problems. "I'm still not ready to agree to any of this silliness yet, but I could have a couple of sharpshooters in place in case Braxton just comes to kill you."

"If he wants to kill me, he'll be long gone on his planned escape route and send someone else to take care of me. However, assassinating me in public could add credibility to the stories that he has to assume I've at least told you. He can't afford to risk anything that could tip off the plan before ten in the morning."

"So killing you on the plane would be better?"

"Depends on whose point of view you're speaking from," Jack said with a wry smile. "That solves his biggest problem and still gives him a reasonable escape. If I were Braxton, I'd be satisfied to circle the *Karpaty* in a light aircraft until after the detonation. Then I'd parachute aboard—he's an expert, you know—and ride out the nuclear exchange on this lonely little ship that loses itself for a few days in the North Pacific."

"Taking one of his helicopters would be a hell of a lot easier."

"Agreed. But then he risks the possibility that on my own I see something in those last couple of hours that tells me it's about to happen."

O'Donnell nodded. "And if he lets you screw up all his work, he might as well be sitting in his office tomorrow morning at ten."

"The KGB didn't put him here for thirty years to fail. He needs to keep an eye on me, and I'm offering him two hours worth of cheap insurance."

"This still sounds too risky," O'Donnell said.

"The first step is being smart enough with what we say in front of the transmitter. We've got to make him believe the first duck he picked has a ten on the bottom."

"You'll still have to be damned lucky to keep him from killing you."

"Maybe, maybe not," Jack said, flashing a fighter pilot's cocky grin. "But it's worth the risk as long as Brown cuts the cables before I run out of ducks."

O'Donnell added, "Or Braxton's score gets to fifteen!"

They decided to use the same room where Christine had left her purse. The discussion would evolve as if they were having a drink while making general plans for the following day. The room was furnished with a wet bar, and Jack would begin the conversation by asking for a drink. Before starting, they asked Dennis Ford if he could jam Braxton's transmitter the next morning. He was reasonably confident that he had the right equipment and enough time to get a small jammer installed in the aircraft.

Jack and O'Donnell waited in the doorway while Ford set up Christine's transmitter. He placed the box on the coffee table. Then he opened the lid of the box and left the room without saying anything. O'Donnell closed the door behind them as he and Jack moved to the coffee table.

Jack wondered if the insulation in the side of the box would block his voice, so he got over the box before speaking. As he started to ask for the drink, he saw the transmitter, and suddenly he was too excited to speak. The transmitter was the beeper Braxton had given to Christine that night at Chaney. Jack realized that she might not have known she had been carrying a transmitter.

"Uh, Colonel," O'Donnell finally said, "weren't you saying you could use a drink."

"You bet," Jack said. "After a day like today, I may need more than one. How about a scotch and water?"

"You got it," O'Donnell said, going to the bar in one corner of the room.

"I suppose you're right," Jack said, "about delaying the call to General McClintock."

"In a day or two you'll know if the police are going to put your picture on the wall in every post office. We can keep you out of sight for a couple of days. I know a pretty good lawyer over in San Jose who'd help arrange a deal."

"I don't want to just sit around. Tomorrow morning I'd like to fly to the crash site and get another look at the Russian ships."

"I can't spare a pilot tomorrow. Wait until Saturday, and maybe I'll fly you out there myself." O'Donnell handed the drink to Jack. "Besides, I hear those guys have been shooting first and asking questions later. Trying to validate the ravings of a senile old man doesn't justify the risks."

"Dr. Whitney wasn't senile," Jack said with more emotion than he intended.

"But, Colonel, his theory about causing an earthquake requires thousands of tons of high explosives. You know damned well that airliner couldn't carry anything close to that weight. Hell, you couldn't get that much there with a whole squadron of C-130s like I flew back in Nam."

"I know," Jack said. "None of this makes sense. That's why I want another look."

"I suppose they could've had a nuclear bomb on that airplane. Maybe it was supposed to go off when it crashed, so they had to pick up the pieces before we found out."

"I have trouble buying that. The Russians wouldn't use a nuclear bomb. The radiation would tell us they'd caused the earthquake."

"Just guessing."

"I know," Jack said. "If you can get a plane for me, I'll fly out there in the morning by myself. I'd go nuts just sitting around here waiting for some lawyer to cut a deal."

"We've got a couple of light planes at the airport south of Napa. That's about fifty miles from the crash site."

"Any problems with fog there in the mornings?" Jack had asked the question to lead to a discussion of the takeoff time. All the same, he was bothered by the thought of being unable to take off as time ran out.

"We'll check the weather tonight, but you should be able to get airborne by eight. If it's foggy, you just get a bottle of Napa's finest and wait until the sun breaks through."

Nice, Jack thought. O'Donnell had established a takeoff time and minimized its importance. "I think another scotch right now's all I'll need to get my mind off the fog."

O'Donnell walked to the bar and clinked a couple of glasses together. "Do you want to take up anything to Miss Merrill?"

"I don't think so," Jack said. "She's exhausted. With the bump on her head that the mugger gave her, I think sleep's what she really needs."

"It's a shame she isn't feeling better," O'Donnell said. "She seems to be one hell of a woman."

"None better. I really appreciate this, Buzz."

"That's what friends are for. How about another sandwich before bed?" O'Donnell spoke as he moved toward the kitchen door.

"Maybe a small one," Jack said toward the transmitter. "But I'm about ready to hit the sack."

Leaving the room, they were met by the electronics expert. Ford went in, closed the box, and carried away the transmitter. Brown was waiting in the kitchen.

Once Jack was sure the transmitter was safely out of range, he said, "Did you see that? That was the beeper Braxton gave her!"

O'Donnell seemed unimpressed. "So Braxton supplied her with a transmitter that looks like a beeper. You'd already guessed he was involved."

"Really?" Brown looked astonished.

"It really was a working beeper," Jack said, ignoring Brown's question. "I'm not sure she knew the beeper was a transmitter."

Brown seemed more confused.

O'Donnell looked dubious. "Aren't you reaching a little, Colonel? You told me she used phony papers to get on the E-4B, and so far she's not admitting to anything."

"She used phonies instead of legitimate papers that had already been issued. Her papers could have been a setup, too. Do you know anything about an espionage case involving someone named Woodson?"

O'Donnell looked stumped.

Brown asked, "Four or five years ago? Silicon Valley?"

"Right," Jack said.

O'Donnell looked at Brown and asked, "Was that the Lange case?" Brown nodded.

"Strange," O'Donnell said turning to Jack. "The FBI arrested Woodson, and right away the Soviets wanted to trade to get him back. We figured that he'd either gotten hold of some secrets the Russians really wanted or he was a lot higher in the pecking order than we'd thought, so we stalled."

"Within a week," Brown said, "the Soviets offered to trade Jeffrey Lange, an agent we thought had been killed in Afghanistan. Before we agreed to the details of a trade, someone tipped Woodson's location and another of their agents slipped in and got him."

Jack asked, "Rescued him?"

"No. Killed him," O'Donnell said. "The KGB wanted to make sure he didn't give us any of the people who worked for him."

"Or who he worked for," Jack said.

"Probably," O'Donnell said.

Jack asked, "Woodson never admitted to anything either, did he?"

O'Donnell asked, "How do you know so much about the Woodson case? Losing him was an embarrassment, so not much was said on the outside."

"I'm guessing. The only thing I know is Woodson was working for Braxton. That wasn't long before Christine became Braxton's number one assistant."

Brown asked, "You think there's a connection between Woodson and Christine? She was sent to take his place?"

"Something like that," Jack said. "I'd say either Braxton is awfully unlucky picking his key help, or maybe Woodson and Christine were awfully unlucky picking who they worked for."

"You're skipping the third option, Colonel," O'Donnell said, "which is he knew exactly who he was hiring, and they knew exactly what they were being hired to do, and we were the only ones getting fooled."

Perhaps, but Jack did not think so. He remembered how determined Braxton had been to keep Christine—and the beeper—close.

"If she had known her assignment was to stick with me, no matter what," Jack said, "she wouldn't have let me slip away at all. Right after she learned I was being pulled off the investigation at Howell, she got paged. A few minutes later her new assignment was to go with me to Alameda. This morning I got away from her to come see you at Alameda. She wasn't with me when I changed my plans, but she got paged within a couple of minutes after I told her. She didn't call in for the message until after she left for the studio, and I was on my way. This afternoon she wasn't carrying the beeper when I told her I was coming back to the E-4B. Braxton sent her after me as soon as he found out I hadn't hung around to take a tour of his broadcasting complex." Jack chose not to mention that she easily could have kept them together through the night at the hotel in Oakland if she had been determined to—or assigned to.

O'Donnell looked more convinced. "It's possible she's been used throughout."

"If she were working the Soviet side," Jack said, "she should have killed me this evening and claimed I'd kidnapped her. The quickest way to kill our investigation was to kill me before I got to anyone who'd listen to what Whitney told me. I gave her a chance at the gun, and she ignored it."

"That must've taken balls," Brown said admiringly.

"Wasn't loaded," Jack said with a smile, "but she didn't know that." Now he was glad that he had been suspicious enough to put the gun within her reach.

"If Braxton's been a mole for more than thirty years," O'Donnell said, "he's bound to have some elaborate cover."

Brown still looked amazed that Jack and O'Donnell were so matter-of-fact in referring to Braxton as a spy.

"Now I want to talk to her," Jack said. "If we can convince her Braxton was just using her, she may be able to help."

"If you can get her to say anything," O'Donnell said, "you'll be doing better than we have so far. She's pretty pissed about being locked up."

Part of the basement of the large house had been remodeled as a holding area. One guard station was outside the section. Inside the main room was another area for guards. That room was subdivided to include two smaller rooms, each with bars across one wall.

The small room serving as her cell was comfortably furnished. She looked relieved, then betrayed when she saw Jack enter the main room. As the guard let him into the cell, she remained seated on the bed and gave him an icy stare. "Why are you letting them do this to me? I demand to be released."

"First of all, I don't control O'Donnell. He's put you into custody because of serious concerns that affect national security."

"Those concerns have nothing to do with me. I've just been doing my job as a reporter, whether you like the way I've been doing it or not. Locking me up's a travesty!"

Jack watched for her reactions as he spoke: "For the last three days everything that's been said to you has been passed to the Soviets." She glared back but did not answer. "The beeper you carried is a very sophisticated transmitter."

She looked astonished. "It couldn't be. It's the one Alex normally carries. Is this some kind of trick?"

"It's a trick Braxton's played on all of us. He—"

She jumped to her feet. "What you're doing to me is bad enough, but trying to shift the blame to Alex is beneath you, Jack." She turned away and walked to the bars.

"For once in this whole mess, I've got some facts to work with. The beeper transmits everything said anywhere near it. That's why you thought I was so smart when you read the accident report provided by the Soviets. I dictated most of their report that night I was trying to explain the accident to you."

She turned and looked at him. Her expression was softening. "Why would the Russians bother to use your words?"

"Medvalev wanted an explanation for the crash that the Americans would accept without question. He assumed there'd be no problem if he offered an explanation the Air Force's top investigator said he'd buy. Anyway, that's not the point. The point is, Braxton gave you the transmitter. He let you take the risks so you'd get the blame if you were caught."

She hesitated, then said, "I don't believe you. I've known Alex for five years. He's like a father."

"Where did you get the papers for your clearance onto the E-4B?"

"Alex got them the night he and I flew to San Francisco. What difference does—"

"Your papers were forged."

"But—"

"What was the cost of the condo Braxton sold you?"

"None of your business."

"One-point-four million dollars."

"Ridiculous. I hardly paid a tenth that."

"It's a matter of public record, and the record shows you paid the one-point-four million in cash."

She froze, unable to believe what she had heard. "Where would I get that kind of money?"

"I have a hunch Braxton made it look like you got the money from the Soviets."

She looked him in the eye and said, "You're serious about all of this, aren't you?"

"I'm damned serious, and we don't have very long to get this all straightened out."

O'Donnell entered the main room. He was followed by Brown and a man pushing a cart with a television set and a video cassette recorder. As the man started plugging in the equipment, O'Donnell came to the bars and said, "My communications folks recorded a news statement a few minutes ago, and I'm told that both of you will find it very interesting."

Once the television set was placed so that it could be watched through the bars, he started the tape.

The scene on the television opened with a shot of Braxton seated on an expensive couch. Jack wondered who Braxton was interviewing, then realized he was answering the questions.

"Of course," Braxton said, "my main concern has been, and continues to be, for her safety."

"But," the off-screen interviewer said, "I understand you've received information that adds even another twist to this evening's strange happenings." Braxton appeared to be struggling to decide what to say and how to say it. The interviewer prodded, "The money?"

"Yes," Braxton said. He paused as if hesitant to put the story into words. "You're referring to funds unexpectedly withdrawn from company accounts."

When he did not continue, the interviewer prodded, "Accounts Miss Merrill had access to."

"Well, yes," Braxton said, "but I'm certainly not ready to accuse her of any wrongdoing regarding the money. You know she serves my organization in an executive capacity in addition to her role in the news department."

Christine seemed dismayed by the inference.

"How much money's involved, Mr. Braxton?"

"We're still checking."

"Don't you have some estimate?"

"Well," Braxton said reluctantly, "one cash account had a withdrawal of fifty thousand dollars this afternoon."

"I sure didn't take his money," Christine said. "I'm not the only one with access to some of his accounts."

"But Mr. Braxton," the interviewer continued, "I understand considerably more money may be involved."

"We're still checking," Braxton said more resolutely. "It's premature to—"

"My sources say nearly two million dollars in negotiable securities are missing. Could you confirm that, sir?"

"Christine's been like a daughter to me. I'm not willing to say how much is involved until I can talk to her and make sure she's safe."

"Where I grew up," O'Donnell said, "we called that 'damning with faint praise.' "

Christine shook her head in disbelief.

"And you don't know where she is, Mr. Braxton?"

"No, I haven't talked to her since she went to Dr. Whitney's home this afternoon."

"Are you assuming that she may have taken this money under duress? I'm referring, of course, to the report that Christine Merrill was kidnapped following the three murders in the East Bay."

"I'm still not willing to assume she took the money at all," Braxton said. "There's more involved than any of us understand right now."

"Would you comment then on reports that the government is investigating the papers Miss Merrill used to gain access to the President's aircraft?"

"I understand she used forgeries."

Christine said loudly, "Ask him who gave them to me!"

Jack responded, "That's not the way this interview's been scripted."

"But the interviewer doesn't work for him."

"Maybe not on any organizational charts this side of the KGB offices in Moscow."

She looked incredulous. "Couldn't be. I've known the interviewer for ages."

"As long as you've known Mr. Braxton?"

She frowned.

While they were talking, the interviewer had asked Braxton what possible motive could have been behind the use of false papers.

The tycoon slumped back onto the couch and seemed to be struggling with how to continue. "That's what the government wants to know. Regretfully, one source close to the investigation says Miss Merrill, whom I have trusted and worked with so closely for several years, may have been an agent for Soviet intelligence since before she came to work for me."

The interviewer continued, "That's an incredible revelation, Mr. Braxton. What would she have been doing for you that could possibly have been of interest to Soviet intelligence?"

"I'm certainly not a target of value, although I learned on more than one occasion that the KGB wanted to silence me." Braxton sighed. "I'm told there are indications she was the contact on this end for a KGB plot that assassinated the Soviet minister of defense, Andrei Valinen, along with others on the Soviet airliner."

Christine just shook her head and watched with a look of betrayal. Jack noticed she was trembling as she stood holding onto the bars. He had vowed to keep his distance emotionally, but he came over and put his arm around her. She leaned her head against his shoulder and took hold of his hand.

The interviewer asked, "The KGB caused the plane crash?"

"Obviously, that's not what Premier Medvalev believes at the moment. However, I'm sure that the KGB had a hand in interpreting the wreckage and helping Medvalev conclude that the crash was an accident."

"If that were her role, Mr. Braxton, then what connection do you see with her kidnapping, the missing money, and the rest of the events this afternoon?"

"One very trusted source surmised that her cell of agents included the scientist who died this evening in the house fire. Perhaps his murder was necessary to keep him from revealing anything about the KGB plot."

Christine said, "I don't believe this!"

Jack took her by the shoulders and said, "He's been manipulating news for decades. This is just a curtain call, and he wouldn't have bothered with it except that he's lost track of you. He's worried that you're the person who could restore my credibility."

The interviewer continued, "If that were true—and that's a big *if* at this point—where does the colonel with the rental car fit in? Rumors are that he did the killings. Is he an accomplice or perhaps an innocent victim of a KGB plot?"

"Frankly," Braxton said thoughtfully, "I'm not sure. I've met the colonel and—"

"Could you give us his name?"

Braxton hesitated, then said, "I'd rather leave that to the police and the Air Force. I can say that he seemed dedicated and intelligent, and he was a highly decorated war hero."

"However, witnesses have linked him to the two shootings after Whitney's murder."

"That's what I've heard, but I would have to see the evidence before I'd believe that."

Braxton paused, and added thoughtfully, "I understand he has served in very sensitive duty as a Soviet expert at the Pentagon during the last year. He was in a position to follow closely military actions that could have been threatening to the Soviet Union."

The interviewer paused as if considering the ramifications. "So if there were a KGB plot, and if the colonel were involved in the killings, are you suggesting, then, that the colonel could be a spy for the Soviet Union?"

"I didn't say that at all," Braxton said firmly. "I'm not convinced yet that he killed anyone. He was under a lot of pressure and had just experienced some reversals in his career. I'm just saying that the actions this afternoon involving the colonel and Miss Merrill have added confusion to what already is a confusing situation. I'm eager to learn the results of the government's investigation of this whole matter. And I think that's all I should say until there's been an opportunity for more facts to surface over the next day or two."

O'Donnell said, "Colonel, I think you just got a little of that damning with faint praise, too."

The picture switched to a narrator announcing the end of that special news report. O'Donnell stopped the tape and said to Jack, "You and I need to talk some more."

Jack nodded. "Give me a few minutes."

As the equipment was taken away, Christine stood silently staring beyond the bars. Jack waited. Finally she said, "I don't know what to say. Why would he—I feel so betrayed."

"Braxton's betrayed everyone," he said as he put his arms around her and held her close, "but he's betrayed you more than anyone else."

"The things he said about you were terrible."

"That's unimportant. What's important is that we get ahead of him and stop what he's doing. Anything you can tell O'Donnell's people may help."

"What can I offer? Nothing ever made me imagine he could be a Soviet spy."

He was certain now she was innocent, but could not afford to reveal his plans or to tell her about the *Iskra* timetable. "I need to see what I can do to try to clear us both."

He started to step away but she kept her arms around him and kissed him. "I'm sorry I thought badly of you. Really, I am."

He felt the same way about her, but could not say the words. He kissed her and then pulled away.

Chapter 26

Thursday Night, 10:15 p.m.
Iskra plus 8:15

O'DONNELL AND BROWN MET JACK IN THE OUTER HALLWAY. "THAT guy's fantastic," O'Donnell said. "In two minutes he's cast doubt over anything either of you might say or anything Whitney had said."

"When you spend thirty years building a reputation as Mr. Super Patriot, you should be able to get away with one big lie. Anyway, I believe there are at least two areas where Christine may be able to help. Once you get names of the companies linked to the four Soviet merchant ships, she may be able to link the companies to Braxton. Also, try to find out how the Vice-President got invited to Wrightwood for the next couple of days."

O'Donnell looked uncertain. "What's the connection?"

"Someone's put the Vice-President right on the San Andreas. If she can link Braxton to the invitation, that'll strengthen our argument for what's going to happen at *Iskra* plus twenty."

"I'll go add those questions to the list," O'Donnell said.

"I believe she's on our side," Jack said.

"If she gives us enough right answers, I might be convinced."

"Now," Jack said, "we need to get a game plan together for tomorrow's mission."

A few minutes later in a briefing room, Jack saw several maps on a table. He selected a topographic map that showed the depth of the ocean in the area west of Point Reyes and the underwater canyon Dr. Whitney had described. Brown pulled a small notebook from his pocket and crosschecked notes he had written earlier. "The latest position report on the *Karpaty* indicates she's a mile southwest of the canyon."

"Makes sense," Jack said. "If I were on the *Karpaty*, I wouldn't want to be right on top of the explosives. You should be able to navigate to the canyon, then find the cables extending southwest toward the *Karpaty*." When O'Donnell joined them, Jack said, "We need to agree how to handle communications tomorrow. I expect the Soviets will try to monitor anything they can."

"If you don't forget that fool notion about taking Braxton along," O'Donnell said with a frown, "you'll have trouble communicating anyway, but let me tell you what you'll have, and you can decide how to use it."

He explained that his communications center would monitor Jack's aircraft and any transmissions made from the *Karpaty*. The minisub was equipped for normal communications through cables to another ship on the surface. However, since secrecy prevented using another ship, Brown could communicate only by UHF radio and only when the minisub was on the surface. Moreover, the UHF radio used normal, unscrambled signals, so the crew on the *Karpaty* might monitor and intercept any conversations between Jack and Brown on a UHF frequency.

Jack's aircraft was better equipped. Along with a UHF radio, the aircraft had a secure VHF radio. That radio included a small microprocessor that automatically split the transmission several times a second, moving the signal across the frequency band. Frequency hopping made the signal difficult to jam or intercept. When Jack transmitted on the secure VHF, his words could be understood only by someone with a similar radio with the appropriate codes. Thus, he would be able to talk in secret with the communications center and with other aircraft, such as the AWACS.

O'Donnell pointed out that the aircraft had been modified with a small panel that allowed the exchange of silent communications. Located near the pilot's left knee, the panel had a red and a yellow light that could be turned on and off by a signal from O'Donnell's communications center. There was also a switch on the panel. Jack could use the switch to send a signal that would turn on a light in the communications center.

These lights permitted the exchange of messages agreed to before takeoff. Even if the Soviets detected that signals had been sent between the communications center and the aircraft, nothing in the signal indicated what the message meant.

As Jack listened, he considered how best to use the radios and the signal lights. If Braxton were aboard—and Jack hoped Braxton would be—the signal lights could be helpful. The communications equipment on the submarine was the main limitation. After Brown submerged beyond the breakwater, he was going to be incommunicado until he surfaced. Jack hoped that was not a significant problem. Until the Soviets discovered the minisub, Brown would have to maintain radio silence anyway. Once he surfaced, he would have accomplished his mission—or have failed.

Gesturing toward Brown, Jack said, "We'll all have to maintain radio silence until you get the cables cut."

"Or," Brown said, "until the Russians discover I'm there."

"When the *Karpaty* detects your minisub," Jack said, "I should see activity on deck. I can turn on the light in the comm center when I see the Soviets responding to you."

"So the comm center will have some warning, but I won't," Brown said with a frown.

"You're on your own," O'Donnell said, "until you're back on top."

Jack said, "The main thing I'll want to know is if the captain on the *Karpaty* asks for permission to detonate early."

"If he asks," O'Donnell said, "we should hear the *Karpaty* transmit on HF radio. Unless the Soviets slip new codes in on us at the last minute, we should have the exact text within seconds of the transmission."

Jack considered how best to get that information while operating under radio silence. "So, the comm center can turn on the yellow light in my cockpit when the *Karpaty* makes the request."

"And the red," Brown said, "if the captain gets permission to detonate early."

"Intercepting the answer coming back to the *Karpaty* will be trickier," O'Donnell said. "You may know he's gotten permission before we do."

For an instant a look of "how would we know" crossed Brown's face before he recognized the obvious answer. He responded sarcastically, "Great!"

"Then," Jack said, "we should make a few educated guesses about how much time's left after I see the yellow light come on."

O'Donnell and Brown nodded their agreement.

"Let's figure a worst-case scenario," Jack said. "What's the minimum amount of time we'll have after you've been discovered? Assume the *Karpaty* asks for permission, my yellow light's turned on, and our clock starts. *Minsk* receives the message and requires maybe two minutes to decode. Then they carry the message from their comm center to the bridge, and the admiral takes a look."

"Give them at least four more minutes to get it to him and talk it over," Brown said.

Jack continued, "The admiral says, 'The American's are onto us. Transmit coded message number one to the comrades in Moscow.' "

O'Donnell nodded his agreement. "Okay, so in two more minutes, the next message is on the way from the *Minsk* to Moscow. That's eight minutes after you see the yellow light."

"In Moscow," Jack said, "I'd give them three more minutes to get the decoded message in front of Valinen."

"That's pretty damned fast," O'Donnell said.

"Face it, at that moment the number one thing Valinen has going is waiting for messages from the admiral on the *Minsk*. In three more minutes Valinen's answer should be on the way back to the *Minsk*."

"That puts the clock at fourteen minutes," Brown said.

"By the time that message gets to the *Minsk*," Jack said, "the admiral's going to be standing behind the radio operator, and you can bet a *'Da'* and a *'Nyet'* are coded and ready for transmission."

O'Donnell punched Brown lightly on the shoulder and said, "Once that yellow light's been glowing for fifteen minutes, Russ, you might as well bend over and kiss your ass *da svedanya!*"

Brown responded with a weak smile, then said, "I'm glad those red and yellow lights are in the airplane instead of the minisub."

"No sweat," Jack said. "By then you'll have the cables cut, and the only red lights that'll matter are on the Christmas decorations. Once we have to come up on the radios, we'll need call signs and code words, especially on UHF where we can be monitored."

"We can make up our own," O'Donnell said, "as long as our words don't give away the mission."

Jack asked, "How about state of birth for the call sign? That'd make me 'Texan.' Any conflicts?"

"Alabama," Brown said.

O'Donnell frowned, hesitated momentarily, then said, "Rhode Island."

Brown smiled and said, "Mister Macho?"

"I didn't know anyone was from there," Jack said. "Would you feel better if we go phonetic on that and let you be 'Romeo India'?"

O'Donnell nodded.

"Since you're going to be broadcasting in the clear," Jack said to Brown, "we need words to tell us what you've found and whether or not you accomplished the mission."

"We don't want to talk about earthquakes," Brown said. "How about the name of a volcano if I find explosives?"

"Good," O'Donnell said. "St. Helens? That's easy enough to remember, and you can name a regular mountain if there's no threat."

Thinking of the man of peace he had met earlier in the evening, Jack said, "I'd like to use Mount Whitney as the code word for peaceful."

"Okay," O'Donnell said, "St. Helens and Whitney. Let's use the phonetic alphabet for whether or not you get the cables cut. 'Mike Alpha' for mission accomplished; 'Foxtrot' for failure."

"Agreed," Brown said.

"The comm center will provide a card that lists the frequencies we'll use, and we'll throw in the ones the *Karpaty*'s been using."

"Good," Jack said. "The Air Force should have an AWACS on orbit, too. You should tell them the freqs we'll be monitoring, but make damned sure that anyone on the frequency agrees to maintain radio silence until we start talking. If Braxton's along, I don't want anyone asking me how the minisub's doing."

They discussed the *Karpaty*, and Jack studied pictures of the ship. Since its purpose was submarine rescue and recovery, the *Karpaty* was lightly armed. Above the bridge, the ship carried a pair of twenty-five-millimeter antiaircraft guns that could be dangerous whenever the airplane or the minisub was in front of the ship.

It was after eleven o'clock by the time they finished making plans for the following morning. When Jack got to his room, he found most of the special items he had asked for. A note said the parachute would be at the airplane. He tried on everything to make sure it all fit together. He found that the pistol was not noticeable when worn above his right ankle. He spent the next half hour studying the checklists and flight manuals for the airplane.

O'Donnell was providing a single-engine, high-wing aircraft with side-by-side seating for the pilot and copilot. Jack was pleased with the selection. With the wing above the cockpit, he would have good views of the ocean below. He would also be able to keep an eye on his passenger—if Braxton chose to come along.

It was nearly midnight when Jack turned off the light and stretched out on the bed. Although he was exhausted, he had difficulty shutting down the thoughts that cycled through his mind. The distant sound of waves crashing onto the beach kept regenerating images of the ocean and of the ship with cables reaching beneath the surface. He pictured Brown's minisub maneuvering among cables in the narrow canyon on the ocean floor.

Whenever he cleared his mind of thoughts of the morning's mission, a less desirable image took their place: dimly lit hands struggling. Beyond the hands was the terrified expression of the KGB agent looking into the barrel of an inverted pistol inches in front of his face. Though the street had been dark, the details were etched into Jack's memory as if the flash of the pistol had been a strobe light capturing the instant before death.

As the minutes passed, he shifted from one position to another, but sleep continued to elude him. He looked at the clock on the nightstand near the bed. Twelve-forty—*nine hours and twenty minutes left until* Iskra *plus twenty*. He rolled over again and wondered how Christine was doing. Memories of the frightened look on her face as she sat behind the bars haunted him as he lay there trying to will himself to sleep.

"Colonel!" A loud knock accompanied O'Donnell's voice. Jack rolled over to respond, assuming that O'Donnell had forgotten to ask something. The agent pushed open the door to the bedroom and said, "It's time."

Jack thought he had misunderstood. The digital clock showed 5:32, but he did not feel like he had slept. Somehow five hours had passed, and he still felt exhausted. O'Donnell's next words, however, were the spark that ignited him for the new day.

"The destroyers are gone, and Brown's on his way."

Jack sat on the edge of the bed and asked, "What time?"

"The Soviets started pulling out just after three. We yanked Brown out of bed, and the minisub was in the water by three-thirty."

Jack added the five hours necessary for the minisub to get near the *Karpaty*. Even with perfect underwater navigation, Brown would not reach the *Karpaty* until eight-thirty, an hour and a half before *Iskra* plus twenty. Locating the cables would take additional time.

He said, "That's cutting it awfully close."

"I didn't make the schedule, Colonel. I'm just the guy who's been watching the clock." He appeared to have gotten little, if any, sleep.

"You watch the clock all night long?"

"Almost," O'Donnell said, leaning against the door frame. "Your lady friend's given us some interesting info. She helped answer your question about the Soviet merchant ships."

"You traced them to Braxton?"

He nodded. "The four ships had three different destinations. Between our computers and what Christine knew about some of Braxton's holdings, we linked him to all three. She described his airplanes, helicopters, and cars, so we should be able to see him coming if he visits the airport this morning. She also made the connection to the Vice-President's invitation to Wrightwood."

He explained that Braxton and the host, a well-known industrialist from California, had worked on several political fund-raisers and on three advisory boards for the state governor. Christine had heard Braxton suggest to the industrialist that a holiday invitation to the Vice-President was the politic thing to do.

He continued, "I think she knew more about Braxton's business than he realized."

"I want Christine airborne before nine."

O'Donnell looked as if that were more of a precaution than he had planned, especially if she were still under suspicion.

Jack continued, "I'll have enough on my mind. I don't want to worry about her in that basement if a tsunami sweeps through here."

"Okay," O'Donnell said, "but you and Russ make sure the tide stays out." He stepped into the hallway and said, "The chopper'll be ready to depart for the airfield at six forty-five."

Jack dressed quickly, then went to the communications center to call General McClintock. His boss was waiting for the call.

Jack asked, "Did you have any luck with the chief, sir?"

"Initially General Raleigh thought I was as crazy as you were. But the chief understands how to connect the indicators, and you gave us one hell of a list."

"I'm seeing a few more," Jack said, "especially where Mr. Braxton's concerned, but I still don't have anything you can see and touch."

"We're picking up a few things," McClintock said. "Just after midnight, the Strategic Air Command sent a recce bird out of Beale to take pictures. By five-fifteen this morning, we had some good oblique shots of the *Tibor Szamueli* and the *Julius Fucik*. Both ships are headed home empty. Whatever they were carrying in the Navy photos is gone."

"Do the Soviets know we were snooping around, sir?"

"Negative, Jack. The bird was offset well to the side and using infra-red."

"Were you able to get a pre-emptive strike authorized?"

"We're still trying," McClintock said. "We're so worried about leaks that this information is being shared with very few people. The President has authorized a backup plan, which I hope will support whatever you're planning."

Jack outlined his plan and the importance of the word St. Helens. They agreed that the AWACS would monitor the minisub's frequency while maintaining radio silence.

"I'd assumed you were going out to take a look for yourself," McClintock said, "so I've ordered Lieutenant Colonel Buchanan to take a couple of his Jolly Greens out of Chaney and do a little low-level training off Point Reyes."

"If I stir up any trouble, sir," Jack said, "I'll need more than a couple of Jolly Greens."

"You'll have it," McClintock said. "The Jolly Greens will be escorted by a flight of Apaches. Those four gunships will be carrying enough firepower to take on a battalion of Soviet tanks."

"That'd be great," Jack said with a hint of sarcasm, "if I expected to find a battalion of tanks. I still think we'd be better off with a couple of Harpoons fired from beyond visual range."

"The President's worried that you may not be right. This way, if the Soviets do any shooting, he'll say the Apaches attacked in self-defense. Then if there aren't any explosives on the ocean floor, we haven't risked World War III by hitting the *Karpaty* without provocation. The President just feels we don't have enough evidence for what obviously would be a premeditated attack with Harpoons—especially after we shot the missile at Soviet National One."

"But what if the captain on the *Karpaty* sees the Apaches coming and blows the explosives before the helicopters hit him. That's a hell of a price to pay for being overcautious."

"The President feels he can still face down the Russians before they launch the nuclear strikes. If we hit the *Karpaty* without provocation, the President's afraid that he and Medvalev together may not be able to keep us out of a shooting war that would escalate quickly to World War III."

Jack understood, but he was not satisfied with the conservative plan chosen by the President. "I'd suggest, sir, that someone needs to tell the Apache pilots that if I call for them, they'd better come in low and fast."

"Roger that," McClintock said. "By the way, don't let the news reports or the morning papers scare you."

"I haven't heard or seen any this morning, sir."

"You're providing one hell of a cover story, Jack. The papers tell how I've been called on the carpet at the Western White House to explain to the President why we can't get you under military control."

"But that's not what happened?"

"Negative. The chief's still back at the Pentagon. He decided I personally should discuss with the President our concerns about *Iskra*. There'll be a statement in an hour and a half announcing that the President's flying over to the E-4B. Supposedly he wants an update on your status, and he's going to do a little 'Commander-in-Chief visit' to acknowledge the crew's dedication in being away from their families during the holiday season."

"And you'll have the President airborne before ten."

"We'll be off at nine-thirty, unless you stir things up earlier. Once we're airborne, the President plans a call to let Medvalev know that an earthquake at ten will not be interpreted as an act of nature."

"That may be too late for Medvalev to back down."

"That's what I tried to tell the President."

"Well, boss," Jack said, "I appreciate your loyalty."

"You just 'fly safe' out there this morning, Jack."

After leaving the communications center, Jack went to Christine's cell. When he entered the guard's area, she was stretched across her bed. As he asked if she was sleeping, she stirred and looked toward him. Immediately she came to the bars. He placed his pistol on the guard's table.

As the guard let him into the cell, she asked, "Where are you going?"

He exaggerated a look of concern and said, "I've been so busy this week, I haven't had time to finish my Christmas shopping."

She looked at his pistol on the table and then looked him over. Parts of his wetsuit showed at his wrists and neck. "You're going out there, aren't you?"

He walked over and put his hands on her waist. "There's just no fooling you reporters, is there?"

She did not move but looked straight into his eyes. "You're going out there to get killed."

He pulled her close and asked, "Is that a question or an answer?"

"It's true, isn't it." She tried to pull from his grasp, but he would not let her.

He held her close for a few moments until she stopped struggling. He realized it was much easier to fly combat when the wife was half-a-world away than to say goodbye to someone he cared for while on his way to the airplane. Finally he said, "I like your perfume."

She let out a frustrated yell and pushed until he released her. Stepping back, she said, "Can't you be serious?"

Jack liked the fiery look in her eyes but decided this was not the time to mention how exciting he found her to be. Instead, he said, "What do you want me to say? 'Yes, I'm going out there to get killed.' I'm sorry lady, but that's not the way fighter pilots psych themselves up."

She hesitated, then rushed over and hugged him. "I'm so frightened."

For the next few minutes, they sat holding hands and quietly talking of things important and unimportant. Seeing that it was time to go to the helicopter, he fished the piece of shrapnel from his pocket.

"The fair way to do this," he said, "is to flip for it. Heads, we run away to Tahiti. Tails, I go ahead and do what I need to do, then tell you about it later."

He flipped the shrapnel into the air, caught it, and brought it onto his other hand. Then he raised the covering hand slowly, peeked beneath, and shook his head.

"Maybe you could go two-out-of-three," she said, trying to force a smile as her eyes filled with tears.

O'Donnell entered the guard's area and called out, "Your ride's ready, Colonel."

"Just don't have time," Jack said to her. He took her hand and opened it, palm up. Then he placed the piece of shrapnel into her hand and said, "Keep this for me while I'm gone."

She threw her arms around his neck and held him in a lingering embrace.

He stood, and she stood with him, not releasing her grip. He kissed her softly on the forehead as he pulled her fingers apart from behind his neck. Then he stepped back and said quietly, "I have to go."

He left the cell and picked up his pistol from the guard's desk. Before following O'Donnell out the door, he turned back and winked at her.

"Be careful," she said seriously. "Alex always gets what he wants."

"Not this time."

Chapter 27

EN ROUTE TO THE AIRPORT AT NAPA, THE HELICOPTER PILOT CON-firmed that there was no unusual police activity. Indeed, it was still early for activity of any kind on the airfield. The fading darkness was giving way stubbornly to daylight that was muted by low clouds. However, a dark Mercedes matching one on the list of Braxton's vehicles had just parked in the lot near the edge of the flight line.

Jack asked the pilot, "Is he parked close enough to see the plane I'll be flying?"

"He should be," the pilot said, "but I can make sure he notices our arrival."

Reaching the airport, the pilot planned his approach so that the helicopter flew over the parking lot before dipping down to a taxiway near the airplane. During the descent the pilot pointed out two of O'Donnell's marksmen hidden on the tops of two hangars.

As Jack stepped from the helicopter, he was convinced that the occupant of the Mercedes knew that the colonel had reached the airport. As soon as he was clear, the helicopter took off.

Two of O'Donnell's men, dressed in coveralls, were at the airplane. Jack stood in the open talking to them for a couple of minutes, making sure he could be identified from the parking lot. He also wanted to make sure that the men did nothing to scare Braxton away. Jack told them to go to a nearby hangar until he was ready. When he went to the airplane for the preflight checks, he got a glimpse of Braxton lifting a canvas bag from the open trunk of the Mercedes.

Checking the condition of the aircraft, Jack never looked directly toward the parking lot, but with peripheral vision, he followed Braxton's progress to within a few feet. Then Jack devoted his full attention to the inside of the engine compartment so he could seem surprised.

"How about an interview, Colonel?"

Jack jumped enough that he banged his head slightly on the up-

348

raised cover of the engine compartment. With a surprised look he asked, "What are you doing here?"

"Just looking for a story, Colonel," Braxton said with a friendly smile. "Now that the Russians are going home, you're the biggest story of the day. I thought—"

"How'd you know I was here?" Jack looked around as if trying to see whether Braxton had brought the police.

"I'm alone," Braxton said. "As far as knowing you were here, in thirty years I've developed a few sources. Sometimes information requires a little cash, but I usually find out what I need to know."

Jack leaned against the airplane. "Why didn't you bring the police? I thought everyone believed I'd kidnapped Christine."

"I know you didn't kidnap her," Braxton said. "She called last night to let me know she was all right."

Jack was stunned for an instant before deciding that Braxton was lying. The claim about the telephone call suggested that the spy was unaware Christine had been confined soon after reaching the safe house. Or, Jack thought, maybe Braxton knew she would have called if she could, so he might have mentioned the call just to draw a reaction.

Jack felt at a disadvantage when it came to lying. Braxton was so smooth—but then he had nearly forty years experience in deception, hadn't he?

Braxton continued, "As I started to say, I thought you could use a sympathetic ear that could also get your side of the story out in public."

Jack turned to close the cowling. "I'm not sure my side matters anymore. I'd thought I could prove the Russians were up to something out at the crash site. Now that their naval exercise is over and their ships are all going home, there may not be anything left to prove."

"I'd still like to hear your side."

"Right now," Jack said, "I don't have time to talk. I'm on my way to see what, if anything, the Russians still have at the crash site. If I hang around too long, someone may recognize me and call the police."

"There's no more natural place for one pilot to talk to another than in an airplane." Jack looked uncertain, so the newsman continued, "What have you got to lose, Colonel? I'm sure you didn't murder those men on the street. If you fill me in on the details, I can help convince a lot of other people."

"I don't know," Jack said. He looked at the canvas bag Braxton had carried from the car.

Braxton knelt and unzipped the bag. "I assumed you weren't coming to an airport unless you were going to fly, so I brought my own chute. I hope you don't mind, but I'm superstitious about flying in light airplanes without wearing one."

"I understand fliers' superstitions," Jack said. "I know a few pilots who've bailed out a time or two. Some never fly without wearing boots whether they're strapped into a Mach-2 fighter or drinking cocktails in the back of a commercial bird."

"Now I understand," Braxton said.

"You understand what?"

"I wondered about the Wellington boots at the airport," Braxton said. Then with a broad grin he added, "The boots didn't do justice to the three-piece suit you were wearing."

Jack was impressed that Braxton had noticed the boots he had worn when tackling the egg-thrower. Since Braxton had never thanked him for his intervention, he had assumed Braxton was too distracted to see the scuffle. Now he wondered why Braxton had not raised the subject previously.

Looking at the expensive parachute and harness that Braxton pulled from the bag, Jack said, "If I had a rig like that, I'd carry my own, too."

"Just a little something I bought for skydiving, but it doesn't get much use anymore."

"If you don't mind flying with someone who's a little rusty," Jack said, "I wouldn't mind having the company. Maybe when we return, you might even talk me into giving myself up, if you'd go along."

Braxton looked pleased. "I've got a dozen good lawyers. I'll call a couple as soon as we get back."

After completing the preflight, Jack signaled the ground crew that he was ready to start. He got in the pilot's seat on the left, and Braxton sat in the seat next to the door. Dennis Ford came out of the hangar and helped with the wheel chocks and fire extinguisher. His presence indicated that the jammer was covering the proper frequency for the transmitter Braxton was using.

Low clouds forced Jack to pick his way carefully through the hills between Napa and the coast. Over the ocean the clouds were less than two thousand feet above the water, but he was pleased that there was no fog. Approaching the ocean, he saw the Coast Guard cutters strung out in a loose picket line. In the distance, the *Karpaty* was nearer the horizon.

During the flight to the coast, Braxton had done little interviewing. Instead he talked about the enjoyment of flying in the San Francisco area. He spoke of the serenity of flying along the coast at times when he needed to relax. As they left Point Reyes behind, he set a different frequency into the VHF radio.

"When we're VFR and 'feet wet' along the coast," Braxton said, "this is the frequency we monitor. We may not be the only sightseers out this morning trying to get one last look at the Russians."

His explanation sounded plausible. Areas that were popular for pilots filing visual flight rules, or VFR, flight plans often had common frequencies. Monitoring those frequencies was a precaution to help reduce mid-air collisions, since the VFR airplanes were not being actively controlled by the FAA. So Jack might have accepted the explanation if the new frequency had not been on his list of those actively used by the *Karpaty*.

"Good idea," Jack said. He motioned toward the ship just ahead of them and added, "I'm monitoring 'Guard' on the UHF too. I imagine that cutter'll call us momentarily."

The crew on the cutter would see Jack's aircraft entering the restricted airspace around the crash site. Someone on the ship would broadcast a warning on the emergency frequency, which all aircraft were supposed to 'guard' during flight. Jack was planning to use that radio call to mask the slight change in background noise that would occur when he shut down the VHF radio.

Continuing the conversation, Jack scanned the circuit-breaker panels until he located the breaker that controlled the power to the VHF. He turned the aircraft so that the closest Coast Guard cutter would be on Braxton's side when the aircraft passed overhead.

As they flew above the ship, Jack rolled the aircraft slightly to the right to give Braxton a better view. Simultaneously, Jack placed his hand on his left knee near the circuit breaker. Both men were looking toward the ship when the warning message from the cutter sounded loudly in their headsets.

Jack pulled the circuit breaker while the message on UHF Guard dominated the sounds coming into the earphones. After pulling the breaker, he turned off the UHF Guard frequency. That also reduced the background noise in the headsets, making the loss of the VHF radio even less noticeable.

"He's going to keep squawking at us the whole time we're in the restricted area," he said, "so there's no sense keeping Guard on."

Now, he thought, everything was set. The next move was Braxton's.

Beyond the cutters, Jack descended to one thousand feet on a course that would allow him to set up a two-mile orbit around the *Karpaty*. He looked beyond the nose of the aircraft, but he also used his peripheral vision to watch Braxton. Though the newsman talked normally about the ship ahead, Jack saw him reach into the canvas bag, which was between Braxton's seat and the door. Jack also saw something ahead that concerned him: many more cables were hanging over the side of the *Karpaty* than he had expected. Brown was going to have to do a lot more cutting than planned.

Jack suddenly had no time to worry about Brown's problems.

"Keep your hands where I can see them, Colonel!" The voice was cold, betraying only a quaver of excitement.

Jack turned and tried to act surprised. The rush of adrenaline that came from looking into the barrel of a pistol helped. The gun was similar to the one he had taken from the attacker near Dr. Whitney's house. He looked from the gun to Braxton. All the friendliness had disappeared from the newsman's eyes.

Jack had to react, so he asked, "What? Why?"

Braxton ignored the questions. Instead, keeping the pistol trained on Jack's head, he turned off the UHF radio. He then rotated the wafer switch on his intercom control panel so he could transmit on the VHF radio. As he pressed the microphone switch and spoke in Russian, he watched Jack as if seeking the audience's stunned reaction to the climactic revelation of an on-stage mystery.

Jack tried to look stunned as he heard Braxton repeating his code name to the radioman on the *Karpaty*. Jack asked, "What are you doing?"

Ignoring the questioning, Braxton awaited an acknowledgment to his message. After a few seconds he repeated his earlier broadcast. He showed no real concern about the slowness of the response from the *Karpaty* until his third and fourth broadcasts also were ignored.

Seeing the first hint of uncertainty in Braxton's eyes, Jack asked, "What are you trying to do?"

Braxton cycled the VHF radio off and on a couple of times. "What's wrong with this thing?"

Jack shrugged. "It's not my plane. The guy at the hangar said they'd been having trouble with the VHF, but he thought it would work."

"Damn!" With the pistol still trained on Jack, Braxton leaned against the door. His eyes watched every move the colonel made, but Jack sensed that Braxton's entire mental energy was processing options, searching for a way to bridge the gap caused by the lack of a VHF radio.

For the moment, Jack thought, the spy was in check, but the pistol made the standoff far from checkmate. As long as the situation lights by his left knee did not flash to bright yellow or red, however, Jack could wait. Braxton had to make the next move, and he needed to concentrate. Jack was determined to interfere with that concentration as much as possible.

Jack said, "I don't understand why. You, of all people."

Braxton ignored the comment as he raised against his seat belt to get another quick glance at the *Karpaty*. He seemed to be looking for a way to approach the ship. Then he responded in a tone that was both unemotional and tutorial, "Surely, Colonel, you don't expect all spies to come in twirling their handlebar mustaches." He shook his head as if expecting his adversary to be more savvy. "When the bear comes to live with the sheep, he does not dress in the coat of a wolf."

Jack was impressed by how easily Braxton had slipped into a different persona. The confidence and hint of brilliance were still there, but the charisma displayed when getting acquainted en route to Chaney was shut down, just as surely as the open circuit breaker had shut down the VHF radio.

"Buzz them," Braxton said. "I want to get their attention."

"You may not know it, but your comrades have a pair of twenty-five-millimeter guns above the bridge." Jack moved his hands away from the control wheel. "You want to buzz them, buzz them yourself."

"I don't have time for your obstinacy, Colonel," Braxton said as he pulled the hammer back on his pistol. "Fly as I tell you."

Jack took hold of the controls. "I'll fly as you say until the gunners say different."

"Descend to five hundred feet."

Pulling his seat belt tighter, Jack said, "The maneuvering may get a little violent, so how about letting down that hammer? You shoot me, and you may end up in the water before you can do anything about it."

"Approach her starboard side at about her two o'clock," Braxton said as he eased the hammer from the cocked position.

Jack maneuvered the airplane to get ahead and to the right of the *Karpaty*, hoping Braxton's directions complied with a standard procedure the Russians used for identifying friendly aircraft with inoperative radios. The course Braxton chose would give the captain on the bridge a good view of the approaching aircraft. Jack's main concern was that the gunner above the bridge had an even better view.

As Jack rolled the aircraft and lowered the nose toward the ship, Braxton said, "Aim just ahead of her. I want to fly across her bow at five hundred feet and give her captain a good look at us."

"Unless you know something I don't know," Jack said, "we haven't got a prayer."

"Waggle the wings as we get in closer."

Jack started rolling the control wheel back and forth immediately.

There was no way, he thought, that a nervous captain on the most important mission of his life was going to let an unidentified aircraft swoop down on his ship. If he were the Soviet captain, he would still want some identification even if Braxton had called ahead.

Jack believed that the gunner would fire sooner if the aircraft looked more like a threat, so he pointed the aircraft toward the bridge. Since he expected to be fired at, he wanted to entice the gunner to fire as quickly as possible. The increased range would reduce the gunner's chances of hitting the small aircraft. The greater range would also let Jack start evasive maneuvers farther away from the ship.

"More to the right," Braxton said. "I want to fly across their bow, not over it!"

Jack banked right, but simultaneously eased forward on the opposite rudder. He rolled out with nose pointed ahead of the ship but the rudder kept the aircraft skidding toward the bridge of the *Karpaty*. Rocking the wings back and forth made the skid less noticeable to Braxton, but would do little to confuse the captain who could watch the aircraft track steadily toward the bridge. As the airplane got closer, the trick would become more obvious to Braxton, but Jack expected the gunner to react first.

He concentrated on the gun position above the bridge. His aircraft was less than a mile out, well within the effective range of the guns. Since he was giving the gunner a head-on shot at a 120-mile-per-hour target, he knew there were few things a gunner could screw up. There were no lead angles for the gunner to mentally compute; he just had to keep the aircraft within the rings on the sight and keep pressing the trigger. If the gunner lacked experience, he probably would underestimate how much the shells would fall in the two to three seconds required to reach the aircraft.

Jack realized he had a death grip on the control wheel. He relaxed slightly, but remained poised to act. In a moment, sparkles above the bridge contrasted with the dull gray morning, and he reacted instantly. Rolling the control wheel left, he jammed the left rudder and control wheel to their forward stops and shoved the throttle forward.

"Look out," he yelled. He wanted to make sure that Braxton knew there was danger if he had not seen the gunfire from the *Karpaty*.

Pop, pa-pop, pop, pop—

Jack noticed the noise of the first few shells going by, although his mind discounted the sounds of the rest. The nose of the rolling aircraft kept him from seeing the shells that were streaming past at the rate of six per second, but the direction of the sound told him that the gunner's aim had been accurate, though low. If he had not maneuvered the aircraft, the shells would have been extremely close.

Maintaining the dive, he kept the aircraft turning until it pointed away from the *Karpaty*, finally leveling off less than fifty feet above the waves. The tail view of the aircraft, which blended in with the dark ocean background, would make the gunner's job more difficult. He saw tracers passing above and to the left, with the shells splashing harmlessly in the water ahead.

He glanced sideways at Braxton and shouted, "I hope you don't want to try that again."

"You fly like you drive, Colonel."

"Negative," Jack said with a cocky glance in Braxton's direction. "I drive like I fly."

"For now, we'll keep circling."

Jack waited until the ship was more than a mile behind before he climbed toward the clouds and began a steady turn around the ship. Studying the ocean, he saw no signs of Brown's minisub.

He resumed the questioning that had been interrupted by the pass at the ship. "So you've orchestrated everything for years?"

"Let's just say I've sometimes caused things to be interpreted differently than they otherwise might have been."

Jack thought of their first personal encounter in the crowded terminal at San Francisco International Airport. "The guy with the eggs?"

"We thought about having him take a wild shot at me," Braxton said, looking amused at the recollection, "but we never would've gotten a gun through airport security. Actually I preferred the wild shot. The eggs were such a mess. Thank goodness you stopped him before he got to the paint capsules."

"Jesus," Jack said, "I've been willing to accuse the media of some pretty childish hype in my day, but—"

"We had to get control of the crash site for the next few days, and we didn't know how much disinformation I'd have to spread to support the Soviet fleet. Medvalev planned to base his case on the American fighters being in pursuit when the aircraft crashed mysteriously. We assumed I'd need to emphasize how much sense that made to the Russians and how in this case we should back off to show our innocence."

Jack just shook his head. Braxton looked pleased.

"We needed to remind the other networks I was around, so that when I spoke, the other networks would listen. By that night in the airport, of course, your F-15 pilot had already given Medvalev all the rationale he needed for bulling his way into the crash site. The KGB at the consulate already knew Captain Benes had fired, but it was too late to tell me before my broadcast. Had I known in time, I could've done away with the eggs and saved the dry cleaning bill."

"Then the KGB was the source of the information Christine passed to Kane about the missile." Braxton looked surprised at the statement, so Jack added, "She told me she gave Kane the story."

"That's a confidence she wasn't supposed to share," Braxton said curtly.

"Did Kane make the Czechoslovakian connection on his own?"

"Kane?" Braxton said with disdain. "That yuppie caricature of a newsman wouldn't have known the real Eduard Benes from Edward the Eighth."

Jack increased the bank to keep the aircraft from drifting farther from the *Karpaty*.

"I still have my original question. Why? You were Austrian. What allegiance did you owe to the Russians?"

"Surely, Colonel, you couldn't get to your rank without being a student of the wars of the twentieth century. Before the Russians liberated Austria in 1945, the Nazis had been there for seven years. My father had been a soldier in the German army. He died fighting against Patton in North Africa. My mother was a Jew. The Russians . . ." Braxton paused. "They were the liberators." He paused again. "And the Russians offered the chance for vengeance."

"But you've become one of the richest men in America. Surely you've had second thoughts."

"When the party arranges for you to inherit the money and tools of capitalism, you do not receive a clear title."

Jack assumed the reference was to arranging the plane crash that killed Braxton's stepmother and stepfather. "For chrissakes, Braxton, those people took you in and were your family for nearly twenty years."

Braxton ignored this outburst of anger and responded instead to the earlier comment. "When I started, I was too young to know better. By the time I'd seen enough to know better, it was too late to have second thoughts. When I was starving in Vienna, if I'd known I could have become an Alexander C. Braxton by taking another path, I might have chosen differently. But, Colonel, most people our age would choose different paths if they could do it all over again."

"Sure!" Jack considered challenging these rationalizations, but the gun convinced him to let Braxton do the talking.

"You're a man of considerable skills, including some of which we had underestimated, as I discovered last night."

Suddenly Jack's blood seemed to run cold. Did Braxton know all along that the transmitter had been compromised? He struggled to come up with a response, but his throat had gone dry.

Braxton's expression suggested that he was enjoying his adversary's discomfort. "You had no idea that I'd witnessed your surprising display of martial arts. Our dossier on you was incomplete."

As a sigh of relief started to escape his lips, anger suddenly exploded inside. "You murdered Whitney?" Jack fought to control the rage that nearly overwhelmed him.

Braxton tensed. "His blood's on your hands, too, Colonel. If you'd left him alone, I would have left him alone."

"Bastard!" Jack growled the word through clenched teeth.

Watching his adversary closely for a few moments, Braxton finally continued, "Your intellect also has been both a concern to me and a stimulating challenge. I have known you for only days, yet I hold your capabilities in higher regard than does your Air Force, to which you've devoted your adult life. Even before this week, your career was stagnated by a bureaucracy that expects its senior officers to be married and that gives the command of its fighter wings to men like Robert Radisson. Now you've become a public embarrassment. Your generals are ready to cut you loose to distance your precious Air Force from my colleagues in the press."

His comments struck Jack deeper than expected, but he refused to be distracted by the probing. "You sound like you're trying to recruit me."

"A good choice, perhaps," Braxton said, "at another time and another place. Now I don't need you."

"Just for the record," Jack said, "bureaucracy or no bureaucracy, I can't think of a choice I'd have made that would've put me anywhere else this morning besides right here."

Braxton shook his head as if disappointed in Jack's lack of personal ambition, and Jack sensed that his adversary had grown less concerned about the dilemma that he faced. Jack assumed that as an experienced pilot, Braxton had recognized that the UHF emergency frequency was the obvious solution to his problem. The crew on the *Karpaty* would be monitoring the frequency. He could wait until a few minutes before the time for the explosions, then broadcast his identity, and tell them he was going to parachute aboard the ship. The crews on the Coast Guard ships would also hear the message, but by the time they learned what the Russian message meant, it would no longer matter. Unless Brown's minisub surfaced, indicating all the cables had been severed, every passing second was in Braxton's favor.

Jack checked the clock on the instrument panel for what seemed like the twentieth time in the last ten minutes. *One hour and eleven minutes remained until* Iskra *plus twenty.* Concealing his increasing concern about the timetable, he said, "And Christine. She's just another pawn in your game?"

"If you mean inexpensive or inconsequential, 'pawn' is the wrong term. For four years I've given her everything she could need or want. Half the people in this world would sign on with the devil himself for a year of what she's had."

"How about expendable, then?"

"Unfortunately."

"I still don't understand her role," Jack said, "unless she was your mistress and her job was to divert inquisitive colonels who came nosing around too closely."

Braxton let out a small laugh. "You're much closer to the truth than you realize."

Having hoped Braxton would deny the accusation of her being his mistress, Jack had not expected that answer. He was unable to hide his disappointment. Once again, he wondered how much she had lied—especially about her relationship with Braxton.

"Don't look so sour, Colonel. You're not the first influential man I've guided her toward. It's incredible the things that men of power will brag about to impress a beautiful woman—things they'd never think of saying in front of me. Anyway, she's actually quite taken with you."

Jack sighed sarcastically and said, "Oh, the sacrifices one makes for Mother Russia."

"I couldn't afford to have her as my mistress," Braxton said, adding, "not that I wouldn't have found the idea most appealing."

"With half a billion dollars, you're telling me you couldn't afford to have any woman you'd choose?"

"Oh, I did, Colonel. I most certainly did. However, Christine was business, not pleasure."

"Business ethics held you back? I'm not that naive."

"I didn't say business ethics, Colonel. I said business. You can have a woman as your mistress or as your business associate. If you try to keep her as both, you'll end up with her being neither. I had to keep Christine close. I couldn't afford some silly lover's quarrel causing her to break away and pursue one of the offers she had back East."

"With your money, you could always buy someone else."

"You're missing the point, Colonel," Braxton said. "She was my current Woodson, and you don't create a new Woodson overnight. You are familiar with Woodson?"

"His name's come up." Jack's expression did not betray how much he knew since he wanted to hear as much as possible that might clear Christine.

"Even with the precautions we'd taken, the FBI got damned close to me just before he took the fall. After he was eliminated, we decided that my close-in cover should be a woman this time. Christine was perfect. You should've seen your face, Colonel, when I told you she'd been inside the Kremlin. I could've spent the next ten minutes praising her loyalty, and you'd still have harbored just a little doubt.

Anyway, in the last four years, we've built a delicate web of evidence and misleads around her. The FBI could've come looking for me from a dozen different directions, and she was who they were going to find."

"You son of a bitch."

Braxton ignored the remark. "I suppose you noticed she lives more comfortably than her salary justifies."

"She said you gave her some extra help."

"Oh, I did. She thinks I'm generous, and I am. However, if the FBI had ever needed to look into her background, they'd have found an interesting set of records. The large checks that my corporation accepted as her payments for the condominium are traceable—with the appropriate level of difficulty, of course—to an account in Zurich belonging to the Czechoslovakian embassy."

Jack was becoming angrier than he had planned. "She's looked up to you like a father. Don't you have a conscience?"

"Colonel," Braxton said in the tone of an overworked professor who had been unsuccessful with a slow student, "in forty years of this, you can learn to rationalize away anything your conscience still bothers to bother you with."

Jack was squeezing the control wheel so hard that he could feel the hardened plastic starting to buckle. He tried to relax his grip and asked, "Do you have a cigarette?"

Maintaining as much separation as possible, Braxton adjusted his position against the door. He brought down his other hand, steadying the grip he had on his pistol. "Come now, Colonel. I've seen all the old movies. There's only so far that I will permit you to distract me."

As Jack struggled to control his desire to attack, he glanced at the *Karpaty*. Earlier, the deck had appeared abandoned. Now he saw a number of seamen working around a small submarine and the crane at the stern of the ship. He was surprised by the activity and took a quick second glance that stirred Braxton's attention.

"What's happening?" the spy asked, straining against his seat belt to get a look at the ship. When Jack did not respond, Braxton grabbed the control wheel on his side of the cockpit. He rolled the aircraft into a steeper bank so he had a clearer view of the *Karpaty*.

"Nothing," Jack said, knowing Braxton could now see as much. "Maybe they're going fishing."

Jack was sure the captain on the *Karpaty* knew someone else was in the water with them. He scanned around the ship, but saw no indication of Brown's submarine. If Brown had been discovered, he thought, he must be having some effect on the cables.

He glanced at the status lights. Neither was illuminated.

He leaned forward as if trying to see something ahead of the *Karpaty*. Braxton tensed in reaction, dividing his attention between Jack and the area ahead of the ship. Jack lifted his right hand as if shielding his eyes from reflections on the windshield.

Cocking the pistol again and leaning as far away as possible, Braxton said, "Don't try anything."

Jack acted surprised. He raised his right hand slowly and leaned against his side of the cockpit. As the raised hand drew attention, his left grasped the small toggle switch by the status lights. "Just looking," he said. At that moment his fingers pushed the switch up, signalling O'Donnell's Command Post that the Russians were aware of Brown's presence.

"You just fly the airplane," Braxton said. "I'll do the looking."

Jack shrugged in agreement and took hold of the control wheel. He glanced at the ship again as if to reestablish his reference for keeping the aircraft nearby. He saw that they were lowering the submarine into the water.

Moments later, the yellow light on the status panel flashed on.

Jack felt as if another electrical signal had jolted him simultaneously. A tingle rushed through him as he tried to mask the excitement and dread he felt. He glanced at the clock: eight fifty-two—Iskra *plus 18:52*. The captain of the *Karpaty* had asked for permission to detonate one hour and eight minutes ahead of *Iskra*'s schedule.

Noticing that something had distracted Jack, Braxton scanned the instrument panel until he spotted the yellow light. "What's that?"

"You think we're low on gas?"

"The fuel gauges say otherwise." Braxton nodded toward the instrument panel. He strained to see if markings near the status lights gave a hint to the lights' purpose, but the status panel was unmarked. "I've flown this model before, but the other planes didn't have those two lights."

Trying to hide how serious he knew the situation had become, Jack said, "Then why are you asking me about the fancy stuff? I haven't piloted a plane in eighteen months."

Braxton looked shocked. "The FAA would . . ." He stopped, apparently realizing how ridiculous the statement was.

"Hell," Jack said, trying to distance Braxton's thoughts as far as possible from the glowing yellow light, "I was looking forward to finding out if I could land one of these machines."

The spy did not look amused, and that pleased Jack. The banter had helped him calm down enough to start spurring Braxton into action. Looking toward the *Karpaty*, Jack noticed that the Russian minisub was submerging ahead of the ship and moved his left leg so that the circuit breaker for the VHF radio was more visible from Braxton's position. "You really didn't think we knew, did you?"

Braxton looked as if he had misunderstood. Before he could ask for the question to be repeated, his expression changed, indicating he suddenly understood the words but not their meaning.

Jack mimicked the conversation he had staged in front of the transmitter the previous evening. He assumed that Braxton had listened to the conversation or to a tape of it before making his decision to come to the airport. "Didn't you say you wanted a drink, Colonel? Sure. Make mine a scotch and water."

"You bastard!" Braxton spat out the words, almost overwhelmed by the implications of this discovery.

"I got tired of having you at my six o'clock all the time," Jack said resolutely, "so I decided to get you out where I could keep an eye on you."

"But," Braxton said, less confident than before, "you're not flying an F-15, and you're at the wrong end of the gun." All the same, he looked more like the hunted than the hunter. His eyes darted around the cockpit until he spotted the circuit breaker extending beyond the rest of the breakers on the panel near Jack's knee. Then he read the words "VHF Comm" below the circuit breaker.

"Reset it." His voice rebounded in confidence and authority, since he now had the answer to communicating with the Russians on the ship.

"Reset it yourself," Jack said, ready to spring into action if Braxton tried to reach across. "You've gotten the last bit of help out of me that you're ever go—"

Taking Jack by surprise, Braxton fired the pistol twice in rapid succession.

The first bullet slammed into the side of Jack's jump suit. The second ripped through his arm, just above the elbow, before lodging near the first slug in the flak vest. The force of the bullets and his spinning away from the gunfire threw him against the left side of the cockpit. His head hit the post that separated the side windows, and for a few moments he was stunned.

Braxton kept his distance, waiting to see if he needed to fire again. Blood was splattered over the blue sleeve and the side of his adversary's flight suit. The blood, coupled with Jack's labored breathing, made it appear that the injuries would prove fatal.

Still watching his wounded adversary, Braxton reached toward the circuit breaker panel on the far side of the cockpit. "Damn!" he cried as his shoulder harness and the parachute pack in his lap kept the panel beyond his reach.

Jack's injuries looked worse than they were. Although one rib was broken and another was cracked, the flak vest had stopped both bullets. The second bullet had passed through his arm without hitting any major blood vessels. Forcing himself to breathe less deeply, he eased the burning caused by each breath. Anger and adrenaline fought off the shock that otherwise might have immobilized him. He made his left hand tremble as he slid it slowly toward where the bullets were lodged in the flak vest. At the same time he let his head roll against the headrest as if he were unconscious. With his eyes barely open, he saw Braxton release his seat belt and shoulder harness.

The older man reached toward the circuit breaker panel, but it was still beyond his fingertips. He glanced at Jack, then extended the barrel of the gun toward the circuit breaker.

When Braxton's full concentration was on touching the circuit breaker with the muzzle of the gun, Jack kicked the right rudder against its stop. Simultaneously he slashed his left hand at Braxton's neck. The sudden movement of the rudder forced the airplane into a sideways skid, however, throwing Braxton against the control wheel and causing the blow to strike his cheek. Although not the disabling chop to the neck Jack had hoped for, the impact stunned Braxton momentarily, knocking off his glasses.

Braxton's body had jammed the control wheel against the forward stops, forcing the airplane into a steep dive, but Jack's first concern was to disarm his foe. Grabbing the little finger on his gun hand, Jack bent the finger back as hard and as far as he could. Braxton, still off balance against the instrument panel, tried to twist his gun hand to relieve the pressure and the pain. Jack had the leverage, however, and he jerked as hard as he could. Tendons and cartilage snapped, and Braxton screamed in pain. The gun fell to the floor and slid into the darkness beyond the rudder pedals. At that moment Jack tried to force his right hand to the gun strapped to his ankle, but his injuries kept him from reaching his gun.

Braxton grasped his injured hand trying to relieve the pain. He pushed away from the instrument panel, and the control wheel returned to neutral. The airspeed, which had increased during the dive, raised the nose of the aircraft and stopped the plunge toward the water.

Jack swung again with his good arm, but his opponent blocked the blow with his shoulder. Lunging forward, Braxton winced in pain as he grabbed Jack's neck with both hands. The weight of his body kept Jack's injured arm pinned between them, but the colonel felt the cold metal of the D-ring on the front of Braxton's parachute. He hooked his fingers around the D-ring, thinking, *even if he wins the fight, he'll have a hell of a time bailing out if I pop his parachute.*

Using his free hand, Jack fought the grip on his throat. Even with the broken finger, however, Braxton's hands were strong, threatening to crush his windpipe. He grabbed Braxton's collar and yanked him closer. At the same time he snapped his head forward, slamming against Braxton's nose.

Feeling his nose shattered by the sudden blow, Braxton cupped his hands to his face and jerked away toward the far side of the cockpit.

Jack held the D-ring firmly, and his enemy's motion pulled the cable attached to the ring. A set of pins ripped free from the linkages that held the cover of the parachute in place, and the springs within the parachute pack expanded. The pilot chute popped away from the rest of the pack as it would during a normal deployment of the parachute. In this case, however, since there was no rushing air to fill the small chute and pull the main canopy from the pack, the bright blue miniature chute dropped harmlessly between them.

"Damn you," Braxton shouted.

Releasing his seat belt and lunging forward, Jack landed a punch to Braxton's head. Before the older man responded, Jack twisted the handle that held the side window closed. The airflow caught the window, slamming it up against the latch on the bottom of the wing. Rushing air swirled into the cockpit.

With his good hand, he grabbed the collar of Braxton's jump suit and pushed his head toward the open window.

With blood streaming from his nose, Braxton reacted in a blind rage. He slammed a fist against Jack's wounded arm, producing a paroxysm of pain that broke the grip.

The traitor grabbed again at the throat. This time Braxton buried his face against his biceps. The maneuver, a common defense to protect one's eyes when applying a choke, also protected his broken nose from another assault.

Jack stiffened the muscles in his neck and tucked his chin against his chest. He only needed to hold Braxton off for a few more seconds. As the spy struggled to force his fingers into the soft parts of the throat, Jack grasped the blue pilot chute for Braxton's main parachute. Jack flinched backward, as if trying to withdraw. Braxton resisted, pulling the other way—the way the colonel wanted to go. Jack thrust his hand forward, and the small chute flew out the open window.

The bright blue material remained limp for a moment before catching the wind, billowing to its full size, and yanking free of Jack's hand. The cords connecting the pilot chute to the main canopy produced a slashing flurry of red silk and white nylon as the canopy fought to free itself from the parachute pack between the two men.

Jack rocked back, trying to get hold of something solid and to escape from Braxton's grasp.

Braxton's head jerked away from his arm as the friction of the nylon cords rushing by burned his neck. His eyes flashed wide open as the parachute risers broke free of the pack and snapped across his shoulders. For an instant, however, the main parachute draped across the tail, spilling some of the 130 mile-per-hour air that had filled the canopy. His hands dropped to the quick-release latches on the parachute harness. His only chance was to disconnect the parachute from his harness before the canopy pulled free from the aircraft. He had just clawed open the safety covers protecting the quick-releases from inadvertent actuation when the canopy slipped off the tail.

His scream was intermingled with the sounds of tearing metal. As the parachute yanked him backward from his seat and through the side of the aircraft, his feet snapped toward the ceiling, striking Jack in the head.

The colonel was stunned momentarily as he felt the aircraft rock violently to the right, then swing to the left.

When he could see clearly again, Braxton was gone. The door also had disappeared. The first two to three feet of the side of the airplane aft of the door had been peeled out as if made of aluminum foil, and some of the jagged edges were smeared with blood. Through the open side of the aircraft, Jack could see the horizontal stabilizer. Moments earlier, the leading edge had had the sleek, rounded shape of a carefully designed airfoil. Now the smooth curves were gone, buckled inward and crumpled, indicating where Braxton had smashed into the stabilizer before being yanked free of the airplane.

Jack looked for Braxton's bag, but it was gone too. There was no need to worry any more about the transmitter.

As Jack settled into the pilot's seat, he looked at the clock. Nearly nine minutes had passed since the yellow light had come on. He also discovered that during the struggle the aircraft had descended to four hundred feet. He strapped in, pushed the throttle forward, and banked into a climbing turn. The airplane was still controllable, but he was concerned about how much more stress it would take with the gaping hole in the side. Air rushed noisily past the hole, causing some buffeting. He pulled his headset on, turned on both radios, and tuned the UHF frequency for the minisub.

Straining to see the ocean behind the plane, he saw a patch of red silk riding over the top of a swell. The rectangular canopy of the steerable chute was spread out across the water with Braxton's body at the end of one set of risers. One of the quick releases had apparently come free of Braxton's harness, causing him to plummet into the ocean with the useless canopy streaming above him.

Coming from behind the *Karpaty*, Jack steered the aircraft toward the left side of the Soviet ship. He was high enough and close enough to see something break the surface nearly a mile ahead. In a few moments the outline of Brown's minisub was visible.

Almost immediately the radio crackled to life through the overhead speaker. "Texan, Texan. This is Alabama. Do you copy?" Before Jack could respond, Brown called again, "Texan, Texan. Alabama is St. Helens. Say again, definitely St. Helens. Do you copy?"

Jack had been certain that the explosives were there, but hearing the code word, St. Helens, still sent a rush through his body.

Ninety-five miles to the northeast, Major Melanie Thompson sat at a console in the back of an orbiting AWACS aircraft. When she heard Brown broadcast St. Helens, she keyed her microphone and said crisply, "Regal Fox, this is Skybird. St. Helens, St. Helens. You are 'Go' for Cedar City."

Cedar City signified a wartime scramble of the President's Airborne Command Post.

In the cockpit of the E-4B at Alameda Naval Air Station, Lieutenant Colonel Rich Jenkins heard her message. As he flashed the landing lights at the ground crewmen standing by in front of the aircraft, his navigator acknowledged to the AWACS that Regal Fox had received the message.

"Starting number one," Jenkins said into his microphone as he began the starting sequence for the number one engine.

In the President's section of the E-4B, General McClintock had also heard Major Thompson's announcement. He pushed one earpiece of his headset aside, dropped the microphone out of the way, then said, "Mr. President, we have confirmed the explosives on the ocean floor."

"Put all military forces at DEFCON One, General. As soon as we're airborne, I want a call placed to Premier Medvalev."

Chapter **28**

JACK PUSHED THE TRANSMIT BUTTON FOR HIS UHF AND SAID, "TEXAN understands St. Helens. Are you now Mike Alpha?" He hoped Brown had come to the surface to report mission accomplished.

"Negative, negative, Texan," Brown said. "Alabama is Foxtrot; say again, Foxtrot on St. Helens. There was too much. Look o—"

Jack saw two streams of tracers arc from the bridge of the *Karpaty* and splash in the water near the minisub. Tuning the VHF radio to the frequency that McClintock had given him to contact the AWACS, he switched to secure VHF and transmitted, "Skybird, Skybird. This is Texan."

"Roger, Texan. Skybird. Go."

"Skybird, Texan reports status as St. Helens, and the friendlies are taking ground fire. Request immediate support."

"Stand by, Texan."

Stand by, Jack thought. He checked the clock—9.02. The yellow light had been on for ten minutes. *Less than five minutes remained.* He switched to the UHF transmitter and called, "How are you doing, Alabama?"

"Alabama's taking hits," Brown said. "I don't think we can take many more!"

Before Jack could answer, O'Donnell's voice—with the sound of helicopter rotors in the background—broke in: "Texan, this is Romeo India. Alabama's transmission was broken. Say again his status?"

"Some damage," Jack said. "Also, Christine *is* innocent. Do you copy?" He wanted that message to get back even if he did not.

"Roger, copied," O'Donnell said. "Have you got anything new?"

"Foxtrot on St. Hel—" Jack stopped when he heard the AWACS controller responding.

"Texan, this is Skybird."

Jack switched to VHF and acknowledged.

366

"Roger, Texan. Skybird clears you to execute with Gunslinger. Meet Gunslinger on secure, one-thirty-two-decimal-five."

"Texan's going one-thirty-two-five, Skybird."

As he dialed in the new frequency, he noticed that the clock had gone beyond the eleventh minute. *Perhaps less than 240 seconds remained.* "Gunslinger, Gunslinger, this is Texan. Are you there?"

A new voice responded, "Texan, this is Gunslinger Lead, with a flight of four Apaches. We're carrying a full load of Hellfires, some Hydra 70s, and thirty millimeter guns. What do you have for us?"

"Gunslinger, your target's a surface ship of the Soviet Navy." He checked the display that showed how far he was from the navigational radio on the Point Reyes peninsula. "Gunslinger, I need you at the two-five-zero at twenty-seven miles off the Point Reyes VORTAC. The target's about seven miles west of the Coast Guard cutters. What's your location, Gunslinger?"

"About five minutes southeast of you, Texan."

Jack checked his clock. He assumed the *Karpaty* would receive clearance from the *Minsk* in less than five minutes. "Push your throttles to the firewall, Gunslinger, because I need you in low and fast. There's a command center beneath the bridge that has to be taken out with minimal warning. There are a pair of twenty-five millimeter guns on top of the bridge. Right now the gunners are busy shooting at a friendly minisub."

"Copied, Texan. We're on the wave tops about four minutes from first launch."

"Say your attack heading, Gunslinger," Jack said.

"Lead's running in on three-one-zero."

Good, Jack thought. The *Karpaty* was holding its position pointing northeast toward the explosives-filled canyon, and the helicopters would attack almost broadside.

His aircraft was nearly a mile abeam the *Karpaty* on the opposite side. Looking beyond the ship, he tried to pick out the helicopters. He was not sure if the dark blurs he saw near the Coast Guard cutters were the helicopters or his imagination. He had to make sure that the Apaches attacked the right ship.

"Gunslinger, where are you relative to the Coast Guard?"

"Gunslinger's coming up on the picket line. We'll pass abeam in less than a minute."

The yellow light had been on for thirteen minutes, and the Apaches were still more than two minutes from launching their Hellfire missiles. Would the *Karpaty* receive clearance to detonate before the anti-armor missiles from the Apaches hit the ship? For that matter, would the captain discover he was under attack and detonate the explosives on his own? Jack had to speed up the action in spite of his injuries and the damage to his aircraft.

A radio call from Brown gave Jack a third problem. "Texan, Alabama needs help."

Smoke was coming from the blue minisub, and the black minisub that the *Karpaty* had launched a few minutes earlier had surfaced about two hundred yards abeam of Brown's sub. A Soviet crewman was firing an automatic rifle from the minisub's conning tower.

Jack switched to the UHF radio and said, "Turn left, Alabama. Turn left. I'll check on air rescue."

"Understand, left turn," Brown said. "We'll do our best."

The turn away from the Soviet minisub would look natural, but it also kept Brown from getting farther from the guns on the *Karpaty*. Jack had decided that everything possible must be done to draw the attention of the *Karpaty*'s crew to the left—away from the approaching Apaches. He prepared to do his part, but first he had to make two more radio calls.

Switching to the attack frequency, he said, "Jolly Green, this is Texan. Are you on this freq?"

Lieutenant Colonel Buck Buchanan responded, "Roger, Texan. This is Jolly One. We're a flight of two, orbiting just southeast of the cutter *Munro*."

"Roger, Jolly. I need you to monitor UHF two-thirty-seven-decimal-eight. I have a blue minisub crippled on that freq. However, maintain radio silence until after the Apaches strike on this freq."

"Understand," Buchanan answered.

Jack then explained to Gunslinger about the second submarine, but ordered him to delay attacking the black minisub until the primary target was destroyed.

He saw that both the *Karpaty* and the black minisub were firing at Brown. As Jack pulled his seat belt tighter and locked his shoulder harness, he wondered if the *Minsk* had received approval yet from Moscow. The yellow status light had been on for almost fourteen minutes. *Barely a minute remained.* In the distance he saw the whirling rotors of the four attack helicopters.

He yanked the throttle to idle, and the engine backfired loudly. He revved the engine two more times to attract the attention of the lookouts on the *Karpaty* as he pulled the aircraft around in a tight 180-degree turn. Coming out of the turn, he let the nose drop into a steep dive.

"Gunslinger, this is Texan. You're cleared in hot. This may be my last call. Continue your attack until the target is destroyed."

"Roger, Texan."

O'Donnell's voice came over the VHF radio. "What are you doing, Texan?"

Jack realized that O'Donnell had managed to switch to the attack frequency. "Time's running out, and I'm going to try to take some of the heat off Alabama."

"Somebody here wants me to tell you to be careful."

Jack double-clicked his mic button, acknowledging that he understood the transmission—Christine was with O'Donnell.

Continuing the dive past the stern of the *Karpaty*, he watched the guns above the bridge. His aircraft was descending through five hundred feet, about a half mile abeam the stern of the ship, when the gunners started paying attention. They stopped shooting at the minisub and swung the guns toward him. He was in a diving turn around toward the stern by the time the guns fired in his direction. However, much of the area behind the gunners was blocked by the ship's funnel and the big kingpost amidships, which was used to lift the diving bells into and out of the water. He leveled at two hundred feet and slipped into the edge of the protected airspace that the guns could not hit. He wanted to tempt the gunners enough to keep them from swinging the guns around to the other side—and perhaps seeing the approaching Apaches.

He looked toward the southeast and saw the blurry images of the four helicopters racing across the dark ocean. The gunships were closer than he expected. Maybe the Apaches would strike in time, but he was already committed—his only way out was through the waiting tracers of the guns on the bridge. He wondered if he would also have to fly through debris and explosions caused by the first round of Hellfire missiles.

He checked the clock. The yellow light was into its fifteenth minute. *Seconds remained.*

The stern of the ship seemed to rush at him as he scanned the antennas above the bridge and the kingpost. He picked out the antenna that he assumed was for the long range, high frequency radio. He hoped he could take enough of the top off the antenna with his landing gear to make the radio inoperable without actually crashing his airplane.

He had almost reached the high stern of the *Karpaty* when he swung to the right, lowering the nose and the landing gear at the same time. Even before the gunners on the bridge started bringing the guns around to the right, he reversed the controls, pointing the aircraft toward the HF antenna.

"Damn!"

Sparkling flashes of automatic weapons fire from two soldiers on top of the stern hoist caused him to flinch, involuntarily trying to make himself a smaller target. The *rat-a-tat-tat* of the guns and the banging of bullets against his aircraft were almost simultaneous. He glanced toward the gunners, then back toward the antenna and the heavier structure of the kingpost. The momentary distraction had brought him in too low. With the throttle full forward, he could still miss the kingpost, but he was going to hit the antenna with more than the landing gear—perhaps with the propeller.

In the background, someone called out that his Laser designator was locked on. The Apaches were about to launch the first of their Hellfire missiles.

Not sure the damaged aircraft would hold together, Jack yanked the control wheel back, rolled left, and for just an instant kicked the right rudder. The plane skidded right, and the propeller missed the antenna by inches. The right landing gear snapped off as it slammed into the antenna's supporting structure. The antenna sliced into the leading edge, imbedding nearly six inches into the right wing.

The aircraft shuddered as it smashed through the tubing, then broke free. He saw the gunners duck as the plane screamed overhead, but he knew they would not stay down long. As he fought to maintain control and keep the aircraft a few feet off the water, lines of tracers flashed by on both sides, and the firecracker-like smell of cordite filled the cockpit. The shells splashed geysers of water all around.

The aircraft shuddered as the gunners finally scored. Pieces of sheet metal from the left wing shredded into the air. He saw fuel streaming from holes on the under side of the wing. He was even more concerned when he discovered that the trailing edge was twisted near the wing tip. The left aileron, one of his two main control surfaces for causing the aircraft to roll—or stopping it from rolling—probably would not stay on much longer.

He pressed the right rudder, trying to evade the tracers, but the aircraft did not respond. Shells had also hit the tail.

Scanning the cockpit for indications of damage, his gaze riveted on the status panel. The red light glowed brightly—the *Minsk* had forwarded a clearance to detonate.

A moment later, the tracers stopped, and he heard a thunderous explosion.

Then he heard a quick succession of explosions, even before he turned to see the *Karpaty*. Black smoke billowed from the ship, and the superstructure forward of the funnel was engulfed in flames. Severed and burned cables were sliding over the railings and into the sea.

As he eased his damaged aircraft into a slow climbing turn, he saw the lead Apache swing up over the bow of the *Karpaty* and start strafing the black minisub. Flaming tongues of red reached out from the chin turret on the copter as thirty-millimeter shells streaked forward at the rate of eight hundred rounds per minute. The water around the Soviet minisub boiled with exploding shells while the second helicopter started attacking the *Karpaty* with enough Hellfire missiles to destroy sixteen main battle tanks of the Soviet Army.

Jack tried to nurse his airplane to a safer altitude as he heard Buchanan's voice making contact with Brown on the crippled minisub. Two miles behind the last Apache, Buchanan's rescue helicopter had climbed to three hundred feet. He and his wingman were heading for Brown's sub. Jack wondered how much longer he could fly before he would need the services of a rescue helicopter.

In the main ballroom of the Officers Club at Howell Air Force Base, Colonel Robert Radisson stood proudly in the receiving line at the commander's Christmas reception. He was pleased to show off the members of his wing to General Harper, who had accepted the colonel's invitation to be in the receiving line.

Everything was perfect, Radisson thought as he looked across the festively decorated room and scanned the gathering of his young fliers and their ladies. Immaculately dressed in his ceremonial uniform, he was only mildly concerned about how much sharper his appearance was than that of General Harper. Harper was wearing the regular uniform he had brought along four days earlier on the emergency inspection visit.

Radisson had read the morning papers and the stories of how much trouble Jack Phillips was in. What a great day, Radisson thought. He could not remember having had a better one in years.

As he stood greeting the people in the line, he heard the sounds of jet engines. He cursed silently. He had ordered "quiet hours" from zero-eight-forty-five to eleven-hundred. No flights were scheduled. No one was to be running engine tests during that period. He did not want the noise disrupting his reception.

Shaking the hand of a major who had just reached him in the receiving line, he said, "Richards, go find out who's making all the noise and tell them to shut it down until quiet hours are over."

"Yes, sir."

Before Richards broke away from the receiving line, there were two nearly simultaneous bursts of noise as first one, and then another, F-15 pilot pushed the throttles of his Eagle into afterburner. The deep-throated roar of four F100 turbofan engines sent out vibrations that were felt in the Officers Club. No one but Radisson paid any attention to what seemed like a commonplace occurrence at any home base of the powerful fighters.

The noise decreased as the two Eagles got farther down the runway and hurtled into the air—but all the noise did not go away. *What in the hell is happening?* Radisson thought as he continued listening. He still heard the nearby sound of other jet engines.

The movement of people through the line had stalled because he had stopped shaking hands. "Bob," his wife said, trying to get his attention back on his guests.

Moments later, there were two more bursts of noise, confirming what he was subconsciously trying to deny—someone had just ordered his alert force into the air.

With the sound of the third and fourth F-15s roaring along the runway in the background, he stepped from the line just as one of the duty officers from the Command Post came jogging into the ballroom.

The excited young captain carried a piece of paper in his hand. Giving the message to Radisson, he said, "Sir, two are airborne to fly close-in cover for the AWACS. The other two have been ordered to cover the President's Airborne Command Post."

Radisson scanned the message. "Hit the lights, Captain."

"Yes, sir." He rushed to a switch panel behind a curtain near the entrance to the ballroom. The DEFCON status lights on panels in each of the main rooms in the club switched from Four to One, and a Klaxon activated on the public address system. For a moment everyone in the room stood in shocked silence, then the captain yelled, "This is for real. This is not an exercise."

His words jarred the crowd into action and almost everyone hurried to the exits.

Radisson handed the message to General Harper. Though it did not mention Phillips, Radisson's instincts told him that his long-time adversary was responsible. When Harper had returned from Alameda the previous evening, he had said that Phillips still thought there was some kind of a problem even though everyone else believed the Russians had ended the crisis. Radisson's response had been to ridicule Phillips as being the problem, and now he said in amazement, "Can you believe that, General? I think the son of a bitch pulled it off."

Harper finished reading the message, then said slowly and deliberately, "Bob, I suggest you get out of your peacock feathers, put on some fighting clothes, and start earning your pay."

Fifty-five miles east of the burning *Karpaty*, the E-4B thundered over the morning traffic on the Oakland Bay Bridge and climbed northward across San Pablo Bay. Leonid Petrov chattered in Russian into a microphone linked through relays and communications satellites to the hot line between Washington and Moscow.

In a few moments, the translator turned to the President and said, "The premier is not available. They are unsure when he can be located."

"Tell them to try the command bunker at Lytkarino. Be sure they understand where you are calling from and that you *are* airborne. Tell them that if Premier Medvalev isn't available, I'll speak with Minister Valinen, since he's also in that bunker."

Fifty-one hundred miles away near Lytkarino, a grim-faced Medvalev sat beside Valinen. Behind the Plexiglas map on the front wall, the status keepers had abandoned using written descriptions for new activities at American bases. Instead the sergeants were marking luminous blue Xs where there were reports of American forces reacting to the change from DEFCON Four to DEFCON One. Above the blue Xs that flooded across the United States and Western Europe, the two *Iskra* timers continued their countdowns. One showed forty-three minutes; the other twenty-four hours and forty-three minutes.

A general wearing a headset turned toward Medvalev and said, "*Minsk* still reports no contact with *Karpaty*, and agents on the ground report everything is still normal in San Francisco."

Medvalev's interpreter added, "The American President is pressing for an answer."

Crumpling a piece of paper in his hand, Valinen formed an upraised fist. "You must answer by ordering all forces to strike now!"

"Their President is beyond your reach," Medvalev said firmly. "*Iskra* cannot succeed."

"You must not wait!" Valinen hurled the paper toward the front wall.

Medvalev turned away and picked up a headset that connected him to the hot line. In stiff English he said, "Mr. President, why have you ordered your forces to take such reckless and provocative positions?"

"We have discovered the explosives," Cunningham said distinctly. "And the guns on the *Karpaty* have fired on American aircraft. I have ordered the ship sunk."

"I do not understand you. The *Karpaty* is a rescue ship that—"

"Then, Mr. Premier, I suggest you ask Minister Valinen to explain. He has prepared a nuclear attack, and I am prepared to respond. You should understand that I have ordered the American ICBM force to be prepared to launch on warning."

Cunningham could not have made a more frightening threat, and

Medvalev shifted uneasily in his chair. Every Soviet strategy for nuclear attack depended upon destroying most American intercontinental ballistic missiles in their silos. The President had guaranteed a crippling counterattack as soon as the Americans confirmed the launch of Soviet ICBMs—like the attack scheduled in less than twenty-five hours. Looking toward Valinen, Medvalev cursed himself silently for agreeing to this scheme. Valinen stared back angrily. Fortunately, Medvalev thought, he had also planned for failure.

He made sure his microphone was turned off, then said, "We have lost." He paused. Nodding toward the chief of his personal bodyguard, he said quietly to Valinen, "And you have lost."

Several guards drew their pistols and closed in on Valinen. The Beast stood without a struggle, and the guards pushed him toward the door.

"Immediately," Medvalev said to the chief guard. The guard spoke quietly to his assistant, and the assistant joined the group that escorted Valinen from the room.

After the doors had closed, Medvalev activated his microphone again, then said slowly, "Mr. President, I have learned at this very moment that Minister Valinen may not have died in the plane crash. I am told that he may have plotted to bring about a war between our two nations. That plot may involve the *Karpaty* and its captain, who has loyalties to Minister Valinen."

"The plot involves much more than the *Karpaty*."

"You have my pledge that I shall stop Valinen's plotting. I will understand any actions you take against the traitors on the *Karpaty*. I want to ask you, Mr. President, to trust me. I give you my personal word that I shall discover his plans and stop them."

"Let me help, Mr. Premier. The nuclear strikes are scheduled within twenty-five hours, at which time some of your naval ships will be covering several patrol areas for our missile submarines. You can help restore my trust by ordering each fleet to reduce its speed by two thirds for the next three days."

"That will be done, Mr. President," Medvalev said reluctantly.

"Mr. Premier, the plotting also involves an invasion of the state of Hawaii by the fleet headed by the *Minsk*. If the *Minsk* does not alter her course within the next thirty minutes, I shall consider that that fleet is also filled with seamen loyal to Valinen. Our attack submarines shadowing that fleet will act accordingly."

"But Mr. President—"

"Thirty minutes, Mr. Premier."

Medvalev nodded in resignation. He looked toward one of his admirals and said, "Order the change of course immediately."

*   *   *

Jack had coaxed the crippled aircraft to twelve hundred feet and turned toward Point Reyes. Below him, the black minisub had cracked open after being hit by one Hellfire missile and disappeared beneath the waves. The second Apache was using its Laser designator to mark points just above the water line on the hull of the *Karpaty*. One at a time, the fourth Apache sent twelve more Hellfire missiles against the aim points designated by the second Apache.

Lieutenant Colonel Buchanan's helicopters were over Brown's minisub. The smoke from electrical fires had forced Brown and the other crewman to abandon the sub, and they were floating nearby in a life raft. The Jolly Green hovered a few feet above the waves, and a pararescue jumper dropped into the icy water.

In the distance Jack saw the Coast Guard cutters getting underway and turning toward the battle. He was glad the ships were coming closer. Initially he had hoped to fly his aircraft at least to the beaches of Point Reyes. Now the vibrations had increased so much that he was unsure he could reach the picket line of cutters.

Checking the damage, he was sure he could not fly much longer. Most of the fuel had drained from the left wing, and the outer edge of the left aileron was being pushed back by the airflow. He was sure that it was only a matter of minutes before the control surface either jammed or broke free. There was enough other structural damage that he feared the buffeting could break the aircraft apart. His best chance to survive was to bail out while the aircraft was still under control.

He unlatched the seat belt and flipped the shoulder harness out of the way, then slid over to the copilot's seat. Moving caused more pain than he expected. He pressed the mic button. "Mayday. Mayday. Mayday. This is Texan bailing out about two miles east of the *Karpaty*."

He waited only long enough to hear the first words of the responses before diving through the open side of the aircraft. As soon as he felt the airflow slam against him, he spread his legs to stabilize himself.

With his right arm dangling uselessly at his side, he had grabbed the D-ring with his left hand before leaving the aircraft. Now, he pushed the D-ring as far away from the chute harness as possible, but the parachute cover did not release. For an instant he panicked, unsure he could pull the D-ring far enough with his left hand to deploy the parachute. Parachutes were designed for right-handed people. Normally, a parachutist simply extended his right arm out to the side, and there was more than enough movement to free all the pins holding the parachute in place.

As he fell faster and faster, the rush of air made it difficult to see, but he grabbed the woven wire that led from the D-ring into a metal tube within the parachute pack. The grease, which made the wire slide easily through the tube, made it difficult to get a firm grasp on the wire. However, his adrenaline added to his strength, and he jerked and twisted the wire out another six inches.

The water looked dangerously close as the parachute billowed free. The opening shock yanked the harness tight across his broken rib, and he passed out from the excruciating pain.

Moments later, the cold water of the North Pacific revived him. For an instant, he was unsure where he was. The water was much colder than that in the Gulf of Tonkin, the last time he had parachuted, but he faced the same problem as before. The wet parachute threatened to entangle him and pull him under.

He reacted more on instinct and training than on conscious thought. First, he took a deep breath before being dragged under. As a wave washed over him, his left hand found the tabs on his Mae West. He pulled, freeing the compressed air into the chambers of the life vest. Even before the life vest filled, he opened one of the covers that protected the quick-releases for the parachute harness. Slipping his fingers through the loop of wire, he pulled. Immediately the pressure on his body decreased as one riser broke free of his harness. When he pulled the other quick release, he was free of the chute and bobbed above the surface.

He gasped in several breaths of fresh air. Hearing the roaring of a nearby helicopter, he rolled over on his back. Kicking his feet steadily, he tried to put as much distance as possible between him and the partially submerged parachute. He did not think that the soggy parachute could be sucked into the whirling rotors, but he did not want to take chances.

The tornado-like winds whipped up by the approaching helicopter increased the cold that was already numbing the parts of his body not protected by the wetsuit. By the time the helicopter hovered above him and the crew lowered the "horse collar," his hand was too numb to grab the cable. Instead, he forced the upper part of his body through the oblong ring and signaled that he was ready to be pulled up. The pain in his side kept him conscious as the winch pulled him higher and higher. Finally he felt the shuddering metal edge of the floor of the helicopter against his back and felt a firm hand grasp the collar of his jump suit.

As soon as he was safely in the helicopter, Christine was all over him. O'Donnell tried to wrap a blanket around him but she was in the way. He finally gave up and put the blanket around both of them as Jack struggled to his feet.

Jack asked, "Were we in time?"

O'Donnell answered, "Barely."

Jack smiled and said, "Looks like I owe you an airplane."

"Don't sweat the small stuff, Colonel."

As Jack hugged Christine close to him, he looked out the window. An internal explosion had broken the *Karpaty* in two, and the stern was barely visible. As the other helicopters swarmed above the scene, two Coast Guard cutters approached the burning ship.

He kissed her forehead, and when she looked at him, he smiled and said, "Looks like the people at Lake Tahoe will get to enjoy their sunrise on Christmas morning after all."

She kissed him on the neck and said, "I hope you're willing to settle for the next best thing."

As he pictured sharing the view of a sunrise from her condominium, he pulled her closer and said, "You got it, lady."

Colonel Jimmie H. Butler served as an Air Force officer from 1965 to 1987, logging over 5,000 hours of military flying and earning numerous combat decorations. THE ISKRA INCIDENT is his first novel. Jimmie H. Butler lives in Los Angeles, California.